STRAYA

Anthony O'Connor

I would like to acknowledge the Traditional Owners of the Country in which I wrote this book, the Gadigal people of the Eora nation, and recognise their continuing connection to land, waters and culture. I pay my respects to the Elders past, present and emerging.

Straya

© Anthony O'Connor and Green Light Productions Pty Limited 2021
www.anthonyoconnorauthor.com

Cover design by Chris Wahl
Internal design by Impressum www.impressum.com.au

National Library of Australia Cataloguing-in-Publication entry
Author: O'Connor, Anthony

Title: Straya / Anthony O'Connor
ISBN: 978-1-922588-03-6 (print) | 978-1-922588-04-3 (ebook)

For Mum and Dad,
who know a thing or two
about raising a mutant

and

Guy N. Smith (1939-2020)
who took shit
from zero crustaceans

STRAYA GLOSSARY (ABRIDGED)

For assistance in fully understanding the poetic and nuanced Strayan language used by the gentle cits of New Sydney.

Beaut	A particularly good example of something
Bee's dick	Tiny unit of measurement
Bewdy	Excellent, outstanding, very grouse indeed
Big End of Town	Where all the wealthy cits of New Sydney dwell
Bonza	First-rate, top shelf, grand
Brasco	Toilet, dunny
Carked it	Died
Ciggies	Cigarettes
Cit	Citizen of Straya
Clacker	Pertaining to the arse region of the body
Clobber	Clothes
Coight	Sphincter
Cunce	Horrible insult to your enemies, term of endearment to your mates
Deadset	100% serious and undeniably accurate
Derros	Surprisingly organised clan in the Downlow
Dinkum	A true statement or objective reality
Doover-fish	NanoCorp-created organism used to purify water
Downlow	An extremely unpleasant district in New Sydney. Very murdery
Drongo	A moron, idiot or otherwise dull-witted cit
Durries	Used to express surprise, distress etc. "Durries, I didn't see that coming!"
Exy-stencil	Existential

Fang	1. A powerful drug favoured by Mongrels, 2. Throwing something
Fark	Exclamation/swear used to express all manner of emotions
Flash	Fancy-looking, expensive
Fug	The more conversational version of 'Fark'
Fuggen	See 'Fug'
Gander	Have a look
Garn	"Go on"
Gawn	Gone
Giz	"Give us"
Gobbie	The beaut act of fellatio
Goey	An amphetamine-based narcotic
Good sort	Someone attractive, extremely rootable
Grouse	About as good as a thing can get
Grunter	NanoCorp-created creature, very cute, bit weird
Guvmint	Government. Cits who run everything. Quite often a packa cunce
Hossie	Hospital
Inasiddy	The area of New Sydney with the highest population density, quite poor
Jool	Fancy rock
Lobbed up	Arrived, often unexpectedly or without warning
Maggoted	Murdered
Mongrels	Terrifying clan of cannibalistic drug addicts in the Downlow
Moots	Mysterious clan of mutants in the Downlow
Mouth-gear	Spoken information, including speeches and monologues
Murican	Race of people from Murica. Possibly all ex-stinked, thankfully
Murder-poet	Author, writer, person who commands the written word
Mutie	Colloquial term for mutants

Nah, yeah	Yes
NanoCorp	The corporation that runs New Sydney, owns everything
Noras	Boobs, chest-lumps, breasticles and so on
Norgs	See "Noras"
Normie	Normal, non-mutant citizen
Paperybacks	Books constructed from paper. Extremely valuable and rare
Pigs	The law enforcement body who keep NanoCorp safe, demand bribes
Pig's arsehole	Expression describing a situation that has ended very poorly
Pissweak	Soft, lacking intestinal fortitude, not tough at all
Poms	People from England, possibly ex-stinked, poor hygiene likely
Poofteenth	A very small amount
Prozzie	Prostitute
Quezzies	Questions
Rat-onna-stick	Strayan delicacy. Often spiced, very tasty
Roils	Family of inbred Poms who owned half the world long ago
Root	The beautiful act of getting your end in, sexual congress
Ruggies	Young children, kids, tin lids etc.
Scrute	Inspect, closely scrutinise
Spadger	Vagina
Squiz	Look, take a gander, examine
Starkers	Nude, sans clobber
Streef	What Strayans say instead of "street". No one knows why
Tockley	Name given to a bloke's penis. AKA Tocko, todger
Todger	See "tockley"
U-drones	Umbrella Drones. They keep New Sydney cits safe from the sun
Vadge	Affectionate slang for vagina. See also "spadger"
Yeah, nah	No
Yonks	Lengthy unit of time, bit non-specific

ONE

I was scavenging in the waterlogged shopping maw when the Mongrels began to chant. At first, I ignored their noise – hoots, howls, loud swearing; all typical Mongrel behaviour – but my ears pricked up when they started to unite. Mongrels were at their most dangerous when they organised.

"Road scab!" came the cry, echoing through the ruins of Gorge Streef, increasing in volume as more took it up. "Road scab! ROAD SCAB!"

I'd never seen a road scab in the dinkum, although I'd heard stories. It wasn't so much that I *wanted* a squiz, but I was curious. It'd be a tale to tell Ken and the ruggies back at the hab.

I pocketed my meagre takings and walked over to the wall closest to where the chanting emmy-nated, and slowly – all catlike stealthy – peeked through a crack in the concrete.

The Mongrels massed around a lone man. He was a skinny bloke, bony and pale, yelling at them to let him go, shrieking high-pitched into their visors and masks. The Mongrels just laughed.

There was twenny or so at ground level, with dozens more looking on from the empty windows in the crumbling edifices above. The skinny bloke was defo no Mongrel, that much was for sure. But he didn't look like a Derro, Moot or member of any other clan I knew.

Just a poor dumb cit who had the bad luck, or low eye-cue, to wander into Mongrel territory.

The lead Mongrel, a huge slab of a man wearing a leather mask and covered in anatomically graphic tattoos from scalp to sole, pointed at the skinny man, booming: "This here cunce snuck into Mongrel territory. OUR TERRITORY!"

This spurred a chorus of hoots and jeers. The big man, who may have been leading the Mongrels for months or hours – such was the mercurial nature of hierarchy amongst the clan – slapped a meaty fist against his chest, slick with drug sweat from whatever weapons-grade fang he'd been hoofing.

"Why he come? For thievering? For murdering? For rapering? WHO KNOW?"

"Who know? Who know?" echoed the peanut gallery, turning to one another, wide-eyed with affected alarm, gleefully absolving themselves of responsibility for what was to follow.

"Who know?" Big man nodded, arms out wide, expansive.

"I wasn't! I didn't know this was your- I-I would never!" Skinny man didn't know when to shut up, although in the same position I'd have been just as skew-whiff with terror.

It was a timely reminder that I too would be met with rough justice if caught.

You should leave, right now, I thought.

I kept watching.

"Keeping our territory safe, we are. Safe from cunce like these!"

The big fella kept on like this for some time. Lots of mouth-gear about invading hordes of undesirable cits, as if the Mongrels had reason to be afraid of anyone in the Downlow.

"So, what we say, boys? What punishment fit crime?"

Homicidal drug addict and circumstantial cannibal he might have been, but I had to admire the chap's showmanship. He really had his clan fired up.

"Road scab!" came the response. Then chanted: "ROAD SCAB! ROAD SCAB! ROAD SCAB!"

The cit wept openly now, and he'd browned his daks something awful. But there was confusion there, too. Did he not know what a road scab was? There was a certain mercy there, however brief.

Sometime in the last decade, the Mongrels had worked out that if they knocked enough umbrella drones from the sky, they could use the unfiltered impact of the Strayan sun for the purpose of inflicting violence. They'd rigged up a huge bitta convex glass flogged from who-knows-where, attached it to the roof of the shopping maw and aimed it down at a patch of concrete – about four meaters wide – at streef level. The result was a bloody huge magnifying glass that could turn the concrete superhot and deadly to anyone nearby. Certainly deadly to a weeping, barefoot cit who just then seemed to realise the depths of his hellish situation and was making a last-ditch effort to save his skin.

"Wait, wait, please! I didn't mean to enter your, uh, territory. It's just that I'm on a very important mission. Perhaps I could pay you some kind of toll!"

He reached into his pockets, producing a handful of round, glinting objects marked with the letters 'VB', linked by dried, braided seaweed. Durries, they were Moot tokens!

Big man accepted the offerings without comment, which the cit unwisely took as a positive sign.

"Yes, you're reasonable men, I can see that," he said, nodding, "and I have no intention of harming any of you. But you see, what I'm doing is vital."

The stammering man pulled something from around his neck — it looked like a bright blue jool on a chain from my vantage point, but I wasn't close enough to see it proper-like.

"I need to dispose of this," he exclaimed. "You don't understand the damage it could do in the wrong hands!"

"A WEAPON!" A stout Mongrel, ferret-faced with fang-addict keen, shouted eagerly. "HE'S A MOOT ASSASSIN!"

"SNEAKY CUNCE!" the big man roared and slapped the jool out of his hand. It spun through the air and landed on the dusty ground, mere meaters from my hiding spot. Up close, I could see it was no jool or gem but some kind of manufactured thingo… and there was movement inside. Like it contained something living.

"MATTER SETTLED!" Big man shouted, as if this wasn't already a foregawn conclusion, "ROAD SCAB!"

The Mongrels chanted and howled, a number of them started chucking bricks at three specific U-drones, marked with pink paint. The drones fell from the sky, buzzing angrily, trailing their UV-blocking wings like deflated balloons. They'd be replaced by NanoCorp within twenny or so minutes — drone automation was efficient even in the Downlow — but that was more than enough time for a road scab.

The sunlight scorched through the gap left by the displaced drones, hitting the convex glass and blazing down like God's own wrath, superheating the concrete in seconds.

The weeping man was pushed and nudged until his bare feet were on the very edge of the baked white concrete.

"P-please don't…"

But the time for talking or begging was over.

The big man pushed the poor bastard and he took a lurching, involuntary step onto the concrete. The cit hopped from foot to foot, making high-pitched yipping sounds as his bare soles hit the ground. He danced this way and that, almost elegantly at first, but before too long he began to tire. Any attempt to leave the concrete ring was met by Mongrel fists and soon his yipping took on a sad tone.

And shortly he stopped jumping and just stood there, wobbling back and forth, his face ghoulish with despair. It took a few seconds before I could hear the sizzling. And then the screaming. And then the cheering.

The cit's flesh flowed from his bony feet like butter in a pan and I had to turn my face away when he fell to his knees, uttering an inhuman wail.

Judging from the reaction of the crowd, it didn't take long. The screaming stopped and then there just was the hideous skillet sound of baking flesh on white-hot concrete. I took one brief glance when it was done – morbid, impulsive idiot, I am – and, before I chundered, I had to admit whatever murder-poet came up with the name was dead right: a road scab was what he'd become, a blackish-red blood-and-bone smear drying on the infected flesh of the city.

I wiped my mouth and tried to block out the lusty cheers. And then I remembered the not-a-gem. Could be worth something at the markets Maybe even to an uptown buyer. I decided it was worth the risk and, moving my sinewy limbs, reached through the crack in the concrete and spidered my fingers towards it. Nearly nabbed it, nearly, neaaaarly…

"Where he weapon go?" Big man shouted.

I froze. Maybe they'd forgotten in which direction it had flown.

"Over there!"

Not good. But I managed to grab the stupid, probs worthless, thing.

"LOOK!"

Oh, come on, now…

"ANOTHER SNEAKY CUNCE!"

If I just back away, I'll be fine–

"GEDDIM!"

Fark.

I turned around and sprang to my feet, quickly sprinting through the maw. My feet splashed in the hot water as I crested a hill of cars, rusted together into a ramp shape, and sprang from the top. My hands latched onto the concrete ledge that led to the upper levels of the building. I was still climbing over the lip when I heard the first of the Mongrels yelling and gibbering beneath me.

Fark it! I'd hoped for more time. I entered the old office building, tilted at a permanent fordy-five-degree angle, and ran for my life.

What Mongrels lacked in raw speed, they more than made up for in destructive capabilities. I remember thinking that almost admiringly as one of them exploded through the rotten plaster wall of the room I'd just run through, screaming malignant glory-rage.

I was fast, nimble on my feet, but they were hopped up, feeling no pain.

I continued pelting through the mouldy rabbit warren of collapsed office buildings, quickly looking for sideways routes and ledges I could climb. Any way to break their line of sight, to send them on the wrong path.

I jumped out a window and hurtled through space until I landed on another tilted building. This whole area of the "see-bee-dee", as Ken called it, had fallen into a depression – a kind of epic, watery sinkhole – compressing the old buildings together like filthy, jagged teeth in a mouth gawn to rot.

It meant someone nimble like me could move faster than the Mongrels. That was the theory, anyway, but six of them – including the big man – were right behind me, bellowing obscene promises of the things they'd do to my bodily meats, none of which sounded very pleasant.

I shifted direction to a long bridge made by a collapsed building spanning a pit that dropped into a cauldron of boiling sea water. The bridge was thinner than the others and I hoped its precariousness would give the Mongrels pause.

I should have known better. Fang contains superpowered steroids, leaving its users in a permanent state of self-aggrandisement, making them too up themselves to fear death. None of the six missed a step as they followed. Gaining.

Then one of them, an older clansman judging by his leathery skin, tripped on an empty window pane and staggered off the edge. He was screaming obscenities the whole way down, and I fancied I could still hear his mouth-gear once the steaming waters swallowed him, although that might have been my imagination.

Five still followed. More than enough to kill me.

"GET THAT YELLOW CUNCE!" the big man brayed.

I should explain something here: I'm a mutant. Not full-blown monster, I can pass for normie wearing sunnies and a hood, but a mutie all the same. I'm hairless, my skin is a bright shade of jaundiced yellow, my eyes blood-red, and I have double as many joints as you do in my fingers, legs and toes.

I can bend my legs in almost any direction, which can come in handy at times, but on balance isn't worth the hassle of being a genetic freak. See, if there's one thing a Mongrel hates more than a regular interloper, it's a mutie interloper. I knew I had to time the next few steps carefully else I'd be a flaking stain on the concrete too.

I ran the last few meaters into the dead end. Big man hooted with a mixture of anticipation and glee.

"Nowhere to go, CUNCE!"

I licked my lips and stared up at the cliff wall that led to salvation. The edge of the barrier between the Downlow and Inasiddy, a near vertical drop half a kilomeater high from semi-civilisation to the madness of the killzones.

I turned to face the Mongrels, who had slowed down, panting and catching their breath. You could see the early signs of fang poisoning in them: greying skin, blisters and boils – these poor dumb bastards wouldn't live through the year. The masks weren't just for the purpose of intimidation, they hid the corrosive effects of fang – rotten teeth, bung eye and scale skin. None of them could have been over twenny-five. If I'd been a better person, I'd probs have felt sorry for them.

If.

"Gon' think up something special for you, mutie," Big man promised, scratching his left bicep that featured a tattoo of the Southern Cross consty-lation that seemed to be having vigorous sexual congress with a number of apparently delighted sheilas. "Comin' down 'ere. Stealing our stuff. WHO YOU THINK YOU ARE?"

The other Mongrels agreed, nodding and grunting.

"We from here!" Big man cried. "We grew here!"

During this one-way discussion, I'd been slowly squatting down, letting my extra-jointed legs bend backwards and tense, sorta like a kangaroo. I'd only get one shot at this. I threw a quick look upwards, mentally marking my target.

"WE GREW HERE!" Big man thumped his chest in time with his words. "WE. GREW. HERE."

I couldn't resist shooting a cheeky grin as I replied: "And I flew here!"

With that I unclenched my legs, using all the extra energy afforded by my joint mutations, and leapt directly atop the big man's head. He was so shocked for that split second, he froze and gave me the chance to perform another leap – this time straight vertical – high above their heads and grasping hands.

Big man's sweaty sosso-sized fingers almost nabbed my foot, but I was up and over.

I reached out with my fingers spread and latched onto the U-drone I'd left hovering when I'd entered the Downlow hours earlier.

My fingers closed on the thing like a vice and I quickly switched it back to its pre-programmed ascent protocol. The Mongrels weren't the only ones who could play silly buggers with U-drones.

"YELLOW KANGAROO MUTIE CUNCE!" came the cries.

"GET BACK HERE!"

"FOLLOW HIM!" Big man's mask had slipped and his ravaged, ugly mug was like a living rage blister. "DON'T LET HIM GEDDAWAY!"

But it was too late, my drone was hooning up the cliff face, leaving the homicidal sinkhole of the Downlow behind. Big man threw a few rocks at me, but the effort was half-hearted. They were tiring and needed more fang. I'd soon be a half-remembered nothing in their decaying brains.

I hoped so anyway.

I turned my face away from the ruins and watched as my drone carried me upwards, carried me home.

TWO

I smelled the markets at Cliff's Edge before I stepped into them. Once I'd risen level to the Inasiddy, I turned the drone to charge mode and let it hover out of reach for anyone without my jumping range. Not that many people want access to the Downlow. Only the insane or desperate.

I pulled on my goggles and raised my hood, hoping it would be enough to avoid any mutie hate. I'd had about enough of that for the day. Peeking out to make sure no one was watching, I stepped through a break in the safety wall and joined the jostling mass of bodies.

As always, the markets were stifling in a haze of cooking smoke and humidity, a potent mix that seemed to brush rudely into you, making you stagger. After the comparatively open air of the see-bee-dee, it felt crushing and oppressive.

Still, fewer cits were likely to try and murder me here.

I walked past stalls selling dog cakes, rat-onna-stick, fish of various sizes – most of them looked suspiciously deformed to my eyes – and various concoctions that were less easy to identify.

The food stalls tended to favour goods that were spicy and rich, all the better to add flavour to the healthy but bland guvmint-delivered nutrition bricks.

I skirted past the food stalls, the blacksmithing joints, the clothing places, barely glancing at the goods and clobber I would never be able to afford, and over to the anteeks section. Here was where I'd try to get some extra grub for the ruggies back at the hab. I nodded at Lil – "Old Lil" we called her, but not to her face – who ran the best of the anteek stalls. She sold all manner of repurposed and repaired gear from the olden days, at a vastly inflated cost, of course. That said, she also had no problem trading with muties and was happy to pay in nutrition bricks.

"Lil." I smiled what I hoped was my least scary smile.

"Franga." Lil nodded as she finished a transaction. She squinted at me through her greasy thick glasses. "What can I do for you today?"

I upended my satchel on the counter, exposing my unimpressive haul. A couple of intact bottles, an old eye-phone that looked impossible to fix and a toy, pre-golden age by the looks, a spiky-haired, yellow-skinned boy in blue shorts.

"Looks a bit like you, eh?" Lil chuckled as she touched the toy.

I winced and tried to make it look as if I found the comment witty.

Lil saw right through it and grimaced. "Ah, durries, kid, I'm sorry. I'm just a stupid old sheila sometimes."

"S'fine, Lil." I waved her apology away. "Long day is all. So, what'll you give me for this?"

"Three nutes."

"Three?" I didn't have to affect outrage. That was daylight robbery, even for a small haul.

Lil just shrugged.

"Guvmint's cutting down. Doing it tough all over."

I met Lil's bespectacled eye. "Four."

Lil's gaze started steely but something seemed to give as she looked at me, like she felt sorry for joking before or just plain sorry in general.

"Righto, then."

"Righto," I agreed.

As I was walking away, four nutrition bricks richer, I suddenly remembered the not-a-gem I'd flogged from the Mongrels. I almost turned back, that thing would surely fetch me another nute or two, but no, this was something for Ken to see.

Ken would know what to do with it. Unless, of course, he was having one of his dazed days.

I headed to the side of the market and left via the exit nearest Flesh Alley. The Rooting District was safer for muties than the main drag, as cits who were feeling toey generally wanted to get their end in, rather than bash a yellow boy.

Prozzies of all shapes and sizes lined the streefs, selling their wares with smiling mouths and open legs. They all ignored me – only a very desperate proz would root a mutie – except for Gia, who gave me a nod and a small smile that suggested she'd be happy to chat later, but right then she was working.

The alley was dimly lit, a blessing really, as the leavings of quick, anonymous roots tended to benefit from muted lighting. I looked back at Gia, who was now chatting with a burly, hairy-backed cit, and gesturing to a small alcove out back of the alley, and sighed.

Gia always made me feel funny, like I was hurtsome in the trouser region. I had a strange urge to protect her even though she could easily handle herself. I had daydreams about touching her hair.

As usual these feelings left me flustered and distracted, which was not helpful, so I pushed the thoughts down and focused on getting back to the hab.

The kids would be getting hungry.

• • • •

The Ages Home sat quietly, hoping not to be noticed, at the back of two sparsely populated streefs, down a bit from the main drag of the Inasiddy. There was nothing of value nearby and few had reason to approach it.

Even so, spidery graffiti painted across the front of the building read "MUTIE SCUM!" and "FREAKS GO HOME", the latter of which made little sense as it was our home.

We regularly had to clean similar messages off the place. Some folks just flat out didn't like muties, and an orphanage full of them seemed to incense them even further.

Still, the walls were thick, the doors were strong and we managed to make do with the little we had. Supplemented, with increasing regularity, by my trips to the Downlow.

As I reached the front door, I took a moment to compose myself. I had to leave the outside outside and be cheerful and upbeat for the young ones. A quick glance around to make sure no one was nearby, then I fished out the key and entered, closing the door behind me.

The Ages Home was divided into three horizontal layers. Downstairs was an open-plan area with a kitchen, bathroom, piles of damaged second-hand toys and lots of space for children to run around. Upstairs were the beds – usually bare mattresses, some with ancient, moth-eaten sheets – and the third storey was Ken's private quarters. It was a cramped joint, but I had made many happy memories there, and the solar panels Ken had rigged up gave us comparative luxuries like the ability to warm water, run fans and cook using a stovetop.

As I walked into the downstairs, the kids started yelling happily, circling excitedly, a ring of cheery chaos.

"Franga!"

"We was worried about you!"

"Did you bring us presents?"

The kids ranged from six years of age to sixdeen. There were twelve of them, thirdeen if you counted me. However, at ninedeen I felt I couldn't really be counted as a kid anymore; now I was a minder or teacher. There was Flibby, Nug, Belial, Bella, Leesa, Rod, Gruta, Debbie, Dane, Claire, Mason and Tommy. Every single one of them was a mutie. Mostly it was little stuff – webbed fingers and toes, missing eyes, extra nose – but we had a couple of "full monsters" with us.

Debbie was seven years of age and a shaggy carpet of hair almost completely covered her facial features. We needed to shave Debs twice a day just so she could find her mouth and eat.

Tommy was sixdeen years old and looked like a lizard. Deadset scales, forked tongue, not an inch of normal skin. He had a sweet, innocent personality and always helped teach the younger ones when needed, but his appearance guaranteed he'd never find a family.

Durries, most of us wouldn't. The Ages Home called itself an orphanage but really it was a place where the unwanted dwelled.

I felt something tug at my hand and I looked down to see Bella, six years old with one enormous eye and one pure white, constantly weeping one.

"Frangaaaaaa."

"Yeah, Bel?"

"I'm hungryaaaaa!"

I ruffled her hair and smiled. She was cute even with the eye pus. "'Kay, let's get you some grub."

"I'll help!"

With Bella and a couple of the other ruggies, I whipped up a feast of nutrition lumps flavoured with some leftover spicy rat. It wasn't exactly gore-may, but the kids shovelled it down, licked their plates and asked for seconds.

In theory, the guvmint provided every cit with enough nutrition bricks to prevent starvation and give them the energy to find gainful employment and not be a burden on the system. Problem one: fark-all jobs. Employment numbers were in single digits, and low ones at that.

Problem two: they didn't consider muties to be legit cits. So, we had to make do as best we could, with Ken being the only technically legit one of us and me doing some shonky jobs on the side. And, of course, there was our main source of income: the yarts.

Entertainment comes in many forms in Strayan culture. In the Downlow, it's clans and killzones. Up the Big End of Town? Well, who knows what those wankers do, but in the Inasiddy? It's theatre.

Ken told me it used to be telefissions and cinemas, internets and all that, but after the Big Blackout they were all lost, along with ebooks and smart paper. One huge electromagnetic pulse and entire generations of yarts were lost to everyone. Existing only in rare and spensive paper forms, most of which had been flogged by collectors or destroyed in the various quakes, floods and fires that hit Straya after the Big Blackout, or the Water Wars that kicked on over the following years.

None of us kids are old enough to remember those days, but Ken – when he was thinking straight – told us they were bad times, so bad most of the murder-poets wouldn't even scribe about them.

Instead, Ken tried to focus on the good times, on the plays and yarts from the olden days, and the more recent mouth-gear from Renaissance 2.0. The problem, of course, was that Ken's mind was cactus and getting more cactus by the day.

See, back in Renaissance 2.0 the science blokes and sheilas had extended lifespans to two hundred years and more. They used these little doers called nanomachines that improved a bloke's blood, guts and all the rest. Healed diseases, kept your brain heaps smart and that.

The Big Blackout put the kibosh on that something severe.

The nanomachines didn't stop working straight away, but they had been getting worse over time, and that was why Ken was losing his mind, piece by piece.

I'd been trying to hide the truth from the other kids, but someday I was gunna have to tell them. I wasn't looking forward to it.

And I really wasn't looking forward to having to care for the ruggies on my own.

"Are we going to rehearse now, Franga?" Bel wanted to know.

"Soon, love," I assured her. "First, I need to see Ken."

• • • •

Ken Ages wasn't Ken's real name, but he couldn't remember his original monica. The name "Ken Ages" came as an answer to the question, "How long have you been alive?"

"'Ken ages!"

He thought it a suitable response and cackled every time he said it, like it was the first. Eventually, I stopped asking and just referred to him as Ken.

Ken had been taking in mutie kids for yonks, giving them a place to live when their normie parents inevitably abandoned them. Usually they'd be left on the front stoop of the home, although in some extreme cases – Tommy f'rinstance – Ken literally saved their lives.

Tommy's parents were God-botherers – real holy cunce – and decided their offspring was the deadset actual devil. They tried drowning the poor bugger down the harbour, thankfully not during a corrosion tide otherwise he'd have been melted. Two passing fishermen were alerted by Tommy's wails and saved him just in time. After they'd had a squiz at Tommy, they weren't so sure they'd done the right thing, but.

None of us mutie kids had happy stories, they usually began with tragedy and ended with death, addiction or long-term servitude at the protein farms, the army or worse. Most of us moved out of the Inasiddy when we came of age, but at least we'd had some kindness in our lives, if only briefly.

We all owed Ken a lot, which was why I helped him like I did.

That night Ken was fast asleep, snoring like a champion and drooling a little. Believe it or not, that was an improvement on some nights 'when he didn't quite know who he was or what was going on. The fear I saw in his eyes in those times fair chilled my blood.

I gently closed the door to his attic apartment behind me and had a long squiz around the joint. It was one of my favourite places.

The room was full of shelves, "bookshelves" they were called, harkening back to an era when cits had enough books to fill whole shelves!

Of course, they weren't full of books these days, rather Ken's versions of the plays we performed – as best he could remember them – and knick-knacks, keepsakes and treasures we were holding back to sell when things got more desperate or had extreme sentimental or practical value.

Ken slouched in his huge leathery chair, a tiny old man with an endless beard and thin hands. There was one other chair, a plastic thing, and the rest of the joint was cluttered with plays, diagrams and half-finished projects of Ken's. It was chaos, it was glorious and the smell of paper made me happy in ways I can't fully describe. A bit like when I'd think about touching Gia's hair, except less in the trouser, more in the heart.

I moved towards the lowest shelf, where the least-precious cargo sat, and went to my area. Ken had let me keep a small box of stuff there since I turned thirteen and I visited it every day I could.

I sat on the plastic seat and took the box on my knees. I opened it and had a good long sniff of the scent of my slightly spoiled treasures. Books, five of them! Five whole actual paperybacks from times long gawn.

In the box was: *Northanger Abbey* by Jane Austen, *A Tale of Two Cities* by Charles Dickens (which had the final thirdy pages torn out), *A Word of the Day* Calendar from 2027, *Night of the Crabs* by Guy N. Smith and *Crab's Moon* by Guy N. Smith.

I remember first reading them crab books, thinking as bad as things could be in the Inasiddy, I was glad the killer crabs that must have plagued the 1980s had all gawn ex-stinked. They sounded like unpleasant, pincery cunce to me.

I expressed that notion to Ken years back and he laughed so hard he had a coughing fit that left him faint.

"That's fiction, Franga," he explained. "Those people in the books aren't real."

"But, like, they're scribed there. On paper," I'd replied, shaking my head. How could it be, like, not real if it was writ down?

"Franga, fiction is when you tell a story about something that didn't really happen, mate," Ken explained slowly, making sure I understood.

"So, it's bullshit?" I found myself suddenly angry at Mr. N. Smith.

"In a way," Ken said, nodding, "but it's bullshit that lets you know ahead of time, and is trying to tell you a yarn for your enjoyment. I suppose you could say that fiction is... beaut bullshit."

Reading hadn't come easy to me, but Ken spent months learning me up good, giving me solo lessons after he'd finished the hab-wide ones with the rest of the ruggies. He was a grouse teacher, patient and caring, and never made you feel like a drongo for being a bit slow off the mark. And, eventually, I'd got the hang of it.

The result was, I ended up being a voracious reader, squizzing anything I could get my hands on. I thought that Dickens bloke and Austen sheila were pretty good murder-poets but I reckoned Guy N. Smith must've been one of the best ever. On the inside leaf of his books, it said he'd scribed ten other paperybacks on them crabs alone! One day I hoped to be as brave as Guy. He sounded grouse.

After spending some time touching my treasures, reading my favourite passages and smelling the paper, I replaced the books and gently put my box back on the shelf. When I turned around, Ken was awake and looking at me, smiling.

I blushed for some reason, feeling as if I'd lobbed up starkers or something.

"Soz, Ken, didn't know you were awake."

"No need for apologies, son. I like seeing you with your books." Ken smiled that old sad smile that left me feeling confused and a bit simple. "How was the Downlow?"

"Mongrels road scabbed some poor bloody cit."

"Really?" Ken's eyes widened behind his grimy specs.

"Deadset."

"Tell me."

Over the next twenny or so minutes, I told Ken about the road scabbing and my heroic escape. To be honest, Ken seemed less impressed with my fleeing skills and more focused on the Moot tokens and the not-a-gem I still had on my person. He deadset interrupted me when I was explaining my high eye-cue bartering with Lil and asked to see the not-a-gem.

I shrugged and pulled it from around my neck, placing it gently in Ken's withered, ancient palm.

He stared at it for a long time, the light from the lanterns placed around the room hitting the bright blue globe and making it give off a strange, shifting light – like what I imagine sunlight looks like when you're under the sea. That sense that it was living came back and left me feeling a bit unsettled, skew-whiff.

"What is it?" I asked after Ken hadn't said anything for heaps long.

"I… don't know," he replied wonderingly, holding the thing up to the light, just the hint of a smile crossing his face.

"Some kind of gem or treasure?"

"Yes, but no… it's not naturally occurring. This has been manufactured."

"S'what I reckoned," I told him proudly.

"Tell me everything again." Ken spoke with an intensity I hadn't seen in him for ages. "Every single detail, especially about the cit who had this."

So, I did. Again and again. And then again. Describing in exhaustive detail every little thing. Eventually, Ken sat back in his chair, knackered but somehow happy as well.

"So…" I began, "we gunna sell it?"

"Not yet. I need to think on this. I feel as if I'm remembering… something." Ken shook his head as if to clear it of fog.

"Ken?"

"Just go rehearse with the ruggies. Gimme some time with this."

"Righto."

"And Franga?"

"Yeah?"

"Thank you."

I nodded and left Ken with the not-a-gem, staring deep into the shifting blue layers, transfixed and somewhere else entirely.

THREE

"It is New Sydney, Straya, and the Big Blackout is about to 'appen..." Bella, dressed as an angel, announced in a voice barely above a whisper.

"Louder, Bel," I advised.

"IT IS NEW SYDNEY, STRAYA, AND THE BIG BLACKOUT IS ABOUT TO 'APPEN!" she bellowed.

I attempted to turn my throaty guffaw into a cough and mostly succeeded.

"Good, good..."

Three of the ruggies wandered onto the stage, dressed as golden-age era New Sydneyites. This involved holding olden style eye-phones and other gadgets and generally looking preoccupied, which came pretty easy to ruggies. I waved a piece of cardboard over the lantern, signifying the BB had occurred.

"Oh NO!" one wailed. "My access to the innanet has been disconnected!"

"How will I communicate wif my friends and relatives?" wailed another.

The third took centre stage and exclaimed: "How will our futuristical you... youtor... youter..."

"Youtopia," I prompted.

"... Youtopia survive," he said, finishing with, "now that all of our electronic devices have been rendered obsolete?"

This was Bel's cue to come back.

"AND SO STRAYA AND NEW SYDNEY WAS THROWN INTO CHAOS!" she roared, weepy eye bulging with the strain of it. Bel continued on, chewing on the large slabs of mouth-gear with more skill than you'd expect from a ruggie. She'd be destined for the Opra House or beyond in a country that didn't hate muties so much.

The play we were rehearsing was called *Angels of New Sydney* by Kenneth Ages. It was an original work by Ken, and one of the more popular ones. Before Angels, Ken had us performing Shakeyspeare plays as best he could remember them. There was *Hamlit, McBeth, Julius Seizure* and *Two Blokes from Somewhere Poncy.* The problem was Ken couldn't recall whole sections of them, so he'd have ruggies dressed as 'angels' appear and explain a bunch of stuff.

The crowd hated it.

Well, to be clear, the crowd hated the Shakeyspeare, with all his fancy words and confusing language, but they loved the angels. Muties were reviled, except when they were adorable kids struggling with dialogue it seemed.

After trying, and failing, to get the public enthused about Shakeyspeare, Tennis-e Williams and Harold Pincer, Ken "sold out" (his words) and started scribing his own historical works.

We were an instant hit and the 'All Ages Mutie Theatre Troopie' was suddenly in high demand. Ken grumbled and complained but you could tell he was at least a little stoked his work was being appreciated.

The thing is, amidst the jokes and cute angels, he'd try to slip in some, like, commentary on society, solid brain-gear for those with the eye-cue to understand it, even sub-limb-alley.

"See, that's the trick ol' Shakeyspeare always pulled, Frang," he told me one night, while sipping a cup of homemade grog that fair burned my nostrils just to smell it from halfway across the room. "You give the people what they want – spectacle, love, horror – but you also tell them something about themselves."

"Like what?" I wanted to know, desperate to be a smarter bloke.

"Like… that we're cruel. We're a mean-spirited load of cits at the best of times…"

That didn't seem like much of a message to me. I was about to say so when he held up a gnarled finger.

"*But*, we can be better. If we acknowledge our cruelty and try to improve, battle our worst impulses, our darkest nature."

"Like Guy N. Smith battled them big crabs, eh, Ken?" I nodded sagely, but jokefully, on account of the fact I knew fiction was beaut bullshit by then.

"Right," he agreed, smiling indulgently. "Just like that."

Back in the now, Angel Bel was relating the next part of the story: "SO THE PEOPLE OF NEW SYDNEY HAD TO BAND TOGETHER, USING MATESHIP AND YOU-BEAUT AUSSIE SPIRIT!"

All the ruggies linked hands on stage and started singing, pretending to build a new society.

I'd asked Ken about this bit, wanting to know if this was dinkum how we bounced back. Ken laughed and shook his head.

"No, son, no. Mateship is a sweet quality but it doesn't build infrastructure or feed the masses."

"So, like, what did then?"

"In the end, NanoCorp saved us all," Ken said bitterly, sneering at something, or someone, only he could see. "Bringing along with it corporate exploitation, the instigation of a new caste system and fresh helpings of social inequality. In other words, 'business as usual'."

"But, we're here, aren't we? Alive and that?"

"Alive, Franga. But are we living?"

I was genuinely flummoxed by that question. I gave it a long think, then replied: "I don't know any other way."

"No," Ken said, his eyes glistening with tears, "and that's a tragedy in itself."

I didn't know what he meant then, but as Bel stood and acted her little heart out – as all the kids tried their best, spreading a well-intentioned if inaccurate message of hope – I was wondering if maybe I was beginning to.

"And that's how come we live in Straya: the best country in the world."

They all looked at me once they were done. I sniffed away the lump in my throat and smiled at them. "Youse did good. Youse all did… real good."

• • • •

Sleep didn't come easy that night and at around 3am I gave up and decided to go for a walk. The streefs of the Inasiddy were not a safe place for any cit to be out that late, much less a mutie, but I wasn't going to be in the streefs, not for long anyway.

I climbed out through the second-storey window, closed it quietly behind me, and crept along the roof. I glanced below to see if anyone was looking up, but no – the few cits on the dimly lit streefs were furtive and busy with their nocturnal missions.

No one ever looks up in the Inasiddy.

I leapt from the roof of the Ages Home to the neighbouring buildings. They were slate, and taller than most, so my landings weren't likely to get noticed. I moved along like this, catlike stealthy, and then jumped to the next low, sloped roof or corrugated iron shanty lid. If anyone heard anything, they didn't react, and if they looked to see where the sound came from, I'd moved on before they got a decent squiz at me.

I paused, as I often did, at the town well. The wide deep hole had dozens of moisture-gathering tubes that snaked up above it on sturdy, interlinked poles, blossoming into what looked to my eyes like a healthy growing tree. It wasn't, of course, it was just a clever placement of materials, leading down to a deep body of water that swam with the doover-fish that cleansed it of poisons and impurities. Still, it felt like a touch of nature, which was rare in the Inasiddy. I made a mental note to grab some water on the way back – a much safer proposition at night when cits were less likely to arc up about a mutie drinking 'clean normie water' – and kept on going.

This was a trip I'd made many times before and I was good at it. The power in my legs, the release of the leaps and the tension as I landed – it was thrilling. I clambered from roof to roof, mainly walking on all fours, for once not embarrassed by my multiple joints and monkey-like mutations. On clear, quiet nights like this I loved them.

I crept and leapt my way through the deserted markets, past several small breweries where grog was distilled from scavenged ingredients that smelled pure evil, past stables where sickly-looking horses were kept to be rented to those with the dosh, over the habs and towards the harbour and the bridge.

The Harbour Bridge was, according to Ken, a "bloody bewdy" that had somehow survived the BB, Water Wars and more. It was a rusting hulk, really, and no cars travelled along it anymore but it still stood strong and proud.

And very climbable.

This was the part of the walk where I had to be real careful. The bridge acted as a barrier between the Inasiddy and The Big End of Town. The guards were usually hopped up on grog or leaf at this late hour, but I had to be cautious nonetheless. They carried crossbows and no matter how fleet of foot I was, a bolt in the ballbag would make the evening a lot less enjoyable.

As I moved closer to the soaring metal arch, I could see my instinct about the guards was correct. They were fat blokes – uniforms straining at their guts – and almost as red-eyed as me, imbibing from a thermos they passed back and forth and laughing in a languid, loose-limbed way.

I could probably jump amongst them and sing a choon and they'd barely react but I stayed quiet, kept climbing. There were barbed wire barriers and wooden signs proclaiming "KEEP OUT" with skull and crossbones painted underneath to drive home the point. I just jumped over them and moved up the arch.

No one really tried very hard to get into The Big End of Town. Even if you made it across the bridge, there was that much security you'd barely have time to remark on how clean everything was before a crossbow bolt gave you a brand-new nostril, or worse, the Pigs got ya. There were all sorts of rumours about the Pigs, and how they did terrible things to wandering cits. Not road scab terrible, but still – those who were caught were never heard from again.

Besides, I didn't want to go to The Big End, I just wanted to reach the top of the bridge.

My arm and leg muscles ached in a good way, a way that signified I'd been working hard, and once I reached the top of the bridge – where the big Strayan flag flew high and tattered – I stopped and allowed myself to rest and look out at New Sydney.

At night, the city was a beautiful sheila, her flaws and pockmarks smoothed by the lack of the sun's merciless light. The Inasiddy, that cramped cluster, looked all poetic and that, lit by lanterns and the occasional battery-operated light.

The Big End of Town, as always, was better lit and prettier. Close to NanoCorp headquarters, they had access to battery-powered inventions, food, medicine and even their U-drones were better quality.

At the top of the bridge, the canopy of umbrella drones that shifted and writhed in the sky seemed almost within reach. I knew that was an optical illusion and if I tried to jump up and grab one, I'd fall well short, but I stared up at them anyway.

In quiet moments like these, I fantasised about what it must be like to live as a U-drone. You'd float high above the city, above all the cits and their problems and hates, and join with the other drones, creating a flowing fibre webbing that blocked out the worst of the sun's UV rays.

You'd float, you'd protect and you'd charge yourself via that glowering ball of cancer that was the sun.

Sometimes I'd try to visualise what the city must have looked like before the drones, before NanoCorp saved everyone from the fires and roasting death, but it was impossible. U-drones were as much a part of life as my cursed yellow skin and evil-looking red eyes.

I looked out over the harbour waters that seemed so peaceful and calm, but if I dipped my head underneath for even a moment, the face I'd pull out of the drink would be far uglier than the one I had now. And if I did so during one of the sporadic corrosion tides, when the most toxic pollution floated in from the sea? Well, I'd be dissolved down to a screaming puddle.

Everything is pretty at night, from a distance, but the truth is usually toxic or deadly.

The truth of my life was I couldn't remember much before Ken took me in. I had vague images in my bonce that resembled a ghostly woman, me mum I guess, but those could have been added afterwards. Comforting brain-gear my head invented to feel less hurtsome and alone.

I couldn't remember my dad at all.

Yeah, it seemed to me life would be a lot better as a U-drone. You could save people from the sun but not need to be close enough to realise some of them, most of them, might not be worth the effort.

I admit I was starting to feel a bit sorry for myself, up there on that silent bridge. I only noticed the guards were changing when some fresher, thinner blokes lobbed up at the trash barricades that prevented easy entry for anyone walking from the Inasiddy, far below my peaceful perch.

The sun was soon going to be peeking over the horizon, the U-drones moving in flock formation to catch it, and I knew I had to get back home.

There would be breakfasts to make, tantrums to halt and baths for the stinky. I took a long, deep breath and sighed, then began climbing down, back into reality.

I stopped on the roofs above Flesh Alley on the return trip, hoping to say g'day to Gia. I snuck along the pointed peaks of The Splayed Vadge and peered down but Gia was nowhere to be seen. The various prozzies still working looked half-asleep and ready to pass out, wilting on stilt-like shoes and sweating under layers of colourful makeup.

I hoped wherever Gia was she was healthy, well rested and safe.

• • • •

I had first met Gia when I was thirdeen. I was only just starting to take trips outside the hab by myself and still wasn't sure of places that were safe or nah for a mutie. Needless to say, I quickly ran afoul of some cits who were none too pleased to see me.

A group of blokes, a little older than me, called themselves the Ozzy Boyz and reckoned it was their culcharool imperative to, like, nugget cunce they believed didn't belong in the fine upstanding neighbourhoods of the Inasiddy.

This remit involved a fair bit of punching and kicking and chasing of muties. So, once they'd clocked me walking down the streef, bold as you please, they yelled some fairly standard insults and started having a go. I managed to pull away and run – nose bleeding, left eye swelling – but they gave chase and were fast.

I hadn't quite got a handle on my mutations at that stage, so it was only a matter of time before these Boyz caught me and beat me brainless. So, I took a shortcut and ran into Flesh Alley.

I'd heard of the Rooting District, naturally – what teenage cit hadn't? – but even so I wasn't prepared for the sheer level of rudie nudieness that greeted me.

There were sheilas getting about with their norgs and lady parts exposed, a few blokes – tockos out and having a pash with one another – and all manner of bendy-over, come-hithery pozzies being struck. Places with names like The Splayed Vadge, The Masturbatorium, GIZ ROOT and Fug-Knucklez promised a variety of sexy treats, daubed in garish fluoro paint. A band of festy-looking cits played what I imagine they believed to be sexy choons, and the stench of sex and ciggie smoke hung thick in the air.

I was gobsmacked by all of it and stared, wide-eyed, forgetting the Boyz behind me. They helpfully reminded me by smacking the back of my bonce.

"Oi, mutie, stop staring at our normie sheilas!" one of them, the leader by the look of him, shouted. Then he spun me around and punched me right in the guts, and I went down like a sack of spuds.

I coughed and tried to stand up but a swift boot kept me on the ground, which was pretty grotty. I curled up and got ready to take a beating. Sometimes it was just better to let them get it over with, I reasoned.

But the anticipated punching on never occurred because right at that moment, Gia caught a squiz at what was transpiring and came stomping over. She was more dressed than most of the other prozzies – clumpy boots, tiny shorts and a singlet, ciggie hanging from her mouth, goggles around her neck – but she looked real good to me, even lying on the ground in no small amount of pain.

She strode over, glanced at me, then at the Ozzy Boyz, furious. "What the bloody hell is all this?"

"Fuggen just, you know, wanted to stomp this mutie. For perving on youse sheilas." The leader of the Boyz seemed a whole lot less impressive wilting under Gia's incendiary gaze.

"This is the Rooting District. Perving is a big part of what goes on here." Gia spoke to him in the way you'd address a particularly stupid dog.

"But, like, he's a mutie–"

"I can SEE that. I can also see he's on the ground in a three-against-one typea bizzo. Which to my way of thinking makes you lot a packa cunce."

"Fair go, love–"

"Further to that, I think I recognise youse boys. You," she said pointing at the fat one, "you're Jay Patto's kid, eh? And you – you've got the look of a Carpo."

"So what–"

"AND YOU," Gia talked over the top of him, "are *clearly* a Kayden."

"Yeah, what's that got to do with anything?"

"Gee, it'd be a shame if your dads were cut off in Flesh Alley."

That stopped all three of the Boyz. Flesh Alley was pretty much the only outlet for hard-working cits of the Inasiddy. An unrooted dad was an angry dad – and judging by the fear on all three faces, these boys were no stranger to a knuckling from the old man.

"You wouldn't do that…" ol' mate said weakly.

"I would. And so would my friends. Ask around. Ask 'em if youse should piss off Gia Bails!"

That did it. All three seemed to share a telly-pathic communication. Something along the lines of *bugger this, let's get the fark out of here* and off they went, grunting and pushing one another, shooting me filthy looks. But they didn't say a bloody thing.

Gia looked down at me, a strange sorta expression on her face.

"You weren't really perving, were ya?" she asked.

"Nah," I squeaked, then cleared my throat to continue. "I was trynna get away from them."

Gia held out her hand to help me up. I took it, savouring the momentary contact – but letting go as soon as I was up. I didn't want her to think me dodgy.

"Ta," I murmured.

"Durries, you're just a kid."

I shrugged.

"You're not full monster, though."

I shrugged again.

"Those eyes, though. Fark. Like a demon's dirty clacker."

I felt like I was about to shit my freshly broken heart into my daks.

"Look, here's the thing: when you're getting about the Inasiddy, feel free to pop into Flesh Alley. Not many of the prozzies here will root ya, but you'll be safer than out there."

"I just wanted to have a squiz around town." I sounded pathetic to my own ears.

"Yeah, I know. People are cunce, trust me on that." She stared right into my eyes and then grinned, as if inspiration had struck.

She quickly whipped the goggles off from around her neck and handed 'em over.

"What's this?"

"Goggles. Obvs. You a bit thick?"

"No, I mean, like – what for?"

"To cover your eyes, mate. Goggles on, hood up you can almost pass as normie. Better than you are right now anyway."

"I don't have anything to give you–" I reached into my empty pockets.

"Ah, don't worry, I've got shitloads of the things."

Gia turned to walk away as a new group of cits had wandered into the alley from the other entrance.

"Thank you!" I called after her.

"You're right, mate." Then she turned around, flashing a brilliant smile. "What's your name?"

"Franga."

"Gia."

I smiled back.

"You've got a nice smile, Franga. I hope you get the chance to use it more often."

And just like that I'd made a friend. Even though she was older, and a normie, I had made a friend outside the hab. So, despite the beating, I counted that as a pretty good day.

Over the years me and Gia became pretty good mates, although we'd go weeks at a time without hanging out. I'd visit her sometimes when she had a break, even walk her home after a long shift if she asked. She told me about her rough upbringing; I talked about mine. We cracked jokes about some of the weirder requests she'd received, talked about the new prozzies who'd just started, the older ones who'd left. She was genuinely interested in the life of a mutie, and as time went on, she began to regret her earlier comments about my mutations. I guess she could see past the skin and the eyes, the knuckly joints, to the me within.

Naturally, I was madly in love with her. But I didn't say anything about it, nor put the hard word on her in a trouserly way. We were mates and that was good, and I didn't want to stuff that up.

Still and all, the fantasies about running my fingers through her hair – or even the hair of one of her many wigs – persisted, but I kept quiet about it.

Seemed like the most sensible course of action.

• • • •

Moving back onto the Ages Home streef, toting the container full of water I'd drawn from the well, I started to get the sense something was wrong. I was at ground level on account of my heavy load, and the few cits on the streef were moving away from my destination quickly, like animals fleeing a hungry predator. I carefully peeked around the corner and stopped and stared at the helmeted and armoured bloke out front of the home.

The Pigs were here and, judging by the one out front playing guard, they'd made it inside. I wiped my mouth with the back of my hand and just stared, unsure what to do.

Ken owned the Ages Home legit. However, as mutants were not legal cits, the Pigs came to take a bribe in dosh, every month, for the great favour of not having us turfed out into the streef. It wasn't personal – a bunch of New Sydney businesses paid bribes to stay afloat – but it meant I had to constantly find ways to make enough to keep them sweet. But this wasn't right. They'd come early, what was the bloody go?

I thought about leaping in, thought about rushing to the rescue, but what could I do? They'd only want to know what I was doing on the streef so late at night and that would just lead to awkward quezzies and awkwarder beatings.

"Carn," I muttered under my breath, "finish up and fuggoff. Carn. *Carn.*"

They did, eventually. Probs only fifdeen, twenny minutes but it felt like forever. Two other Pigs – square-jawed, helmeted, armour-plated cunce – left with looks of mild smugness on their mugs. Ken closed the door after them, shooting sour looks in their direction. The Pigs upped stumps and buggered off down the streef. I waited until I was sure they were totes gawn and then entered the home.

The kids were crying and carrying on and it took me ages to get them some breakfast. Ken beckoned to me to follow him upstairs, so I did once I'd fed them, telling the children to be calm.

Once the door was closed, I could stop pretending to be all relaxed and I almost shouted at Ken.

"What did the Pigs want? It's not Bribe Day yet!"

"Ah, those wankers. They're increasing the bribe. Doubling it, in fact." Ken snorted dismissively.

I made a noise like a sick dog and slumped into Ken's chair. We were stuffed, good and proper. Ken came over, concerned, and I copped a proper squiz at him. He looked different. Standing up straight, present and seemingly unconcerned by the dark news he'd just shared.

"It's not a big deal, mate."

"Not a big deal? We can barely pay them as it is! I'll have to scavenge even more and I nearly got maggoted last time!"

Ken stopped, knelt down and gently put his arms on my shoulders, looking me right in the eyes.

"You're absolutely right, son. This is a revolting development, but I reckon there's a way we can deal with it. See... I've remembered something. Something important."

"What?"

"I don't know," he sighed. "Well, not specifically, anyway. But I know it's important and that it relates somehow to... all of us."

"Us, like you and me?"

"You, me, the ruggies, hell, maybe more than that. This," Ken pulled the not-a-gem from around his neck and held it up, "it's the key to something big."

"Righto." I shrugged, unsure of what else to say. "What are we gunna do about it?"

"We've gotta go back, Franga," Ken said, eyes bright with excitement. "Back to the Downlow and find out where this bloody thing came from!"

FOUR

Ken moved with a speed I hadn't seen in him for a long time – if ever – bustling back and forth, packing an old leather backpack full of weird gadgets and devices he produced from shelves, nooks and crannies around the room.

He seemed alert and alive, awake for the first time in, well, ages. It was hard not to get caught up in his excitement but I needed to impress upon him the very real dangers of the Downlow.

"Ken, you're old, mate. You're, you know, fuggen ancient. It's not safe for me down there, much less you…"

"Well, son, you'll be there to protect me," he cackled.

"I might not be able to–"

Then he pulled something metallic and rectangular from behind his old chair and held it up to the light. "Plus," he smiled, "I just might have a few tricks of my own."

"What's that?" I was curious.

"Insurance," he told me and slipped the thing into a pocket of his overcoat. "So, are you gunna keep whinging or are you gunna get ready?"

"What about the ruggies?"

"Tommy's been doing a fine job of looking after them, and I'll get Gia to pop her head in when she can."

"Yeah, but–"

"Mate," Ken said soberly, "how long do you reckon I've got before my brain turns to mush? Three months? Six, if we're lucky? And after that, you and the ruggies without a place to live, it doesn't bear thinking about."

He wasn't wrong, but still. "How's this gunna help, but?"

"Whoever this belongs to," Ken tapped the not-a-gem now hidden under his shirt, "is going to be very grateful to have it returned. The kind of cits who can make something like this? They'll have dosh. Lots of dosh. The kind of dosh that could keep the Pigs off our backs forever."

"Or they could just, you know, maggot us."

"That is a risk we'll just have to take."

"This is a bad idea, Ken."

"All the best ideas are bad, Franga."

• • • •

The walk from the hab, through the streefs and markets, felt like a dream. Firstly, because Ken was acting so out of character, but also because a dense mist covered everything. It was a humid cloud that seemed to stick to a bloke's skin, holding on like a clingy, living thing.

It made me wince and sweat, wiping perspiration from me eyes constantly, but ol' mate Ken just powered forward, lugging the heavy backpack with little visible effort.

"How do we even know where to go?" I gasped, trying to keep up.

"You were saying the cit, the skinny bloke, he had a handful of Moot tokens?"

"Yeah, s'what it looked like."

"How would a pissweak cit like that get his hands on Moot tokens?"

"Good question," I admitted. "Could have just found 'em, I spose?"

Ken considered this. "Maybe. Unlikely, but maybe. Answer me this: who controls the Downlow?"

"Which clans?"

"Yes."

"Durries, lemme think. Well, the Mongrels have the largest share of territory – although it's mostly just ruined buildings and old shopping maws." I was trying to remember details from recent scavenging missions. "Derros have a smaller portion but it's better built, stronger walls and that. And the Moots? Sewers mostly, and places near water. I haven't seen much of them for a while, though."

"Interesting. How long have the Moots been scarce for?"

I shrugged. "I'm not scribing a play about the buggers, just been grateful for the quiet. They're almost as berko as the Mongrels. Worse in some ways."

"Estimate, please."

"Nine months, a year maybe? Last time they hassled me was when I made that good haul at Chrissy last year, you 'member?"

"I do." Ken smiled. "You've always been a good boy, Frang. I'd be lost without you."

I was silenced by this unexpected bit of complimentary mouth-gear. Sook that I am, I felt the beginnings of tears prick my eyes and I was glad for the goggles I wore.

"Uh, thanks, Ken."

"Now, how hard would it be to get into Moot territory?"

I couldn't believe my ears. "For me? Pretty bloody hard. For both of us: near impossible!"

"'Near', you say?" He grinned with frightening zeal.

We stopped off at a few vendors and bartered for some dried food, stuff that would last us the next few days – although if we were in the Downlow for that long, food would be the least of our worries. I'd left Tommy in charge of the kids, and he could be trusted, but I didn't want to be gawn long. Even with Gia's assistance, the ruggies could be a handful.

Although Ken was proving to be a handful himself and he was older than all of us put together.

"Ken, are you on the chems? Necked some goey? Hoofed some fang?" I found myself asking.

"Not quite," he said carefully. "But I do feel... more alive than I have for some time. There's a tickle, a strange feeling, right at the back of my skull."

"Day-jar-voo?" I suggested.

"Perhaps," he allowed, "or maybe I'm truly remembering something. There's only one way to find out."

We'd come to the wall that overlooked the Cliff's Edge drop. A quick glance around showed us no one was watching, so together we slipped through the gap in the safety wall, away from the smells of sweating flesh and cooking meat.

"It's... quite a long way down, isn't it?" Ken sounded less than sure of himself for the first time that day, as he stared down at the sink-holed catastrophe of the Downlow. "Like a demented child's domino collection, smashed together after too much red cordial."

I didn't know what dominos or red cordial were, so I just nodded wisely, as if that was the very observation I too was about to make.

"You don't haveta do this, Ken. I can go alone."

"I have a feeling the people who made this... object will respond better to me." He nodded to himself, sorta confused but determined.

"Righto." I leapt out over the emptiness, latching onto my noodling umbrella drone. A couple of switch flicks and I guided it back to Ken. "You latch on and I'll get on behind you."

"You sure you can hold on?" Ken asked, concerned.

"I'm fine." I waggled my multi-jointed fingers in a way that usually freaked out normies and delighted muties.

Ken latched on, holding on tight and closing his eyes. I got on behind him and twined my arms around him and his bag, forming a human belt that would tether us to the drone.

I just hoped Ken wasn't going to freak out on the way down and shake us off. Multiple joints are very useful but they do bugger all in the face of gravity's cruel indifference.

"Just keep your eyes closed, Ken. It'll be over soon," is what I said.

One way or another, is what I didn't say.

"Three… two… one!"

We both stepped off the edge.

Ken spent the whole trip down swearing under his breath and shivering with fear. Still, he kept a tight grip on the drone and we landed without too much fuss. I looked around to make sure we weren't being watched, then set the drone to wait and recharge, ready for us when we came back.

If we came back.

"You're pretty handy with that thing," Ken said in a shaky voice.

"I had a real good teacher." I smiled, remembering the long, patient process Ken had gawn through, learning me up on hacking drones and other tech.

If anything, the mist was thicker in the Downlow and I told Ken we'd have to move slowly and carefully. Sound would carry in the blanket of stinky fog and we didn't want to give ourselves away.

"Giz a look at the map, eh?" Ken said.

I fished the map out of my back pocket and we looked at my hand-drawn piccie of the Downlow. Ken used a red pen and, with my help, traced a red line through the safest route to Moot territory. It still looked pretty bloody dangerous to my eyes.

We started walking, slowly and cautiously, moving over the bridge of collapsed buildings, the sea water roiling and bubbling beneath us, the stink of singed salt pungent and intrusive. The mist started to clear and I judged it safe enough to talk softly.

"What was this joint like, before the quakes and that?" I'd already talked about this with Ken dozens of times but figured it wouldn't hurt to keep him engaged.

"Pre-golden age it was… lovely, really. Right next to the water, lots of people milling about – restaurants and cafes and all the rest. A good place to bring the family, albeit a bit expensive."

Ken struggled over a series of broken windows, spread horizontally over the ground, glass shards poking upright and ready to scratch. He moved carefully but quickly and managed to avoid impaling himself, which was good.

"Closer in, where we are now, the see-bee-dee, was where people worked."

"In office buildings?"

"That's right." Ken said, nodding. "People flocked in from the suburbs, commuting and working late. Of course, that was pre-golden age. Once Renaissance 2.0 kicked in money no longer existed, and cits devoted themselves to their passions, creative pursuits, sciences and whathaveyou. It was even more beautiful here then, Frang. A gleaming city on the edge of the sea."

He went quiet for a bit so I asked, "And then?"

"And then… well, we don't know for sure."

Ken followed my lead, creeping underneath a canopy of old rusted girders, raising one hand to find the ceiling and not scrape his bonce.

"I know the Seppos, Muricans, had a whole bunch of bullshit going on. They were always getting into blues with other countries about this or that. Anyway, war broke out, or *something* broke out, because we lost contact with that half of the globe all at once. Rumours were the best we got, but something nasty happened, of that we can be sure. Something went horribly wrong."

We'd moved through the tunnel of buildings and come to a depressing vista – dozens of broken old buildings leaning at odd angles, like the toey drunks in Flesh Alley. Ken gestured at them, as if he'd timed the conversation and was hitting his cue.

"Then, before we could lob over to investigate, everything started going pig's arsehole. The Big Blackout hit and most of our technology was cactus. The energy based on renewables kicked in, but it wasn't enough. People started fighting, rioting about food and water…"

"That was the Water Wars, right?"

"Weren't wars so much as nasty, desperate skirmishes, to be honest. We might have wiped ourselves out, all because we couldn't share, but then the quakes came and half of the city was suddenly underwater."

"That helped?" It seemed strange to me.

"Ironically, yes. It was as if our possible extinction became a reality, we had to band together, to a degree at least."

"Plus, NanoCorp started the protein farms and that?"

Ken nodded, pursing his lips as if he'd just tasted something foul. "Protein farms, U-drones, doover-fish for water purification. All of it appeared overnight."

"But that's good, yeah?" I couldn't figure Ken's mug, grumpy somehow when talking about a positive thing.

"It is. I mean, we survived. So that's… good." Ken sighed. I waited for him to keep going but he said nothing more.

For a while we walked in silence, Ken's tale oddly unfinished and the mood suddenly glum.

• • • •

"We're getting close to Mongrel territory," I observed, as we rounded a creaking pile of cars.

Ken nodded and swung his backpack to the ground. He rummaged around for a moment and came up with a thin metal box that he slipped into the front pocket of his daks.

"What is that thing?" I wanted to know.

"Insurance. Like I said."

I didn't honestly know what insurance meant. Most of my vocabulary came from Ken and the *2027 Word of the Day* calendar and them other books I'd read. I was wordier than most other Inasiddy cits, but there were still big gaps in my education. From context I reckoned insurance was, like, protection from the future.

Ken shrugged his backpack back on and we kept going. I consulted the map and pointed at the red line, then raised my yellow finger to the road ahead.

"So, we skirt around the most populated parts, hopefully running into no bastard." I traced the finger back over the map, illustrating the route.

"Got it."

"Keep your eyes open," I told him. "If you see anything suss, lemme know and we'll stop and see what's what."

"Okay."

"Remember to breathe."

"I will."

"Let's go."

And we walked together, heads swivelling, ready for death to come from every side.

About twenny minutes later, we were walking through a corridor formed by two buildings that had deadset smashed into one another. We had to climb a pile of dry garbage to squeeze through a tiny crack in the concrete. Normally I'd just climb and jump over the top, but Ken was having a hard time, so in solidarity I crawled along ground level with him.

We were halfway through the pitch-black hole when we heard a scratching sound. Both our eyes were wide and shitscared as we looked at one another.

"What was that?" Ken whispered.

"Shhh!" I hissed back.

At first there was nothing. Then nothing some more. I was about to give the signal to keep moving when the scratching got louder and closer and we both froze, ready to meet whatever threat it was.

I clenched my teeth. Ken grabbed my shoulder, hard… and then a grunter wombled into view, snuffling through the piles of empty fang canisters and ancient garbage. It was a genetically created creature that looked like a cross between a wombat and a pig, hairless and harmless.

The grunter looked up at us, mildly interested, but more intent on absorbing nutrients through its pasty white skin.

I made a whistling noise, like I was deflating, and Ken started shaking. At first, I thought he was having a sook but then I realised those were tears of mirf.

"Do you really think this is funny, Ken?" I squeaked in a voice that barely sounded like my own.

Ken was laughing too hard to answer, but he nodded his head as tears ran down his cheeks.

A moment later I joined in, laughing in low volume his-terrics, as the grunter made grunter noises and imbibed a couple of patches of sickly-looking vegetation. The bloody things were ridiculous looking, one of NanoCorp's less successful but utterly benign experiments, an attempt to create a creature that fed on toxic waste. They did what they were supposed to, mind you, but tended to have a habit of just buggering off randomly. The little fella certainly didn't seem to mind us laughing like a pair of galahs.

Once we'd calmed down a little, my stomach sore from the laughter, we kept moving through the hole and flopped out on the other side, on hands and knees.

I helped Ken to his feet, dusting off his jacket, and clocked he was staring at something behind me, eyes wide.

"What?" I said.

Ken just pointed with one shaking pink hand.

I turned around and found myself staring into the open-mouthed, hideous mug of the big man – leader of the Mongrels.

FIVE

I managed to bite off the scream before it got too loud, instead coming out like a dog's wounded yelp. I fell on my arse, though, and that big ugly face was staring, mouth open, right at me.

Right through me, actually.

See, while it was the big man, he ended from the neck down. His bulbous bonce had been severed from his massive body and shoved onto a sharp metal spike. Evidently the other Mongrels had decided his leadership was no longer effective and had taken power the only way they knew how: by judicious application of carnage.

I turned to Ken, who seemed to be getting himself together.

"Th-through the fog, I thought he was coming for us," Ken muttered.

"Me too. This is the one who almost killed me last time."

"Why did they mount his head like that?"

"Mongrels are into some rough politics."

Ken nodded, looking distinctly green around the gills.

"Carn," I said. "Let's get out of here."

We moved on, trying and failing not to look back at the grisly monument to the big man.

• • • •

We walked the red line, turning in and out of the edges of Mongrel and Derro territory. For hours we didn't see anyone, just the occasional desiccated skeleton or curious grunter. Something about the Downlow seemed to let the little fellows thrive, gave them plenty of waste to absorb.

Ken pointed to one that had a patch of grass and a single blue flower growing on its back. It wobbled along, a tiny garden growing on its dimpled, sickly looking flesh.

The grunter, oblivious or apathetic to our presence, kept pottering along on its wee stumpy legs. Then, after a moment, we carried on as well.

"The Downlow was originally a prison, you know," Ken was telling me, as we walked past a wall decorated with strange tribal graffiti.

"Oh yeah?"

"After the earthquakes, we used it to house the worst of the worst, cits who just couldn't integrate with society. Some of them went mental after the Water Wars, unable to come back after all they'd seen and done. Others were just arseholes. But after a while a strange thing happened: people started heading to the Downlow voluntarily."

"To visit or live?" I wanted to know.

"Both. A lot of cits wanted the freedom. The Pigs stopped patrolling it and as long the cits didn't bring their crimes up cliff, it was just allowed to sit and fester and get more and more horrible. It's maybe not the best solution, but everyone sort of agreed it was better than having the crazy bastards live amongst the civilised."

Ken gestured to the graffiti, which featured a lot of violence and unpleasant-looking rooting.

"Originally I imagine it was everyone for themselves but after a time, tribal instinct kicked in and clans were formed."

"Why would anyone want to live like this?" I couldn't get my head around it.

"I… don't know, honestly. I just don't."

A skeleton hung from a nearby lamppost. It was missing its legs and jaw, and the bones clacked in the thick breeze like a psychopath's windchime. The skull's empty eye sockets seemed too wide and awake to me and I turned away from it, frowning.

I hoped I wouldn't end up adorning some crazy bugger's wall or hanging from a post. I didn't want my death to be decoration.

We eventually came to a small hill that looked comparatively clean and unlikely to poison us immediately. A few car hulks rusted together to form a makeshift shelter and we sat down to eat a fairly unappetising meal of dog jerky between sips of warm, salted water. We ate in silence, the sound of gristly chewing our only conversation, and after I'd finished eating, I gestured that I was going to take a piss.

Yoorinating a discreet distance from our sad picnic spot, I looked at Ken, squizzing the back of him in particular. He was hunched over, his spine curved from years of bad posture, and he looked frail and old to me again. Then I noticed something just underneath his hairline. It was a scar, a big one, that seemed to trace around the back of his skull.

I shook the wee off me tockley and came back, wiping my hands on the back of my pants.

"Nasty scar you got there, Ken."

"Scar?" He looked up, mouth still full of jerky.

"On the back of ya bonce."

Ken reached a hand up to touch the old wound, frowning. "Oh yes, it is quite impressive, isn't it?"

"Where'd you get it?" I wanted to know.

Ken frowned, with a far-off look in his eye, and answered in an almost childlike voice: "I don't… remember… isn't that funny?"

"WELL LOOK WHO IT IS!" came a throaty voice filled with malicious intent.

Ken and I turned to see the stout Mongrel, the ferret-faced bugger from my earlier trip, stepping into our midst, wielding an enormous plank of wood wrapped with barbed wire, grinning beneath a leather mask.

"G'DAY, CUNCE!"

My first instinct was to flee, whatever the cost, but I had Ken to think about. We both backed away from the Mongrel. Ken reached slowly into his pocket and carefully rummaged around for something.

"Stall him, I need to get... just stall him..." Ken muttered, barely audible.

"G'-g'day, mate," I managed to stammer, "h-how ya going?"

He laughed, a sickening sound that made my ballbag shrink right up into my body.

"GET OVER 'ERE, BOYS!" the Mongrel shouted, then turned to me, rasping: "We're gunna have some fun with you, mutie."

Emboldened by having literally nothing to lose I said: "Like you had fun with your old boss, eh? That looked like a good time."

The stout one actually looked taken aback by this. "Shelvan was weak, he was. He let mutie go and take the weapon with 'im." Then he slapped a hand on his chest: "BUT TRAYVOR IS STRONG, EH."

"Trayvor?" Ken said, voice dripping with disdain. "Did your parents call you that?"

"Yes," Trayvor said proudly. "RIGHT BEFORE I ATE THEM."

"Yeah, I'd have killed anyone who named me that too."

"What," Trayvor spoke in an even more chilling tone, "did you say to me?"

"What the fark are you doing?" I hissed at Ken, but he just smiled.

"Are you deaf as well as stupid?" Ken chirped, smiling even wider.

Just then, out of the mist, four enormous shapes appeared. They soon resolved themselves into four Mongrels. I wasn't sure if these were ones I'd met before, or freshies, but they looked just as nasty and terrifying as every other bloody Mongrel.

"The things we're gunna do to youse…" Trayvor chuckled.

Ken was pressing buttons on the front of the shiny metal box thing he held in his hand. Sweat beaded on his forehead but he still wore that crazy grin.

"So how many of you does it take to kill an old man and an ugly mutie?" he asked, bold as buggery.

"There's five of us, cunce, but believe me IT'LL JUST TAKE ONE OF US TO ROOT YOU IN THE EYE SOCKETS AS I PEEL THE SKIN FROM YOUR BACK AND PULL OUT YOUR SPINE AND—"

I'll spare you the rest of what Trayvor promised. Needless to say, it was all very graphic.

"Yes, yes, very nice," Ken said. Then his metal box made a loud *PING* and he looked at me, dead serious. "Get down, Frang."

I dove to the ground and rolled onto my back. Ken pressed a button on the device and there was a sound as the air was split by five projectiles that zoomed, almost faster than my eyes could see, out of the device.

Then there was a kinda *zzzzzttt* sound, like U-drones make when you hack them, and four of the Mongrels fell to their knees, groaning. Trayvor was hardier than his peers and took one faltering step towards us, uttering, "Cuuunce…" before he fell face down on the ground and promptly voided his bowels in an explosive and prolific fashion.

The other Mongrels also went down for the count and, judging from the smell, many of them had also browned their daks.

I almost spewed in my mouth from the smell, but I was too shocked to do anything but look at Ken and go: "What… was that?"

"I told you before: insurance."

"Where did that thing come from?"

"I…" Ken shook his head, like he had it on the tip of his tongue. "I think I might have invented it, Frang."

"When and HOW? And…" I trailed off, looking at the Mongrels. "Are they dead?"

"I don't think so. Just unconscious."

I walked over and kicked Trayvor. He groaned, low but audible, defo not dead.

"Then we should go before they wake up, eh."

Ken replaced the device in his pocket and grabbed his backpack. "That is an excellent idea."

We moved quickly, putting the whip to shank's pony.

"Did you know it would make them shit themselves?" I had to ask.

"That side effect was a happy accident," Ken replied.

"It didn't smell very happy," I muttered.

SIX

Words failed us both when we saw Derro Town. Ken and I stared, wearing identical expressions of awe and disbelief.

The Mongrels were about what the average cit would expect from a Downlow clan – low eye-cue, poor sense of self-preservation, crazy as a rat with its clacker sewn shut. Mongrels lived in loosely affiliated ruins, with little in the way of infrastructure or development.

Derro Town, however, was something else altogether. It was a walled off mini-city, comprising half a dozen buildings – all over five storeys and in relatively good nick – surrounded by a thick border wall.

A sign read, 'DERRO TOWN – DERROS ONLY' with three decaying Mongrel corpses hanging below it. Each building had dozens of thick plastic chutes leading from them, down to a central area that appeared to be a pit, extensively excavated. Derro Town cits milled around the main plaza, which even had stalls and vendors, although we were too far away to see their wares.

"It's civilisation," Ken murmured, breaking the silence. "A rough sort, but civilisation nonetheless."

I hadn't seen Derro Town before, as I tended to skirt through higher, more isolated places when on my own in the Downlow. It inspired a strange mixture of shock and admiration, like maybe we had got the

Derros wrong. They were a coarse band, at least the ones I'd met, usually wearing armour crafted from scavenged car parts or pots and pans. The blokes tended to have long, greasy hair and bushy beards and the sheilas all with dark mania in their eyes and their teeth filed to points and yet… here was evidence of higher thinking, logic and reason.

"It almost makes you want to visit," Ken mused, stroking his beard thoughtfully.

"'Almost', though, yeah?" I asked, then: "*Ken*?"

"Yeah, mate, yeah. Of course. We have a mission."

I couldn't help but notice a certain tone of regret in his voice. Like maybe he wanted to stay, explore, understand. A noble urge, but in the Downlow it would likely prove a fatal one.

I gave him a gentle push, he grunted and we kept moving.

● ● ● ●

Night fell and we set up camp many hours away from Derro Town. We'd made good time, and moved further than I expected, but I could see Ken was starting to fade. The idea of him having one of his episodes in the Downlow was too sketchy to contemplate. On bad days, Ken could pitch a fit, start foaming at the mouth and even yell out whole conversations with people who weren't there, all of which wasn't as bad as when he'd just go blank for hours, staring at nothing, like his mind was gawn. So I tried to keep his brain busy by chatting.

"Did you have a sheila, back when you were young, Ken?" A little cheeky, but it seemed to bring him back to the present.

"Ha, mate, I'm not sure I was ever young. But yes, I was with a woman for… for… a long time. Mei… Mel… Marny… something like that. I can't remember her face well but her smell stays with me, like mandarin peels and honey."

I didn't know what a mandarin was, but honey came from a bee's clacker, according to a book I'd read, and that seemed less than ideal.

"Were youse together long?"

"In the golden age, because everyone lived so long, things were more fluid. You could be with dozens, hundreds of people, in some cases in a kind of flowing, overlapping way. Monogamy was an option, certainly, but not one many people took voluntarily." Ken sighed.

I hadn't been with even one woman, either with my heart or trouser, so the idea of hundreds was at once shocking and deeply exciting in a secret sort of way. I'd kissed one sheila who used to live at the hab, back when I was thirdeen, but I was too young for it to mean much more than one mutie smushing lips with anothery. She'd left the home since, adopted by a strange family, and rumours suggested she'd been sold to slavers, although I didn't know for sure that was dinkum.

"Didn't anyone get jealous and that?" I asked Ken softly, not wanting to betray my complete lack of knowledge in this dangerous area of conversation.

"When you live that long – theoretically indefinitely, although more realistically a few hundred years – your sense of scale changes. So, something that could make you jealous in a life lived for eighty years is quite different to how you feel living three or four times that. Plus…"

Ken trailed off here, smiling to himself.

"Plus?" I prompted.

"Plus, we all liked to root a lot, son." He laughed. "I mean, we'd cured all known diseases – sexual and otherwise – we'd mastered our bodies, our planet and our… rooting parts. Seemed wasteful not to use the bloody things as often as possible."

I closed my eyes and tried to imagine what the golden age had been like. When you had so much time and life and you didn't need to scratch in the dirt for a feed. It sounded grouse but yet again, I couldn't see it in my head, I just came up against a wall in my mind.

"Sounds like a beaut time to be alive." I spoke wistfully.

"It was and yet… I think we were the architects of our own destruction in some ways."

"How so?"

"We were cocky, son. We assumed things would stay good. Assumed we'd tamed our darker natures, just because we'd created paradise. But we also created the Garbage Plains, that huge vista of trash and neglect, and poisoned our environment, always thinking there'd be time to set it right."

Ken gestured around the dark expanse of the Downlow. "You can see how that turned out."

"You did alright, Ken. Took me in. Took all us muties in." Ken sorta nodded and grunted, unwilling to take a compliment for some reason. He was funny like that.

"What about you?" he asked.

"What *about* me?"

"Have you got your eye on a sheila?"

"Nah, not really," I lied.

"What about that Gia? You're always hanging around with her."

"It's not like that with us, eh."

"Why not?" he scoffed. "She's spunky, smart, great with the ruggies. I thought she'd be right up your alley."

I grumped silently for a moment, face burning, and then replied:

"Too beautiful for me, Ken. She wouldn't have a bar of me."

"Why not?"

"Because I'm a catshit yellow mutie with eyes like blood clots," I blurted.

"Now, mate, it's not how you look–"

But suddenly I was furious, and words seemed to shoot out of my mouth like a righteous tide: "Now, don't you be laying any fuggen mouth-gear on me about 'how you look doesn't matter, it's what's inside that counts' because we both know that's some ruggie-comforting bullshit! Maybe you even believe it when you're a little tacker, running around with other muties, but when you're outside – Inasiddy-like – you find out *exactly* how fuggen much it does matter. When people you don't even know spit on you, or won't let you into their store because of what you are, how you look? That's when you find out the truth, because it does matter, Ken, it means bloody everything."

I was breathing hard and I could tell Ken wanted to speak, but he kept listening and I kept talking.

"Don't get me wrong, I can pass better than most – and I'm glad of that – but deep down normies will never accept me. Never, Ken. And a sheila like Gia? She might be my mate, but she'd never be with me, heartful-like. Never."

I could feel tears running down my cheeks and I was glad Ken couldn't see them in the dark. I wiped them away and sniffed.

"You've never asked her, though, have you?" Ken spoke softly, gently.

"No," I admitted.

"Never even brought the subject up?"

"... No, spose I haven't."

"People can surprise you, Frang. That's the last I'll say on it. But they can. Most of the time in powerfully shitty ways, but every now and then…"

He trailed off here and after a few moments I asked: "Every now and then?"

But my only answer was the sound of an old man snoring.

I sighed and decided to sleep too. I'd need the rest and besides, I thought, maybe I could dream of a world where being a mutie didn't matter.

I didn't, but. Instead, I dreamt about being torn apart by giant crabs.

It was shithouse.

• • • •

Next morning both Ken and I woke up cranky. Me with visions of crabs dancing in my head and Ken feeling the aches and pains of a body long past its prime.

He started the day, as always, by dry-swallowing a handful of colourful pills. They kept him going, he said, but never gave me the specifics.

Maybe he didn't think I'd understand.

Maybe he could no longer remember.

Either way he necked them like a champ and seemed to brighten somewhat.

"Reckon we'll hit Moot territory by this arvo." I spoke through mouthfuls of jerky. "Do you have any idea what we should be looking out for?"

"I'll know it when I see it," Ken assured me, as he boiled water for coffee.

So that's a 'no' then, I muttered internally, but nodded and smiled in the dinkum.

Twenny minutes later, we'd packed up and were on our way.

SEVEN

We'd been staring at the Moot village for over an hour before Ken said, "Bugger it, let's take a look."

It had taken us most of the day to get there, hard yakka for the pair of us, and the sight of the primitive village – with its barnacle-encrusted structures and mouldy walls – initially spiked feelings of fear and unease. Unease became curiosity, which then became boredom and finally frustration.

The bloody place was empty, not a single Moot, grunter or any bastard about.

"Nevertheless," I opined, "could be a trap."

Ken stood to investigate. "Pretty elaborate trap to capture an old bloke and a young fella."

He had a point.

I stood as well and, cautiously, heads moving all around, we traipsed down the hill to investigate the seemingly deserted village.

Moots were a mutie clan who lived in sewers or near the sea. They constructed their villages from waterlogged materials, some of which they'd dragged from the ocean or the shore, and tended to stay away from the other clans, preferring to be isolated rather than violent.

No one was entirely sure if they were muties first, or if the water had mutated them over time, but they were a bunch of ugly bastards either way.

I'd run into a Moot hunting party a couple of years before, three of them there were, all dressed in rags with fishbone ornamentation that made them look tough, smell bad and cause bulk fear. Any bugger who spent time in the sea was either tough as nails or crazy, and I suspected both were true in the ones I saw.

The party had seen me but didn't say a word, just stopped as one and grabbed bows and arrows from their backs. They were firing fishbone arrows at me before I'd had a chance to get my bearings and it was just dumb luck that I managed to get away; a convenient hole to dive in here, a large wall to clamber over there.

Despite my initial escape, they'd tracked me for a whole day, keeping a consistent pace, and only stopped their pursuit once we'd reached the edge of Moot territory. Even then there was no anger, no promises of violence, just a silent vigil as I ran quickly, making a solemn promise to myself that I would never again enter the territory of Moots.

Until that very moment when I did so with Ken.

It was a tense old trek through the village, every creak or cracking noise had me and Ken on our tippy toes ready to pelt off, but after a while it became apparent that every Moot was just… gawn.

Tools still lay about, unfinished meals rotting in pots, abandoned weapons… but no people. Just an eerie silence and a sense that something very wrong had occurred.

"What do you think happened?" I spoke mainly to hear something, to remind myself I existed.

"No signs of violence. Whatever it was happened fast."

"What could take out an entire Moot village?"

"What indeed."

I stared at a building crafted from the hull of a ship, perhaps some deep-sea fishing vessel, the only kind that made any dosh these days as the catches close to shore were always too polluted to consume. From the look of the building, its comparative fanciness, I reckoned the village elder or war chief had lived there. I pushed aside the musty-smelling canvas door flap and looked inside.

A cot, shitbox, a few weapons of various sizes and a bowl full of Moot tokens. I grabbed a handful of the latter, stuffing my pockets, hoping to trade them for dosh in town. Having a squiz around the joint, I could see the Moots lived simple lives and yet… what was that?

I moved further inside and looked at the wall above the elder's bed. There were paintings on the rusty wall of the hull, crude pictures of fish-headed villagers walking in a line to the shore. Then, in the second piccie, something, some kind of creature, rose from beneath the water – with huge red bug eyes and a massive monstery mouth. In the third, some of the fish heads were calmly entering the mouth of the beast.

In the fourth, the entire village had wandered inside its hungry maw.

"'Slimy things did crawl with legs, upon the slimy sea,'" a deep voice intoned behind me. I spun around, eyes wide, but it was just Ken bunging on a fancy voice he sometimes used when quoting poetry.

"Fark, Ken," I panted, but Ken was staring at the paintings.

"It's like they're… going into the belly of the beast. Voluntarily. Voluntary sacrifices to some kind of…"

"Big watery cunce?" I suggested.

"I was going to say 'ancient sea God' but yours is good, too."

We exited the rusty dwelling and started moving, instinctively, towards the sound of lapping water.

"You don't really reckon there's a sea monster out here, do ya?" I managed to keep most of the fear out of my query.

"No," Ken said.

But he didn't sound too sure.

We walked a short distance to the shore. Rocky sand crunched underfoot – it was all stained an inky black – and the smell of corrupt water rose up like a pongy ghost, tickling our noses and the backs of our throats.

We both stood and stared out at the water that stretched into the distance, occasionally interrupted by a partially sunken rusted hulk of a boat and, in one case, a plane – fuselage sitting up vertical like a raised middle finger.

As the small waves hit the shore and retreated, they left behind a kind of purply-green skin, see-through and shiny, it was actually a bit beautiful if you ignored the fact it was poisonous.

Neither of us spoke for ages. Just stood there, thinking those kinds of thoughts you think when the world lifts its skirt and shows you how empty and lonely things can be. It wasn't a bad feeling, not really, but it wasn't the kind of thing you'd want to have running in your mind every day, otherwise a bloke'd never get anything done.

After another ten minutes of silent contemplation, I had to take a piss. I moved a few meaters down the beach, so Ken could continue looking poochy-faced, and let loose a stream of yoorin into the scummy waters.

After a couple of seconds pissing, the waters began to bubble in a wide area that began where my yoorin splashed and then widened much further out. Some kinda chemical reaction, maybe? I kept the stream focused on the bubbles and they got bigger and then bigger again.

"Heh."

It was funny at first but the size and violence of the bubbles began to increase to a point where I realised it wasn't my piss at all, there was something moving under the water.

Something big.

My stream died to a dull trickle and I tucked my still dripping tockley away hastily.

"Ken?" I spoke in a quiet voice.

"Hmmm," Ken answered in a distracted way.

"KEN," I said more firmly and he looked over.

By now the bubbles had increased in volume, like the water was boiling from the inside.

"What the bloody hell is that?" Ken spoke in a shaking voice as he joined me.

We watched in gape-mouthed shock as something huge – like, the size of a boat, bigger even – rose from beneath the murky waters.

I was thinking, *the Moots were right. They did have a sea monster living near 'em, and we're about to meet the fuggen thing.*

It rose up, huge red bug eyes staring at both of us, and a shiny bronze body gleaming in the sickly sunshine. I was ready to scream and start running but when I looked over at Ken he was laughing.

Laughing!

But I wasn't! The size and shape of the monster reminded me of crabs. Like my dream had come true, like I was living in a dinkum account of Guy N. Smith's nightmares and this one was coming to grab me in its enormous bloody pincer. As the full bulk of the thing burst out of the water, I let loose a scream that I barely recognised as my own.

"It's okay, Frang," Ken said, inexplicably.

I couldn't speak but stared at the monster that had eaten a whole village of Moots, and waited for it to charge towards the shore and make me its next dinner.

Then its mouth started to open and a bright light shone from within.

I closed my eyes and waited to die.

I kept on waiting and, after a fair bit, opened my eyes again. Now that I'd had time to suck in and shoot out a few breaths, I could see the watery cunce for what it really was: artificial-like. This wasn't some ancient sea God but a —

"Submarine," Ken said, nodding towards it. "That right there is a submarine."

What I'd taken for a mouth was, in fact, a large metal door and it was opening, spilling out cold blue light. I could see figures silhouetted on the inside and they looked, from a distance, to be just your normal cits.

"This is what we've been looking for, isn't it, Ken?"

"Yes. It is." Ken reached into his shirt and stroked the not-a-gem. He had an odd smile on his face, sort of happy but also worried. I didn't really understand it but there were more pressing matters.

The submarine moved over to us, close to the shore, so we could see the people inside better. They were dressed in clean, white clothes. The sort of pressed, laundered clobber that reminded me of…

And then it hit me: the road scab bloke. He had looked like he belonged to them.

There were three cits inside. Two sheilas, one bloke. The older sheila and the older bloke waved, and the younger sheila – red-haired and wearing glasses – stepped forward, right to the edge of the door that had turned horizontal and become a platform on which she could stand.

"Uh, hello!" she said, looking nervously at me and then Ken and then back at me again.

"Hello there." Ken smiled broadly. "Shouldn't you say 'we come in peace' or something?"

"Oh. Hahah!" the sheila said, blushing. "I suppose that would be rather appropriate. We come in peace."

"Us too," Ken assured her.

"We've been watching you two for a while, unsure on how to proceed, but then we realised who you were."

"Who are we?" I wanted to know.

The sheila looked at me then and I suddenly felt real self-conscious. She eyed me up and down like I was a specimen on a tray, like she couldn't wait to dissect me.

"You're, well, you know. Hah. Don't you?" The sheila was getting frazzled.

"We're the blokes," Ken said, reaching a hand into his shirt and pulling out the not-a-gem, "who have this."

The not-a-gem sparkled in the light and I could see all three of the sub crew look at it with a kind of yearning wonder.

"Oh, thank God," I heard the bloke mutter.

The other woman nodded to the younger sheila. "Let's get them on board, Eva. We don't have time to waste."

The sheila – Eva was her monica apparently – stepped onto the black sand and shook Ken's hand and then mine, all the while nodding like a nervous bird.

"Sorry, yes, quite. Let's get you on board *The Raw Prawn*."

I looked at Ken and he looked at me. My expression was asking if we should go and his nod assured me that, yes, this was legit. He was still holding the not-a-gem up, like some kinda statue, when there was a whistling noise and something moved through the air, right near Ken's head – and then zipped past me.

Suddenly half of Ken's hand seemed to vanish and Ken, Eva and I were all covered in bright red… something.

Blood, it was blood.

Time froze for a sec, and then as I looked down at the dirty ground, where a pile of Ken's fingers lay with the not-a-gem – I realised everything had just gawn pig's arsehole in a serious way.

"FOUND YOU, CUNCE!"

We all turned to see Trayvor and the shitpants Mongrel crew running through the Moot village, ready for violent retribution.

"Ken, get your box thing—" I started to yell, but Ken was staggering towards the submarine, blood jetting from his ruin of a hand, which was now just a thumb and some nuggety-looking gore. Thinking fast, I snatched up the not-a-gem and shoved it into my back pocket just as another whistling sound shot past my ear and then Eva started screaming.

I turned to see she had a boomerfang – a razor blade-edged boomerang – sunk deep into her thigh, shooting out red stuff and causing her to fall to her knees.

I grabbed her arm, ready to pull her with me when another whistle and this time something struck me, hard and sharp, in the small of me back.

"Fark!"

I landed hard onto the sand, Eva falling with me and a dull throbbing in my back suggested another boomerfang had sliced me just above the clacker. I raised a hand to Ken, who had gawn white and fallen over. The older sheila and bloke were helping him inside the submarine, when the sheila pressed something and the sub started hissing, the platform turning back into a door, making itself vertical again.

"WHAT ARE YOU DOING?" Eva screamed. "WAIT FOR ME!"

"Ken…" I murmured.

But Ken had fallen over, out for the count or dead, and the two other cits were dodging boomerfangs as the door sealed its occupants inside.

"Oh God, oh God, oh God," I heard Eva moaning in pain and terror.

I, somehow, wasn't feeling either. It all seemed like some dark dream I'd stumbled into, and like a dream it would soon fade and be forgotten.

I remember thinking, *we bloody well should have killed these blokes*, as the Mongrels surrounded me and Eva, looking down at us and grinning.

If I could do it all again, I remember thinking quite philosophically, *I would defo kill these blokes very much.*

"Gotcha, mutie!" I heard.

And then Trayvor's massive booted foot filled my vision and cracked me square in the bonce. And for a sweet merciful time I thought and felt nothing at all.

73

EIGHT

I was a bit surprised to wake up at all. But I did, and immediately wished I hadn't.

I was trapped, upside down, somewhere stuffy. And moving. My body kept slapping against something hard, rhythmically, like I was a dog's wagging tail or the dangling ballbag of a trouserless giant. A quick check of me pockets showed the not-a-gem was gawn, likely flogged by the Mongrels.

It took me a few moments to work out I was inside some kind of sack, made of a coarse fibre, slung over the back of someone wide and nuggety. I suspected it was Trayvor. This suspicion was confirmed a moment later when he chortled: "I can feel ya squirming back there, mutie."

I stopped moving.

"Wriggle all you want. We'll be home soon and then the fun can really begin."

Trayvor laughed and was joined by a couple of others, rough barking guffaws.

"Gunna have some fuggen fun with youse both."

Both. So that Eva sheila was still alive, somewhere. Probably in a different sack, bleeding. I licked my lips and instructed me brain to come up with a daring escape plan for us both.

A moment later, I realised I'd slipped back into unconsciousness, probs the result of a con-cushion or similar. I pinched the skin on my hand, hard, so I'd become more alert. It did bugger all other than hurt my hand, but.

I could hear someone crying and figured it had to be Eva.

"You'll be okay!" I croaked out, loud as I could.

"No, she won't!" Trayvor laughed, sneeringly.

The crying increased in volume and I blacked out again, dipping my toes into a dark land I'd likely soon live in permanently. Unless there was a heaven for muties, which seemed unlikely. I hadn't given much thought to death, other than as something to avoid in the immediate sense, and I was having a miserable time, upside down, feeling sorry for myself and wondering what, if anything, happened after a bloke carked it.

I even had a little sook. Quiet, but, so Trayvor and crew wouldn't hear it. I reckoned if I was gunna have to die horribly, I'd try to do so with a bitta dignity and that, but deep down I wasn't sure if I'd be able.

I wondered how many other cits had thoughts like these on the eve of their maggoting. Probs shitloads. It was a grim thing to consider.

Soon the uncomfortable rocking had me back under and I drifted off.

When I next came to, something had changed. There was a tension in the air, or perhaps all the blood had gawn to my bonce and I was thinking crazy.

"Shut up, I heard something." One of the Mongrels. He sounded edgy.

"I bloody didn't." That was Trayvor, but he didn't sound too sure of himself.

"Wait, what's th–" The other Mongrel was cut off suddenly and then I was moving everywhere, like Trayvor had started running, jostling my swollen head something fierce.

There were shouts, Trayvor grunted and then a slapping sound, metal hitting meat.

Then the world was tits up and I hit the ground hard, with what felt like a boulder on top of me.

No, not a boulder, Trayvor. The bugger was crushing me. I wheezed and gasped, trying to catch my breath in that stinking sack. This was a rotten way to end it. Crushed by a Mongrel in a whiffy bag! But then, mercy, a weight lifting. I could breathe again, and then the sack was gawn, snatched off me.

I squinted at the new brightness, trying to blink away the tears and see who it was standing above me. Man-shaped they were, tall and hairy, but I couldn't make out the finer details, my peepers had been in the dark too long.

"It's okay," said a calm and pleasant voice. "You're going to be fine."

And for a strange wonder, I believed him.

• • • •

When I was a ruggie back in the hab, Ken used to love recalling a story about the first time I saw a Jesus stick. It was around the neck of a missionary sheila who'd come to visit and tell us the "good news".

I was real keen to hear what she had to say, because I couldn't remember the last time I'd heard any good news – and thought perhaps this particular news would end with me getting a present of some kind. However, it turned out she was saying a bunch of mouth-gear about this real grouse bloke, Jesus, who came back from the dead some years after he popped out of his mum's virgin spadger, which all sounded a tad suspect to me, and certainly not news I reckoned qualified as 'good'.

After a few minutes of her blathering on, I asked this sheila, "Why is there a monkey on that stick?"

She looked down at the Jesus stick around her neck and turned bright red. Turns out the monkey was a representation of this Jesus bloke during his crucyfixin', and just wasn't very well made.

Ken laughed so hard he had to have a lie down.

I'd always been fascinated by this Jesus fella, but, and the way – in other books and piccies I'd seen – he looked real gentle and serene. His eyes somehow comforting and friendly, his beard unusually devoid of crusting mucus, leftover food or dried blood.

I mention this because that's who was standing over me, holding out a hand, ready to lift me up.

"Jesus?"

"Not quite," the bloke answered, smiling. "You can call me Redmund. The Lord lay blessings upon you."

"Franga. Cheers, ta."

I staggered to my feet with Redmund's help, looking around, blinking. Eva was being helped to her feet by a greasy-looking sheila with sharp teeth and, with a shock, I realised something.

"You're all Derros!" I exclaimed, before I could snap my stupid mouth shut.

Redmund smiled, though, and it seemed genuine.

"That's correct, child, but we have seen the folly of our former ways. You have nothing to fear from us."

And to be fair, it seemed like he was telling the truth. There were a dozen or so Derros, standing around, calmly. They were busy tying the limbs of the unconscious Mongrels with occy straps but didn't seem inclined to do the same for us.

"No, we won't be tying you up," Red said, as if reading my mind. "We are hoping you'll come with us voluntarily."

"What for?" I asked, suss as.

"For a meal, a night's rest. You will be able to leave tomorrow in peace. Leave with the Lord's blessing."

I looked over at Eva, who was staring back at me, shaking and confused. I walked over to her and put a calming hand on her shoulder. She flinched but didn't push it away.

"You alright?"

"I... think... I..."

"You hurt?"

She looked down at her thigh. It was a nasty-looking wound. She turned her face back to me, about to say something, when her eyes rolled back in her head and she literally fainted in my arms, body limp and unexpectedly heavy.

Before I could call for help, two Derros, a bloke and a sheila, came over with an improvised stretcher, laid Eva down on it and lifted her up.

"Your friend is hurt." Redmund looked genuinely sad about this. "We can tend to her wounds and yours when we get back."

From the sticky feel of me back, it seemed like my wounds were shallow and starting to scab over already. Eva on the other hand...

"Okay, I guess we'll come with you," I sighed, seeing no other option.

"Praise be the Lord."

"Bless Him mightily!" chorused the other Derros in yooni-sun.

Never thought I'd see God-botherers in the Downlow, but I had to admit, right at that moment, I didn't hate it.

"Where exactly are we going?" I asked, but suspected I knew the answer.

"Why, Derro Town, of course," Redmund replied.

• • • •

We must have made a strange procession walking through the Downlow. In the lead, a band of rough-looking Derros, who were dragging a group of trussed-up Mongrels. Then there were two Derros carrying a fancy-looking sheila on a stretcher, and finally a Jesus-y bloke with a yellow mutant.

I had so many questions for Eva. I had so many questions for Redmund. And I had one other big question for myself: where was the not-a-gem? Still on Trayvor's limp body or had Redmund flogged it? I was gunna ask him but, like, how much could I trust this bloke? I mean, a clean beard didn't mean good intentions.

The indecision and that on my mind must have shown on my face because Redmund looked at me strangely, saying: "You seem troubled."

"It's been… a long day. I want to go home."

"To the Inasiddy?"

I shrugged vaguely, neither confirming nor denying.

"I understand you have little reason to trust me."

Too bloody right, I thought.

"Your people are not well loved in the land above." Red gestured to the cliffs that loomed over us.

"We're not exactly well loved down here, to be honest," I muttered, nodding towards Trayvor.

Red frowned. "It's true, the Downlow has been a cruel place for far too long. But understand the new way of things: the colour of your skin and your mutations matter not to the Lord."

"Bless Him mightily!" came the response.

"I've gotta say, I'm surprised to see Derr- uh, you blokes adopting, like, a degree of religiosity," I said, looking at Redmund's calm face.

"Because we don't deserve it in the Downlow?" He spoke without anger, genuinely curious.

"No, but… it's unusual, you have to admit that."

"It is, and I do. But then you're unusually articulate for a mutie, are you not? I suspect you weren't formally educated? Muties are still not recognised as full citizens up cliff, I imagine?"

I grunted noncommittally, careful not to give anything away. He nodded as if I'd answered regardless.

"A religious Derro and an intelligent mutie, truly it has been a day of wonders."

"Well, look, I do appreciate you saving us from the Mongrels," I admitted.

"It was genuinely my pleasure, and the will of the Lord."

"So, did youse, like, learn about the Lord from a missionary or something?"

Meanwhile, thinking, *did you guys eat the missionary?*

"No missionaries in the Downlow anymore, too dangerous." Redmund once again came eerily close to echoing my thoughts. "But we've been blessed. The Lord came to us and we let Him in."

"Into your hearts?"

"Into our village."

NINE

The walk to Derro Town felt different to the one on the way in with Ken. There was no hiding or skulking, no peeking around corners and questioning every sound. I felt like I was getting a glimpse of the Downlow from the perspective of a clan and, honestly, I could see the appeal. There really was strength in numbers. A feeling of power.

I imagined forming a clan with the ruggies when they were older, a mutie clan who would take no crap from the normies. It was a nice idea, although one I'd never pull off, and after the initial happy feelings, I began to get homesick for the hab. I missed the ruggies, I missed the Inasiddy and I missed Ken. Was he even alive?

Of course he is, I reassured myself, *injured, yes, but with the submarine people. They'll look after him. He'll be fine.*

Still, I couldn't help but wonder a bit sookily if I'd ever see home again.

Focus up, Franga, I admonished myself, *you've got more immediate concerns.*

I did. Eva and the not-a-gem. And I was about to take a risk regarding one of them.

"I say, Redmund?" I tried my best to sound real casual.

"Yes, son?" He smiled blandly.

"Did youse search the Mongrels, when you caught 'em, I mean?"

"We took all their weapons away, if that's your concern."

"Well, no. I mean, that's good youse did that, but they, uh, also flogged something from me…"

I briefly described the not-a-gem to Red, making sure to emphasise how it only had sentimental value and wasn't worth a pinch of shit. The Derros conferred with one another, but nah. None of them had seen the glowy orb and I wondered bitterly if, after all the fuss and heartache, it'd just been lost on some random patch of ground in the Downlow.

I was so caught up in my own thoughts I didn't realise we were within cooee of Derro Town and it came up on me, all of a sudden-like.

It was even more impressive the second time around. A genuine mini-city, or at the very least a suburb, built up and thriving in the last place anything should be able to do so.

"It's quite something, isn't it?" Redmund spoke with evident pride.

"It is," I had to admit.

"I can't wait to give you a tour."

"Great." I smiled but inside was wondering just what the hell I'd gotten myself into.

• • • •

As we approached the Derro Town gates, cheers came from within. Redmund waved and smiled. They seemed awful pleased to see him.

"Truly the Lord has seen fit to grant us a beautiful day, friends," said Redmund.

"Bless Him mightily!"

The thing is, it *was* a beautiful day. The sun was bright but not too stingy, even beaming through the lower-quality Downlow U-drones, and the air was clean, crisp. There was only the vague stench of rot on the breeze. You could almost imagine you were somewhere normal, safe.

I looked closely at the Mongrel corpses hanging from beneath the 'DERRO TOWN – DERROS ONLY' sign.

Redmund followed my gaze and nodded grimly. "Old habits die hard, I'm afraid. These men attacked us and we were forced to defend ourselves."

"Were you forced to hang them up like Chrissy tree decorations?" I wondered out loud.

"I'll be hanging youse both, from your tockos!" came the guttural rasp of Trayvor, still bound, but now awake and extremely angry.

"Peace, brother, you will find peace in Derro Town, I promise," Redmund assured him.

Trayvor launched into a mono-log about all the nasty stuff he was gunna do to Red and me and everyone else there, save the other Mongrels, but it sounded half-hearted at best, and he soon gave up.

I reckon he thought he was about to join his mates hanging from the sign. I reckoned that wasn't such a bad idea.

If the exterior of Derro Town was impressive, the inny was even more so. My first thought was *this is like Cliff's Edge, this is their own market!* and I wasn't far off. The whole place was assembled from the large hole outwards, with walkways around the hole leading to market stalls standing in a circular formation.

The stalls sold all manner of thingos: food, weapons, what appeared to be toys of some kind of a lumpy bugger with big eyes, handcrafted from leather and cloth. The place was chockers with Derros, all of 'em scary-looking at first glance but then you saw the big, happy smiles on their faces. Their eyes bright, shiny. Their grins genuine, not sarcastic or mean-spirited.

"Redmund!"

"Welcome home, brother!"

"Bless your happy return!"

"Bless the Lord!"

"Bless Him mightily!"

The air rang with positive hollering as everyone seemed to reckon Redmund's return was beaut. There were even some Derro ruggies milling about. If I squinted, they looked just like the ones back at the hab, although the filed teeth and the human half skull one wore as a hat spoiled the illusion a little.

Every now and then, one of the Derros would drop something into the pit. A chunk of meat, a piece of bread, sometimes even a bit of armour or clothing, and more of those toys. Seemed like an awful waste to me and the sound me guts were making suggested I was more than a little hungers.

"If you are hungry, you may eat, brother," Redmund told me.

"Don't have anything to trade." I'd somehow even lost the Moot tokens I'd nabbed earlier.

"You won't need to."

"I can just… like… go get stuff?"

"You're my guest. Everything here is free for you."

It felt like a trap, it sounded like a trap, it almost certainly was a trap, but fark I was hungry, so I decided to throw caution to the wind. Minutes later, I was munging down on some kind of meat onna stick – I didn't dare ask what – and drinking a sweet green juice. It was delicious going down, and I managed not to think about where any of it came from. Once I'd finished the feed, licking juice off me fingers, I remembered poor bloody Eva.

I hadn't seen which way she or the Mongrels had been taken and a sudden spike of panic hit me. Looking left and right for Redmund, I pushed through the throng of Derros, desperate and lost.

"Excuse me," I said to an old sheila who looked the least able to snap me in half, "do ya know where Redmund and that are?"

The sheila smiled a toothless smile and pointed to one of the tall but crumbling buildings nearby. I nodded thanks and grabbed another meatstick from a grinning vendor. I figured Eva'd be hungry too and if she wasn't, well, that was seconds for me.

After the noise and crush of outside, the building seemed eerie to me, as I looked around the cluttered lobby. Everything was smashed to buggery and there were small holes in the walls, ceiling and even the floor. I heard the sound of voices upstairs so I moved up the metal steps. One time, Ken told me these were known as escalators, on account of the fact they moved using electricity and that, which seemed insanely lazy, but such was life back in the day.

"Redmund?" I called out, not liking the way my voice echoed all the way through the building.

"Up here, brother!" came the reply.

I shrugged and made my way up, noting that the holes were all over everything, like someone had taken a chisel and hammered it in. Maybe some kind of culcha and yarts-based gear?

The only alternative was they'd had some massive bullet-based blue, which would be crazy as! Bullets were a valuable resource, you'd never spray 'em around all willy-nilly. I also noticed a bunch of those plastic chutes that led from the buildings, down and into the pit. They were quite wide, I could fit in them and only have to crouch down a little, but what the bloody hell were they for?

It was a confusing climb and I felt as if I'd missed some vitally important part of the puzzle. I cursed myself for being a drongo, wishing I was smart like Ken.

Eventually, about five or six storeys up, I found Eva and Redmund and some specky Derro who was stitching her leg up as she lay on an operating table made from three ironing boards strung together with occy straps.

"She okay?" I wanted to know.

"Doc?" Red asked the specky bloke.

"The wound is deep, but I'm cleaning it, stitching it, she'll be fine for the offering."

"The offering?"

"Never mind that." Redmund waved the question away. "Are you fed?"

"Yeah, uh… I brung this for Eva." I waved my stick meat awkwardly.

Redmund took it off me and laid it down on a dusty bench nearby. "For when she wakes up," he assured me.

I took a closer squiz at Eva, making sure not to focus on Doc's bloody work. She looked pale, but alive. I hoped she'd be okay. I wanted to be there when she woke up but Red was leading me up some more stairs.

"Come, I want to show you something."

I followed. What else could I do?

We walked up through a crumbling fire escape, some wooden steps and finally a couple of rickety ladders strapped together to reach the top of the building. I cautiously walked to the edge and looked down over Derro Town. It was an impressive view, even though I doubted the structural integrity of the building on which we stood.

The markets, the other buildings, the plastic chutes and the pit were all better organised than anything I'd ever seen in the Downlow before. Durries, it was better organised than most of the gear up cliff!

"Do you know the Derros almost wiped themselves out not so long ago?" Redmund spoke looking off into the distance, reading his own yesterdays.

"Really?"

"Not so long ago we were in-fighting and massacring one another. The urge for violence is strong amongst the clan."

That's a bloody understatement, I thought.

"But then, one day, the Lord came into our camp. Walked right in. Bearing fruit."

"Fruit?" I couldn't hide the covetous note in me voice. I'd lop off my own pinky finger for a piece of fresh fruit. These days it was practically ex-stinked.

"Fruit of the Lord. It opened our eyes… so wide. To the error of our ways. All the violence, killing and dismembering of others… to what purpose?"

I vaguely remembered some of the Jesus-stick sheila's Bible lessons. Something about "do unto others and be grouse as you'd hope other cunce would be to you" or similar. No killing, no rooting without a licence, bother God on Sundays – that sorta thing. It was hard to see how any of that would appeal to the Derros.

"And so, we changed." Redmund was getting into it now, preeching. "And we forged a new way. Now when we kill and dismember, we do it for the Lord!"

"... eh?"

"No more pointless violence, now it's violence with a point! A purpose! The way it always should have been!"

"That, uh, that doesn't sound very much like the God-bothering gear I know, Redmund."

"God-botherers? Whatever gave you the idea we were aligned with those irrelevant relics?"

"All the mouth-gear about the Lord and that."

"Not *their* Lord!" Redmund was shouting now but smilingly. "Not their weak God of forgiveness and peace. Our Lord: of violence and fire, pain and strife! Our most holy Lord of the Pit!"

My stomach felt like it was dropping down to the ground floor as Redmund grinned, asking: "Would you like to meet Him?"

TEN

Redmund kept nattering on about how grouse the Lord of the Pit was the whole time we were moving down through the building. I glanced at Eva as we walked past, but she was still out – the doc standing nearby chewing on the meat stick I'd left for her. He glanced at me a little guiltily but didn't stop eating. I was gunna say something, but I just shook my head and kept heading down, half listening to Red and half thinking about ways to escape if the situation turned pig's arsehole.

About a third of the way down, I noticed something: singing. Not, like, proper music with words and such, but a kind of humming chanted gear, all done in yooni-sun by the Derros outside the building.

I looked up at Redmund, questioning him with me eyes, and he nodded, saying: "They sing for the Lord, my son. They praise Him with their voices."

To be honest, the type of sound they were making sounded less like praise and more like an old dog in severe gastrointestinal distress, but I decided to keep that particular observation to myself. By the time we'd arrived back on ground level, the singing was deadset deafening, filling the air with its eerie rhythms. It wasn't nice music, you understand, but the way the Derros all harmonised with one another was powerful in a way I couldn't really explain. You just sorta felt it deep in your guts.

"Can you feel it, my son? Can you feel the power of the Lord?"

"I can feel... something, I spose."

We'd hit the ground floor and Redmund led the way, opening the door back into the holy crush of ecstatic Derros. They all had their smiling faces turned up, chanting and moaning and singing as darkness began to stain the sky, with thunderclouds approaching.

It almost seemed like they were summoning the storm with their voices.

Which is, of course, nonsense, I chastised myself, and yet... that was defo the impression I was getting.

The Derros had donned robes, dyed black fluffy things with names like 'Hyatt' and 'Sheraton' on 'em. I suspected these were the names of ancient Gods that fed into their complicated religion but didn't want to ask Redmund lest I make a tit of myself.

Also, I doubt I'd have been able to hear myself speak over the holy ruckus. Still, it was friendly. Derros patted me on the back or moved out of my way as I walked through the crush. The odours of mouldy clothes and bee-yo were pungent, and the stick meat's stink was cloying and yet I didn't feel overwhelmed. Somehow what should have been a scary situation felt almost normal, safe even.

But you don't want to let your guard down, Frang. That's precisely the moment when a bloke gets maggoted.

Some of the Derros wore hats with sculptures of the blobby toy bloke I'd seen in the stalls before. I wanted to ask Red what that was all about, but he was leading me through the crowd, taking me towards the pit.

The pit itself was a big hole in the ground, obvs, but it was built up, designed with thought behind it. For a start, all the plastic chutes led from the buildings, snaking around their bodies, down under the ground – or just above it in some cases – all leading into the pit. I thought maybe it was a quick way to get offerings to the Lord or similar, but I couldn't be sure.

The hole was deep enough that I could barely see anything at the bottom, other than the familiar orange glow of lanterns ringing around the outer edges. I got the impression there was something large in the middle, maybe a hut or a mound of something… I squinted but couldn't work it out.

Placed at regular intervals around the top edge of that most holy hole were large serving dishes full of what looked like dried dates. Dates! My mouth started watering again, as fruit – even dried fruit – was the rarest of treats. Redmund began handing out these dishes to various Derros, who in turn would take a date, start chewing and then pass the dish on. They seemed to be working to a choreography I couldn't fathom, like me and the ruggies after we'd rehearsed our plays heaps. Everyone knew where to turn, to whom they should pass the dish. Again yooni-sun, like everyone was connected.

Red turned to me and offered a date. He didn't have to pressure me; I just popped it my gob and started chewing.

It tasted real bad. Like rotten bad, and it took all of my self-control not to spit the bloody thing out. After the initial hideous burst of flavour, it seemed to taper off into just low-grade disgusting, and the aftertaste was offset by the fact these dates had clearly been soaked in something sweet like sugar water.

"DID YOU ENJOY THE FRUIT OF THE LORD, FRANGA?" Redmund shouted to be heard over the sound of singing.

No, I bloody didn't, it tasted like unwashed clack.

"YEAH, CHEERS, TA!" I roared back, after managing to swallow the last of the date with a heroic effort. Frankly I was surprised a bloke who offered such foul-tasting fruit wasn't hanging underneath the Derro Town sign next to the dusty corpses of the Mongrels, but I spose his holy teachings must have been beaut or something.

"LET'S GO MEET THE ONE WHO PROVIDED IT!"

"OKAY!"

As long as I don't have to eat any more of those dates.

Redmund gestured to a part of the pit that had a ladder latched to the side. It was a tall, kinda rickety-looking thing – not a lot of builders amongst the Derros, I reckoned – but Red seemed very keen that I get on it and start climbing down, so, shrugging on the inside, that's exactly what I did.

I figured if the dodgy old thing collapsed, I'd be able to jump clear. Besides, heights have never bothered me much. I was climbing down when the whole ladder shook as Redmund started on it too. I looked at him and he gave me a thumbs-up. Then we descended the ladder, into the dark depths of the pit, ready to meet a living God.

Dunno what I expected from the Lord of the Pit, I really don't, but it wasn't what I got. When I reached the bottom of the ladder, my hands sweaty and cramping with tension, I took a moment to look around. I couldn't see much on account of the muted lighting, but what I could see was… odd.

For a start it was real dark. Lanterns ringed the roughly circular sir-cum-frence of the pit, but the middle was obscured and shadowy.

I got the impression of something large there, like a pile of stuff, and a gamey, animal smell, but that was all. Robed Derros milled around silently, offering small nods but no mouth-gear. Redmund completed his climb down and came over to stand next to me.

"Are you ready, my son?"

I was getting a little tired of all the "my son" stuff. I reckon Red was probs no more than five or six years older than me.

"Yep, ready."

Redmund took a lantern from one of the Derros and led me towards the centre of the pit. The first thing was I got a sense of a pile of what looked like white bleached sticks. They were stacked haphazardly in a nest-like formation, and I noticed discarded clothes and those toys the Derros were chucking in earlier.

Due to the lantern's soft light, it took me a while to understand what I was seeing, what I could slowly make out sitting atop this pile.

My breath caught and I reckon Redmund thought I was feeling holy awe. But fair dinkum, my first reaction was baffled disbelief.

Sitting on the nest of sticks and other detritus was deadset the biggest grunter I've ever seen in all my days. It was huge, the height and width of a medium-sized house, and as fat a creature as could ever have existed, but unmistakably a grunter.

It was reclining, on its side like, with its little stumpy legs waving lazily in the air. I noticed there were five or six legs on the beast, making me reckon it was a mutant, which went some small way to explaining the size of it.

I looked from the legs, up its flabby bulk, to its eyes that shone bronze in the dim lantern glow. There seemed to be something in those eyes, a little spark that suggested more eye-cue than your average grunter but, like, at the end of the day it was just a really, really big, fat grunter.

"Isn't He glorious?"

"This is the Lord of the Pit?"

"The Lord lay blessings upon you!" every nearby Derro and Redmund said in yooni-sun.

I gently took the lantern from Redmund and moved even closer, examining the thing. I noticed its mutations weren't just confined to extra legs. It had odd vestigial lumps and bumps down its belly, and on its back and haunches were tumours, dozens and dozens of them, bulbous and seemingly ready to burst at any moment, and a bright, angry red colour, ranging from tiny to the size of a ruggie's clenched fist. They were either infected or a naturally angry red, but they covered the majority of its bulk – and I had to imagine that wasn't real healthy.

"Now do you understand, Franga?"

I was starting to feel a bit light-headed but I shook it off and looked at Redmund, not wanting to offend the bloke.

"Mate, I'm not really sure what you want from me."

"You can't hear His holy voice?"

I turned back to the Lord, and stared into those eyes, that lolling, pouty mouth, and waited for it to say something. For a moment, it looked like it was gunna, sorta sat up a bit straighter and made direct eye contact, but then the Lord of the Pit pooted out a trumpety fart and went back to chewing on something meaty in his nest.

I didn't mean to start laughing, it just happened, natural-like and out of my control. But the situation I was in, standing around with these so-serious Derros, as a mutant grunter – their fuggen deity, no less – farted like a champ, it just struck me as a glorious absurdity. I started cacking myself.

"I certainly heard something from Him," I sniggered.

Redmund didn't look impressed and I tried to control myself, but my laughter seemed to grow and grow, like a wall busted open inside me and the mirf just thundered out.

"It's okay, laughter is a blessed reaction," he said in a way that didn't really sound like he meant it.

"I'm sorry, mate, I just…" I couldn't finish the sentence, just kept on laughing, tears in my eyes.

When I looked up again, Red was grimacing and he'd pulled out a small paring knife from his tunic. The steel was clean, sharp, and I stopped laughing as it glinted in the half light.

"What are you doing?" I asked, managing to keep my voice level.

And yet it seemed to echo... echo... echo in a strange way.

"The Lord has blessed us with a bounty of fruit," Red said to the blade. "Now it's time to harvest."

Redmund took a step towards me and I tensed my legs, ready to leap, but then he turned and walked over to the Lord, bypassing me completely. The stern look on his face wasn't anger at my apparent mockery of his belief system, but something else. The mug of a bloke who had an unpleasant task to perform and was getting on with it.

He climbed up the nest and stood next to the Lord, who was burbling and drooling, chewing on something I couldn't identify.

"See, at first we didn't understand what the Lord was offering. We caged Him just to be cruel. It was in our nature, I suppose." Red gesticulated with his knife, which I found a tad unsettling, and I couldn't help but notice his hands seemed to leave trails in the air.

Trails aren't usual... what's all that about?

"One of our number, a particularly unpleasant fella, name of Mad Dog Seven."

"Why 'Seven'?"

Red shrugged. "Lotta fellas want to be called Mad Dog. They'd fight about it, stab one another over it – so we just add a number, keep 'em all happy."

This struck me as particularly funny and my laughter seemed to leave my mouth as a solid thing, drifting away like a cloud.

"Anyway, Mad Dog Seven – he saw the Lord's fruits and decided to rip them off. Just to be wicked. After he'd rent a few from His holy flesh, Mad Dog Seven decided it would be extremely grouse to eat one of them."

"Oh jeez," I muttered, a horrible feeling of dismay rising up inside me. "Wait, when you say 'fruit' you don't mean–"

"Of course, that was the death of Mad Dog Seven. Undiluted, taken directly from the Lord's body, the juice of the fruit is simply too powerful for a regular human. But removed and dried, drained of most of the fluid and soaked in sugar water – well, that allows us mortals to see the divine and survive."

It suddenly became horribly clear that the fruits weren't literal-like, and that 'date' I'd necked earlier? Not a date. A dried, sugar-soaked tumour from the body of a massive mutant grunter.

I covered my mouth but the foaming sea of chunder poured through the dam of my fingers, and I was spewing my guts up like a sick dog for what felt like forever.

"It's okay, my son," Redmund advised. "Enlightenment can feel like a poison at first."

With that he started hacking at the bulbous growths on the grunter's back, and I bent down again and spewed until there was nothing left.

Everything had trails. My sick-spattered fingers, the puddle of spew, the glistening strands of drool that hung from my mouth, the Lord's nest, Redmund, as he cut bleeding growths off his deity and put them in a basket, and the Lord... the Lord bled rainbows from His wounds. Rainbows that sparkled and glistened like nothing I'd ever seen before, rainbows at night as the storm began to break, the first drops of water – shiny, incandescent – dripping from above like tears from a sooky sky.

"What... did you do... to me?" I asked, my mouth feeling like a foreign thing I'd forgotten how to use proper.

"Gave you the truth. What you do with it is up to you."

I lurched to my feet, the world spinning around me, trailing and pulsing and skittering away in a most peculiar fashion. Like a cockroach fleeing a lantern's light. My movements became erratic, sporadic, as if time itself was being chewed up like a stick of gum, stretching and spreading in strange, new ways.

My fingers moved even when I didn't move them, and when I did move them, they moved even more...

(Moved more... moved more... moved moooooore...)

I looked back at Redmund, who was cutting more fruit from the ample haunches of the Lord, spreading new rainbows, sparkling so bright they hurt my eyes. I turned to the ladder as the rain poured down on me and I decided I wanted to be up top for a bit, so I began to climb.

During my ascent, I first felt as if I was climbing across a horizontal plane, and then downwards and then up again, my sense of orientation changing by the second. As I neared the top *(bottom, middle)*, the warm rain lashed my face like a tongue of sun.

I felt the embrace of the Derro's song, and now the discordant wails seemed to touch something vital and meaningful on the inside of me. I realised I was smiling as wide as they were and I stood, weaving and joined the throng.

"His blessings be upon you!" someone was exclaiming, and then something firm and fascinating was shoved into my hands. I held it up and closed one eye, trying to get a sense of what it was I had gripped in my yellow multi-jointed hands.

"What's this?" I said, or thought.

A smiling Derro answered: "The Lord's tool."

And I realised what I held in my hands was a gun.

Not a little gun, either, but a rifle, from when they made projectile-firing weapons that didn't have any computery parts inside 'em. Before an ay-eye would tell you if you could shoot a bloke or nah.

"What do you want me to do with this?"

"Ascend the building, brother. Ascend and let the Lord's tool deliver him offerings!"

I shook my head, trying to clear it, but it did very little good. I was still confused. And off chops.

"You want me to lob up in the building and shoot some cunce?"

The idea didn't bother me especially – I seemed to be past the stage where things mattered –but it was an odd concept.

Then a hand fell on my shoulder, gently but with firm intent.

"Worry not, my son," said Redmund. "I will show you the way."

Lightning flashed in the sky and, for a second, we were all e-loomy-nated in stark shades of blinding white and darkest black, and the rain came down all the harder.

ELEVEN

Everything seemed to move like a series of still piccies, shuffled quickly in the manner of a deck of cards. A bunch of tiny moments strung together to form a spasming whole. I barely had a chance to wonder why Redmund was out of the pit before he was gently leading me to one of the buildings, not the samey as before but anothery.

I noticed, still juddering in lurching sequence, that two buildings appeared to be lit from within, lanterns glowing in the windows. Other Derros were filing inside the two buildings, which happened to be right next to each other.

They were all armed. Mostly with guns of various sizes and quality, but about half a dozen Derros had rocket launchers and such. They couldn't possibly be loaded. Could they?

"What's all this for, Red?" I asked in a voice that barely sounded like my own, as we entered the building on the left.

"It's the offering, brother Franga."

"Honestly, that's not a huge help."

"The Hour of Power."

Fair dinkum, some blokes can make a lot of noise while saying bugger all.

"I don't know what any of that means."

"It means that for an hour, once a month, we Derros suspend our peaceful attitudes and look back on our violent ways, revisiting them. Temporarily, of course."

I couldn't help but notice Red was grinning and gripping his own gun, a large well-polished black rifle that looked extremely hurtsome, in a covetous, almost sensual way. Like he harboured trouserly feelings towards it.

"It means the strong will survive," he assured me.

"And the weak?"

"Will feed the Lord. As always."

Time shifted again and suddenly we were on a floor near the top of the building, looking at the one across from us. Derros were at every window, aiming rifles, laughing and singing happy choons. This wasn't the ecstatic wailing of earlier, but more recognisable choons with words and such.

I was shivering for some reason, barely able to hold my rifle, and I looked up at Red, who seemed delighted by everything.

"I'm not feeling so good, Red." The colours were fading and a film of sweat covered my skin. It was like I'd suddenly come down with a bunch of flus, stuck together-like, to form one giant, debilitating monster flu.

Red nodded, as if he understood the problem. He reached into his back pocket and pulled out a glass vial.

"Hold out your hand, palm down."

I did. He sprinkled some powder from the vial. It was a bright pink, like a fresh scar.

"Sniff it."

"Sniff it?"

"Sniff it."

I did. It hurt going up but a second later it was like a warm blossoming flower of love had started growing in my head garden, although the back of my throat tasted fearsome.

"What was that?" I managed to croak.

"Powdered Lord," he answered, and for some reason this struck me as both wonderful and hilarious.

"DERROS!" Redmund roared, somehow managing to be heard over the singing, voice booming off the concrete. "It is time."

Everyone cheered. Including me. Especially me.

"The Hour of Power begins in five… four…"

"THREE!" chanted everyone.

"TWO!" cried the universe.

"ONE!" exalted existence itself.

And then all the well-armed Derros in two ancient office buildings turned their weapons on their neighbours and started firing.

Thunder and lightning exploded in the night, but this time they were human made. Bullets flew like buzzing mozzies and right next to me, four Derros jerked back, rainbows bursting from their chests, spattering warmth, light and people juice everywhere.

The wounded Derros slipped to the ground, smiles on their faces, and the ones still standing fired back into the other building, spraying ecstatic violence all over the shop. They were laughing, I was laughing and then something hit me in the bonce.

I realised, with a feeling of delight, that a bullet had grazed the side of me head. Warm rainbows leaked out of the cut, and as I examined it with my fingers, I noted how beautiful the loomy-nus fractals of life truly were.

"FIRE BACK, FRANGA! SPREAD HIS LESSON!"

I wasn't sure where that voice came from, but it sounded like a good idea. I aimed the gun at the blokes and sheilas in the building across from us, cackling like a loon, and pulled the trigger.

Immediately, the gun bucked in my hand like a wild animal and I sprayed empty air and then the mouldy ceiling of the building as I was thrown backwards onto the ground.

From my pozzie on the floor, I watched in calm glee as three, four, five Derros burst open, spraying the good Lord's light everywhere.

"Bless him," I chuckled. "Bless him."

Redmund turned around, aware that most of the Derros near him were no longer firing.

"BODY CHUTE!" he called and the remaining Derros stopped shooting and turned around. Following directives that had been drummed into them over time, the clan members grabbed the fallen, rainbowing bodies and dragged them over to the mouth of the plastic tube. One by one, the blessed corpses were fed into the body chutes and gravity did the rest, the carcasses sliding down a steep incline, lubricated by person juice and stray organs.

"OFFERINGS FOR THE LORD!" Redmund called and everyone cheered. Then they turned back to the window and started firing again, spent shell casings plinking everywhere like burning hail.

I felt strangely apart from them, curious at all that was going on around me but not really connected to anything. I slowly staggered to my feet, leaving my gun where it lay, and wandered towards the stairs, following some obscure instinct I couldn't define. Bullets burst through thin walls and thick Derros, but they didn't feel like a threat. I was fine; I was exploring. I took the stairwell down, the air thick with gunsmoke and religious zeal.

I walked without knowing where I was going, randomly strolling onto levels and back down stairs. Bullet holes had punched through most surfaces and many Derros. Survivors were dragging them to the body chutes and pushing them in, sending offerings to their God via slippery dip.

It was strange, it was beautiful and I walked through it all – untouched, near but not involved. A part and yet apart.

Until I heard a voice, growling: "Mutie. Oi, mutie!"

I looked over and saw a large metal cage, chains around the door. Inside were Trayvor and the Mongrels, although only one stood standing, the rest were on the ground, leaking rainbows.

"Trayvor?" I asked, not frightened or angry… just interested.

"Lemme out, mate. Garn." He seemed to be trying to appeal to my better nature, acting like we were old mates or something. I cocked my head to one side, curious.

"Didn't you want to kill me?"

"Nah, mate, nah. I was… only joking." He stood up straight and reached into the back of his strides. "Besides, if you let me out, I'll give you back your glowy thingo!"

That got my attention, although I was confused. "It's in your daks?"

"I hid it up me coight," he cackled, then winced mightily as he pulled it out of his tradesman's entrance with an audible pop. "Let me out and it's yours!"

The not-a-gem in Trayvor's hands glowed beautifully, the colours extra vivid, albeit lightly browned. I found myself staring into its strange, shifting depths. And then, for no particular reason, I started laughing.

"What's wrong with you, mutie?" Trayvor looked around, frustrated. "What's wrong with everyone? Are youse high?"

"On the Lord's love."

A sudden burst of gunfire hit the floor nearby, shooting chunks of concrete into mine and Trayvor's faces.

"Let me out!" he roared, scared and angry. "LET ME OUT!"

I turned away, suddenly bored by all the shouting. A Derro fell by my feet, glistening with rainbows and very much dead. I decided to do my bit for the Lord by dragging him towards the nearby body chute. He was surprisingly light, or perhaps I was given extra strength by the powdered Lord.

Speaking of, I could go another snoot of that. Where was Redmund again? Two levels up, more? It was easy to get lost in this place…

Just then a series of shouts caught my attention. Trayvor had managed to grab a nearby Derro by the neck and was wrestling his gun from him.

"How interesting…" I murmured, watching.

The Derro fought hard but Trayvor had desperation on his side and grabbed the gun. He laughed and fired the weapon into the Derro, spilling his light all over the shop. Then Trayvor turned the gun on the chains and blasted the metal to pieces, some of which lodged in his chest and face.

He didn't seem to mind, and kicked the cell door open, eyes wide and full of murder. For me. He aimed the weapon and squeezed the trigger, but it was empty. Snarling, Trayvor dropped the gun and charged and I felt the merest hint of alarm. Maybe the Lord's blessing was running out but it suddenly seemed like a good idea to get away from this malignant Mongrel.

"Cuuuuunce!"

I tensed my legs and jumped just as he was about to barrel into me, but it wasn't quite enough. The jump struck Trayvor a glancing blow, sending his momentum off course, but still with plenty of grunt behind it.

He'd also latched onto my leg so, instead of getting out of his way, I'd managed to tangle up with him and we both went staggering right into the mouth of the nearest body chute.

I didn't even have time to yell for help before we flew inside and rocketed downwards.

We twisted and turned, moving fast on a slick trail of blood. I saw the Derros continue to fight through the see-through plastic of the chute. A couple turned to watch us fly past, including one bloke who I swear was Redmund.

It was a sickening, confusing and terrifying ride and both Trayvor and I screamed the whole way down. It musta only been seconds of pure panic but it seemed longer, and after it ended there was just a long fall into the void…. which ended in a crushing landing onto something moist that punched my whole body.

I blacked out for a cuppla seconds and came to, shaking my head and trying to get a handle on the swampy surface on which I'd landed. It was a slick, slimy sorta deal that looked fishbelly white, tinged with orange from the lanterns around the place.

And it moved, the surface moved and seemed to… pull at me.

I sat up with a start. It hit me in a flash of shuddering loathing: I was on top of the Lord of the Pit. Riding the blobbiness of the mega-grunter.

I looked about myself and saw that Trayvor had also landed on the Lord and – for the moment, at least – wasn't moving. I gingerly pushed myself over the moist meat of the beast, nudging my way along, past bulging tumours and gnarly bumps and finally sliding down the side of the creature, hitting the nest of white sticks hard as I landed.

But of course, they weren't white sticks, were they? I should have realised it before, but; they were bones. Bones of the offerings to the Lord of the Pit.

The Lord Himself – because that was how I'd begun to think of Him, as a *He* not an *it* – seemed barely aware of my presence and I backed away, gingerly descending from the nest.

"Oi…"

I turned back; it was Trayvor. He'd woken up and was glaring over the side of the Lord.

"Come back 'ere, mutie!"

His face was busted up, he'd landed badly, and blood oozed from his mouth. He was holding aloft the not-a-gem and sneering. I took a step backwards and he attempted to lunge at me but couldn't move, jerking and grunting to no avail.

He was stuck, you see. Both legs inside the Lord's most holy bonce up to the knees. And the Lord was, well, he was *absorbing* Trayvor. Because that's what grunters do. Especially holy grunters, they absorb poison, turn it into nutrients and discard the rest.

"Soz, Trayvor, but you're about to help the Lord feather his nest, mate," I told him, voice quivering with a mixture of awe and disgust.

"I'll get out and I'll murder ya!" Trayvor yelled, but you could tell his heart wasn't in it. Hard to sound threatening when your body is dissolving.

"What about your glowy thingo?" he yelled, desperate to claim some small victory.

"Keep it," I muttered. "Bloody thing has brought me nothing but trouble."

Of course, had I known then what I know now, I woulda run up and done anything to get it back. But I didn't, so I didn't. I just sat back on my haunches, tired and coming down from the Lord's high, and watched an insane, cannibalistic drug addict get absorbed by a mutant deity.

Trayvor stopped talking soon after his crotch had been absorbed. Without a tockley and ballbag the fight just sorta left him. Torso followed, then chest and arms – the not-a-gem with it – and then his shoulders, neck and finally his bonce.

I'm not sure how long the caper took, and during that time other corpses flew from the body chutes and began to meet the same fate. Oozing into the Lord like ants melting into a pudding's glaze on a filthy hot summer's day.

During it all, the Lord had an expression on His face, like a happy dog with too much food, and licked His lips and sat contentedly, absorbing life from death. It was sort of beautiful in a way, but also unsettling and I decided it was probs time for me to leave.

I didn't get far, but. I found myself sinking to the ground, despite my best efforts. The sound of raindrops and corpses falling, both landing on and around the Lord, to provide Him with sustenance, was strangely soothing to my ears. And every now and then He'd spit out a bone, or a skull, to add to the pile that formed His throne.

"Blessings upon Him," I mumbled to myself and slipped into a brittle blackness.

TWELVE

I was woken up by someone slapping me in the face, hard, and bellowing. It got worse from there.

"What's happened to the Lord?" A vague pinky-gray shape was shouting, a shape that soon resolved itself into the form of Redmund, lacking any of his former serenity.

"Whadyafuggenmean?" I mumbled, too confused to be angry.

"THERE'S SOMETHING WRONG WITH THE LORD!"

"I don't–"

"WAKE UP!"

Smack! Now both my cheeks were stinging and the world was less fuzzy. I could see the gleam of madness and desperation in Red's eyes and knew something had gawn drastically amiss.

"What's going on, Red?"

He grabbed my head and pulled me up onto my knees, pointing at the Lord, his voice his-terrical.

"Look at Him! LOOK, DAMN YOU!"

And to be fair, the Lord of the Pit did not look well. His entire body had turned the colour of a bruise, murky purpling-gray. His face looked crook, too – eyes glazed and distant, thick strand of drool dangling from His mouth – and He was making hurtsome sounds, a low moaning noise.

Aco-lights milled around Him, dabbing Him with cloths and it was then that I noticed His "fruit" – those bulging tumours – had all deflated and were weeping their holy pus. The aco-lights were trying to store the stuff in bowls or urns – but it was happening too quick. Some of 'em were even licking the dribbles, desperate to continue their strange symbiosis with the grunter despite the danger.

"He looks real crook, Red," I murmured, not without sympathy. After all, the Lord had saved my life before by absorbing Trayvor and–

That's when it hit me. Trayvor and the not-a-gem. It had to be related to what was going on, didn't it?

"Oh, durries," I breathed.

"What?" Red was desperate. "Do you know what's causing this? TELL ME!"

"Trayvor had a… a… glowy thingo in his hand, he'd flogged it off me, y'see. Maybe it did… something…"

Just then the Lord started vibrating and wailed a mournful cry. Redmund dashed over and started patting His holy face, licking at a small dribble of 'fruit juice' that descended like a tear.

"Oh, my Lord," he cried. "We have displeased you. Tell me what to do, I beg of thee."

The aco-lights all looked to Red for instruction but you could tell from Red's whole demeena that whatever link he and the Lord had once shared was gawn, and he was just patting a very sick animal.

"This is your fault, Franga, you and your *glowy thingo*."

Was he right? Maybe not totally, but nor was he completely wrong.

"I'm so sorry."

"He saved us all and now He's going to die."

"Trayvor took it and I just… I didn't mean to cause this."

"Well, that doesn't really help very much, does it, mate?" Red turned to face me, paring knife in his hand, face wet from his grief and the rain that still churned above us.

The Lord's whole body was rumbling like crazy, making the entire pit shake.

"What was that thingo?" Red demanded.

"I really don't know, the Mongrels had it–"

"It was a MONGREL WEAPON?"

"No! They flogged it from a fancy science cit and–"

"Are you a Mongrel spy?"

"No! They're all dodgy as buggery! I would never–"

"Did *they* send you here?"

Redmund took a step towards me, knife raised, and I pushed back against the wall. I never did find out whether he would have gawn through with trying to hurt me or whether it was just the emotion of the moment, because right then the Lord began a terrifying transformation. His fruit – now flat, lifeless skin flaps – all sucked inwards, forming holes all over the grunter's bulk.

"What… is… this?"

The holes then began to move, contracting and expanding. They reminded me of something but I couldn't put my finger on it yet.

"Lord, please–"

The Lord's bronze eyes rolled back in His head and the drool turned a dark red. I think the Lord may have died at that moment, or at least crossed some unknowable threshold.

"Please, don't leave us."

Red's prayers were answered, after a fashion. Because the second after he'd made that piteous plea, the Lord's body went still for a moment… and then a dozen glistening, white, dripping spears burst from within His most holy body and skewered Redmund and the closest aco-lights.

The spears looked like they were formed from fat – the yellow-white nugget you see after a kill has been skinned – yet they were firm and strong. Strong enough to kill most of the aco-lights outright, but Redmund lived, staring in horror at the white pointed barb that had ripped through his guts and poked out his back.

"Why...?"

The Lord began shaking anew and the spears – each holding meat onna stick – began to retract into His body. A body that flowed with a viscous slime and boiled with a pressure brought by intense changes beneath its skin.

The first of the Derros was being absorbed into the Lord, and the process proved to be a lot faster than before. One of the poor bastards was still living, screaming the whole time the grunter's skin engulfed and dissolved him.

"We have displeased you, I see that now..." Redmund managed to croak with the little life he had left. "Let me know how we can make amends!"

But if the Lord wanted anything anymore, it was just food, and Redmund provided that, his Jesus-y face squeezing against and then inside the rippling skin of his God.

And then the Lord started making a sound – a kind of screeching ululation, the likes of which no one had heard before. The surviving Derros covered their ears and I could hear cries of alarm from the top of the pit. And all of a sudden, I realised what those holes reminded me of, what they were.

They were mouths, dozens of them, all over the twisting, transforming flesh.

Multiple mouths and all of them screaming.

Just then more glistening spikes burst from the grunter, impaling those who remained in the pit. Not me, but. I was moving, leaping up the ladder and away from the monster that was being born.

Away from the thing that, even as I ascended, was beginning to rise.

I burst out of the pit and slammed into a brace of Derros, who were looking over the edge, trying to understand what was going on.

"Is the Lord angry with us?"

"What are those sounds?"

"Where is brother Redmund?"

I didn't answer anyone's quezzies and pushed past the Derros, desperate to be away from the pit and those horrible wails. It sounded like a herd of cows shrieking in a storm drain while a nightmare chorus played – but even that doesn't do the hideousness of it justice.

It was the worst sound I'd ever heard.

Pushing and jumping when I could, I moved through the thickest of the crowd and took a moment to catch my breath. Even with the rain beating down on me, I felt overheated and panicked. A kind of primal fear washed over me and I started running through the muddy streefs, desperate to be away from whatever was going on.

From whatever I'd unleashed.

I was almost at the Derro Town gates when I remembered Eva. I looked back, torn with indecision for a moment, but ultimately I knew I wouldn't be able to live with myself if I didn't try to save her from whatever was rising from the pit. I sighted the building where I'd last seen her and pelted towards it, glad that most of the town was near the pit and away from me.

I ran up the stairs, leaping a dozen of them at a time. I almost chundered from terror and exhaustion when I reached Eva's level but she was nowhere to be found. I looked from her operating table to the floor, where a thin trail of blood led behind a pillar. Heart in me throat, I strode over, following the blood, but it ended up being the specky doctor lying on the floor, a scalpel sticking out of his neck, his eyes wide open, surprised. Dead.

I looked desperately around the room, searching for Eva or signs of where she might be, but saw nothing. Just a dead doctor and more fuggen questions.

"Eva!" I cried. "EVA!"

But my only answer was echoes and the sounds from the pit. Cursing myself for being a coward, a fool, an idiot who couldn't do nothing right, I descended through the building and ran back out into the streef.

I only looked back at the pit once, but even that was a mistake. There was a break in the rain – however brief – and the lightning was flashing like mad and I got a squiz at the thing from the pit, pulling itself up on one massive, disturbingly human-looking arm.

A human-looking arm that itself seemed to be made, comprised, of humans, like the thing was reforming itself – changing its structure – to accommodate something I didn't understand.

The nearby Derros didn't understand it either and, as that grotesque limb slapped onto the ground, screams of fear and agony rang out.

And then I turned away. I turned away from the panic and the monster and the confusion. I turned away from a hell I'd helped birth and I ran. I ran into the rain and darkness, away from Derro Town and back into the Downlow.

I ran until I couldn't breathe and sank to my knees and wept tears of horror and confusion.

• • • •

Morning's light was creeping up over the busted buildings and garbage piles as I found myself near the Cliff's Edge shortcut I'd created. I'd walked all night in a numb confusion, unsure of anything. Perhaps the effects of the narcotic fruit of the Lord had led me to imagine all manner of terrors. A monster from the pit, created by the not-a-gem? In dawn's light that sounded like sillybuggers. Maybe it was all a big hallucination – after all, I'd been pretty well off my tits, as had all the Derros.

Maybe it was just… like… a shared delusion? Mass his-terrier?

I was starting to like the sound of that idea when I heard the first full-throated roar of the beast from the pit. It rang out with furious glory-rage throughout the atypically peaceful morning in the Downlow, echoing everywhere, loud as could be.

My heart sank and I knew it was all real. But what was it? What abomination was bellowing in this mad place? I was so buggered I took three attempts to jump to the U-drone. If there'd been a single Mongrel present, wanting to maggot me – even a thin, sickly one – I'd have been stuffed, but luck was on my side. Luck, it seemed, favoured cowardly, ugly idiots like me.

As the drone took me back up cliff, I looked, squintingly over the Downlow, trying to get a sense of where the monster might be. I couldn't see nothing, and the roaring didn't repeat. But I couldn't fool myself. I knew something important had changed that day. Dawn rose on a new nightmare.

The Cliff's Edge markets were just starting to be set up as I staggered past, not paying any attention to the cits. I knew I must look a fright – plus I was probs heaps whiffy – but I just didn't care. I stumbled on by, mentally daring anyone to have a go. No one did, but.

By the time I reached the hab, I was dead on my feet. I reached for my key but, of course, I'd lost it. I'd lost everything in that trip to the Downlow. Lost Ken, lost Eva, lost the not-a-gem and the key.

I'd lost it all.

"Because I'm a loser."

I knocked on the door. No reply. I knocked harder. Footsteps. The door opened and I stared down at Bel's puffy face. She'd just woken up.

"Hey, Bel," I croaked. And she screamed and ran inside.

Just then Gia appeared, holding a cricket bat and ready to have a whack at me.

"You fuggen well leave these kids alone!"

"Gia, s'me. S'Franga," I mumbled.

Then I caught a glimpse of myself in the glass of the door, and yeah –
I was a blood-crusted mess, most of my yellow skin covered with blood,
mud and various scum. No wonder Bel had run.

"Sorry," I said, not really sure who I was talking to.

"Franga?" She said it like she couldn't believe it.

And then she slapped me on the face, hard, and shouted: "Where the
bloody hell have you been?"

THIRTEEN

Gia yelled at me for a fair while. There was a lotta mouth-gear about me being "unbelievably irresponsible" and questions like "what were you thinking?" and "did you consider anyone else for even a moment?" and "do you even know how scared the ruggies have been?" and so on. I was too numb to react much to the tirade, other than quietly nodding and agreeing with most of her points. She calmed down an indeterminate amount of time later and I reckon my lack of fight had something to do with it. That and the fact I was dead on my feet and swaying, like a grogged-up cit after the pubs close.

"Are you alright, Franga?" Gia asked, seeming to actually see me for the first time, and recognise the sorry state I was in.

I shrugged.

"You look like shit."

I nodded.

"Where's Ken?"

That's when I started bawling. It was heaps embarrassing, but I just couldn't hold it in any longer. Gia's entire demeena changed straight away and she hustled me past the wide-eyed ruggies, into the bathroom, and started heating up the water.

As the water warmed, I told Gia the whole sorry tale, stopping to sob and wipe my eyes. She sat and listened, attentively, only asking for clarification on a couple of points. Once I laid out the story, I felt a bit better. Not great, mind you, but lighter. As if the story had been hanging around my neck. Like an Albert Tross.

"Righto." Gia nodded at the bath. "Get your togs off and geddin."

"But…" I was shy about dropping my strides in front of her. "Nah…"

"Franga, I see tockleys all day. It's literally part of my job. I promise you I won't stare. Plus, you stink, mate."

"Righto."

I was too knackered to argue, so I peeled my scummy clothes off and stepped awkwardly into the bath. The lukewarm water felt like an unexpected embrace and I sighed as I slipped down into it.

"Crikey, that feels good," I murmured.

"So, I guess you had quite the adventure, then." Gia started soaking a washcloth.

"It was horrible. I made a mess of everything."

"I don't think you can blame yourself, sounds like it was berko down there. Lean forward, I'll wash your back."

I did.

"What I don't get," Gia said, scrubbing the various layers of filth from my back, "is what Ken was thinking wanting to go down there in the first place."

"Well, we need to make some serious dosh if we're gunna keep this place…" but Gia kept talking.

"And who were those people in the submarine?"

"Dunno," I sighed. "I reckon they had something to do with the not-a-gem, but I never got a chance to find out proper-like."

"And you reckon Ken's still alive?"

"Yes," I said firmly, because the alternative was unthinkable. Then, softer, "He has to be."

"Well, that all sounds a bit shit, to be honest."

"It was," I agreed. "So, like, you believe me? Even about the monster and everything?"

"Yeah, why wouldn't I?"

"Cos it's…" I trailed off. What was a better term for 'fuggen crazy'?

"Unbelievable?"

I nodded.

"Franga, you've never been a slack-arse moll or a bullshitter. The fact you and Ken went on this mission was, you know, a bit bloody thick, but to come back here and tell porkies? That's just not something you'd ever do. So, you know, by the process of a-limmy-nation, it must be true."

I felt myself welling up again so I didn't say anything.

"Although," she murmured, "the question becomes: what are you gunna do about it? And who are you gunna tell?"

"I dunno," I shivered, remembering the sound of the monster's roar. "But I've gotta let someone know, eh."

"Your back's done. I'm guessing you can do your own front?"

"Yeah, cheers."

Gia passed me the washcloth and stood to leave.

"I'm glad you didn't cark it, eh," she said, still facing the door.

"Ta. Me too."

Gia left me alone and I finished cleaning myself, thinking how grouse it was to have mates.

• • • •

When I came out of the bathroom, clean and dressed in some fresh clobber Gia had thoughtfully left for me, the ruggies were waiting. I stood there for a moment, looking at them all, taking them in after what felt like such a long time. Then Bel barreled into me like a cannonball, making me woof my breath out.

"I'msorryIdintrecogniseyouFrangaaa!" she squealed, wrapping her arms around my legs and looking up at me with her big, beautiful, weird eye and her blank wee one, both filled with tears.

"That's okay, love, I didn't recognise myself."

"Why have you been gawn so loooongaaa?"

"Ran into some trouble. Bad kind."

She nodded solemnly. And then it was time to hug and greet the rest of the ruggies, assure them I was back, and calm their quezzies. Their many, many quezzies.

Most of them revolved around Ken, who I told them was still "busy taking care of some stuff", and though I wasn't entirely sure when he'd be back, "it could be any day now. Maybe next week."

I was still hoping that might turn out to be true. Because if not, the whole lot of us would be out on our mutant arses, and that would be a deadset death sentence.

There had been a number of dramas since I'd left, a weary Tommy relayed to me, and they were delightful in their banality. Bel had been having nightmares about me and Ken carking it, which was easy fixed on account of me being alive.

Debs was annoyed that Gia didn't "shave her face as good" and had been eating several mouthfuls of hair with every meal. To be entirely honest, Gia's shave job looked fine to me, but I obliged Debs with what she clearly felt was a superior shearing.

"That's the way you do it," she said, looking pointedly at Gia. Happily, Gia found it as cute as I did.

Claire's scale skin had been itching up and she needed some ointment that would have to be bartered for at the markets. Dane's ear infection was worse than before, and as he didn't have any eyes it made life terribly confusing for him. And Gruta – with her catlike claws and sensitivity to light – had been withdrawn and moody. I thanked Tommy for the news and wrote notes to meself to take care of all the sundry, simple problems with a trip to the shops, some canny bartering and numerous hugs to be administered over the course of the evening.

It was work I was more than happy to tackle. Because of all the excitement, I didn't put them down until after midnight, which I allowed due to it being such a special occasion and all.

After they were all asleep, I crept upstairs and sat in Ken's chair, the door open, and drank a cup of weak tea, mentally adding 'tea' to the extensive shopping list I'd probs have to sell a book or two to fill.

I heard a light knock at the door. I looked up patiently, expecting one of the ruggies, but it was Gia, ready for work and looking real nice.

"Like the hair," I said, sipping my not-very-good tea. "Pretty shade-a purple."

It was, too, and I should know as I'd scavenged the wig from a mostly intact mannequin I'd found in the Downlow.

"You think?" Gia flicked her hair in a most enchanting fashion.

"Yeah, grouse."

"Ta. Hey, so, I'm off to work."

"I managed to figure that out," I said, raising the part of my face that would have an eyebrow on it if my body grew hair.

"Ha ha," Gia said, but she was smiling. "But, uh, I was wondering if you wanted me to come back tomoz, to help out and that?"

"You don't haveta do that, G."

"I don't *haveta* do anything, Frang, but I'm asking if you'd like that. If it'd be a help."

"I would and it would, mate."

"Good-o, then. I'll see you tomorrow, sometime after brekkie."

"Have a good shift."

She smiled and flicked her hair again, sauntering out the door with a grin on her face. I was left feeling extremely complicated in various regions of my body, so I picked a few books from Ken's shelf and sat in his huge chair, flipping through the pages, until something grabbed my attention.

I was home, I was safe and Ken would be back soon. Everything would be okay.

Right?

Yeah, right, a darker part of me seemed to mutter, *because that's how things go so often, isn't it? Happy endings all around.*

I didn't realise I'd fallen asleep until a knock at the door in the wee hours woke me up with a start. I figured it was Gia lobbing up early, so I dashed downstairs with a grin, pulling open the door.

And found myself staring into the grim, helmeted countenance of a tall, stern-looking Pig.

"Bribe Day," he sneered down at me.

$$\bullet \quad \bullet \quad \bullet \quad \bullet$$

Ken reckoned that back in the old days, Pigs were meant to protect cits from dodgy criminal bastards and the like. That must've been nice, but a far cry from what they got up to in the Inassidy. Branded with NanoCorp logos, the Pigs were basically a corporate force of well-armed hard cunce who kept undesirable cits out of The Big End of Town and extorted whoever they could for sexual favours and dosh.

I counted myself at least a little bit lucky that they only wanted the latter from me.

Ken had had the foresight to prepare a Bribe Day basket of dosh – consisting of flash junk, some ancient machines and a cuppla paperybacks it hurt my heart to see gawn – so at least I had that to hand over. But the Pig in the door looked curious, leering around the joint at the waking ruggies and me.

"Where's your normie?" he wanted to know.

"Uh, Ken's popped down the shops for some essentials," I lied through my nervous grin.

"Tell him to be back for next Bribe Day." The Pig had a voice like a sharpening razor and a face like a dropped pie. "I don't like dealing with *your kind*."

"Okay, thank you," I stammered and then, because apparently life wasn't already hard enough for me, I said the words: "There's one other thing."

"What?" the Pig growled.

I launched into a heavily edited version of the story of the monster's birth, starring only me and with no mention of the not-a-gem or Ken. Basically, a creature was loose in the Downlow and was maggoting everyone in sight. After I'd finished telling it, I was panting slightly, but glad I'd got it off my chest. I'd done the right thing.

"So, you're telling me," the Pig rasped, "something's in the Downlow killing off all the muties and murderous scum that live there?"

"Um, yeah, but–"

"Sounds like we should be thanking it, if you ask me."

"No, well, like, thing is, if it managed to get up here, then, there could be a big–"

The Pig stepped closer, towering over me, and I briefly considered how he was defo good Mongrel material.

"Now you listen here." The Pig was right up in my face. "That little fairytale has added another ten percent to your Bribe total."

"But–"

"Keep carrying on like a porkchop and I'll make it fifdeen!"

With great personal effort, I managed to keep my gob shut and just nodded. The Pig spat on the floor, looked around once more and left without another word. I closed and locked the door behind him and shut my eyes, hands shaking.

"Yeah, nice one, Franga," I sighed. "Just brilliant fuggen work there, mate."

FOURTEEN

Life returned to a state I called "sorta normal". I looked after the ruggies, restarted rehearsals for their next play, which was due to be performed the following week. Gia stayed some nights and helped out when she could and, in the back of my mind, I made plans to find Ken. I spent time with Gia and Tommy and not one single person tried to kill me.

It was all sorta normal.

But of course, in the back of my mind, the quezzies – *What about the monster? and what if Ken is dead?* – ran around like increasingly agitated rats. Not to mention the problem of how I'd keep the Ages Home from getting repossessed by the Pigs, which simmered in me guts, a low but persistent ache.

I couldn't let it get the better of me, but. I had shit to do.

I managed to barter with Old Lil and get the various goodies I needed to keep life peaceful and even got her to kick in some spices and extra nutrition lumps at no extra cost. I suspected word of Ken's disappearance had done the rounds but I wasn't too proud to take advantage of her sympathy.

A bloke'd be stupid not to take advantage of every chance he gets.

I woke up early most days and went to sleep late, too knackered to think about the future. The ruggies settled down, which was grouse, but my dreams, most nights, were plagued by nightmares about the monster in the Downlow and Ken's unknown fate.

However, and this can't be stressed enough, not a single solitary person tried to maggot me. All things considered, sorta normal was a state I could see myself eventually getting used to.

It lasted just over a week.

The day it all ended started normally enough. I woke up to the sound of screaming mutant children. I went downstairs – I'd taken to sleeping up in Ken's quarters with the door open – and shut them up with a combo of yelling and food. It worked about as well as it usually did, which is to say partially.

By the time I got them settled learning lines or playing various semi-educational games, I'd managed to shove some food in me face and drink a cuppa tea. Then Gia arrived and brought information that changed everything.

"I've got news!" she said, excited-like and panting, like she'd run to the hab.

"Oh yeah?" I drained me tea. "What's the go?"

"Too much to tell ya. Just come down the pub."

"Bit early to sink piss, G, I'm more of an arvo drinker–"

"Franga." Gia's tone suggested I should be mouth closed, ears open. "You need to come right now."

"Righto, then."

Muties aren't strictly allowed in pubs, although Dave-O – proprietor of Dave-O's Beer Hole – usually turned a blind eye to anyone except full monsters. Hooded and goggled – scarf wrapped around my neck – I didn't attract many looks. Gia, on the other hand, garnered approving glances from every bloke and sheila within cooee of us. I felt a momentary petty jealousy, envious of the positive squizzes she must get all the time, but woke up to myself pretty quick.

Dave-O's Beer Hole was probs the least dangerous pub in the Inasiddy. Certainly safer than Piss Sinkers, Grog For Youse or that cave that just has a badly drawn mouth painted above it that everyone calls "the cave", "the mouth" or "for fug's sake, don't go in there!".

People in Dave-O's were mainly there to drink and socialise, and stabbings were rare, although not unheard of.

The attention of the punters was directed to the front of the large, echoey room – all eyes turned towards someone who was standing on the bar, banging on about something. Gia squeezed through the throng, pulling me by the hand.

"Carn, this is the bloke."

"Which bloke?"

"Just listen."

The bloke in question was Pisshead Michael. He was called that on account of his yoorin-blond locks and habit of being half-cut on cheap grog most of the time. He was generally considered to be a harmless but powerful stupid cit, so the fact he had the crowd's attention suggested he had an interesting tale to tell.

"Righto, righto, I'll tell youse, okay, giz a minute," Pisshead was muttering, obviously fearful of the attention he was getting but encouraged by the free drinks. "So this all happened yesterday, when I was in the Downlow diving for treasures…"

Pisshead was one of about fifdy Downlow divers that I knew of. These were desperate cits who'd climb down the cliffs into the Downlow and scavenge what they could, usually to swap it for grog or chems. It was a foolhardy profession, although divers rarely went as deep in as me.

"I knew something was wrong halfway down. There's always some kinda noise coming from the Downlow. Shouts, screams, bitta biffo – always something. But this time, there was nuthin'. It was quiet as the grave."

"Ged fugged, mate!" one of the drunk blokes in the front row jeered, and a bunch of people laughed. Pisshead continued, undaunted.

"I kept going anyhow – figured the quiet could only be a good thing. None of the clans were about. Maybe they were fighting with themselves. I unclipped me rope and started filling the bag, walking froo there. About an hour later, I come across the first of them…"

"First of what?" someone in the crowd asked.

"Probably another bottle of grog!" anothery answered, chuckling smart-arsedly.

"It was a pile of skulls. About yea high," Pisshead held a shaking hand at chest-level, "and covered with, like a… dunno… a kinda slime. Stank to high heaven. Never seen nuthin' like it."

The crowd murmured at this and a cold chill crept up my spine. Gia and I shared a look. That sounded awful familiar. Like the nest of the Lord.

"Still, Downlow's a dangerous place," Pisshead went on, "and I needed to fill me bag, so I kept going, but careful, ready for anything. It wasn't long before I come across a second skull pile, then a third – bigger than the other two put together and fresh enough that it was steaming. It occurred to me then that I should probably bugger off and get back up cliff and that's when I saw it…"

Pisshead's hands were trembling, spilling beer on the bar's ancient counter. Nobody said anything, totes captivated by the story.

"… I-it was as tall as three men, and wide as five. Two arms, that I could see, and two legs, but no way was that a human, normie or mutie. It was like nuthin' anyone's ever seen before. The Downlow was misty that day, so I couldn't make out its face and that, but it was dragging a body behind it, Mongrel from the look of him. Big bastard but messed up and dead – or close to it. But that wasn't the worst of it." Pisshead paused to take a deep swig here. "No, the worst was… when it turned around, looking in my direction, I could see it clearer and it was… it had…"

"Spit it out, y'wanker!"

"It had faces, heaps of faces, and they were all…" Pisshead's mouth moved but it was like he couldn't make the words jump out. He was a fresh-caught fish gasping on a dock. "They were all talking at once!"

This was too much for the assembled crowd to take. Disbelief can be suspended during a pub yarn, but not beaten to a pulp out the back. The spell was broken and the incensed patrons started jeering.

"Bloody bullshit!"

"Off you pop, ya cheeky dog!"

Pisshead shrugged off the attention and headed for the door, still shaking and beginning to have a sook.

"Bullshit, y'reckon?" Gia asked me.

"I dunno, hey," I shrugged. "He loves a drink but…"

"He seemed genuine?"

"Yeah."

"That's what I reckon too."

Over the following five days, more stories of the monster in the Downlow circulated via the pub grapevine. Some of them were certainly bullshit, spread by attention-seekers who wanted some free booze, but others rang horribly true.

One deep-sea fisherman told a tale of coming into port only to have his craft smack into what looked like white islands. A poke with a boat hook showed these islands were in fact Mongrels from the Downlow, horribly burned and deformed by the poison waters. There were dozens of them, maybe even as many as a hundred.

The fisherman shook his head and his voice quivered with disbelief, asking: "Why would they do that? Why would they throw themselves into the water that way? What were they running from?"

What indeed.

Another story that made an impact was one of omission. A group of six Downlow divers, inspired by Pisshead's story, headed down there in group formation, to prove the stories true or nah. Twenny-four hours later and they hadn't returned. Some cits investigated but all they found were their ropes, hanging from the cliff. They pulled them up and every rope had been ripped, the ends tattered and frayed, with spatters of blood spread across their length.

After that people stopped Downlow diving.

There were more stories. The God-botherer who reckoned he saw something huge and unnatural leap through the air, the prozzie who swore blind that something howled from the bottom of the cliff where she'd taken a client for a romantic gobbie, and more and more.

Everyone had a monster story, it seemed, and the tension and excitement in the air was palpable. Boredom is a terrible curse and even bad news is better than no news for the people of the Inasiddy.

Cuppla nights later the roaring began. It was loud enough to echo through all the streefs near Cliff's Edge and even some of the Rooting District. It was a pained abattoir wail that spoke of loss and longing, of hunger and pain, of violence and the extreme desire to inflict it.

Every night, for three nights running, it went on and on – for over an hour – and it seemed to be getting closer.

I'd begun spending a lot of my spare time in Dave-O's pub, more thinking than drinking, listening to the theories and what people reckoned. Cits believed the monster must be dying, maybe it had run out of food, maybe it had contracted some kind of disease – but surely we were all safe up cliff.

Nothing – no matter how fearsome – could scale the pitiless vertical cliff. No, everything was fine, they believed, *everyone* was fine.

The whole situation would resolve itself soon enough.

I appreciated their optimism but I couldn't help but wonder. I headed home after the roaring stopped, thinking I had best get back on track planning my next trip into the Downlow. I certainly didn't want to go back down, but there was a finite amount of dosh I'd be able to use to pay off the Pigs, even if I made that most soul-scouring sacrifice of selling me books.

So caught up in my thoughts was I that I didn't notice the door was unlocked as I entered the hab. I took a couple of steps and then it struck me – I'd entered without using my key.

"Kids!" I called out. "Did one of youse forget to lock the door? How many times have I–"

"Sorry, Franga," a weary voice replied. "It's been a while. I forgot."

I spun around to see Ken, battered, bruised but unmistakably Ken, sitting at the dining room table, smiling wearily.

"Ken…" My mouth and eyes musta been perfect round O's of surprise.

"G'day, Franga."

And with that Ken fell forward onto the table, his head hitting the wood with a solid, echoing thunk.

FIFTEEN

It seems to me that life is timed all wrong. Stuff should happen one thing after another, sequential-like, but instead it seems to come at ya all at once or not at all. Case in point: Ken's return, the monster in the Downlow and the latest production by the All Ages Mutie Theatre Troopie, *Angels of New Sydney*, at New Sydney Arr Ess Ell.

Any one of those could be hard yakka, but all three occurring in the same bloody twenny-four-hour time period felt like a particularly cruel jape.

Of course, I wanted to prioritise Ken, but he wasn't having a bar of it. After I'd managed to get him upstairs – the bloke seemed to weigh less than a laundry basket half full of festy undies – he woke up and seemed a little better. I made him drink water and passed him a handful of his pills. I gave Ken a brief summary of events he'd missed, the monster and the Pigs and so on, and he absorbed the information wearily. He was about to slip into sleep when I told him I'd cancel the play the next day.

"Don't you bloody dare!" he cried, suddenly alert and wide-eyed. "Those kids have worked so hard for so long. Don't take that away from them."

"Righto, Ken. Jeez, mate."

"Promise me, Franga."

"I promise, bloody hell. Where have you been, anyway, what's happened?"

"I'll tell you," Ken raised a hand, "when you get back. Tomorrow night, I'll tell you everything. Just let a bloke get some rest, recover a little."

I fussed over him a while, made a couple of sangers and left them near the end of his bed in case he got hungry. It didn't seem real having him back like that and I felt something deep down in the core of me unclench, my whole being relaxing a poofteenth.

I lay down on the floor at the bottom of the stairs, keeping an ear out for Ken should he need help. I didn't anticipate I'd get to sleep at all, but in the end, exhaustion got the better of me and I drifted off.

• • • •

I woke up to Bel looming over me, dripping eye juice onto my face with a soft *plipping* sound.

"*Franga,*" she whispered in a manner that was not intended to minimise sound at all.

Plip.

"Yes, love?" I said, grimacing and wiping cloudy tears off my face.

"*It's time to get up because we're doing the play today.*"

Plip.

"Okay, let a bloke wake up, would ya?"

"*Okay, but then can we rehearse because I'm very neeervousaaa?*"

Plip.

I soon realised there would be no more sleep for me, so I sighed and sat up, drying my face with my shirt. The ruggies always got feral before a performance. Nerves, tension and anticipation led to tantrums and all manner of dummy-spitting. I spent the morning trying to corral the youngsters, making sure they were fed and at least vaguely clean, but it was quite an effort all by myself. Gia was evidently still working and

Ken had decided he wasn't going to tell anyone he was home just yet. Considering the shape he was in, I didn't think it was such a bad idea.

Eventually everyone was made ready and we left the hab in a big group – hands linked and eyes open – the full monsters amongst us covered up. We stuck mainly to back roads to avoid any potential nugget with cits, but even so, the streefs were unusually deserted for that time of day. A scrawny, hungry mongrel dog and an old sheila off her guts on chems were our only companions on the fordy-minute walk to the Arr Ess Ell, and though I was glad of this fact it was undeniably strange.

The Arr Ess Ell was basically a big shed with a multi-tood of smaller huts spun off it, in various colourful, frequently impractical ways. In theory, it was a place where veterans of the Water Wars and more recent conflicts could be kept housed, fed and away from other cits. In reality, it was a dumping ground for ex-soldiers who were now too damaged – either physically or mentally – to be much use to the guvmint or society in general. That said, they'd always been a good customer for us – we performed at the Ahry a half dozen times a year – and the staff and vets were pleasant, for the most part.

Interestingly, the Ahry was the place that muties felt least judged and that was because of the state of most of the soldiers. Put kindly, they were a rough-looking bunch. In the three full rows of cits who sat, waiting for the play to begin in the Arr Ess Ell's main room, I reckon there might have been two who weren't missing at least one limb. The rest were multiple amputees, skin scarred with chemical burns or flesh degraded by one weaponised poison or another. There was one poor bugger in the front row– "Stumpy" they called him – who had no limbs at all, and his lower jaw had been dissolved to a twisted little nub of flesh. He was friendly, but, and when the ruggies took the stage he clapped as best he could, his stumps making a rasping papery sound as they thumped together enthusiastically.

"It is New Sydney, Straya, and the Big Blackout is about to 'appen..."

The play ran without a hitch. Everyone remembered their lines, hit their cues and delivered the finest version of *Angels of New Sydney* that I'd ever seen. I was proud beyond words. The audience seemed to enjoy it and yet... there was something off. Yes, the applause was strong and they oohed and ahhed in the right places, but there was a sense of tension, of preoccupation that seemed to hover over everything, damping down enthusiasm.

During intermission, the bar sheila, serving me my one complimentary beer, told me why.

"It's the bloody monster, isn't it?" she murmured, handing me a rather stingy pour.

"They know about it here?" I was surprised.

"They can *hear* it."

"They can hear it this far up cliff?"

"Yep. Unsteady Eddy did his block."

Unsteady Eddy was the Arr Ess Ell's physically whole but mentally broken soldier of a recent skirmish out in the Garbage Plains. Not a lot of information existed on the conflict but every bastard who came back seemed deeply disturbed by the experience.

"Can I talk to him about it?" I wanted to know.

"You can try, but I wouldn't."

I noticed the bar sheila deliberately placed the glass on the bar and snatched her fingers away before mine could get close, as if my mutations were contagious, like the flu or mega-herps. I was probs feeling a little over-sensitive about it, so I wandered over to Unsteady Eddy, who was staring out a grimy window at a depressing view of a wall and a dead bird.

"How ya goin', Eddy?"

"Yeah, good, mate, grouse and that, good to see ya, yeah."

Eddy spoke with a robotic repetition, his eyes flicking back and forth and rarely settling. It was confronting, but you could get used to it. Sorta.

"Um, so… heard you were a bit skew-whiff about the, uh… noise from the Downlow."

"Skew-whiff? Screw it. Everyone… everyone… ponytail… lies."

"Sorry, mate?"

"You don't apologise. You didn't do nothing. Something was done, though. To you. They should apologise."

"They who?"

"They too. To you."

I took a deep breath. This wasn't much help at all and Eddy's edgy twitchiness was starting to make me feel light-headed.

"Righto, mate, I'd best finish this play and that." I clinked my drink against Eddy's and turned to leave when his hand lashed out like a snake and gripped my arm. His fingers were strong, like steel, and I winced and hissed in pain.

"I saw it out in the plains. I saw it, saw it, saw. IT."

"Eddy, that hurts. Please let go."

"Seek. Rit. In the plains. Seek. Rit."

"Righto…" I was trying to pry Eddy's fingers off. Even using all my strength, I could barely shift the pinky.

"That's where I found out the truth. Who we were fighting. Why we were fighting them. The big. Seek. Rit."

"Fine, *fuggenhellpleaseletgoyabloodyfuuu–*"

Just then two of the burly orderlies grabbed an arm each and lifted Eddy off me and off the ground with seemingly little to no effort. Eddy came back to himself, confused but entirely pleasant.

"Oh crikey, boys." he murmured. "Did I go berko again?"

I rubbed my arm, the bruise already beginning to form, and assured Eddy and the orderlies I was fine. To be honest, it hurt like buggery, but there didn't seem much point laying that on Eds. Ol' mate Eddy had seen some shit, and it had clearly left him a bit off.

"Anyway, second half of the play to put on." I wince-smiled and trotted back to the stage.

If anything, the second half of the play went even better – laughter, cheers and even a few tears, especially at the end. But I couldn't help but notice that tension, just around the edges of every interaction.

And Eddy was nowhere to be seen.

After the ruggies said hello to some of the veterans, and a few of them had a run around what they called "the back paddock", but in reality was a mostly concrete enclosed area – where the dead bird was a big hit entertainment-wise – it was time to head back home.

Once again everyone linked hands and I led them outside and into the back streefs as the arvo sun slipped behind some greasy-looking clouds.

There were a few more cits on the road but they barely looked at us, which seemed a strange reaction to a bunch of muties. Again, I wasn't complaining – it was all for the best – but it was unusual.

As we neared the hab, I noticed someone had a horse and cart out front. My heart started hammering in my chest, and I began to worry that the Pigs had come back, but nah – that was an old, sad-looking mutant horse and the cart was similarly unimpressive.

What shocked me was when I recognised the cart's driver. It was Ken!

"Uncle Ken!" Bel squealed and launched herself at the bloke, which encouraged the rest to do the same. Ken's face seemed to grow younger by a decade as a beaming smile crossed his chops, and all twelve ruggies joined him in a big beautiful group hug.

"We were so worried, Uncle Ken."

"Where have you been?"

"I'm here now, kids." Ken's eyes shone with tears of joy. "I'm here now and it's so good to see you all."

They stayed like that for a long time, a perfectly blissful moment. But it eventually ended and Gia herded everyone inside with the promise of grub, which left me and Ken staring at one another.

"Come for a little ride, Frang?"

"Righto." I shrugged.

I sat on the cart next to Ken as he braced the horse with a snap of the reins. The horse, a fearsome ugly bastard with a tiny vestigial head next to his normal one, snorted and slowly moved to a trot.

"How'd you afford the nag, Ken?"

"Sold a cuppla books," he said and then, reacting to the horrified look on my face, "none of yours, they're still safe."

"How come you reckon we need it?"

But Ken ignored the question, sighing, "Let's just ride for a little bit first, son."

The horse dragged us through the Inasiddy streefs in silence as the sun slipped below the horizon.

SIXTEEN

We travelled for about an hour without saying a word. Ken was distant, contemplative. He either watched the scenery turn more wild or stared down at the bandaged stump of what used to be his hand. I opened my mouth to say something, to try to start a conversation a dozen times, but nothing came out. The air was thick with a tension I didn't understand, so I let the slow and steady movements of the mutie horse lull me into a kind of waking slumber. A listless state of being.

I watched as the scenery changed from urban to suburban, the houses spread farther apart, many of them ruined husks. The lanterns of the Inasiddy faded away and the landscape was almost pitch black, save for the lights of the stars that beamed down at us from on high. The moon was a fingernail sliver, but a bright one, and the road – such as it was – remained visible enough for travel.

We came across a corpse, some kind of animal – probs a horse – and scattered an intrusion of cockroaches the size of lanky dogs. They scuttled in all directions into the night, making a soft rasping sound as their antennae slid across the bitchy-man road.

Cicadas filled the air with their endless drone-song, and the night was alive with shapes – large and small – that performed their furtive, nocturnal rituals. I shuddered to think what might be lurking in the tall grass and weeds that grew either side of us, creatures brimming with mandi-bulls and strange purpose. Ken had told me that before the Big Blackout, Straya had the largest concentration of poisonous insects and animals anywhere in the world. It was a fact I reckoned hadn't improved in recent years.

I didn't like how nature made me feel. People could be deadset fugknuckles but at least in ways that made sense. How could you reason with a giant cockroach? A hungry spider? What argument can you make against a snake that just wants to fang you full of poison?

Just then an animal screech filled the night air. I couldn't tell what kinda creature it was, but something had caught it and was maggoting it good and proper.

The screams got higher, and madder, and then stopped all of a sudden. Nature's dance of death concluded and the cicadas kept singing.

"Used to be beautiful country, this."

Ken's voice was so unexpected it made me jump with fright. I looked over at him, but he was still looking straight ahead.

"Farmland. Vineyards. 'God's country', they called it. I don't think they were far wrong. Except if there is a God, he stopped giving a shit about us a long time ago."

I didn't know what to say, so I kept not saying anything. We rode on for a spell. I was beginning to think that was it when I heard, "I'm going to tell you what happened, Franga."

Ken was looking at me now, something weighing heavily on him, something he had to cough up.

"And I need you to listen, real careful, and not distract me with a hundred questions."

"Why–"

Ken raised a hand. "What did I just say?"

I opened my mouth to answer but instead just nodded.

"Very good."

Ken turned to face the road again, giving the reins a little flick.

"It's not... easy... to start telling this. So, I suppose I should begin where we parted ways for a time. The last thing I clearly remember is my severed fingers falling onto the black sand and then everything going very wobbly indeed. Later on, I realised I was in shock as a result of losing fifty percent of my upper digits thanks to a boomerfang attack." Ken raised his bandaged stump. "But at the time it was more abstract, vague. I certainly didn't want you to think I'd abandoned you."

I didn't realise I'd needed to hear Ken say that until he did. I didn't say anything, but. Just let Ken tell his tale.

SEVENTEEN

After taking a deep breath and letting it slowly out, Ken began:

"I woke up in a small, hard bed, lying on my back, eyes closed. I could hear voices around me, male and female. One of each.

'Is he alright?' That was the man talking.

'He's a fighter, Garold, you know that,' the woman replied.

'I know he is, but perhaps *he* isn't.' I didn't understand that comment but kept listening.

'What about Eva?'

'No word yet.'

'Christ, what a mess.'

The sound of pacing. The man, Garold, I think. He continued: 'I need to get back to it.'

'Any progress?'

No answer. Maybe he shrugged or nodded or shook his head. Regardless, what followed was a hissing, a door of some kind I judged, and the sound of footsteps moving away. Then nothing but the woman moving softly through the room, metallic clinks and drawers opening and closing. After a while, the woman's footsteps receded and there was that hiss again, the door.

It felt like I was alone so I opened my eyes, slowly, cautiously.

'Hello, "'Kenneth'",' said the woman, leaning over the top of me. 'Glad to see you're awake.'

I'm not sure why I had been playing possum. I can't explain it even now, but it felt like the right thing to do. Maybe I was just being overly cautious. Or maybe I had an inkling something was amiss. Either way, it hadn't worked and the woman – one of the three people from the submarine – looked down at me with a grin that was sardonic and somehow familiar.

'I've always known when you're awake, Ken.'

'Always?' I murmured in a voice that sounded like ground glass in a rusty tin can.

The woman, tall with a handsome, somewhat stern face, handed me a bulb of water, which I drank from eagerly.

'Do you remember where you are?' she asked.

'Submarine?' The water was soothing my throat but it still hurt to speak.

'That's right. We were attacked by a band of savages. Garold, yourself and I managed to submerge before they caught us.'

'Frang-a?'

'Excuse me?'

'My… friend. Yellow… skin.'

'Oh, the mutie? With Eva. They were taken by the savages.'

I tried to sit up then but the world spun crazily and I had to lie back down.

'Don't try to move; you've lost a lot of blood. And appendages. We're sorting you out, though.'

For the first time I noticed I was hooked up to various machines, tubes and IV bags. Apparently, I was in a bad way.

'Franga…' I said sadly.

'He'll be fine. Eva is… more than she seems at first glance.'

'Who… you?'

The woman seemed hurt by this question. Her face took on a curious cast, as if a longtime family member had said something cutting and barbed, a comment rendered all the more potent by familiarity. And that expression… triggered something in me. Like maybe I did know this woman. But how and from where?

'You truly don't remember?'

For a second, I almost did, but no. It was a fleeting thing. I could remember advertising jingles from my teens but not the identity of this woman.

'Sorry.'

'That's quite alright.' She spoke with an affected indifference. 'I am Minerva. The gentleman is Garold. You're aboard *The Raw Prawn* and we're soon going to dock with Research Station Alpha.'

'Underwater?'

'I've found that's where submarines usually work best, yes.'

Minerva grinned and it changed her face from imposing and severe to something else entirely. It was a nice smile.

'As for your health, you'll be fine. But you need to rest. There will be plenty of time to talk later.'

'But Franga–'

'Your affection for that mutie is… odd but I can see it's genuine. We'll do our best. I'll do *my* best.'

'Thank. You.'

Minerva gave me that odd look again, but it left her face quickly – skulking away like an awkward party guest. I suddenly became aware of how bone tired I was and closed my eyes, for real this time, slipping off into a chemically assisted period of slumber.

Next time I woke up the whole of *The Raw Prawn* was shaking. I sat up, eyes wide. There was a sound like something enormous clicking into place. Footsteps came down the corridor. I looked over just as the door hissed open.

'Don't panic,' Minerva said, smiling cryptically. 'We're just docking with Alpha.'

'How long was I out?' I asked in a much less painful voice than before.

'Twelve hours, give or take.'

'That long?'

'You needed it.'

Twelve hours. Where was Research Station Alpha that it took so long to travel to? I thought about asking but I suspected obfuscation was the order of the day. Minerva didn't trust me, which was fine. I didn't trust her or Garold either, and yet… there was that tickle at the back of my brain again, that sense that I knew them both.

Maybe in a past life. Well, that was an odd thought. I don't believe in things like that.

'Can you sit up?'

I tried it and the result was unpleasant but manageable. Minerva helped me up and manoeuvred me to the edge of the bed on which I lay. I noticed for the first time a fancy-looking wheelchair, chrome and steel, and a rather uncomfortable-looking arse cushion.

Evidently my displeasure showed in my facial expression.

'It's just for ease of movement, Ken. Let me give you a hand.'

I allowed myself to be awkwardly levered into the wheelchair. The cushion was as unpleasant to the buttocks as it was to the eyes, but otherwise I was comfortable. I looked down at my old body. Clad in a hospital gown, it looked like the last chicken in the shop, knock-kneed and pasty.

'I take it you've got my clothes?' My tone was snappy to hide my embarrassment at the undignified position I was in.

'Being cleaned. They were covered with blood. And vomit. Mostly yours.'

I nodded and looked down at the bandaged stump.

'I do appreciate you helping with the arm. Bandaging me up and so forth.'

'We did quite a bit more than that, dear,' she said, in a clipped, precise way.

'What do you mean?'

'I'll let Garold explain.'

With that, Minerva positioned herself behind me and began pushing me down the light green utilitarian hallways of *The Raw Prawn*. We moved swiftly and soon found ourselves at the airlock. Minerva entered a code into a keypad and a second later the large, round door hissed open.

Garold – stout and short, eyebrows arched and hirsute – greeted us with open arms: 'Welcome to Research Station Alpha.'

The research station was a large, round space shaped like an enormous metal doughnut. It had clearly been built pre-blackout but that raised numerous questions about how it was powered. And powered it most certainly was; the mechanical thrum of electricity shooting through the guts of the thing was unmistakable. It made me feel nostalgic and confused all at once.

There was a central habitation area on one side of the ring, where a series of couches and bookshelves surrounded a kitchenette and a television. A bloody telly, Franga! I almost kissed the thing, it'd been so long since I'd even seen one. The other side was divided into two laboratory areas, both blocked off by heavy-duty doors that required key codes. The entire station was suffused with a light greenish hue, probably designed to be calming, but I found it faintly sinister.

'You're wondering how this place even exists, aren't you?' Garold grinned toothily.

'I really am. I mean, how do you power something this size?'

'Nothing about this place reminds you of anything?' Minerva had that odd look to her again.

'It reminds me of life back in the day… pre-blackout, but no, I can see that's not what you mean.' I sighed, frustrated. 'Minerva, I'm sorry, but I can't remember a lot of things. Why would I remember this joint?'

'Because, "Ken", you bloody designed it,' Garold spoke nastily.

'Garold!' Minerva was incensed.

'Oh, come on, we can't keep tiptoeing around it like this. I feel utterly absurd treating him like a bewildered grandmother.'

'Yet again, it's all about you, isn't it, Garold?'

'That's not what I meant, I just– come on, Min, this isn't messing with your head just a little too?'

'Of course it is!' Minerva snapped. 'But I don't see how you're helping matters any.'

'Um, excuse me.' I spoke softly.

'I think a short, sharp shock might help his memory, is all.' Garold seemed more than a little afraid of a newly angered Minerva.

'Your attempts at altruism are noted,' she said in a tone that didn't so much drip sarcasm as have sarcasm gushing out of every orifice.

'Hello, yes?' I actually raised a hand like a school student. 'I don't mean to interrupt... whatever this is, but if either or both of you could explain what's going on it would be sincerely and emphatically appreciated.'

Garold slumped into a comfy-looking chair, groaning. Minerva sat on the edge of one of the couches primly. They looked at one another. Garold shrugged and Minerva nodded.

'The thing is, Ken, you're well known to us both. Very well known, in fact.' Minerva seemed to search for what to say next, so Garold stepped in.

'Research Station Alpha was created by four scientists to facilitate a project designed by the Strayan government with extensive funding from NanoCorp. The principals involved were Garold Evans, Minerva Stampforth, Gabriel Little and Stephen Blentiff. Do those names mean anything to you?'

'Should they?' I was beginning to feel light-headed. As if I knew what was coming.

'Well, one of them should, dear.' Minerva's eyes were wide and intense. 'Because your real name is Stephen Blentiff.'

'You're one of us, Stephen. Or Ken. Or whatever it is you want to be called. It doesn't change the fact – you're one of us.'

'That can't be true…' I said in a voice that sounded far away to my ears.

'Oh, for God's sake…' Garold stood and stalked over to the kitchen area, rummaging through drawers and blaspheming absently. Minerva patted me on the leg.

'I know this must be very confusing. I wanted to break it to you more gently.'

'AHA!' Garold had found something and was striding back. 'Right, then. If I'm talking shit, then tell me, in the name of Jesus-farting-Christ, who is *that*?'

Garold shoved a framed photograph into my hands. The picture showed four people standing in front of the partially submerged *Raw Prawn*. Garold, Minerva, a skinny-looking chap and…

My breath caught and I couldn't believe my eyes.

'That's… me.'

It was. Younger, fitter and considerably healthier-looking but unmistakably me. Wearing the kind of cocksure smile a man wears when he's doing work he considers important. Also, the languid way I had my arms draped around Minerva's shoulders made me realise something.

'You and I… we were…?' I asked her.

'Yes. Very much so.' Could I remember her now? Was there a little piece or something coming to mind or was I just looking for it, hoping for it all to fall into place? Hoping for something.

'I'm sorry, I don't blame you for not remembering,' she assured me. 'After what you did to yourself…'

'What did I do to myself?'

'Well, that,' Garold said, retrieving a cigarette from his coat pocket, 'is the question, isn't it?'

'I should have thought the better question,' Minerva mused, 'is *why*.'

I spent the next hour and a half listening to two strangers describe decades of my life that were simply missing from my memory. It was simultaneously confronting and strangely numbing. What was curious was how much of it tracked with my vague memories but deviated from others. I, Stephen Blentiff, was a talented biologist who believed the future was in 'wet tech': a bold but unpopular branch of research that tried to meld technology with living organisms as opposed to exclusively machine-based hardware.

'It was furiously unpopular before the Big Blackout,' Garold reminisced over his third or fourth cigarette. 'People thought you were mad. Or a cretin. Or mad *and* a cretin.'

'But then,' Minerva continued, stealing Garold's cigarette and taking a puff, 'the Big Blackout changed everything. In an instant our reliance upon machinery was laid bare for the hubris it was and everything we had – our support systems, our infrastructure, the very nanomachines that kept us living such long, comfortable lives – was stripped away. And we were left like idiot children in the ruins of our own making.'

'Figurative ruins, of course. This was pre-Water Wars. Before things got really bad. Back when we still had hope.' Garold smiled, remembering better times.

'And suddenly,' Minerva's smile echoed that of her partner's, 'your eccentric branch of scientific thinking didn't seem so mad. In fact, it was beginning to look like the only thing that would save us all.'

'Ours wasn't the only research station, of course. There are half a dozen all over Straya, deep enough underwater that the effects of the Big Blackout are negligible. We were suddenly given carte blanche to investigate ways to get us back to working order. Can you guess what our first triumph was, Ken?' Garold seemed very eager for me to correctly answer the question. It took almost a full minute of furious internal speculation, but I smiled when I realised.

'The U-drones,' I murmured. 'It has to be, yes?'

Minerva and Garold beamed.

'I think this calls for the good scotch.' Garold chuckled and stood, heading over to the kitchen.

'It's in your lab,' Minerva called over her shoulder.

'Right, right, yes,' Garold replied, walking over to one of the heavy bulkheads and entering a code. As he entered his lab, Minerva leaned forwards, excited.

'The U-drones weren't just us, of course, all the research stations contributed to that one. But your research into the area of what you called BAI – Biological Artificial Intelligence – gave us the breakthrough we needed to make it work.'

'But umbrella drones aren't biological… are they?'

'Partially,' Garold called, re-entering the room, holding aloft a bottle of scandalously good single-malt scotch. I noticed he'd left his laboratory door open but didn't think much of it. 'There are mechanical components, of course, but their flocking instinct, the way they know to cover an area in the sky in such a way that delivers the most efficient blocking of UV rays over the most populated areas, that requires too much improvisation and lateral thinking for a simple machine. However, if you program an AI, augmented with the brain cells of seagulls and magpies, well, the results speak for themselves.'

Garold poured three extremely generous glasses of the scotch as I sat back, reeling.

'Bit of a shock to the system, love?' Minerva smiled.

'I really need this drink,' I agreed.

We clinked glasses and I sipped deeply of the wonderful drop.

'So,' I began, savouring the flavours in my mouth, 'what other life-changing discoveries did I come up with?'

They laughed.

'Other projects you *assisted* on?' Garold smiled. 'Doover-fish for a start. New Sydney can thank us all for their drinking water, not that they ever will. Oh, and grunters! That most adaptable of organisms that can survive in a pitiless wasteland is a classic Blentiff concept.'

'One that required an insane amount of actual hands-on work by your poor bloody coworkers,' Minerva grumbled good-naturedly, 'and in the end the little buggers were always too curious to program effectively. Live and learn.'

'And of course, there was your masterpiece…' Garold murmured.

'Oh?' I looked at them both, burning with curiosity.

'Our nanomachines were beginning to fail. Even underwater their descent into entropy was all but guaranteed. But, you wondered, what if nanomachines could be completely biological. Grown rather than built, evolved rather than constructed, impervious to EMP damage, giving us the ability to regrow dead and dying cells with even more efficacy than ever before…' Minerva trailed off, enjoying keeping me in suspense.

'Well?' I practically shouted.

'Well, what?' she cackled wickedly.

'Did the bloody things work?'

'You tell me. Take off your bandage.'

I looked down at my bandaged stump and then looked back at them. They were grinning eagerly, eyes gleaming in the green light.

I began unwrapping the bandages, pulling them off in a circular motion and dumping the soiled dressings on the floor. I expected to see a ragged stump, well-cleaned but grim nonetheless. Possibly stitches and the red scar tissue of recent physical trauma. Instead, as the final wrapping was pulled off, I was looking down at… a human hand.

An infant's human hand, I might add. About the size of three-year-old's. But when I tried to move the fingers, they wiggled. When I made a fist with my mind, the tiny hand made one too.

'What is… this?' I whispered.

'Your new hand, Stephen,' Garold crowed. 'The bio nanos have been instructed to grow it from infancy to adulthood, over the next six weeks or so. You won't feel any sensation in it until it's complete. Growing pains are a bitch, so we've had all pain signals blocked.'

'But at the end of that time,' Minerva said, putting her hand rather unsubtly on my leg, 'you'll be as good as new. Better, actually.'

'It probably hasn't escaped your attention that Minerva and I look, well, pretty good for people whose age runs into three digits.' Garold drained his scotch and poured a new one. 'Whereas you look like a hatful of arseholes. No offence intended.'

'I feel like there was *some* offence intended,' I muttered, still transfixed by my tiny, numb baby hand.

'We're both full of bio nanos, Stephen,' Minerva said, encouragingly. 'Your grand design worked.'

I looked away from my hand and asked the question that burned me to the core: 'Then why on earth did I leave this place?'

Minerva and Garold shared a look, something passing between them.

'Should I tell him?' Garold asked.

'It's better coming from me,' Minerva replied. Then she turned to me and opened her mouth.

And that's when an alarm started blaring and the green lights turned red.

'What's going on?' I shouted as Minerva and Garold lurched to their feet.

'Eva?' Garold asked.

'Has to be,' Minerva replied, all business now.

'Put it up on the monitor.'

They moved over to the television area and I wheeled myself after them.

The telly flicked on, showing black and white footage – grainy and crackly – of a young woman moving swiftly and looking towards the screen.

'Eva!' Minerva cried.

'Thank Christ for that. Can you hear us, Eva?'

The woman, Eva, nodded and shouted to be heard: 'I'm okay. Wounded but mending. Sorry it's taken so long to check in. There's been a development...'

'Well, go on!' Garold snapped.

'The initial group of savages who kidnapped us were themselves attacked by a larger group who have constructed some kind of...' Eva stopped here, trying to find the right words, 'belief system based on hallucinations brought about by a series three grunter.'

'Fascinating,' Minerva murmured.

'Where's Franga?' I asked loudly.

Minerva and Garold glanced back testily.

'Excuse me?' Eva yelled.

'The bloody yellow mutant. Is he okay?' Garold asked in a manner that suggested he cared very little about the answer.

'Last I saw, yes. This second group of savages were... organised. They'd become peaceful... I'll give you a full report when I get back.'

'Why aren't you back now?' Garold was becoming increasingly agitated.

'There's been a development,' Eva said ominously.

'Where did you last see Franga?' I yelled, becoming fairly bloody angry myself.

'Stephen– Ken, please. This is important. Can you give us a minute?' Minerva phrased the question like a command and I sighed, wheeling myself away from them. You were alive, Franga, and that made me feel better. Although my guilt over leaving you there and drinking with these two like old friends was a knife in my guts. My thoughts were a roiling tempest and I barely heard Eva exclaim: 'There has been a Shelley-level event, repeat: a Shelley. Level. Event.'

The effect of this statement was instantaneous. Both Minerva and Garold suddenly started rushing about, retrieving electronic tablets and asking a million questions.

'Describe the interaction between host and instigator.'

'What was the effect on the immediate environment?'

'Did the host remain intact or was it compromised?'

'Was self-awareness established?'

And on and on. I suppose I should have known what it all meant, but I simply didn't, and I felt like an intruder on their big moment. So, I wheeled myself away from them and into the doughnut proper. And that's when I saw Garold's open laboratory door. Perhaps there'd be something inside that might trigger a memory or two.

Perhaps I just wanted to have a bit of a sticky beak.

'Why not?' I murmured softly. And, as there was no one there to give me a compelling reason, I wheeled myself over there."

EIGHTEEN

Ken stopped talking for a moment and sighed deeply. For a couple of minutes, I thought maybe he couldn't go on, wouldn't be able to finish his tale, but in the end, he shook his head, sat up straight in his seat and kept going.

"I didn't know what I was seeing at first. It was incongruous in the context of the pristine laboratory I found myself in. Here a shelf of microscopes, there a desk covered in neatly organised samples – and then, in the middle of all this rigorous organisation, was… chaos. At first, I thought it was an area open to the lab proper, but then I saw the sheen of transparent plastic containing it all. It was a sort of enclosure, large enough to house three people in relative comfort, or six squeezed in like sardines. Bark chips on the floor, muted lighting and surprisingly lush plant life, tendrils and fronds and whatnot, framed a single person – skinny, nude – leaning against a tree stump, facing away from me.

I remember wondering, *where on earth did they get a tree stump and why is it glistening so?* Which, of course, was the least important of my legion of questions, but the mind can be funny like that.

I stood and moved towards the enclosure and my shadow fell across the naked figure. She – it was a 'she' I could see that now – partially turned around and tried to look up at me, wincing as if she was in pain. I raised my bandaged hand, a strange reflex, and placed it on the thick plastic. I wanted to help this human in pain; I wanted to ease her suffering if I could.

'Hello?' I croaked. A ridiculous thing to do. No doubt the enclosure was soundproof. Probably airtight as well. But the girl, a woman actually, seemed to understand that I was trying to communicate, however poorly. She turned even further, moving her face and neck, clearly causing her discomfort, and looked up at me.

She had large grey eyes. The saddest eyes I've ever seen in all my days. She opened her mouth and called out, or cried out, or maybe just whispered and then I spotted something I hadn't been able to see before.

The 'tree stump' wasn't a tree stump at all. It was a chaotic lump of living flesh. *Her* flesh, the woman's, because it was attached to her. It was the hideous fusion of her two arms and upper torso, morphed into something grotesque and unbearably alive, shiny and viscous on the floor of this wretched display.

I took a faltering step backwards, light-headed from the shock, and it struck me that the plant life around the woman wasn't flora at all... it was flesh.

Mutated beyond belief in some bastard God's twisted joke conducted on living tissue. But not a bastard *God,* rather a scientist, because for all its seeming wanton cruelty this was clearly...

'An experiment,' I whispered, staring at the vines of living tissue that intersected in what I'd taken to be a thin tree trunk but on closer inspection was a human face, unable to move but still horrifically aware. 'Some kind of human experiment.'

'That's right,' Garold said cheerily as he entered the lab from behind me. 'It's actually fascinating, you know. What you're looking at is the "before" part of the experiment. The "after" is, right now, marauding around the Downlow.'

'What did you do to them?' I asked, not taking my eyes off the slick, ruined flesh that melded in ways never dreamt of by nature.

'What we did to them was attempt to introduce early variants of the Bio AI into their living bodies, using them as a testing ground.' Garold gestured around the enclosure like a proud papa. 'What you're looking at are the last three living members of the Moot clan. They literally lined up for this, you know. Thought we were some kind of god beneath the waves. We didn't disabuse them of the notion, of course. Religion really is marvellous for keeping the peasants docile.'

'But why this torture? To what end?'

'Bio AI needs to learn on the job, as it were. It needs to gain knowledge in a more evolutionary fashion, and evolution is chaos, requiring sacrifice. But worth it, I assure you.' Garold's grin widened. 'I mean, just think of the applications. This isn't just extending life or curing disease, this is creating organisms that can not only survive in the world outside but thrive in it! Imagine the upgrade from our old failing nanomachines. We would be able to stride along the land above like gods!

'How many did you butcher to become a god?' I asked, teeth grinding.

Garold finally seemed to understand that I wasn't delighted with his experiment. He cocked his head to one side and sneered.

'Are you feeling sorry for these savages? For God's sake, Stephen, they'd have eaten your flesh if they'd caught you in their territory. They're bloody monsters, the lot of them.'

'And this,' I shouted, slamming my hand against the clear plastic,. 'What kind of creature does this to another human?'

Garold looked me right in the eye. 'One just like you, Stephen. This is your experiment. These are concepts that you wanted to explore before you went crazy. So, before you get on your high horse, maybe remember who the bloody hell you are, *Stephen.*'

'My name,' I seethed, 'is Kenneth.'

And with that I clobbered the smug bastard over the head with a microscope I wasn't even aware I'd been holding. He went down like a sack of potatoes and left me standing, panting and wondering what the hell I was going to do next.

I knew one thing: I wanted to be out of there. Away from these people, this experiment and the links it had to Stephen Blentiff's life. My life.

I found the gun to the immediate right of the enclosure, in a small recessed panel that opened at a touch. It was lightweight yet clearly far more advanced than anything I'd seen on the surface. In fact, it looked more than a little bit like my shocker device. Which made sense, because they probably all came from the same place. I hefted it in my hand. It felt good. I looked down at Garold but, although he was clearly breathing, it didn't seem like he'd be waking up any time soon.

I walked out to the main area, legs strengthened by rage and resolve. Minerva was concluding her communications with Eva. She hadn't yet noticed me standing behind her.

'Do you think it's containable?' Minerva was asking.

'Doubtful. The power of the thing, the speed… the drone footage doesn't do it justice. It's a force of nature.'

'No, not nature, not quite,' she said softly, then louder. 'Head back here.'

'Ma'am?'

'Look, it's not the specific circumstances we'd planned for, granted, but the end result is the same. To test the catalyst out where collateral damage doesn't matter. From that perspective, I'd say it's going spectacularly well.'

'Ma'am.' Eva nodded and vanished from the screen.

Minerva turned and at first was surprised to see me. The 'O' of her mouth crept up in a smile. She was glad to see me. Momentarily, at least. It lasted until she saw the gun.

'Stephen.' She tried to smile again but it wasn't taking. 'Why do you have a gun? Garold?'

'He's indisposed.'

'You killed him?' Minerva was shocked and I felt no guilt about that, but I didn't want to draw it out. I wasn't like them. I wasn't.

'He's alive, which is more than he deserves considering his little science experiment.'

'Ah, so you saw.' Minerva sighed, the penny dropping with a thud. 'That was rather ill-timed.'

She took a step towards me but I raised the gun. 'Don't.'

'You know how to use that thing?'

'I'm a quick study and I'm not playing around.' I aimed the gun at her face.

'I can see that. Well, what do you want?'

'My clothes. My stuff. A way out of here. In that order.'

'You understand there's something wonderful but catastrophic occurring in the Downlow… it's dangerous for a man of your age…'

'I'll risk it.'

'If you died because of an excess of emotion, the loss to science, to humanity, would be incalculable.'

'I saw precious little humanity on display in there,' I growled.

'It's absolutely surreal having this conversation with you,' she laughed. 'You're literally the architect of the very thing you're objecting to.'

'I've been thinking about that,' I admitted, 'and here's my conclusion: that's bullshit. Or at least not the whole story. Because if that were the case, if I was so on board with Team Whatever The Hell You're Doing Down Here, then why did I leave? Why did I… do whatever it is I did to my own mind? See, I reckon it's because I opened a door I didn't like the look of and I tried to close it and back away. But then you and ol' mate in there decided to keep the dream alive with these sick experiments. That sound about right?'

'I… don't even know where to begin,' she sniffed. 'That's a terribly simplistic–'

'Clothes. Stuff. A way out. Please and thank you.'

Sensing my mood, she didn't dally. Walking ahead of me, under my close supervision, Minerva placed my clothes and my bag on a bench and took a few steps back. I awkwardly pulled my clothes on, ready for Minerva to pounce, but she didn't, and I was soon dressed and feeling less exposed. I had a quick look through my bag and everything seemed to be present and accounted for. I slipped the shocker into my left pants pocket and hefted the bag over my right shoulder.

'So how do you imagine you're getting to the surface?' she asked. '*The Raw Prawn* is charging. It'll be hours before it's ready for another journey.'

I thought for a moment and smiled.

'Do you know the one idiot-proof part of any ship or installation, Minerva? It's the escape apparatus. Because it's designed to be used under extreme circumstances, you see. Be a dear and direct me to the nearest escape pod, won't you?'

The look on her face told me all I needed to know. My intuition was correct and soon I found myself being led to a circular hatch. I gestured for Minerva to open the door, which she did without complaint, and then stepped back. I was about to enter the pod when a wave of anger hit me like a fist and I turned to her, rage in my eyes.

'What happens to those people? In the lab, what happens to them?'

'I- I don't know what you mean...'

'Can they be cured?'

'Well, no, your– er, Stephen's BAI was meant to reconfigure living tissue. At best they could live another six months, in the most awful pain. I'm not without sympathy for their plight but their suffering produces extraordinary insights and useful data–'

'End them. Humanely. Do it today, do you understand?'

'I can talk to Garold–'

'End it. Or I swear to you I will come back here and do things to you and Garold you can't imagine.'

Minerva was shocked into silence. Something in my face or in my eyes had her actually take a step back. And then, because despite myself, I felt a strange sort of pity for her. 'Please. If I – if we meant anything to you… if you think of me fondly at all, don't let that harrowing display continue in my name.'

She nodded with tears in her eyes. 'I will, Stephen.'

And I knew as clearly as I'm sitting here right now, Franga, that she was lying right to my face. Lying with the practised skill of a sociopath.

I sighed, lifted the gun calmly and shot her in the chest.

All the breath woofed out of Minerva and she slumped to the floor. She was alive but unconscious, stunned.

I returned to Garold's lab and walked over to that cursed enclosure. Scanning the console, I quickly found the 'purge' button. I took one last look at the woman and the plant things and offered a silent apology for the sins of my flesh. Then I elbowed the button and the enclosure filled with fire. It was a horrible end to a hideous life and I turned away as the vines started twisting and melting to the ground, blackening, falling around the Moot woman who I desperately hoped had finally found some peace.

I went a bit mad then, I'm sorry to say. The rage at the inhumanity of these old friends of mine, the torture they'd committed, it sent me over the top. I turned the gun up to its highest setting and walked around Research Station Alpha in a daze, shooting everything that looked expensive or important. The cables that conducted electricity mounted on the walls, the various screens filled with information, the books that collected research, even the bloody telly. I spent extra time burning the framed photograph of me with my colleagues.

By the time I was finished, I was out of breath, the station's lights were flashing, various alarms were blaring and several sprinkler systems had activated. Reckoning it was time to leave, I started back towards the escape pod. Which is when I saw Garold, drenched from the sprinklers and glaring, holding his head with one hand and pointing an accusing finger at me with the other.

'Do you,' he spat, 'have any idea what you've done here?'

'I know,' I muttered. 'You can't take me anywhere.'

Then I shot him. He flew backwards, landing in a puddle, and I stood over him for a moment, giving serious thought to killing him. But no, cold-blooded murder struck me as a bridge too far.

So I shot him twice in the scrotum instead.

I pulled myself into the cramped circular escape pod and closed the door after me. It hissed shut. I looked at the controls. As I had intuited, they were simple. A lever to launch and a lever to open the door once I'd hit the surface. I pulled the launch lever. There was a lurch, a clunk and suddenly I was free of Research Station Alpha, surging into the polluted water like an air bubble and rising to the surface.

Despite the rage that seemed to be heating my blood, I actually fell asleep on the way up. There's something soothing about water surrounding you, even if it is a carcinogenic shit swamp. I was jerked awake when the pod broke the surface, bobbing like a cork. Looking out of the round porthole window, I could see shore in the distance, gradually getting closer. The escape pod must have been designed to move towards the closest land mass. I sat and watched as an unfamiliar shore grew larger in the window and, when finally I felt the rough embrace of land, I pulled the second lever and clumsily made my way out of the pod.

I flopped onto a black sand shore, and for a moment thought I'd found my way back to the Downlow, but no. This was altogether more desolate. Hopefully less full of angry clans as well.

I soon realised I was at the outer edges of the Garbage Plains. A fair hoof back to the Inasiddy but one that I could manage, despite the exhaustion that was blooming in my bones. I got up and slogged my way back here. It took a couple of days but eventually I made it, although a little the worse for wear. You saw the state I was in. And so… that brings us to the present, doesn't it?"

At some point during the story Ken must have turned the cart around, because when I looked up, the lantern lights of the Inasiddy were glittering up ahead. We were close to home and I hadn't even noticed because of the yarn being told.

"Durries," I murmured. "I... dunno what to say, eh."

"I know the feeling, mate." Ken smiled sadly, and we rode the rest of the way in silence.

NINETEEN

Next day, Ken was in a grim mood and the ruggies were bouncing off the walls. Tommy and I knew the only way they'd be getting any kip that night was if we tired them out, so we took 'em on the mostly deserted back streefs to play 'the game'. This was when we chucked an old rubber ball really far away and they ran after it and brought it back. Shit game, you might think, but it was surprisingly effective.

After fanging the ball, Tommy ran with the ruggies and I enjoyed some momentary peace and quiet.

"Oi," I heard from behind me, and turned to see Gia looking bright and sparky. And spunky.

"G'day."

"Ruggies are full of beans."

"Yeah, they're excited for the Roil Easter Show." I sighed with a resignation borne from years of the bloody thing.

"Rolls around every year, Frang."

"And every year I hope it won't," I muttered quietly just as Tommy ran up, panting and holding the rubber ball aloft like a prized treasure. The other ruggies were close behind, so Gia quickly snatched the ball out of

Tommy's scaly hand and chucked it down the road, far further than my throw. I made a mental note to up my game in the next round.

The ruggies ran off after the ball again and we resumed our conversation.

"So… Tanya's coming to town." She smiled widely.

"Oh," I replied.

"Don't be like that."

"I'm not being like anything," I insisted. I was, but. I was no fan of Tanya.

Point of fact, I reckoned she was a deadset moll.

Tanya was Gia's younger sister and I'd known her, vaguely and mostly from a distance, over the last five or so years. When I first met her, she had been an awkward, knock-kneed kid just coming into her adult body and resembled a baby giraffe. Not that I'd ever seen a baby giraffe in the dinkum, but I'd squizzed pictures.

The first time I met her she was friendly and sweet and full of enthusiasm. Gia told me later she had a bit of a crush on me, which was really flattering and cute. I reckoned she was a bit like Gia, rough past but ultimately a top sheila. She proved me wrong the next time she came to stay a cuppla years later.

That time around, Tanya had come into her looks. She was gorgeous, a deadset stunna, but she'd developed a coldness and a manipulative streak that I reckoned I could see, a) because I wasn't blinded by familial love, and b) because, as a mutie, you encounter the darker stuff of humanity more often.

Long story short, by the time Tanya stopped crashing at Gia's joint she'd flogged a lot of her favourite clothes and all of her savings. Gia was forced to do double shifts in Flesh Alley for the next three months just to hold onto her poky little place.

It hadn't been a good time and I had figured that would have been that, but Gia loved Tanya and gave her another chance. And another.

And another.

And every time she gave her a chance, Tanya would, in ways both large and small, betray her and break her heart anew.

And apparently Gia was about to give Tanya yet another chance.

"She's really got herself together this time." Gia was talking in a tone suggesting she desperately wanted it to be true.

"Oh yeah?" I didn't mean to sound sarcastic but it just came out that way.

"Yeah. She's stopped taking chems and has discovered religion."

"Tanya's a God-botherer?" That was a legit surprise.

"Nah, a Hendoist."

Hendoism was a relatively new religion that had sprung up around a reportedly grouse bloke named Hendo who, legend has it, got lost on a trip into the Madlands and managed to survive, walking back into New Sydney. And, of course, he had a beaut book all about it that you could buy for a price. It was one of those cults that sprung up in the Inasiddy, suckering in the more suggestive cits, so it didn't surprise me that Tanya was into it.

"Good-o." I was frankly a little surprised how sincere I managed to make that sound. "When's she get into town?"

"Tomorrow."

Fark.

"Great!"

I really didn't want to see Gia left hurt and broken-hearted by her shit sister again. Still, if it happened – *when* it happened – I'd do what I could to help out.

Just then Bella ran up, holding the ball – bless her – and managed to lift me out of my cranky spell.

"Bella!"

"Frangaaaa!"

"How'd you manage to get ahead of the pack, love?" Gia asked. Bella was a wonderful actress and a spectacular singer, but sporting pursuits had never been her thing.

"Um," she giggled. "I haccidently tripped Tommy."

As if on cue the high-pitched, unmistakable sound of a teenager having a loud and angry sook filled the air. Gia and I shared a weary look and started walking towards the din, with Bella leading the way.

"Oh." Gia suddenly remembered something. "I almost forgot to tell you about the monster."

"Bloody hell," I murmured. On this normal-seeming, pleasant day I'd almost forgotten about the damn thing.

"No, it's good news. Word down the pub is it's all over."

"Fair dinkum?" I was excited.

"Lotsa people 'round town reckon the thing died of starvation or just swam away."

"Jeez, that'd be beaut, wouldn't it?" I very much wanted these pub theories to be true.

"Yeah. Situation just took care of itself, maybe."

"Maybe."

And fool that I am I even let myself believe it, just a bee's dick.

• • • •

Later that night I brought some grub to Ken, who was sitting with his eyes closed. At first, I thought he was asleep, but after a moment he spoke softly.

"Franga…" he started, then paused, and then kept going. "Franga, what do you want to be in life?"

I pondered that, gave it some hard thought.

"Well… I'd like to keep looking after the ruggies…" But Ken was shaking his head.

"Don't tell me what you think I want to hear, tell me the truth. If the ruggies were looked after and safe, what would you want to do? Perfect world."

"I spose I'd like to travel. See more of New Sydney, yeah, but also – like – see the rest of Straya. Hit up Melbs, visit the ruins of Queensland, just have a squiz at the whole caper. Maybe do some scribing about it, try my hand at being a murder-poet. Maybe, like, one day, own my own place. Even meet a nice sheila who doesn't mind muties, pop out a cuppla ruggies…" I trailed off. Even my unambitious dreams felt like deluded fantasies. How would any of that happen, things being the way they were? "They're just dreams, though, eh."

"Dreams are the things that keep us going, Franga," Ken said softly. "Dreams are what keep us from losing hope."

It was a nice idea, and I got where he was coming from, but it sounded a bit too simple to me. Still, I didn't want to piss on a bloke going through a rough trot.

"I'd like to be a lot like you, Ken, to be honest."

I was hoping to raise a smile or make him feel good but the words seemed to have the opposite effect.

"Be better than me, son," he spoke emphatically. "Be a lot better."

TWENTY

I'd barely put my head down on my hard pillow and it felt like I'd blinked, when there was a sudden knock at the door. Trundling down the stairs, I realised the "blink" had in fact been a full night's sleep, and the knock was coming at a fairly decent hour. I hoped like buggery it wasn't the Pigs, as Ken and I hadn't yet prepared the next Bribe Day offering.

Plus, if they raised the price yet again, we'd be stuffed.

I walked past Tommy, heading to the front door to see who it was and, bless him, he asked if I wanted help with breakfast. It was a small gesture but it made all the difference. I opened the door.

"Hey, Franga."

It was Gia. Always a welcome face.

"Yeah, G'day, Frang. Howscarn?"

I frowned and looked over Gia's shoulder to see Tanya, looking smug and spunky.

Fuggen hell.

"Hey, Tanya," I said, not even attempting to hide my weary disdain. But then Gia shot me a warning look and I turned my expression into something approximating a smile.

"We're here to take you and the ruggies to the show."

The Roil Easter Show. Bloody hell, yeah, nah, bugger that. Hopefully the ruggies didn't hear and I can talk these sheilas out of it—

From behind me came a cheer of youthful excitement.

"Easter Show!"

"Aunty Tanya!"

"Did you bring us presents?"

"Grouse," I muttered.

• • • •

So it was, on one of the hottest days in the oppressive Strayan Summer, me, Gia, Tanya and twelve excitable ruggies went wandering over to the Roil Easter Show. The ambitious beano was hosted on a sprawling patch of land that comprised the Cliff's Edge Markets, most of Flesh Alley and the disorganised shopping district, the borders of which changed like the tides.

The whole caper was the Inasiddy's chance to dress itself up and show off a little, usually via the means of selling stuff and/or demonstrating skills and talents.

"Who were the Roils?" asked a small voice next to me. I turned to see Debs, her hair pulled back into two adorable but slightly heartbreaking pigtails. I could already see the regrowth beginning on her chops, and I'd shaved her barely fordy-five minutes earlier.

Back to the moment, mate, she's got questions.

"They were, like, a packa inbred Poms that owned Straya heaps long ago."

It wasn't my most elegant teaching, but to be honest, I was struggling to remember what Ken had said about the Roil Family. The phrase "cousin-rooting parasites" came up a lot as I recall.

"But," Debs looked nonplussed, "if they was Poms, why come they owned Straya?"

"Poms used to own all sorts of gear, Debs, loads of countries and that. Fair almost took over the whole world, I'm told."

"Then why come they wanna put on a Roil Easter Show for us?"

Crikey, she had me there, that was a really decent question. My significant shortcomings as a history teacher became glaringly obvious. Much to my surprise, Tanya came to my rescue.

"The Poms weren't our enemy, Debs, at least not back then. They flogged the land off the Firsties and then filled it up as a penal colony."

"Firsties" was what we called the first people, the Aboriginals, who had lived in Straya from way back in the day, long before the Poms had invaded and took over the joint. You still saw Firsties around the place, though way fewer since the Uluru Free State declared independence from the rest of Straya and walled off their sacred site.

"What's a penal colony?" Debs asked, which I wasn't sure of myself.

"A prison."

"The whole country was a prison?"

Tanya nodded and Debs was clearly blown away.

"The Roils probs wanted to keep us sweet by bunging on shows and that. But after a while we cracked the shits and took the place back." I was about sevendy percent winging it, but it sounded familiar and possibly right.

"Okay then," Debs said, that serious expression on her mug. "Thank you."

Debs wandered back to her friends and Tanya shot me a cheeky look.

"Joo just pull that out of y'arse?" She smirked.

"Little bit, maybe. Sounded about right, though."

"It was pretty close," she admitted.

"Since when are you such an expert on history?" I'd never known Tanya to be a bookworm. I mean, she wasn't a drongo or anything, but never what you'd describe as well read.

"Hendoists have a pretty healthy-sized library."

Fair dinkum, the word "library" is spunky. Images of a huge, book-filled space permeated my noggin. The musty smell of pressed pages. The satisfaction of stacked volumes. The collection of knowledge, wisdom. Perhaps the complete works of Guy N. Smith. Paradise.

"We believe in reading, learning, loving one another."

Yeah, I've heard this bloody song before.

"But you need to cough up some dosh, or maybe a limb or something, don't cha?" I kept my tone light but I reckon Tanya could tell I wasn't a fan.

"We're not like the God-botherers or the kiddy-fiddlers, Frang, really we're not." Tanya's earnest expression was so genuine I had to turn away. It felt like her bright green eyes were seeing inside me. She pulled at her sweat-stained headband, ruffling her frizzy blonde hair. "This headband represents the brother- and sisterhood that unites us all. All of us, normie and mutie alike. Hendoists believe in a simple doctrine: 'don't be cunce'. You should think about joining up, eh."

So that was her game, trying to recruit me.

"Thanks, Tan, but I've had all the religion I can stomach." Even thinking about my time in the Downlow and the Lord of the Pit made me feel ill, so I increased my stride and moved up, walking next to Gia.

She clocked me and, without looking away from the ruggies, nodded, saying, "Hope you're being nice to Tanya."

"Yeah. Just talking history."

"Did she try and recruit you?"

"Yeah."

"Did you tell her to get stuffed?"

"Not in so many words but, you know..." I trailed off.

Gia made an amused snort at this but dropped the subject. We walked in companionable silence for a bit, then she said, "You got dosh for the show?"

"Yeah, Ken set a bit aside."

"Tanya's given us some too, to spend on the ruggies," said Gia. And then, at my surprised look, "Shocked me too."

"Be nice to get them some showbags for once."

"Showbags!" cried Bella, stealthily walking close behind us both, hoping to catch juicy snatches of adult conversation.

The cry was taken up by the other kids, and soon they were cheering and talking over one another excitedly. I laughed, so did Gia, and we crested the hill that led to the start of the improvised showgrounds in a better disposition than when we started.

"Durries…" I breathed, taking in the sight before me. It seemed like the entire Inasiddy had come to the show and it was impressive to say the least. From the hill on which I stood, the ground sloped down to the entrance of the show, where brightly clobbered clowns and cits dressed as rabbits cavorted, handing out colourful catgut balloons to giggling children. Further on, there were booths with games to play, some rides – sit in the wobbly bucket, fall onto the pile of mattresses, that sorta caper – and even some yarts gear, mainly consisting of short plays and opra singers. I should mention here that despite throwing our hat in the ring every year, the "All Ages Mutie Theatre Troopie" had never been invited to perform. It was a sore point, and Ken had shared many a choice word on the subject after he'd necked a few.

I felt the tug of ruggie fingers on me hands and looked down to see excited faces looking up at me expectantly.

"Righto, then." I spoke loud enough so everyone could hear. "Let's go in, eh."

We headed through the front gates, the kids practically tearing my arms out of the sockets with their excitement. Gia and Tanya struggled to keep the group together, and it was both funny and a bit scary. The crowd was a mass of sweaty flesh and the spectacle of so many muties in a single place caused eruptions of amusement and disgust. A particularly round, potato-shaped sheila with a brood of equally squat, red-faced wobblers hissed at the sight of a grinning Bella, and made gagging noises to her lanky, dead-eyed husband.

"Bloody filth should stay away from us normies," she said in a tone designed to attract as much attention as possible. As usual I was briefly dumbstruck by the capacity of people to be deadset shithouse for no good reason. I struggled to think of a good comeback, all the while keeping focused on the ruggies, who had, mercifully, been too distracted to clock what was going on.

Gia stepped forwards, smiling a big happy smile, and put her arm around the woman's clammy shoulders. In a friendly tone, she said: "Would you like a kick in the slats?"

The woman gaped, mouth hanging open like a broken shutter. "Eh?"

"Because talk like that will get this boot," Gia showed off a shapely leg and thick-soled boot, "to travel at a considerable velocity fair up ya manky slats."

The husband opened his mouth to say something, more out of obligation than any genuine sense of chivalry I reckon, but Gia silenced him with a look. Most likely he was a frequenter of Flesh Alley, or perhaps Gia just scared him.

She could do that at times.

"Message received?" Gia asked, in that same cheery-but-I'm-about-to-eviscerate-ya tone. The husband nodded dumbly and the hefty sheila mumbled, "Yeah, righto, then, wasjusthavingabluttyjoke…"

The whole family toddled off, quickly lost in the crowd. I smiled and nodded at Gia. She grinned back, but I could see the exchange had affected her.

"I'm sorry." She sighed.

"You don't need to apologise for, like, all normie kind," I told her and meant it.

"Kinda feels like I do."

And then we were again distracted by the bellowing from the ruggies. They'd just seen the showbag tent and were fair foaming at the chops. I laughed and let them drag me along, deeper into the show's humid heart.

Showbags were hemp sacks filled with, like, toys and knick-knacks and such, painted or designed around various themes. There was the Grouse Ozzy bag, which featured toys and necklaces made from rat and cat skulls, all painted in the colours of the Strayan flag. Another favourite of the ruggies was the Cute Little Doers bag, which contained all manner of animal friends with wobbly eyes, pasted atop the skulls and skeletons of the creatures who'd carked it. Ken always reckoned that was heaps morbid, but I reckon his squeamishness around death and such came from the old days. These days it was play with a painted skull, manage to get your hands on some of the spensive anteek toys or bloody well go without. The kids knew which option they preferred.

Stupid Bird bag, Join the Army bag, New Sydney Is the Best bag and so on. A lot of variations on the same theme but the ruggies went absolutely berko for it and honestly, I was pretty bloody delighted to see that.

"You'll spoil them," Tanya warned half-heartedly as she tried to wrestle a couple of Girls Are Grouse bags for the young sheilas amongst them.

"They could use some spoiling," Gia replied, all tight-lipped.

"Fair enough," Tanya answered, eyes wide and backing away. I tried very hard to suppress my snigger. Didn't work, but. Crikey, Tanya shot me an evil look.

Throughout the whole showbag-wrangling bizzo, we'd copped looks from regular normie cits. They weren't always obvious – and no one was as dog-arse rude as the sheila near the front gate – but it's the kind of thing that wears you down after a while, like a slow-acting poison. Still, as we finally wandered out of the dripping heat and humidity of the tent into the slightly less moist environs of the show proper, I had to admit I enjoyed the rare joy on the faces of my charges.

There was Bella, wearing a beaut painted necklace of rat skulls, announcing she was "the rat queen" and all should "bow down before her". Tommy wore a hood to cover his face, he knew to do that without me asking, but he also wore a grin thanks to the dog-headed sceptre he wielded, swinging it back and forth, playing some game he'd invented, with rules known only to himself. Gruta wore a pair of cheap sunglasses adorned with Straya flags, and the bright colours against her parchment-white skin made it look like she was lit up. These weren't high-quality goods, you understand, they were cheap and tacky and disposable. And the ruggies loved them.

Something caught my eye and I looked up to see Tanya staring at me with a strange look on her face.

"What?" I was ready to get defensive but she just shook her head and smiled.

"Nuthin'."

"S'gotta be something."

She sighed, irritated, and then spoke in a way that suggested she was doing so at great personal cost: "You're real good with them. The kids."

"Oh." I genuinely didn't know how to take this unsolicited pleasantness. "Um, thanks, Tan."

"S'alright." She shrugged, a little self-consciously. Then her smile grew and she laughed and flicked her hair. I was very pleased that I managed to witness the event without drooling.

"Reckon we should go see the animals?" I croaked the quezzie to Gia, my mouth suddenly extremely dry.

"Yeah, sure." She nodded and helped gather the ruggies together. I decided to tamp down my heart and trouserly confusion by getting on with it.

Shortly afterwards, me, Gia, Tanya and the kids all stood at a rusty iron fence, staring at a group of half a dozen mildly mutated shetland ponies, who were strolling in an amiable parabola around the dusty paddock, letting anyone who wished pat their flanks as they ambled by.

The front rows were mostly full of kids and I noticed something interesting. The normie kids didn't react to our mutie kids for more than a second or two. They'd clock them, react honestly and then move on to more interesting eye-gear: in this case, adorable animals. A smarter bloke would probably be able to scribe a beaut moral to that story, but for me it suggested something nice. I shared my observation with Gia and Tanya and, after a few moments, they saw it, too. One of the mutie ponies walked by and Bella trailed her fingers through its fur. It moved past Bella and into the eager fingers of a normie girl and her friends. They smiled at one another and then went back to looking at the ponies.

"Jeez…" Gia murmured, mellowed by the moment.

I caught the eye of the girl's mum and she winced initially but then gave me a small nervous nod, like a bird pecking at suspect seed. But still, better than nothing. Better than abuse.

I turned to see if Gia noticed and saw that both she and Tanya had. I smiled a bit and opened my mouth to say something. I'm not sure what it was. Maybe a dumb joke to lighten the mood, maybe an attempt at something deep and meaningful. I guess I'll never really know. Because right at that moment, all throughout the showgrounds, a sound rang out. A sound that silenced everyone, mutie and normie alike, a sound that seemed to stop even the animals in their tracks, as everyone's instinct to fear predators kicked in.

It was the sound of the monster's horrific wail, ringing out loud across the paddocks and the grounds, through the stalls and shops, past the eateries and mobile pubs.

It was the wretched sound of the other, the thing we thought had left or died and vanished from our collective nightmares.

And, judging from the volume of the shattering shriek, the way it seemed to claw its way into your ear holes, something was very clear: it was close. Horribly so.

The monster had finally come to the Inasiddy.

TWENTY-ONE

Everyone around us in the tightly packed crowd paused a moment, looking about, tense and nervous. The conversation near me came in halting whispers, overlapping.

"Did ya hear that?"

"Sounded close."

"Wassit the monster?"

"I thought it was dead."

Gia's wide eyes mirrored my own and I spoke in a low, urgent tone. "We should get the ruggies out of here."

"Yeah, yeah, yeah." She nodded, then said to the kids in a friendly fashion, "Hey guys, let's start moving to the exit, 'kay?"

I expected the youngins to begin sooking but they seemed aware that something wasn't right and we all began to move, slowly, through the corridor of fleshy faces contorted with fear and confusion. Urgent whispers filled the air but most people were rooted to the ground like trees. I wanted to smash bonces and elbow necks to get past but I kept breathing slow and steady, slow and steady, pushing politely but firmly through, and passed.

We'd barely moved two meaters when the second scream rang out. Closer than before, longer, it lingered in the air like a haze, spreading crimson threads of anxiety throughout the crowd. I had a sense that everyone was about to panic, an animal instinct,I suppose, and hundreds of terror-mad cits running in all directions would result in injury and worse, especially for the ruggies.

"Everyone just calm your tits and keep moving," I spoke loudly in a voice that was far more confident than I felt. I was speaking to the ruggies, but hoped my words were loud enough to be heard – and heeded – by all. Far in front of me, I spied a break in the crowd. If I could just lead my family there, we could take cover, get clear of the crush. If I could just get through...

"I CAN SEE IT!" A quavering voice somewhere behind me. Then there was an almighty *CRUMP* and the ground shook under my feet. One of the kids, probs Bella from the sound, squeaked out a fearful noise.

"It's okay, love, just keep walking, straight ahead, good girl."

"IT'S HERE–" The latest cry was abruptly cut off and turned into a nerve-shredding shriek.

The third roar belted out behind us and this time it felt close enough to shake our skulls. I opened my mouth to shout a bitta advice to the kids, tell them which way to run, where to hide – but it was too late. The crowd entered panic mode and surged up against me like a wave, an unstoppable force.

I managed to wrap my long arms around as many of the kids as possible before all hell broke loose, bodies pelting everywhere, trying to escape a nebulous but nightmarish-sounding fate. Of course, hundreds of cits with the same impulse and little in the way of forward planning meant bodies were being trampled left and right. Screams were choked off under a sea of boots. Jagged elbows thudded thoughtlessly into my bonce, having me seeing stars and snarling angry curses. I saw one sheila, the mum of the kids from earlier, blood streaked across her face, as she tried to keep up with the pace of the crowd. She actually made eye contact with me for an instant before a fat bloke in a blue singlet dragged her down.

She screamed once and briefly and that was it, the crowd rolled over her and we were moving on, roughly pushed by the fear-mosh.

A knee to my back, a fist to the kidneys, I thrashed around to no avail. Nek minute the crowd was pulling me away on a sea of his-terrical meat seasoned with terror-sweat, little ruggie hands vanishing from my grip. I cried out, desperate not to let them out of my grasp, but the mob ruled and I was carried away. I realised with mounting horror that if I stayed with the herd, I'd be splintered on the ground within moments. I gritted my teeth and pushed down the dismay rising up inside, and tensed my legs, willing as much muscular tension as I possibly could given the constantly shifting state of the surrounds.

With a desperate yorp, I unleashed and jumped with all I had. It barely got me above the shoulders of the crush around me but that was enough to clamber up on heads and start to run like a cattle dog atop a flock of sheep.

This particular flock were none too pleased that I was riding on their heads, jumping from bonce to bonce, but I tried to tread as lightly as possible and ignore the sweary, outraged, fearing faces below me.

I was completely lost. Even with the higher ground, I couldn't make head nor tail of where I was. So, I just lurched on wobbly legs heading for the closest break in the crowd, reasoning that I'd loop back around and find the ruggies–

(Dead or alive?)

–then. I almost lost my footing on a bald, sweaty scalp and staggered awkwardly towards the nearest open area. I jumped again, a profoundly unco lurch through the air, and tumbled to the hard ground, arse over tit.

I sat up straight away, head onna swivel, looking around to orient myself. It was the plastic tarp overhead that gave it away. I was all the way back at the Cliff's Edge markets. The terror-mass of cits had plonked me further than ever from my family.

And then I remembered, I was exactly where the monster's screams had been coming from.

A feeling like ice water being poured down my back splashed all over me. I directed my gaze from up high, down to the stalls, and noticed the cloud of dust that suffused the area. The sounds of screaming, fleeing cits faded into somewhere below the point of caring and I staggered to my feet, my eyes darting around, trying to make sense of what I was seeing.

I took a step towards the dust cloud when a strong, gnarled hand wrapped around my ankle. I was about to cry out when two more hands appeared, one covering my mouth, the other on my shoulder and I was dragged roughly to the ground.

"Geddown, ya bloody idiot!" A pair of spit-flecked lips hissed into my face. I jerked back to see the owner of the lips, a wiry-looking bloke I vaguely recognised from the markets. Behind him, one of Old Lil's idiot sons and a sheila I didn't know held fingers up to their lips in the universal symbol of "shut ya fuggen mouth!"

I got the message.

We were all crouched behind an overturned stall, hand-carved goods scattered all over the place, and everyone's attention seemed directed at something on the other side. I peeked around the edge of the stall to get a squiz and immediately saw what had them shitscared.

Standing amidst a cloud of dust, towering over everything around us, was the monster. Mercifully, the thing was turned away from us, giving me a chance to take it in without being spotted. But even squizzing it with my own eyes, I couldn't believe what I was seeing.

Pisshead was telling the truth, I marveled. *If anything, he was under exaggerating.*

The monster was easily five times my height, with broad shoulders and powerful-looking arms that spanned three or four of me in width. It had the kind of strong, taut physique you'd expect to see in a great ape, except that, like me, the bloody thing was hairless. Skin wasn't yellow but, rather a sickly white with pink patches and covered with a layer of viscous slime that rippled even though the monster itself was standing more or less still.

What's harder to describe is the way I felt looking at it; an overwhelming sense of wrongness swept over me, a deep-down desire to flee from this hideous thing.

What was it doing? I turned to the wiry bloke and mouthed that very question at him but he shrugged and gestured for me to get down.

The monster was moving now, body quivering, like the inside of it was experiencing seismic changes, complete with a loud cracking and a vibration that shook the very earth around us. It made a disgusting wet choking noise and then, all of a sudden, turned around, giving me a proper look.

The monster had no head; its shoulders led to a bald, featureless triangular outcropping of flesh where a bonce might sit, sans face. Its "facial" features were all over its massive broad chest. And they were hideous beyond belief.

Huge bronze eyes, a wretched bastardisation of grunter eyes, sat either side of the chest, just below each shoulder. Below that a round and vicious mouth, a pit of teeth, really, took up most of the surface area of the torso. The mouth chewed and drooled, every part of its sir-cum-frence in continual agitated movement. Worse was what the mouth was chewing: half a human body – poor bugger had entered the mouth head first… except 'chewing' wasn't quite right. The rows and rows of teeth were masticating the bloke, no question, but strange fleshy tendrils stuck into his thighs, legs and feet and they seemed to be… absorbing him.

Just like the Lord of the Pit except there was nothing of the Lord's gentle, farty-calm and no fruits on that slimy skin.

This was a beast with an entirely different agenda.

With a slurp that had the nameless sheila nearby quietly chundering in a koala-shaped basket, the monster quickly swallowed the back half of the bloke, mouth closing and healing like a wound, leaving the torso eerily blank… but only for a few moments. That internal seismic repositioning occurred again, the monster's whole body shifting and pulsing, and then with a sigh it formed a new orifice, lower on its body.

Clacker height.

I realised we were about to see how the monster went to the dunny.

I almost cackled then. A dangerous, high-pitched terror giggle that would have no doubt led to my unpleasant end. Instead, I managed to clap a clammy hand over my traitor mouth and bit down until the his-terrier passed and tears flowed from my eyes.

Within seconds the beast squeezed a full human skeleton from the excretory orifice, lubricated by the ghastly-smelling slime, and the devoured bloke's togs swiftly followed, plopping down in a pile of bones and clothes.

I felt light-headed and had to turn away when the monster let loose another roar, ear-splitting in volume. But this time, close as I was, I could hear something in the scream. It was… not quite words but something like them.

"WHAAADAMMMIIII!"

The creature's bellow was evidently one step too far for the sheila hiding nearby. She stood and ran, pelting like a champion towards an alley that dog-legged off the main drag of the markets. At first it appeared as if the monster hadn't heard her, hadn't sensed the escape; it didn't seem to register her at all… until it did.

It turned its odd triangular nub in her direction and its mouth straightened, tightened and then it was gawn. Just like that. I blinked, it was no longer in front of me and I turned in time to see it land from an insanely fast pounce, crashing down in front of the now-screaming sheila and raising another cloud of dust.

The sheila was losing it – wailing, crying, all the rest – as the monster picked her up by the back of the shirt with one huge hand. She kicked and spat and swore. None of it helped.

"WHAAADAMMMIIII!!!" It shrieked in her face, mouth a horrifically wide circle, spewing noise and saliva.

"WHAAADAMMMIIII!!!"

Then it gripped her legs with one hand, her neck with the other and cracked her in half, almost snapping her body into two separate pieces.

It threw the dead mess inside its gob, assisted by eager tentacles, and within moments she was gawn, absorbed and feeding the beast.

I never did learn her name.

Seconds stretched into strange, new units of time. Time that was both madly fast and full of information. The creature seemed momentarily lost, looking around. Almost like it was confused, like it wanted answers.

Its large bronze eyes were… sad, somehow. This wasn't just some dumb animal, that much was for sure.

WHAAADAMMMIIII!!!

Was there a message there? I was probs insane to even think in that direction and yet...

WHAAADAMMIII.

WHAD. AM. I.

Or even,

What. Am. I?

Could it be my imagination? Or was it… asking a question? Possibly the question. One we all want answered.

The monster was vibrating again, flesh rippling and pulsing, especially on its chest… and then faces began to appear. Bulging out like gurning tumours they rose from within and manifested in the slimy skin, facial features distorted but clearly present and unique. Multiple faces, five, six, more?

They erupted into being and tried to move their mouths, to speak.

And the messages came through. Not from their own mouths – those were under shifting slabs of translucent body meat – but from the wide, toothy, reopening monstrous mouth, they came in different cadences… in different voices.

"Can you hear me? It's so dark… What's happening?"

"…Please… Lord… why have you forsaken me?"

"*Mu-mmy… is that you?*"

"Cuuuuunce!"

Just then a shunting sound had me glance over the other side of the markets. A stall that had been hanging precariously up against a wall slid down, revealing a number of hiding cits. Cuppla blokes and Old Lil, all staring wide-eyed and open-mouthed with horror at the monster.

"CUUUUUNCE!" One of the voices became louder and was it my imagination or did one of those faces push forwards further than the rest, and didn't it look familiar… didn't it look like Trayvor? And now that you mention it, didn't it sound like Trayvor?

This is important. If you get through this – which seems unlikely – remember.

The monster moved then, with that same unbelievable speed, shooting across the market and grabbing a bloke in one fluid movement. The poor bugger screamed as the monster shoved him inside its mouth, worrying his body like a dog, and absorbing that which wouldn't fit straight in his gob. Then it turned its bronze eyes and multiple faces towards Old Lil, who was panic-waddling as fast as she could.

"Mum…" I heard one of the idiot sons whimper to my left.

The monster pounced again, lifting Lil's squealing form up in the air.

"WHAAADAMMIII!!!" it screamed into Lil's scrunched-up, terrified face. "WHAAADAAMMMMIIII!!!"

"Who know?" cried a foolhardy voice in an eerily accurate impersonation of Shelvan, the former leader of the Mongrels. "WHO KNOW?"

And then I realised the mad bastard who was making the noise was me.

I'd come out from behind the stall and yelled at the monster, operating on the basis of some half-baked drongo idea that I could... communicate with it somehow?

This is a profoundly fuggen stupid way to die.

Two things happened real quick. First, the monster dropped Old Lil. She thumped to the dusty ground, rolled to her feet and scarpered far faster than I'd believe of a woman of her size and age.

Then the monster turned and looked at me like... it recognised me. Just for a second, mind. And its body quivered.

And it screamed.

No words this time, just a brain-melting shriek, far louder a noise than any living thing should be able to make. It grabbed the triangular growth at the top of its body and screamed, snarled once and then, just at the point when I thought the ghastly sound would go on forever, it jumped twice. Once to barrel through the markets like a runaway train and a second time to vanish over the lip of the cliff, leaving the devastated markets in an eerie, ear-ringing silence.

I sank to my knees and started shivering, shaking so hard, like I was freezing to death. I curled into a ball and covered my eyes and shook and shook. I felt as if I was going to shake so hard, I'd break apart into a million disbelieving pieces and fall away into nothingness.

TWENTY-TWO

Best I can describe it is, I went away for a while. Mentally-like. Something about the combined horrors of the rushing crowd, the fear of losing the ruggies and then coming face to faces with the monster overloaded the meat mechanisms inside me bonce.

I blew a gasket and went to another place for a time and, apparently, the pieces reassembled more or less correctly. I came back into myself lying on a small, hard mattress in a long, thin room lined with other small, hard mattresses on which lay sickly-looking cits.

I was in the fuggen hospital!

Ken once told me that back in the day the hospital had been a grouse place. You'd go in, doctors would tell you what was wrong and they'd pump you full of beaut chemicals – or cut you up, in a positive fashion – and she'd be apples. Hossie in the Inasiddy was a whole other kettle of cats. Most of the 'doctors' were chem addicts who might, now and then, stumble onto helping someone, but it was almost always accidental. Generally, hossies were places for sick cits to either get well or cark it on their own, far from the eyes of everyone else.

Footsteps alerted me to the fact someone was approaching, and I turned my head to see a long-haired, bearded bloke approach. He wore a lab coat that may have once been white but was now a mucky light brown, and a stethoscope – broken from the look of it – around his neck.

"Ah, you're awake." The doctor smiled at me distractedly and took a syringe out of his coat pocket, flicking the tip and holding it up to the light.

"I… spose so," I croaked. "What's going on?"

"You were brought in with a bunch of other injured cits. From the attack on the Roil Easter Show."

I looked around, straining to see through oddly blurry vision and a piercing headache, but none of the patients were people I recognised.

"Where's Gia? And the ruggies? And Tanya? Did they make it? Are they alive?" My voice was getting more and more shrill.

"I have no idea who any of those people are."

"What are you gunna give me?" I looked nervously at the syringe, still held in the doctor's hand.

"Oh. This isn't for you." The doctor scoffed and began to roll up his sleeve, exposing a number of fresh-looking track marks.

Yeah nah, healthcare in the Inasiddy was not great, hey.

"Franga!" A sheila's voice called out. I smiled, then, because I recognised it.

"Gia!" I managed to rasp and then she was on top of me, smothering my face and chest in a warm, friendly hug.

"Not dead then, eh?"

"Not yet."

"Well, that's a bloody weight off."

First things first, the ruggies were fine. Well, like, not 'fine' – Tommy's leg got scratched up something fierce, Bella had a black eye (the big one) and most of the others had bumps and bruises of varying severity, but everyone was still alive, miraculously. "Healthy enough to have a whinge" is how Gia put it, and it was music to my ears.

The rest of the Inasiddy didn't get off so lightly.

Due to the brief but memorable attack by the monster, some sixdy-three cits lost their lives. The monster was only directly responsible for a dozen maggotings, mind you. The rest were crushed in the panicked exodus of people from the showgrounds. Twelve more looked like they'd be succumbing to their injuries before the day was through, not to mention the poor bastards who were severely injured, physically or mentally, and would survive with those afflictions for the rest of their lives. I wasn't the only person to have a brainmelt and in fact Old Lil, a woman as hard as stone, had been inconsolably terrified in the twelve or so hours since it had all transpired.

Add to that the fact that no one was labouring under the delusion this would be the only attack. Word of my strange, albeit briefly effective, distraction had spread, but I doubted it was a permanent solution.

Some cits had headed over to the Harbour Bridge to see if they could get the Pigs to send some help. Best of luck and all, but I didn't anticipate much of a response. Pigs protected NanoCorp and the Big End of Town, mainly using the Inasiddy as a source of income.

Which begged the question: what were we going to do?

A thought struck me. "Where are the kids now?"

"My joint," Gia answered. "Being looked after by Tanya and Ken."

"Righto, best get back to it then," I sighed as I struggled to sit up. "I reckon we should prob– bloody hell, where are my pants?"

Gia looked over at the doctor, who was now slumped next to a bed, in narcotised bliss.

"Oi," she called. "Where are my friend's pants?"

"I dunno, fuggen somewhere… look aroun', ya molls…" he trailed off, clearly out of his tree.

Gia and I shared a look.

Ten minutes later, we left the Inasiddy hospital, Gia dressed in casual clothes and me wearing a shirt, undies and a spiffy, albeit stained, lab coat.

I reckoned it made me look rather distinguished.

• • • •

Gia's apartment was the nicest pad I'd seen in the Inasiddy. Prime real estate, right next to Flesh Alley and the markets, with a grouse view that was fiddy percent Downlow and fiddy percent an abandoned bus depot full of screaming addicts, either happy about going up or freaking out when they started coming back down.

The place itself was one bedroom with a large lounge area and a brasco that had a chute leading down the side of the building, all fancy. Squizzing the place as we approached her building, the various dunny tubes reminded me of the body chutes in the Downlow and I shivered a little.

"You right, Frang?" Gia asked, putting a hand on my shoulder.

"Yeah, just wobbly, and my vision's a bit blurry."

"You've got an impressive-looking shiner," she mused, looking at my face. "From the monster?"

To be honest, I think it was probably from some rando cit's elbow in the crowd, but I said yeah anyway.

Upstairs, I had the expected reunion with the ruggies – hugs, tears and assurances we'd never be apart again – and Tanya – cordial nod, very little else. I saw Ken dawdling in the kitchen and he smiled when he felt my gaze.

"Hey, Franga. Got a minute to chat?"

As it happened, I did. So, we adjourned to the roof barbie area, which was empty save for a scrawny ginger cat who glared intermittently at the pair of us. Ken took a flask from his pocket and we both had a swallow of some powerfully spensive-tasting whisky.

"Don't ask me how old it is," Ken insisted.

I didn't.

We sat for a moment, appreciating the flash grog, and then Ken clapped his hands, like he wanted to kick things off.

"Righto. Tell me the whole story. Leave nothing out."

I nodded, cleared my throat and laid the whole caper on him, pausing only to answer very specific questions where Ken would grill me for details. I didn't mind. I could see his big brain working, putting together theories and – hopefully – coming up with a plan.

We'd polished off the whole flask by the time I was done.

"Fark," Ken breathed.

"Yep," I agreed.

Ken fished out a second flask, had a pull, then handed it to me.

"What do you reckon?" he asked. I was a bit surprised by the question.

"Who cares what I reckon?" I was incredulous. "What do you reckon? I'm not the smart one, Ken."

"I'm not so sure that's true. You were the one who thought to appeal to the part of the monster that seemed to be controlled by the Mongrel, Trayvor. I wouldn't have thought to do that and I'm quite bright allegedly. You've got an instinct for this kinda thing, Frang, the ability to think on your feet. That's not to be underestimated."

"I appreciate that but... I dunno, eh." I handed the flask back. "It wasn't a well thought out plan. I was just reacting."

I stood and wobbled on my feet for a moment, realising with a kind of agreeable surprise that I was quite drunk.

"Durries..." I murmured.

"Still can't hold your liquor, though!" Ken laughed.

I smiled back and enjoyed the sense of boozy camaraderie I felt with him. The circumstances were pretty bloody far from ideal but it was nice all the same. Or course, that coulda been the grog talking.

I walked to the edge of the roof area and looked down at the Inasiddy, now mostly hidden by the night. The druggies were screaming in the old bus depot, but they seemed happy as they danced, fought and rooted amongst the flaming barrels that lit them, broken bottles sparkling like shonky diamonds. Maybe they weren't happy precisely but they were excited – probs too off their tits to be worried about the monster's return –

or maybe they just didn't give a shit anymore. Maybe not giving a shit was the true meaning of life. No one can hurt you if you don't care.

Yeah, or maybe you've just had a skinful and are talking out your arse.

"It hurt him," I spoke softly.

"Hurt who?"

"The monster. It hurt him to remember. I think…" I trailed off.

"Go on." Ken was eager, insistent.

"I think in that moment it remembered who it used to be, or at least part of him did. And it hurt. The memory wounded him somehow. Like the awareness of it was too much."

"That's interesting. Was there a sign of a dominant personality, a sense of who was in charge?"

"In the angry moments, it was Trayvor. Pure glory-rage and malice. But the rest of the time, it was like… a whole bunch of them in there. Reckon I heard worshippers of the Lord of the Pit, Redmund, some people I'd never met… maybe even a ruggie. Poor little tacker."

"'My name is Legion, for we are many.'" Ken had his quoting voice on.

"Bible or poet?"

"Beg yours?"

"Every time you quote something fancy you bung on that voice. And, like, it always ends up being a quote from the Bible or a poet."

Ken looked at me askance for a moment and then burst into uproarious laughter, surprising me and causing the ginger cat to flee, yowling.

"You know, lad, I think you might know me best of all in this world, I do declare. You were quite right, by the way, it's from the Bible. About demons."

"I don't reckon it's a demon."

"No?"

I shook my head. "Nah, demons are evil, yeah? That's what the God-botherers reckon, anyway. This thing is… confused. I don't think it hurts because it's angry or, like, malicious. It's more that it just doesn't know where it is, *what* it is."

"Whad. Am. I."

"Right."

I wobbled back over and sat on the ground near Ken. I was feeling pleasantly fuzzy and more than a little sleepy. I stifled a yawn and blinked myself alert.

"When was the last time you slept through the night?" Ken asked.

"Dunno. Seems like a while. What day is it again?"

"That settles it. You need to get some sleep."

Ken stood and ignored my protests. He sauntered down to Gia's apartment and demanded to know if any of the other prozzies were working all-nighters. Turned out a bloke on the level above – Gaz – was away for at least twelve hours. After a few quiet exchanges between Ken and Gia I was a bit too drunk to fully comprehend, Gia agreed to let me have a bed.

"I don't want to cause a fuss…" I murmured but real soft-like because the idea of sleeping by myself in a one-bedroom apartment sans ruggies, friends dropping by or indeed any distraction sounded like a slice of heaven.

It seemed like no time had passed at all before Gia and Ken were letting me into Gaz's spotless place and walking me over to the bed.

"He's dead on his feet," Ken muttered, an implied blame hanging in the air.

"He's been working the job of two blokes," Gia countered, giving as good as she got. Ken grumbled but you could see he took her point.

"Give it a bone, you two," I sighed as I sat down on the bed. "Or argue very, very quietly, please."

The soft mattress and its flowery purple pillows and gloriously smooth sheets were about the best things I'd ever felt.

"Night, Franga." Ken spoke kindly.

"Sleep well," Gia purred.

I nodded, pulled my shoes off, dropped the lab coat on the floor and crawled under the covers. I reckon I was out before my head even hit the pillow and I slipped into the land of nod, bothered by no bastard dreams at all.

• • • •

I was woken by the sound of someone entering the apartment at some point in the early morning. It was still dark out but the air had the smell of approaching dawn, still a few hours off but defo on its way.

At first, I figured it was Gaz arriving home early, but the shadowy figure's physique was clearly that of a sheila. I judged by the bob on her bonce it was Gia, wearing one of her more fetching wigs. I started to raise my swollen head, blinking.

"Gia, whatzgoing on? S'everything ok–"

"Shhhh."

I closed my mouth and lay back, well-rested but entirely willing and able to slip back under the doona and explore nothingness some more. Gia stood there, staring at me, her features impossible to make out due to the dark and my blurry vision, but I had the strange sense she was smiling. Wickedly.

Then she started dancing. To whatever music was in her head presumably, swaying and undulating in a fashion I found extremely pleasing. A little too pleasing, if I'm honest. Her movements caused a stirring in my trouser area, and I suddenly felt exposed, despite wearing undies and being covered by sheets and a doona.

Maybe Gia had had a few at work? Or a bit of a cheeky smoke? I tried to surreptitiously hide my mounting stiffy, lest I turn the sheets into a tent, but the bloody thing had a mind of its own.

I opened my mouth to say something and hopefully distract from my social foe-par when Gia began shedding her clothes.

First, she pulled off her top, then her strides – dropping the items of clothing on the floor and kicking them away – then she began shedding her undies. All the spit in my mouth seemed to boil away and I stared – wide-eyed – as Gia dropped the last of her smalls and stood – a beaut starkers silhouette – standing with one hand on her waist. She cocked her head to one side and nodded towards the now straining pyramid of my engorged tocko.

I hoped the gesture meant 'do you mind if I hop on that?' rather than 'I'm about to beat that thing with a stick' because I answered in a shaky voice, "Uh, yeah. Yeah, garn."

She pulled the sheets off with a savage jerk and moved up my body, using her knees, until she was straddling me. I raised a hand to touch her face but she slapped it away. My hand had to go somewhere, so I placed it gently on Gia's right norg, which she seemed okay with.

I was pretty fuggen okay with it too.

Nek minute, she'd grabbed my undies and reefed them down past my knees. She grabbed my groaning tockley with a firm hand and slid herself onto me. She was warm, wet and tight. It was grouse and I moaned happily. Deadset, I wasn't even sure this was real or a shockingly vivid dream, and I didn't much care. We were joined at the crotch and Gia rode me and I did my best to make a decent accounting of myself, despite a complete lack of experience other than many, many fond fantasies while knocking one out on the sly.

I reckon all told, I lasted sevendeen seconds before a wave of sweet release shuddered through me and I exploded inside her.

Gia stayed astride me long after I'd gawn soft and seemed content to just stare down at me. I noticed with a sort of distracted awareness that she wasn't wearing shoes. I'd never seen Gia barefoot. It struck me as strange.

"Your feet are–"

"Shhhh."

I shhh'd and lay on my back, feeling pretty good about the whole experience. Within five or so minutes, I was barring up again and this seemed to be the signal Gia had been waiting for. We went for another round and this time I got to experience the entire caper without my brain screaming *HOLY FUGGEN SHIT IT'S FINALLY HAPPENING! IT'S REALLY FINALLY HAPPENING*! endlessly.

I lasted way longer and this time Gia actually got something out of it, climaxing roughly with a whispered moan and then finishing me off once more. My ballbag felt as empty as an old windsock and the sense of relief and contentment that washed over me was like nothing I'd experienced before.

Gia lay down next to me, sheets still tangled on the floor, and I stroked her sweaty skin, and moved my fingers up her face and into her hair. I fell asleep like that, curled up next to the woman I fancied, nude and satisfied. If I'd died at that very moment, I probably would have considered life worth the effort.

I didn't, but.

Some time later, with early morning lighting the apartment much more comprehensively, I woke up with Gia's wig still in my hand. Its owner was prowling around the place, putting stuff in a bag from the sound of it.

I sat up, looking around: "Gia?"

Her shadowy form turned towards me.

"What's going on?" I asked.

"Tell her I'm sorry," she said.

"Tell who?"

Then the form stepped into the light and showed me what I should have worked out much earlier.

The bare feet, the silence, the very fact she wanted you – ya bloody drongo!

It was Tanya. Tanya inexplicably pretending to be Gia to, what, seduce me? Why?

"Tan?" I hissed, my brain a seething cauldron of conflicting emotions.

"Tell her I'm sorry," she repeated.

"Who?" I asked. But I knew she meant Gia. But sorry for what? Rooting me? Then I took a closer look at Tanya's bag. It was heavy and bulging and Tanya was fully dressed.

"No, Tanya, come on– don't…" I stood up and tripped over the tangled sheets on the floor. I swore and pulled myself free, making a mess of it. By the time I was standing up again the apartment door yawned open and Tanya was gawn.

I tried to give chase but she wasn't in either stairwell and I couldn't see hide nor hair of her outside. She'd scarpered good and proper. With a sickening realisation, I ran downstairs and hammered on Gia's door, not caring that I might wake the ruggies.

The door opened almost immediately and Gia was standing there, shod but wigless, with red eyes. She'd been crying, a lot by the looks.

"Tanya–" I began.

"I know," Gia said tiredly. "I know."

Turned out, Gia hadn't been quite as ready to accept Tanya back with open arms as she'd implied. She'd hidden the bulk of her dosh and scrap in a secret spot she wouldn't even reveal to me, but left a small amount in her usual stash place. Tanya had fallen for the ruse and flogged some of Gia's gear, plus whatever she got from Gaz's joint. By way of a note, she'd left behind a flyer for Hendoism. Amidst the various mouth-gear, it explained that one of the major tenets of Hendoism was breaking ties with family and friends.

"You don't break ties with family more successfully than flogging their stuff," Gia muttered bitterly while I read the pamphlet. I opted not to remind Gia that Tanya had been a thieving moll long before Hendoism. Didn't seem the time. There was something I did feel I should mention, but.

"She, uh, she said to tell you she was sorry," I mumbled.

"Sorry for what?"

I took a deep breath and gave her the whole story. The dancing, the pretending to be Gia, the rooting. I was blushing all over by the time I finished and not sure where to look.

"That. Absolute. Scrag," Gia hissed.

"I guess she reckoned we were an item, maybe? That's the only reason I could think of for her to apologise." I was looking at my bare yellow feet.

"Mate, I'm so sorry."

"S'okay." I was horrified to realise I was on the edge of having a sook.

"It's not. That's awful and manipulative."

"I should've known, eh. A sheila like you would never love a bloke like me."

"Oh, Franga. I do love you. With all my heart." Gia lifted my face up, looked me right in the eyes.

"But just not… in a trouserly fashion?"

"No."

"Because I'm an ugly mutie?"

"No!" she exclaimed, hurt and angry. "Franga, no."

"How come then?" My eyes were fair brimming, it wasn't a good look.

"I'm…" Gia sighed. "Franga, I'm asexual."

"A sexual what?"

"No, like, asexual. It's a thing. When you, like, don't wanna root. Anyone."

The concept fair boggled my mind. "Gia, I hate to be the one to tell you this, but you're a *prozzy-toot*."

Gia started to laugh. "Yeah, thanks, mate, I am aware."

"Correct me if I'm wrong but a big parta that job is rooting."

"It is. And I do it well, make all the right moans and noises and whatnot. Wear the sexy kinda outfits… but it just does nothing for me. Trouserly-like. I don't hate it, but it's just a job. And in real life, when I'm with someone, it's the same. Bloke, sheila, whoever – it all amounts to me kinda lying there a bit bored. I want to make them happy but they can, like, sense that I'm not into it and so it never lasts. Haven't you ever wondered why I've never had a boyfriend or girlfriend in the whole time I've known ya?"

To my eternal shame, I hadn't. Too self-absorbed with my own feelings.

"An asexual prozzy-toot, eh? Crikey."

"I still love you, but," she said without looking at me. "I hope you'll still be… my friend."

I realised with a shock that Gia was crying again and trying real hard to hide it.

"G, mate, of course. Of course!" And I meant it. "Maybe you're not meant to be the love of my life after all, but you're deadset my best mate. Nothing's gunna change that."

"Fair dinkum?"

"Fair dinkum."

"Thanks, Frang. I needed to hear that."

We stayed up for a while longer, me rolling Gia cigarettes and making cups of tea while she lamented having an arsehole for a sister. By the time the sun was properly up, she'd regained her composure and was acting normal, this latest hurt absorbed by a body adept at soaking them up and moving on.

Besides, whinging was a luxury we could little afford. We both knew the monster would be back.

It was just a matter of time.

TWENTY-THREE

The first sign something was skew-whiff occurred after breakfast. Everyone had been fed and Ken was helping the ruggies clean the dishes in Gia's cramped kitchen area, leaving her and I a modicum of privacy. Although we hardly needed it. Gia was in control of her emotions again, typical of her. If I hadn't witnessed her crying myself, I'd never have known it had even happened.

"Where's Gaz?" she said suddenly, stubbing out a cigarette and standing.

"Work still?"

"It's half nine. He should have been back a cuppla hours ago at least."

"Maybe he walked past us when we were talking…" But even as I said the words my heart began to thump insistently. Gia and I hoofed it upstairs but Gaz's apartment was empty. We shared a look.

"Maybe we should–" I began.

"–get the ruggies back to the hab?" she finished.

"Yeah, let's get it going."

We headed back downstairs, moving at a speed you could describe as "calm but brisk". Happily, Ken intuited our joint mission and we got everyone ready for a "fun walk in the city" that promised to be anything but. In the back of my mind, I could almost hear a clock ticking, counting down the seconds to… what?

"Something bad," I whispered.

Bella looked at me tying her shoelaces. "What's that, Franga?"

"Nothing, love, nothing." I shot her my best fake smile, which seemed to work.

Within minutes me, Ken and Gia were herding the ruggies out of Gia's building and down the shadowed streefs that led off it. I'd always found this area of town a bit sinister, the olden-style tall buildings felt like massive tombstones to me, and there was an eerie quality to the sound. It echoed strangely, the noises coming from places they ought not. Perhaps I was letting my imagination run away with me, although judging from the looks on Gia and Ken's faces they too felt the tension.

The unnameable dread.

"Why are we walking so fastaaaa?" Bella grumbled.

I was about to answer when I saw someone appear on the streef ahead. Actually, stumbled was a better way to put it, they stumbled into view, ran a few steps and then stood, panting and coughing.

It was a lanky bloke, tall and bald, wearing a loud shirt and a pair of strides that hadn't been properly fastened. His fly was undone and though I didn't investigate the issue too closely, he appeared not to be wearing undies.

"You right, mate?" I called, manoeuvring myself in front of the kids in case he turned out to be a dodgy bastard.

The man looked up, eyes wide, and just stared for a moment.

"You okay?"

"F-flesh Alley," he spluttered, struggling hard to breathe normally. "Flesh Alley…"

"What about it?" Gia stiffened.

"It's fuggen cactus!" the man cried. "The monster's tearing it up!"

Taking a moment to spit, calm down and – upon Gia's insistence – zip up his dick window, the bloke gave us an abbreviated version of events. He'd been visiting Flesh Alley to get his end in, and a fine time he'd been having too, rooting his favourite prozzie at The Tradesman's Entrance. Him and the prozzie (not Gaz – we checked) were thrown off the vinegar stroke when the whole brothel began to shudder and screaming broke out.

"We uncoupled and ran to the door when we heard the most horrible growling. It was different to the sound at the Easter Show but still… defo the monster. I pulled the window open and started climbing out. Trent was right behind me, I swear. Just… a second behind me."

The very room exploded behind the bloke and he ran through the Rooting District in a panic, the sounds of terror and painful death dogging his steps.

"I swear I didn't mean to leave him," the bloke sobbed and I patted him awkwardly on the back.

The ruggies had watched the exchange with wide, mostly uncomprehending eyes. Ken moved close to me, saying: "We've gotta take 'em home, son. Further from Flesh Alley, better protected."

I nodded.

"I'm staying. I have to help." Gia was staring up the alley the bloke had come down.

"That's a bad idea, love," Ken offered.

"That's my place of work. They're… they're my friends." Gia's chin was set in a determined fashion.

"Righto, then, I'm coming with you." I stepped forwards.

"That's two exceptionally bad ideas in a row. The pair of you. I understand how you both feel but…" Ken gestured at the kids, at my family. "You know."

He was right. I knew he was right. And yet… the idea of Gia running into danger alone was like a punch in the guts.

"Look," Gia began, but whatever the end of that sentence was to be, we never heard it, because there was an almighty crash and a bunch of cits came running down the alley, pursued by a cloud of dust. Many of them were bloody, battered. One poor sheila was missing an arm, the stump still bleeding. She had a dazed look in her eyes, like she couldn't believe what was happening.

Moving as one, me, Ken and Gia grabbed ruggie arms and started pelting in the opposite direction, running as fast as we could while remaining upright.

No one said a word, we just ran. More sounds of death and destruction ringing out behind us, bouncing off the concrete and seemingly coming from all sides.

A chorus of terror.

The trip back home was a tense trek through hell. We were constantly looking behind us, starting at each and every unexpected sound. People were coming out of their homes, confused by the noise. We just told them the monster was coming and they should run. Everyone should run.

We made it back the hab and bundled the ruggies inside with Ken. Me and Gia stood on the streef staring back the way we'd come.

"Everything's changed, hasn't it?" Gia wasn't really asking. We knew. We both knew.

The world had transformed that day, into something darker and weirder than we'd ever imagined.

● ● ● ●

Back at the hab, Ken got the ruggies to pack a bag of "essentials" in case we had to leave in a hurry. We weren't keen on the idea of fleeing, mind you. Keeping twelve ruggies safe on the streefs of a panicked city would be no small task, and for all we knew the monster would be moving in the same direction. We needed solid info before we acted – where the monster was going, where it had been, that sorta thing – so Gia and I headed to the one place we'd be sure to get it: the pub.

We got the full story of what transpired talking to various sources. Some of these witnesses were reliable, others were deadset full of it, but we talked to enough people to get the whole caper described to a degree of accuracy that, we reckoned, was mostly not bullshit.

And that's about the best you can hope for most days.

Despite, or perhaps because of the attack from the day before, Flesh Alley had been doing a roaring trade. Many fear-gobbies and proximity-to-death roots were traded, which was bonza, but it did mean everyone was rather distracted and not at all prepared for what was about to happen.

The first joint the monster attacked was Nudie Rudies – one of the softer places that was more about naked sheilas and drinking, rather than getting on the job. Consequently, the place was almost empty when the monster struck, taking out one whole wall and bursting inside. No one survived.

Nek minute, the monster crossed the streef and hit The Splayed Vadge – a place that catered to both voyeurs and those who fancied a root. Place was packed, when the monster hit it was like a bomb went off – prozzies and customers flying everywhere, total massacre. One sheila who managed to escape unscathed by sheer luck would tell her story to anyone who bought her a drink and a vial or two of goey. It was cheap stuff and I barely needed to hock a paperyback to get the whole tale.

"I'd just finished up with one of me regulars. Nice bloke he is– or was. We were done and I was walking him out when I realised I was a little… drippy, if you know what I mean."

I did but chose not to interrupt. The sheila – Charm was her name – was on the way up, pupils dilating as the drugs entered her bloodstream and she was talking fast and smoking furiously.

"So, I grabbed a spunk rag and mopped out me spadger, told the regular to hold up but he either didn't hear me or wasn't listening. Blokes don't listen so good once they've had their end away. There was this huge *BOOM* and suddenly the whole place was lit up, like by daylight.

"Normally the whole joint is pinky coloured, like it's the inside of an actual vadge. That was Craig's idea, he was the owner, had a lot of grouse ideas like that – anyway, I knew there was trouble because the only place that light could have come from was the roof. Which was suddenly gawn.

"Anyway, fuggen hell, I looked down and there's blood everywhere and cunce lying all over the floor. Prozzies, customers, the whole box and dice. In the middle of it all was that monster. It had Craig by the neck, poor bugger, and was shoving something into his mouth, down his throat. Next thing I know he's smoking from, like, the inside. Burning and that, right down to his skellington! I looked away but something weird caught me attention, the monster said something… like speaking to Craig, not just yelling and that."

"What did it say?" I prodded.

"Dunno. Sounded like 'Loorblay Blezing' and then 'Aponyew'. It said it again and again, as it took something from inside its mouth and shoved that stuff inside me regular, and some of the other girls as well. But – and this is what was confusing – it didn't seem angry or like it was *trynna* hurt anyone. Its eyes were different from the attack at the Roil Easter Show. It had a… I dunno, gentle look about it. In my job, you get real good at reading eyes."

Gia nodded in agreement at this.

"But I wasn't gunna stay to get fed that burning shit, no matter what its eyes looked like. I spose I shoulda tried to help the people still alive. I thought about it, fair dinkum. But in the end, I just ran. Jumped out through the roof hole and hoofed it the fug out of there. I'm staying with me nan and pop now. Fuggen shithouse."

Charm's story was echoed by witnesses from The Horse's Hoof, The Tradesman's Entrance and GIZ ROOT. All three places were demolished spectacularly, with various cits being force fed the chunks of meat, the flesh of the beast. And every time that same statement: "Loorblay Blezing. Aponyew."

Lorb. Lay. Blezing. Apon. Yew.

Lord. Lay. Blessings. Upon. You.

Fark.

"It's fuggen Redmund," I muttered, sitting back in my chair. "Somehow Redmund is now in charge of it."

"The churchy bloke from the Downlow?" Gia asked, doing her best to hide the utter exhaustion in her voice.

"That's him." I nodded.

"How does that help us, but?"

"No fuggen idea…" I admitted, draining my beer. "But maybe if I said something he remembered from his former life… I could distract the bloody thing like before."

"Wait, if *you* said something? You're thinking of going near that thing?"

"Maybe?" I shrugged helplessly.

The monster hadn't returned to the Downlow, squatting instead in a temporary nest constructed from the rubble of Flesh Alley. The whole Rooting District was, essentially, gawn – now home to a monster that was absorbing the flesh of its victims and growing bigger and stronger. Many cits had been displaced and were moving steadily away from the danger zone, Inasiddy refugees, but what would happen when it started cracking on again?

"Franga, you barely got away the last time, you had a massive freak out." Gia was exasperated.

"I dunno. It just feels, like, eventually someone's gunna have to do something!"

"Why does that someone have to be you?"

"Can you suggest anyone more appropriate?" I gestured around the pub, which was now brimming with pissed locals, exaggerating stories of heroism and terror. It's funny how quickly devastation and horror become a good drinking anecdote.

One particularly arseholed chap was taking a piss on the bar, mistaking it for the brasco no doubt. No bastard seemed particularly bothered and he ordered another drink with his yoo-rinating tockley still dangling.

"That bloke, maybe?" I shot Gia a quizzical look. "Reckon he'd give it a good go?"

"Righto."

"He could have a slash on the monster, distract it that way, maybe."

"Righto, I take your point. It's just… you're not a fighter. At all. You're… you know… you're *you*. You care about people and jump real good, and it'd be a fuggen shame if you got maggoted."

Gia looked into her beer and I barely heard her add: "And I'd miss you."

We ordered another round and swore it would be the last, but despite the desperate baccy-nall vibe of the pub, it was nice to be out and drinking with Gia. It was nice to be anywhere, to be alive.

"What would you say?" she asked after a companionable silence.

"To who?"

"To the monster, to Redmund."

"Maybe something like 'praise his name'."

"Why that?"

"The Derros said it a lot. They were all about that kinda gear."

"And you reckon he'd react?"

"Dunno. Seems like he's trynna offer some kinda yoocharist to the cits of Flesh Alley, so… maybe?"

Gia pursed her lips angrily. "Fine."

"Eh?"

"I'll stay with ya, protect ya. But if it doesn't work and we get maggoted, I'm gunna have the shits something fierce."

I was about to say something stupid like "I don't need protecting" or a similar bitta nonsense but the door to the pub slammed open, cutting off my potential idiocy.

"Oi!" A red-faced young bloke shouted. "It's the Pigs. The fuggen Pigs are comin' to the Inasiddy. They're gunna kill the monster!"

Gia and I looked at one another.

"Oh, thank fug for that," she said.

"I really didn't wanna do it either," I admitted, laughing.

"What were we thinking?"

"Let's have another drink!" I suggested.

The relief spread around the pub and throughout the Inasiddy. The Pigs were gunna take care of it. Everything was gunna be, well... maybe not good, but regular, normal.

The situation was under control.

TWENTY-FOUR

Watching the Pigs march from The Big End, through the streefs of the Inasiddy, on a non-Bribe Day-related matter no less, was wonderful to behold.

The crisp uniforms, the body armour, the helmets gleaming in the bright glare – it made you feel real good, especially because they weren't coming after you. These blokes and sheilas were obviously the best of the Pigs, fit, strong, armed with decent guns – old but powerful, probs very loud – and ready to dispatch the monster in short order. A giddy sense of anticipation swept through the crowd and cits started to shout encouragement as sevendy or so Pigs marched past.

"Go get 'em, Piggers!"

"Tear it to pieces!"

"Rip its ballbag off, ya cunce!"

That last one was Gia. I looked sharply at her and she blushed, grinning.

"Got caught up in the moment, eh." She shrugged.

I laughed; I couldn't help it. It finally felt like the adults were stepping in, taking care of a volatile situation. Then a thought struck me. "Oh, bloody hell."

"What?" Gia was still smiling.

"We should tell 'em about 'praise his name', help out that way."

She nodded. "Yeah, good call. Oi!"

Gia started pushing people out of the way, shouldering through the crowd to get to the Pigs. I followed in her wake. The upbeat nature of the mosh was such that most people moved and let us through; I even got a pat on the back from some rando. It was actually quite nice. We made it past the front row and Gia waved at a Pig in the middle of the group.

"Sorry, love." The Pig – it was the stern bloke with a huge chin who had paid me an unpleasant visit at the hab, I noticed with some trepidation – addressed Gia. "We can't stop for roots beforehand. Afterwards though. This shouldn't take long."

Gia rolled her eyes but shook it off, saying: "Nah, you should listen to this bloke. He's had a run-in with the monster before."

The Pig looked at me sceptically and kept marching but inclined his head to show he was listening.

"Say 'praise his name' to the thing," I advised. "Do it all churchy-like. It, uh, seems to distract it."

"It's a monster," the Pig sneered. "We're just gunna shoot it until it's dead. Fuggen mutie."

With that, the Pig turned his helmeted head forwards and kept marching. I felt a bit gutted as I slowed my walking pace and wondered what to do next, when I heard a whistle. A sheila Pig from the very back row gestured for me to come over.

"Don't worry about him, citizen," she told me. "What was the phrase you recommend?"

"'Praise his name,'" Gia answered for me.

The Pig nodded. "Appreciate the help."

It seemed like she meant it too. The Pigs kept on moving, down the streef, into the area that was currently the monster's nest. Soon the various buildings obstructed our view but we could still hear the sound of marching. After that had dwindled too, the crowd became less vocal and looked around, at a loss for what to do next.

"Beer?" Gia asked.

I checked my pockets to see how much dosh was left. Quite a bit as it turned out. Bewdy.

"Beer," I agreed.

• • • •

One beer became two, then three, then many more. Which was how I ended up coming to at the table in the wee hours of the morning, the sun just starting to have a cheeky perv over the horizon.

"Durries," I groaned, "we didn't make it home."

"Mate, we didn't make it off the table," Gia burped, her eyes still closed.

"I'm pretty crook, G," I admitted.

"Me too." Then inspiration struck her. "Got any of that goey left?"

I checked my bag and indeed there were two capsules that I hadn't used to get more story out of Charm.

"Giz." Gia gestured impatiently. I handed them over and she emptied the two pills into the sludgy dregs of our warm, unfinished beers. She then swished the extremely festy contents around and handed me one of the glasses.

"Garn then."

"I'm not drinking this," I insisted.

"Garn. Then."

"Well, when you put it like that…"

We both skolled our piss-warm bevvies and I swear it tasted worse than the Lord's fruit. I kept it down, but my belly was rumbling and I could feel me gorge rising.

"Try not to think about it," Gia advised. "Just imagine a nice place."

"I'm imagining my wonderful life five seconds before I decided to drink this swill," I muttered, but I felt better shortly. It might have been my imagination but my head began to clear as well.

After a couple more minutes, the rumbling had become a distant hum and I was beginning to feel like a real human again. I managed to visit the brasco and empty my swollen bladder, which was a huge relief.

When I got back, Gia was sparky as well and we decided to walk outside to see what was going on. The humid air smacked into us, and I reeled slightly. You never really get used to it, you know, that smothering sensation.

A cuppla blokes were standing around staring down the road where the Pigs had gawn, but other than that sweet fug all was happening. I'd never necked goey before but, crikey, I suddenly had the urge to chat with everyone something fierce.

"G'day blokes," I said chirpily. "What's going on?"

"Nuthin'," one of them – the older one – answered.

"Where are the Pigs?" Gia asked.

"Dunno. Went in. Heard some gunshots. Didn't come out though, eh." That was the younger one's input.

Gia and I looked at one another and stepped away from the two blokes, who barely noticed.

"That's sevendy Pigs, G. Seven. Dy."

"And none of 'em came back." Gia was gnawing on her fingernails.

"Should we check anyway? Real quiet-like?"

"Yeah. Yeah?"

"Yeah."

We nodded at the blokes and made our way down the streef, early morning steam rising from the cracked concrete. Even through the chemical haze of amphetamine confidence, I had a feeling like, maybe, this was not gunna end well at all.

We hoofed it along another few meaters and then slowed down, in yooni-sun.

"You know, we should really wait for a few more cits to come with, eh..." I ventured.

"Yeah, yeah, let's head back to the pub for a bitta liquid courage," Gia rationalised.

We headed back inside and necked not one, but two beers a piece. It actually felt great, equalising the energising-but-twitchy goey feelings with numbing booze. While there, we chatted with the few upright cits about our mission and managed to rope two young blokes and an older sheila into our half-baked plan.

Emboldened by increased numbers and beers, the five of us exited the pub and headed down the streef, just as the sun was burning its way through the clouds and heating the concrete and flesh of a new day.

• • • •

At first everything seemed to be fine. Or at least, lacking evidence of horrific events. The first few blocks were deserted and eerily quiet, sure, but no bodies lay splattered around and the streef didn't run red with blood or any of that sorta nonsense.

About ten minutes later, as we approached the area in Flesh Alley that we knew, anecdotally, had been transformed into the creature's nest, we all went quiet. Our chattiness evaporated in the face of a strange atmosphere.

I looked over at Gia and she gave me a quick, thin smile of encouragement and patted me on the elbow. It wasn't much but it was nice, and I nodded back and did my best not to look as daks-browning shitscared as I felt.

Flesh Alley was silent as the grave and all the bodies had been cleared out, presumably by the monster to be–

(consumed)

–used however it saw fit. Something else struck me, though, something about the way the rubble appeared to be uniform, organised.

"Has it…" I spoke, startling everyone with the sudden noise. "Soz. But, like, has it been… cleaning?"

A cuppla my traveling companions scoffed at the idea but then they too saw the unnatural symmetry, the brush marks in the concrete dust. A deliberate sense of organisation, albeit a bit half-arsed and haphazard.

"Has it been sweeping?" Gia asked, eyes wide in abject disbelief. I barked out a laugh. The incredulity on her face combined with the image of the monster doing a few outdoor chores was too insane to take.

The laughter dried up pretty quickly, but, once we came across the first Pig helmet.

It was sitting alone in the middle of the streef, on the ground – incongruous in the two blocks of baffling cleanliness through which we'd just been walking.

It was turned away from us, giving the unsettling impression the Pig had been buried up to his neck in the concrete. Durries, maybe he had – it wouldn't be any weirder than anything else that had been happening.

We all stopped in our tracks, waiting for a sign from above – some indication of what we should do next.

"Could go back to the pub?" one of the blokes suggested, beating me to the punch by a bare second.

"Nah." Gia shook her head. "Let's see what that is."

"It's a helmet. I can see that from here." That was the other chap. Both were skittish and ready to run. I couldn't really blame them.

I sighed deeply. "I'll go."

"You sure?" Gia looked at me, head cocked curiously.

"Not really." Nevertheless, I started walking towards the helmet.

"Wait!" Gia called. I turned around. "Don't touch it with your hands. Use a stick or something."

Seemed like good advice, so I picked up a chunk of wood, that was probs a knocking shop door at some point and now sat in an oddly prissy pile of refuse. Moving as if in a dream, I headed towards the helmet, wincing as sunlight glinted off it. The surface was slimy, covered in the stuff. I mentally thanked Gia for the stick idea.

I moved close enough to the helmet so that I could use the stick, but with enough distance to jump away and pissbolt if things turned pig's arsehole. I didn't know what could happen – maybe the bloody helmet would grow legs and come after me like a narky spider – but I was ready for anything.

Then, with aching care, I poked the slimy helmet with my stick.

It moved a centimeater to the left but other than that, no reaction.

"Nothing happened," I called back.

"Hit it harder," the old sheila suggested.

I did with very similar results, although I caught a glimpse of something under the helmet. It didn't seem dangerous, though, so I bent down to get a closer look. The helmet was deadset dripping with slime, monster spit I reckoned, and as I moved around to the front of it, I could see the unmistakable off-white of bone glinting in the sun.

"What is it?" Gia was moving closer.

"A skull." I sighed, relieved and a bit disgusted.

"Whose skull?" one of the blokes wanted to know.

"One of the Pigs?" I shrugged. "Couldn't really tell ya which one."

"Well, that one certainly didn't kill the monster. Still, it can't have got all of them, right?" Gia was trying to hide her tension with chatter, and if I didn't know her so well, it might have worked.

"I'm sure there are some left ahead," I said.

But I wasn't so sure at all. In fact, I was beginning to think we'd be better off turning around and running like buggery.

We unconsciously moved closer to one another as we walked down the streef, eyes moving back and forth – ready for anything from anywhere. Curiosity was fighting fear inside me, and I was starting to think I should throw in the towel and concede the match to fear. Safer that way.

My heart was smacking into my ribcage and I was drenched in sweat by the time we turned the corner and we all stopped, gaping at what was in front of us.

It took a few moments to work out what I was looking at. This was partly due to the full brightness of the sun blasting into our eyes but also the strangeness of the scene. At first it seemed like the wide area in which we stood – an area clearly excavated and tamped flat – was a graveyard of some kind. Tiny tombstones stood in neat, precise rows in a rough triangular formation, with the pointy end faced away from us. But, of course, they weren't tombstones, they were–

"Helmets," I said to no one in particular. "They're Pig helmets."

Although I didn't count them, I would have put good money on there being sixdy-nine gleaming, slimy Pig helmets arranged just so. I toed one that was close to my foot and glimpsed a skinless skull beneath it.

Gia, following my cue, lifted anothery – same story. A wide-eyed human skull, preserved in monster goop, underneath the helmet. We all breathed in the scale of the… what, trophy display? Warning to others? Some kind of modern yarts gear?

Just then a cloud moved over the sun. Or what I thought was a cloud, but when I followed the gargantuan shadow back to its source I realised, with a spasm of nightmarish dismay, that it was the monster, now massive after gorging itself on the Pigs, and moving slowly around its domain, in an oddly distracted, contemplative fashion.

Its back was to us and it hadn't seen us yet so, I reasoned to myself, if we backed out the way we came real slowly and didn't make any sudden movements, we had a chance of walking out of this. I specifically made eye contact with Gia, the sheila and the one bloke.

Wait, *one* bloke? Where was–

Flap flap flap flap flap flap flap flap.

I followed the sound with my eyes and watched in horror as the other bloke pissbolted down the streef, away from us, thonged feet slapping on the ground. I snapped my head back to the monster and was relieved to see it hadn't turned around. The relief was short lived, but. Because just then two slits appeared in the huge expanse of rippling back meat. They lengthened, grew and then, with a wet, ripping sound, pulled open, revealing two huge, bronze eyes glaring. I heard Gia gasp behind me and felt her arm grip mine hard, but I couldn't move. I was frozen to the spot, those eyes boring into my very soul.

Then movement around them as holes, no – mouths – many, many mouths – peeled open and started hissing angrily, a riot of angry flesh. Gia jerked me, hard, and I came out of my stupor blinking. There was nothing for it but to–

"RUN!"

I'm not proud of what happened next, but I reckon it's important that I tell the truth of it. The whole caper reminded me of a thing Ken used to tell me – it wasn't quite a story and it wasn't quite a joke, but it had elements of both of those things.

Two blokes are in a forest when they hear a tiger roar and they can tell it's getting closer. One of the blokes starts stretching and getting ready to bolt. The other bloke says, "You reckon you're gunna run faster than a tiger?"

First bloke replies: "I don't need to run faster than a tiger, just faster than you."

It's an old story by all accounts but something about it always struck me as very revealing of the nature of humanity and that. Well, that story was running through my head even as Gia and I were outrunning the bloke and the older sheila. I caught something of betrayal in her eyes as we passed her, and it stung, but it didn't stop me pumping my legs and moving onwards. Predictably the monster got her first, landing with an enormous thump right in front of her. It opened its arms wide and dozens of tentacles shot out of it, wrapping around her like living occy straps and absorbing her within seconds. I dared to glance back once to see it fully consume her, snarl and start racing towards us again.

I didn't see the bloke behind us get taken, but I heard his scream abruptly cut off and then a nauseating squelching sound.

We turned the corner to see the bloke who'd run first had tripped over the single helmet and done himself a mischief. He was clutching his ankle in agony and attempting to get to his feet, tears streaming down his face as his body refused to obey his commands.

I'd like to tell youse me and Gia grabbed an arm each and helped the fella to his feet. That we carried him between us, because if you lose your humanity in the face of terror, what point is there to humanity anyway?

I'd *like* to tell youse that, but I'd be speaking out my arse.

We ran straight past the bloke, barely pausing to look back at him, and ignored his outraged cries. We weren't running faster than the tiger, but we were faster than him. Poor bastard.

We felt a thump as the monster landed and I might have heard a scream but to be honest I wasn't really focused on anything other than putting one foot in front of the othery. It became clear we'd escaped, at least for the time being, when we were running past the pub. Gia and I turned around to see an empty streef and no sign of the monster. Still, we weren't gunna hang about.

The two slow-talking cits from earlier were still outside, sharing a ciggie and looking vacant. I slumped to my knees, panting and looked at the older one.

"T-tell everyone inside," I panted, "tell e-everyone you see…"

"Tell 'em what, mate?" he asked, seemingly oblivious to the terror in mine and Gia's eyes, and the desperate state of us.

"Tell 'em…" I trailed off. What should we tell them?

"Tell them," Gia spoke in a stable tone, "that the Inasiddy is lost. The monster's won."

TWENTY-FIVE

Gia and I slogged back through town, towards the hab, like two soldiers returning from a particularly debilitating battle. The goey had mostly worn off – taking the quick way out of our systems via the terror-sweats – and now we were left with a comedown, hangover and exy-stencil dread combo.

It was shithouse.

A few cits watched curiously as we shambled past but, due to the heat of the day and the rumours of impending monster attack, it was a mercifully event-free journey. We were a cuppla blocks from home when Gia finally spoke.

"What are we gunna do, Frang?"

"Get home. Tell Ken. Make plans." I'd been wondering the same thing but was putting on a brave face.

"There's no way to beat that thing." Gia spoke with a defeated tone I'd never heard from her before. "Like, it's too much. It's too… I don't even know how to say it."

I didn't either but I think I got what she meant. It was too huge a concept for an individual person's brain to grasp, this strange, malevolent thing.

This terrifying *other*.

"Ken will know what to do." I spoke in my most reassuring fashion, but I had to wonder. Had the situation spiralled out of control?

Was I just kidding myself?

We flopped in through the front door and sunk into the closest seats. I could hear the sounds of the kids playing outside but I was just too knackered to say g'day, plus I was enjoying the peace. A few moments later, Ken came inside and clocked me and G. He nodded once and started busying himself in the kitchen.

"Looks like you two could use a feed." He spoke without judgement or reproach, which was real nice given the circumstances.

"Thanks, Ken. That'd be grouse. Wouldn't it, G?"

But when I turned to Gia, she was dead to the world and snoring. I looked up at Ken, who was faced away from me and busying himself, and tried to find the words to explain our predicament.

"Ken… things are… like… not good."

"Save it, mate. Food first, then talk."

I sighed and slumped back into my chair. Despite everything, it felt good to be home. I closed my eyes and somehow managed to fall into a light doze right there at the table.

• • • •

Around the same time as Ken was cooking me and Gia a hearty feed, less tasty events transpired in the Inasiddy. It wasn't the monster that kicked off the next disaster, or at least not directly. The crowd from the pub – the cits G and I had warned – headed over to the Harbour Bridge barrier to tell the Pigs that their brothers and sisters in arms had been maggoted by the monster. Or at least, that was the idea. I don't doubt that the original intent had been to just inform the Pigs of the bad news and inquire as to what might be the next logical step in remaining alive. However, the mob that headed over there grew in size and seemed to lose focus, especially when early-morning pissed and high cits added to their number.

An individual can be grouse. A group of people are mostly okay. A mob, however, is usually a packa cunce, no matter how righteous their cause.

By the time the large group – just under a hundred strong if reports are to be believed – lobbed up at the barrier, some had started chanting, others fanging rocks, so the reception they got from the Pigs was... less than friendly.

Adding fuel to the growing fire was the fact the barrier had been reinforced since the day before. Almost as if the Pigs had abandoned us to the monster, fortifying their own lofty position in the Big End, leaving us to cark it. Regardless if that was the goal, or just what was infurred, things kicked off in short order and a riot commenced.

It was a little half-hearted and disorganised, due to its impromptu nature and the fact it was real early, but it was the beginning of something potentially wider, nastier and more far-ranging. Veterans of the Water Wars in particular would have recognised the all-too-familiar signs of bloody revolution.

When the blue ended with lots of injuries but mercifully no loss of life, the cits nearby likely breathed a collective sigh of relief. The Pigs were bruised but alive with their barrier intact, the cits were bleeding but still walking, having expressed their discontent. Perhaps the day wasn't such a bad one.

That's when the monster entered the scene.

Of this particular attack we don't know very much as the majority of the witnesses were killed. Those who later told us the story were mainly ensconced around the outer edges of the danger zone. What we can gather is that the monster – enormous and bristling with glory-rage – entered the scene armed. I mean that literal-like *and* metaphorically. It had somehow grown more arms, stories have it as either six, eight or "a fousand" – that last one from an unlikely source of information, though. Each of these new limbs held a weapon – a Pig gun – and after the damn thing landed on the streef, it opened fire, spraying projectiles all throughout the crowd, bursting bodies left and right.

The gunfire continued for nigh on fifdeen minutes, the creature reloading and firing anew, stitching the concrete with holes and knocking the edges off buildings. A rumour that each of the heads that swarmed in the monster's bulbous mass wore a Pig helmet spread for a while, but have since been mostly dismissed as the embellishments of overactive imaginations. What can be confirmed is that all of the cits involved in the riots were maggoted with extreme prejudice, and not a single Pig was harmed.

This was an important detail as even the dimmest of cits could now grasp the nature of this thing. It was taking on aspects of the personalities it consumed.

Most of the Pigs fled, but the one who remained a little longer was heard to describe the monster's consumption of the corpses as, "A meat orgy… a fuggen meat orgy… swirling… chaos… horrible… horrible…"

We'll never know for sure what happened, but what can be confirmed is that the beast consumed those it killed and began to tear through the Inasiddy streefs, punching enormous holes in crumbling buildings and tearing storefronts to pieces.

In a very real way, the monster was having a riot of its own.

• • • •

I knew nothing of the monster riot at the time, of course. As the pub crew were heading over to the bridge barrier, I was waking up to a steaming plate of Ken's 'special stew', itself a bit of a meat orgy, but one I would defo enjoy.

Summoned by the smell of fresh-cooked grub, Gia snapped awake. Ken served us both brimming bowls and we ate them down like a cuppla starving dogs. The sound of the ruggies playing cricket, or some variation thereof, was a nice accompaniment to our sloppy munching noises.

We were both on to our second helpings when Ken sat down across from us and began speaking.

"So, things are bad then?"

"Very," I mumbled between mouthfuls.

"Pig's arsehole," Gia agreed.

"Tell me." Ken smiled at us. So we did. It took a while, me and Gia shared the storytelling duties, tagging in when the other wanted to continue eating, but we got there in the end. Ken stroked his chin, staring off into the distance.

"So different personalities keep vying for control," he mused. "Do you know if the Pigs tried appealing to the Redmund consciousness?"

"No idea," I admitted. "Maybe they tried and it somehow set the monster off. Or maybe they didn't try at all and it just killed them anyway, used their bodies as decorations. That kinda gear is pretty common in the Downlow, so it's hard to say."

"This thing, this catalyst, it's designed to thrive in any environment, but I can't believe this rage, this lust for destruction, was intended. It doesn't make any sense. We need to speak to someone involved in its creation, see if there are any potential weaknesses we can exploit," Ken murmured.

"Reckon you might have burnt your bridges with Garold and Minerva, eh, Ken."

"That I have," he agreed. "But there's someone else we haven't talked to yet. First things first, Gia? I need you to get the ruggies on the wagon I've hired, and their gear, and head over to the Arr Ess Ell."

"What good is that gunna do?" Gia asked.

"For a start, I'll be paying you a shitload for it," Ken told her. "Secondly, whatever happens here will be bad news for the kids. Even if it all goes to plan, there's going to be things they just… shouldn't see. Besides, if it goes badly here, you'll have some ex-soldiers around for protection."

"Righto, then." Gia nodded and licked her bowl.

"This isn't a venture I enter into lightly, you understand," Ken continued, "but things aren't gunna get better by themselves."

"So, what's the actual plan, Ken?" I was curious as to why he'd remained so vague on the details.

But before Ken could get into it, Tommy and Bella, giggling like lunatics, ran in through the back door, squabbling good-naturedly, and we had to do that thing where we all pretended we weren't talking about scary adult shit.

The kids were happy to see me and G, and we were happy to see them. We started spruiking their big exciting trip to the Arr Ess Ell, making it sound like a fabulous getaway and not a calculated retreat designed to give them their best chance of living through the ongoing disaster. It was surprisingly easy. Kids, even mutie kids with rough pasts, tend to want to believe in the essential good nature of the adults who control their lives. I don't think it's optimism so much as a way of retaining innocence for as long as possible. It was a conspiracy I was happy to help feed, because these kids deserved the best possible chance they could get. They deserved every chance at happiness.

So, let's make them feel excited and happy, and not scared and alone.

So, we played. G, Ken and me, we played with all the ruggies like we'd never played before. Indulged their whims, accepted their weird game premises and gave each one of them an unusual amount of personal attention. Hugged them, made it clear we loved them all and they were important to us.

We mighta laid it on a bit thick because Bella got wary.

"Why are you guys being so friendlyaaa?" she asked, her eyes slitted with suspicion, a dribble of fluid running down her face.

"We're not!" Gia exclaimed, about three octaves too high.

"Just happy to see youse kids, is all," I replied, breaking eye contact in a very suspect fashion.

"Franga," Bella intoned, her eyes barely even open now, "are you gunna come with usaaaa?"

Shit.

"Um, well, like… eventually I'll join youse at the–"

But it was too late. Bella had started crying, which set some of the younger ruggies off and then even the older ones began to sook. It was a bloody disaster. By the time the three of us had shouted, coaxed and cajoled the various tantrums down to weepy grumping, we were exhausted all over again.

One frenzied crap-pack later, we bundled the puffy-faced ruggies into the wagon, administering forehead kisses and hugs, along with promises of a reunion soon. Gia gave me a look of exaggerated pain as she stepped onto the back of the wagon.

"Why am I doing this again?" She spoke at a level only I would be able to hear.

"A shitload of dosh, wasn't it?"

"Ah yes, right you are." Gia smiled. "I'll see you soon. Look after Ken, yeah?"

"Always," I answered, trying to ignore the horrible premonition that I'd never see her again.

The wagon started moving, mutie horse clip-clopping away, and just before it rounded the corner, Bella shoved her head out the back of the wagon and yelled: "I LOVE YOU, FRANGA! I'LL MISS YOUAAAAA!"

"I LOVE YOU TOO!" I yelled back. "AND I'LL SEE YOU SOON!"

Then the wagon turned the corner and they were out of sight, and I was wiping tears from my eyes.

Ken pretended not to notice and we stood there in rueful silence. I was about to say something when a sound rang out, louder and longer than before.

It was the monster's roar, of course. After it had taken care of its bloody business, it filled the heavens with its noise, either crowing triumphantly, wailing sadly or some unknowable third option.

We stayed outside for a bit, and soon the streef was filled with mutie horses pulling shonky-looking carts as refugees displaced by the attacks moved through the night, attempting to find safe harbour on the outskirts, and presumably further afield if forced.

"Hey, where's the monster now?" I called out to a family of four who were piled into a very structurally unsound-looking contraption pulled by a donkey the size of a fat dog.

"It killded our hab!" a sweet-faced boy intoned, bottom lip a-quiver. His mum pulled him closer and glared at me.

"Fuggoff mutie!" the dad yelled and went back to slapping the backside of their tiny mule. Bloke musta bought the thing on special, because not only was it small, it looked likely to keel over at any moment.

"Good luck," I called back, too tired and sad to be angry. The daughter smiled up at me.

"You too," she said, "and we're from Central."

"Cheers, ta."

The dad slapped the daughter but she didn't cry and looked defiantly back at him. He turned around and they kept moving along in silence. I waved once and then they were gawn, swallowed by the dark.

Central was barely six blocks from the hab. Judging by its movements thus far, the monster could be coming in a matter of hours.

"Won't be long before it destroys the whole Inasiddy," sighed Ken.

"Spose we'd better hear this plan of yours then, eh?"

"I suppose so."

TWENTY-SIX

All told it took about an hour to assemble the "special room". Ken helped as best he could but after twenny or so minutes he sat down and assisted in more of an advisory capacity. That is: told me where to put stuff and offered "constructive criticism" when I got it wrong.

What I had to do was place Ken's big leather chair right in the middle of the hab's second floor. Then around the chair I set up a complicated apparatus consisting of a bewildering array of occy straps, sturdy chains and little metal boxes that all led to a collapsible tripod with an empty mount behind the chair.

I asked Ken what he was gunna put in the mount but he just muttered, "All in good time" and went back to moody silence punctuated by occasional instructions. Ken reckoned the end result looked like an old-fashioned electric train set, but the way he said it suggested it was more of a personal observation and not anything that required my input.

"So, we done?" I asked, standing and stretching, my back muscles popping from the strain.

"One last piece of the puzzle," Ken replied, holding a small black box in his hands, "and I have some instructions for you."

Ken handed me a folded sheet of paper on which he'd scribed a list of questions and notes. They were a strange lot and I couldn't make head nor tails of them.

"What are these for?"

"The interrogation," Ken said sombrely.

"Who are we interrogating?"

Ken looked into my eyes, all serious-like. "Me."

I reacted as you might expect. Asked him if he was mental, what the hell he was talking about – had he been necking grog on the sly, that sorta thing. Ken nodded as if expecting these questions and wandered over to his chair and sat down.

"Forty-odd years ago, I walked away from my life. From the job of a lifetime, from a relationship with someone I loved, because of something I'd done," Ken said, gesturing with the black box. "I changed my identity and even removed the memories of whatever it was from my brain. I've been storing them, along with a bunch of other inventions from my previous life, in the back of my chair."

This was news to me and I wondered briefly if Ken was having one of his turns.

"I think, from my recent aquatic misadventure, I can work out, broadly speaking, why I did it: guilt or horror at what I'd unleashed. Somehow, technology I helped create has caused what's roaring and killing and smashing up the Inasiddy. Well, I want to know if there's some way to stop the bloody thing and the best way to do that is by asking Stephen Blentiff."

"Jeez, Ken," I spoke softly. "That sounds awful drastic."

"It needs to happen, mate." Ken sighed wearily. "Plus I'm sick of my history having a big question mark hanging over it."

"Like the sword of Damo Cleese," I mused, stroking my chin.

Ken smiled sadly. "Just like that, Frang."

"So, what's the go with all the chains and widgets and stuff?"

"I don't know how I – or rather the old me – will react to being woken up in my body. I – he – could be violent or aggressive or mad with sorrow and try to kill himself. Myself."

"You reckon it could get that bad?"

"Mate, I removed part of my brain – actual living tissue – to get rid of these memories. That and my trip to Research Station Alpha suggests… this ain't gunna be a picnic."

"So, your memories and everything… in that box, yeah?"

Ken nodded and opened the box, sliding the dark lid back and pulling out a silvery contraption that looked a bit like a metal carrot, with a razor-sharp blade at the pointy end. Inside a clear section of the thing, I could see a mound of reddish-grey flesh. The muted light in the hab made it seem like the thing was… moving, twitching, but that wasn't possible.

"Is that your… like… brain?"

"Tissue, memories, the other me. Clearly, I wasn't ready to off myself entirely," Ken said and then held out the metal carrot.

"What do you want me to do with it?"

"Bung it on the tripod, turn it on and then stand right the hell back. It'll know what to do."

"How do you know that for sure?"

"I don't know… I just do. Whatever the memory erasing process might be, it's far from an exact science and some stuff just… stuck around. Now go on, do as I say."

I reluctantly took the carrot. It was heavier than it looked. Ken began strapping his legs down and fastening them with chains.

"I'm not smart like you, Ken, but deadset this feels like some shonky business."

"I know," he muttered, strapping his stump down with his good hand. "Can you do my othery?"

I nodded and strapped Ken into his own chair. I tugged on the restraints. They were secure. I walked around to the back of the chair and gingerly attached the carrot to the mount. Nothing happened.

"Did it click?"

"No."

"Push it in until you hear a click."

I didn't like holding the damn thing; it was warm and the flesh inside made me uncomfortable, plus the blade at the front of it looked like it could do a bloke some serious mischief. Still, this was Ken, so I put a little more pressure on it and it clicked into place.

Nothing happened.

"Huh," I said, "maybe it's broke–"

That's when it sprang to life.

If it'd resembled a carrot before, it quickly took on the appearance of some kinda insect, like a mechanical cockroach. Six silver "legs" sproinked out either side and quickly clamped down on the tripod, holding itself tightly in position. Meanwhile, the front end opened up and a bright red dot appeared on the back of Ken's bonce, moving around as if searching for something. The dot came to rest on Ken's old scar and the thing jittered closer, making an eerie buzzing noise. I got the unsettling impression the carrot was alive, sniffing at Ken's flesh and eager to do… something.

"It seems real interested in your scar, Ken." I tried to keep the note of warning light.

"That makes sense, son."

"Oh yeah?"

"Yeah, it needs a way in."

"Eh?"

Four more legs popped out from the top of the cockroach and formed a rough square on the part of Ken's head that contained the scar tissue and latched onto his skin. Ken hissed slightly and I began to wonder if I should find a length of wood to smash the strange thing to pieces. Just then the thingo shot forth another appendage, singular this time, that whipped from its face and into Ken, dribbling a blue fluid.

"Durries!"

"That's just the anesthetic. Everything's fine."

The buzzing noise ramped up and the blade at the front started spinning in a circular motion, becoming a deadly steel cutting device. It moved towards the section of flesh it had clamped, heading down to the bottom of the scar and pausing, briefly, as if double checking its location.

Then, with an almighty lurch that almost knocked over the tripod, it shot upwards, drawing a red line the entire length of the scar. A line that, a second or two later, started oozing blood, then gushing it. More legs emerged from the device and grabbed either side of the skin flaps and reefed them open like grisly curtains.

I confess I had to turn away for a moment here as I was feeling funny in the head and didn't want to faint. A couple of deep breaths later, I turned back to see that the thingo had stitched up the worst of the injury – which still seeped a lot of the red stuff – but was more focused on a specific section of skin right at the back of Ken's skull.

"Don't untie me until you're sure it's really *me*, Frang." Ken's voice sounded a bit mushy, but otherwise fine.

"Righto," I agreed.

Then the thingo drilled right into the back of Ken's skull and opened up, real wide, inserting the thin tube that housed Ken's – or Stephen's – brain into the recently dug opening. There was a sickeningly wet shunting noise and an equally disturbing thunk as the tube found a home. Ken lurched and jerked and then flopped in his seat, unconscious. The thingo was ready for this and moved accordingly, tending to the bleeding gash and stitching up the worst areas. I realised this was technology the like of which I'd never seen, from the olden days, and for a moment I felt untethered from everything I'd always believed to be reality. This was a thingo from a time when a bloke could extend his lifespan, cure disease or regrow limbs. It was like magic and I was both scared and fascinated by it.

But as awe-inspiring as it was, I had a job to do, and I made sure the list of questions was still in my pocket. My sweaty palms found it and I squeezed it to reassure myself. I cleared my throat and walked around to the front of Ken.

Speak in a loud, clear voice, the note at the top of the question sheet said. *Be polite but firm. Don't leave the subject with any doubt as to who is in charge.*

I re-read the instruction and nodded to myself. Righto, then.

"Stephen Blentiff? Can you hear me, Stephen?"

He remained slumped over, breathing but unconscious. The only sound was the whining of the thingo, tending to the very wounds it had created.

"Stephen. I need you to wake up. I have questions."

Still nothing. I began to panic. Had something gawn wrong? Was the thingo busted? Had I made a mistake? Had I killed Ken?

"Stephen? Ken?"

I moved close to Ken's face, practically touching it with mine. "Mate?"

Ken's head jerked up; his eyes looked directly into mine. He opened his mouth and started screaming.

Ken's scream echoed through the hab, flying off the walls and ceiling like a trapped pigeon. He maintained an impressive volume for a surprisingly long time, his wide eyes shooting from his surroundings to his bindings, to me, and back again, with an erratic energy borne of fear.

I had a quick squiz at my notes, then turned my attention back to Ken.

Stephen! The man in the chair is Stephen. Ken isn't here right now.

I had to keep reminding myself that no matter how much he looked or sounded like Ken, this man wasn't my mentor or the closest thing I'd had to a proper parent.

This was a stranger. A potentially dangerous one at that.

"Breathe, Stephen, take deep breaths and try to calm down."

Stephen didn't reply but he seemed to hear me, his breathing going from shallow and rapid to deeper and slower. He was clearly still terrified and confused, but that was better than screaming, I reckoned.

"I understand this must be very confusing for you," I said slowly and softly, like he was a ruggie I was trying to calm down after a particularly bad nightmare. "But I want to assure you that you're not in any danger."

Pretty bold claim to make to a bloke who was tied up in a chair, but my demeena relaxed Stephen to the point where he looked at me and actually seemed to see me as real, as a person, for the first time.

"Where am I?"

"I suppose you could say we're in the hab of a mutual friend." I smiled.

"Jesus, what's wrong with your eyes?"

I tried not to flinch. Every stranger who reacted to my mutations made me feel a bit shit, doubly so when they looked like Ken.

"Have you been in an accident? A particularly cruel and violent one?"

"My eyes are just like this. I'm a mutant, y'see."

"A mutant..." The way he said the word was strange, like it was an exotic dish or the name of some far-off country.

"Yep. Yellow skin, too. Plus, I can jump real good."

"A mutant... but... wait... what year is it?"

I told him and the colour leached out of his face and he looked like he was about to faint.

"Don't forget to breathe, Stephen."

I walked over to the side of the hab and grabbed a plastic crate. I was going to use it as a seat, because I had a feeling this was going to take some time.

Stephen took a while to calm down. I managed to get him to swallow some water and breathe deeply. He was still pale, but alert, when we resumed our little chat.

Using Ken's notes as my guide, I began. "Stephen, what's the last thing you remember?"

"Why am I tied up?"

Ken had anticipated this question, writing: *If he asks about his bindings, explain that...*

"It's for your own safety," I told him, reading from the sheet verb-ate-em.

"That sounds like a rehearsed response. Safety from whom?"

"From yourself. From potential harm and that." As I was saying the words, they seemed to come out wrong, weak – like they couldn't stand under the weight of their bags fulla bullshit.

"Seems to me I'm in a room tied to a chair with only you for company. Not a lot of harmful influences. Other than yourself."

I was incensed. "I wouldn't harm ya!"

"You don't have to lie." He looked me right in the eyes, sympathetic-like.

"I'm not!"

"You're a mutant."

"So?"

"You're clearly here for revenge."

"I'm not... what... eh?" Fuggen hell, this was all going tits up. I was confused and defensive. He'd somehow turned the tables on me within seconds, although to be fair, Ken had warned me he might.

The line *Ask a question instead of giving him an answer* was underlined three times on the sheet, so I figured I'd give it a go.

"Why do you think I'd want revenge on you?" It wasn't just an interrogation technique, but. I was legit curious.

"You're a mutant. I imagine most mutants would wish me a great deal of harm, and worse."

"How come?"

Stephen narrowed his eyes. "You really don't know?"

"I'm asking the questions here," I said, attempting to assert an authority I didn't feel. "Now, why would mutantkind have a vendetta against you?"

"Because…" Stephen seemed unsure of how to proceed. He stopped, took a moment and then restarted. "Because I created you."

My heart stopped. It didn't make any sense, but I asked anyway: "You're me dad?"

"In a manner of speaking," Stephen explained. "I'm the father of all of you. I created mutantkind."

TWENTY-SEVEN

"It wasn't on purpose of course; it was an accident." Stephen spoke with far more confidence than you'd expect of a bloke tied to a chair. "Minerva, Garold, Gabriel and myself had been working nonstop. Desperately trying to finish before the damage to New Sydney became too great. You've got to understand, we were trying to save the city! The Water Wars were dreadful – both to civilians and infrastructure – and we needed some way to arrest the constant fires and debilitating disease the sun was causing now that the ozone had been stripped from the sky.

"Previously, NanoCorp had put all its resources into building a dome that would cover New Sydney and the attendant suburbs. The plan was to consolidate and rebuild as best we could. But the sheer destruction and loss of personnel put paid to that plan. So, we had to try something desperate… something unique and seemingly mad."

"The U-drones," I murmured.

Stephen nodded. "A branch of freak science. A perfect biomechanical organism. I suppose NanoCorp were of the opinion that if the whole project went spectacularly badly, they could blame it on the strange underwater scientists who came up with the idea. I was so sure of my genius that I risked becoming a pariah."

"And it worked, didn't it?"

"Not without a few missteps. The first flock of drones we released into the air had too much autonomy and simply flew away. We never did recover them – bold bastards." Stephen chuckled to himself. "But in retrospect the stumbles were minor and the results borderline miraculous. Within days of the launch proper, we had a self-aware canopy that blocked the worst of the sun's UV rays and flocked to the places with the highest population density. It wasn't hard. The Water Wars had reduced our numbers to barely one-tenth of what they once were. Plus, with the augmentations we added to the drones, the sun's rays literally powered the bloody things, allowing their wingspan to grow organically. A perfect combination of biotech and genetic engineering and... I can see by your eyes glazing over that I'm losing you."

I snapped upright. "Soz."

"It's fine." Stephen smiled. "I spend too much time with scientists. I forget how much you civvies are deeply unenthused by shop talk."

"So, the U-drones were grouse," I prompted him. "Everything was beaut, yeah?"

"Yes," he agreed. "At least at first. And then it happened. The same thing that always happens when humanity reaches a new milestone: greed entered the equation. Sure, it's great to provide shelter and safety freely to a group of fiscally diverse cits... but what if one could deliver superior shelter to those who could pay for it? And, while we're on the subject, do those dreary proles really need all that shade? I mean, they're not doing anything with it, are they? Lowering property values and such while they lounge around in squalor... perhaps we should restrict the better U-drone tech to geographical areas that deserve it. And so on and so on..." Stephen made a circular gesture with his stump, a motion that seemed to indicate the hopelessly cyclical nature of mankind's endeavours.

"So why did you go along with it?" I asked in a soft voice.

"Why do you assume I did?"

"I looked out this window, had a squiz at the sky. Saw the difference between what's hovering over the Inasiddy versus the Big End of Town."

"Everyone has their price."

"What was yours?"

"A virtually limitless budget and unfettered access to the best equipment in continuing my research into biological nanotechnology: thinking, living machines purpose-built to assist in the betterment of all humankind."

"Or at least the type of humankind who can afford it?"

"Quite." A toothy smile appeared. "You catch on quickly."

"So, what went wrong?"

"At first? Nothing. It was all like a dream. Doover-fish cleansed the wells, grunters roamed the land and U-drones filled the sky, and my newest enterprise looked to be even bigger, more important. And then the dream turned into a nightmare and I became aware of something to which I should have been paying far more attention: the side effects."

Stephen winced as if the very act of reliving the memory caused him physical pain.

"I didn't hear the first reports of birth defects until I was five years into the project, although from what I can gather they'd begun mere months after the drones were launched and had been kept, quite deliberately, from my attention. It wasn't so much the drones themselves but the pollution from their manufacture that was the problem. The disposal of the dangerous chemicals we used took place far from the laboratories and NanoCorp headquarters. Theoretically, they were meant to be confined to the Downlow. However, people got lazy, or they weren't paid enough, or... who knows? Point is, lots of toxic materials were being improperly dumped in areas of the Inasiddy, close to dense population centres."

"Not in the Big End of Town, though, eh?"

"No," Stephen admitted. "Initially the mutations were fairly standard but as time went on, it became clear that this was quite unlike anything we'd seen before."

"So, what'd *you* do?" I found myself becoming angry. "Why didn't you try to stop them?"

"I did." He looked at me grimly. "I marched into NanoCorp headquarters and even saw the CEO, Bazza Lornville. Ghastly man, I sincerely hope he's dead now. But it was all to no avail. Part of my contract for the U-drones removed me as owner of the technology and any side effects that may have occurred were simply beyond my control."

"But there were ruggies, kids and that, being born mutants. Surely that's against the law!"

"There wasn't much law at the time, and certainly the notion of being sued was beyond ludicrous. I suppose they thought it was just easier, an acceptable price to pay."

I cracked the shits then. Got right up in Stephen's face and angled a lantern at my eyes, enjoying the bitter triumph I felt as he tried to turn away.

"Does this look acceptable to you? Ya fugger, does this look ACCEPTABLE AT ALL?" Spit trickled down my lips but I just kept staring into his eyes, boring into him.

"Of course not. After Bazza brushed it aside, I headed back to the research station, fully intent on galvanising Minerva, Garold and Gabriel into action."

"So, what happened?"

Stephen made a sound then. A strangled sort of noise that was a weird hybrid of laugh and cough.

"They knew." He spoke in a disbelieving voice. "All three of them were completely aware of it and none of them cared. Oh, Gabriel was probably the most sympathetic, but ultimately it was all for show – wringing his hands but doing nothing."

Through Ken and Stephen's combined stories, I'd worked out that Gabriel was the poor, pale cit who got road scabbed back at the beginning of this whole sorry affair. I didn't exactly feel good about his hideous maggoting – very few cits deserve such an end – but I certainly felt less sympathy for him than I had previous-like.

"In fact," Stephen continued, "in Garold's case, it spurred a new series of experiments using… using living mutants as test subjects."

But, wait a second, I thought, *when Ken was telling me about his time underwater, didn't that Garold bloke reckon that was Stephen's idea?*

"What'd you do then, Stephen?" But I already knew, didn't I? The overlap between Ken's story and Stephen's was almost complete.

"I came up with an astonishingly foolish scheme. It started off as a suicidal impulse: if I killed myself, I'd be off and unaware, I'd be able to cause no more harm and yet… I couldn't quite bring myself to accept that finality. I didn't want to die. Besides, my research had already been adopted, the damage was done and continued to be done, perhaps not in my name but with my discovery. So, I couldn't live with the memories of what I'd caused and I couldn't die… so I created a third option."

"Chopped your brain up." I whistled. Whatever I thought of Stephen, he was, in his way, a brave bastard.

"Not quite." Stephen smiled. "I managed to isolate certain chains and synaptic networks associated with memory to be placed in a cryo-crib that would sustain the living tissue, keep it active if unaware, to be reactivated if and when it was ever needed. Suicide without a corpse. The reversible death of my specific identity but not the knowledge and experience that went with it."

"It didn't quite go according to plan, Stephen. Ken's mind was always a bit… skew-whiff."

"Ken?" Stephen raised an eyebrow.

"Kenneth Ages. Your… replacement. When we asked 'im how long he'd been alive, he'd always answer–"

"Ken Ages!" Stephen cackled uproariously, just like Ken would have. "That cheeky bugger. Well, look, it was a rush job. If I'd had more time, I could have created a better mind map and been more surgical about the whole thing, but…"

Stephen tried to shrug but the bindings made it seem like fidgeting. I understood his intent.

"Why not stay and fight as Stephen? You were well regarded, a prominent scientist and that, surely you could have had more impact as that than a blob of meat in a tube."

"I've been alive for a fair whack of time and in that not insignificant period I've realised something: you can't beat the system. Not in a direct, head-on battle. As much as you want to break its walls and tear it to pieces with your bare hands… it's beyond you. Beyond any individual. Futile. So, I did the best I could. I took my dangerous mind off the table, to make a better world or, at the very least, allow one to grow." Stephen took a deep breath and sat back in his seat, taking the minimal amount of comfort he could find.

"That's some schmicko mouth-gear, Stephen," I said, meaning it.

"Thank you."

"Pity it's bullshit, eh?"

"What do you mean?"

"Look," I said, standing up, "I reckon you probs were heaps appalled by what was going on but you didn't fang your brain into a metal carrot because you couldn't beat the system – you did it because you were scared. You left the hard yakka up to a version of yourself you'd never meet and kept your old self safe and able to be, like, reactivated at a later date. Like now. I'm not saying I woulda done any better – maybe not – but you should have done more. 'Make a better world' my festy clack! You should have stuck around and even if you couldn't tear NanoCorp to pieces, you could have, at the very fuggen least, assisted with the muties you bloody created!"

"In a way I did–"

"NO, MATE, NO." I was fair bellowing into his face. "*Ken* fuggen did. And you don't get to take credit for his goodness!"

I turned around and started kicking the crate that had been my seat and kept on laying the boot in until I'd given it a rough journey around the room. Stephen said nothing and I took a moment to calm down, get my breathing under control.

"I'm sorry," Stephen eventually whispered.

"Righto," I muttered noncommittally and felt slightly ashamed as I walked over to pick up the crate, which frankly looked none the worse for wear at all despite my best efforts.

"I honestly thought I was doing what was best," he sighed.

I grabbed the crate and carried it back to my sitting place in front of Stephen. We had a lot more ground to cover and I couldn't keep spitting the dummy every ten minutes.

Deep breaths, Franga. You've got this, son.

"Let's move on. I've got a lot more to ask and limited time." I tried to sound professional.

"For what it's worth–"

"It's worth nothing." My voice was icy. "The only good you can do is help me and Ken. After that you can bugger off back to your stick. Now, tell me about the monster."

"Monster?" Stephen looked legit flummoxed.

"Yeah, one of your mates, that Gabriel bloke? He pissed off to the Downlow with one of your little projects. Got maggoted, but."

"Which project?" Stephen became very still.

"It was a shiny type of thingo. When it came in contact with a massive grunter, it made the thing go berko, started absorbing Derros. Now it's this big monster."

"The catalyst?" Stephen asked in a hushed, awed voice. "You're talking about the catalyst."

"Yeah, that's the one."

Stephen sat up as straight as he was able, straining against his bonds, face tense. "Did they get it to work? Is it out there? Tell me!"

I was so shocked by his abrupt change I almost fell off my crate.

"I need details," Stephen hissed, his entire body rigid. "Tell me everything you know!"

I opened my mouth to say something when an arm as strong as steel suddenly curled around my neck, holding me in a vice grip. I could barely move, and was thinking, *the bloke holding me must be bloody enormous,* when a woman's voice spoke close to my ear:

"No. Don't do that."

I thought I was about as surprised as a bloke could be when Stephen, looking at the sheila who held me, said: "Hello, Eva."

"Hello, Stephen," she answered.

TWENTY-EIGHT

I tried to turn my face up to Eva, but her grip was utterly unbreakable, so I just squirmed for a bit, like a grub on a fish hook.

"Are you going to behave if I let you go, Franga?" Eva spoke sternly.

I was bloody behaving before, ya moll.

"Yiss," I managed to gasp.

"Okay, but any sudden moves and I become extraordinarily unpleasant."

The vice grip stopped all of a sudden and I gasped out a few breaths, trying to get rid of the tingly, light-headed feeling that had me all wobbly-like. I shook my head and had a squiz at Eva. She was wearing a strange kinda outfit, black and shiny, that flowed over her skin like an oil slick. The material was like nothing I'd ever seen, and in the dim light it appeared somehow alive. Around her neck was a lowered hood made of the same material. She had a small satchel on her back and held a large, frankly terrifying-looking pistol in her hand, casually, though, not aiming it at me – for which I was grateful. Her red hair was pulled back in a severe-looking bun and she seemed very different to the wounded, terrified sheila I'd met before.

"Hello, Eva," I croaked. "I'm glad you're alright."

She winced, a fleeting look of sympathy crossing her face.

"Sorry about the neck, I thought you might be a little more… vigorous in resisting."

"The only reason he wasn't is because he doesn't understand why you're here." Stephen spoke in a cold manner.

"What do youse mean?" I asked, turning from Stephen to Eva and back again.

"Franga, I have a job to do here. It's a very simple job – one which doesn't concern you all that much – but if you get in my way, I'll be forced to take actions you won't like."

"What's the job?" I asked with a heart-sinking sensation.

"I need to retrieve an individual." She spoke in precise, clipped tones like them military cits who'd sometimes be down the pub.

"Who?"

Eva nodded towards Ken/Stephen.

"You can't have Ken!" I said in a voice that was far tougher than I felt.

"I don't want Ken." Her tone was impatient, dismissive. "I want Stephen."

"But I need to ask him more quezzies, to find out what's going on with the monster."

Eva sighed so slightly I thought I'd hallucinated it. Then she stood up ramrod straight and spoke in a flat, dead-eyed fashion: "The storage device currently attached to the individual known as Kenneth Ages contains proprietary materials and information that is the property of NanoCorp under Intellectual Property Act 1-2420138. Any attempt to withhold said materials or information will be met with level four retribution: that may feature retaliation up to and including severed limbs, broken bones, decapitation, defenestration, disemboweling and all other acts of physical force that may result in severe injury and/or death. Pursuant to said Act, this E.V.A may use her own discretion in the application of same."

I stared at Eva for a long time.

"Eh?" I eventually answered.

Eva sighed and started to raise her pistol.

"Her name's not Eva, we just call her that for simplicity's sake," Stephen said quietly. "She's an E.V.A – Enhanced Variable Assassin."

"*Assistant*," Eva snapped. "The 'A' stands for 'Assistant'."

"If you say so," Stephen muttered. "Do assistants always carry heavy ordinance?"

"You're an assassin? But, like, when we were in the Downlow you were wounded, scared shitless…" I couldn't get my head around it.

"She was faking," Stephen sneered.

"I was adopting the most useful affectation for demographic infiltration." Eva spoke firmly but not unkindly to me.

I remembered how terrified Eva had been – how absolutely out of her depth she'd looked – but then I also remembered the fact she was gawn when I tried to rescue her, and the specky doc was dead with a scalpel poking out of his neck.

"You… killed that specky doctor, didn't ya?"

"It was the only way to escape; the action was prudent."

"I thought you were in danger. I tried to rescue ya."

Her expression softened.

"Thank you, Franga. Sincerely. You acted with bravery and a sense of honour, which is not to be underestimated these days. It would be a genuine shame to have to kill you."

"Yeah, that would be a shame, eh."

"So, please, retrieve NanoCorp's intellectual property, place it in my hand and I won't be forced to fire projectiles through your face."

"Righto, then."

Ken had given me instructions, both verbal and written, on how to detach the carroty thingo. I was pretty sure I knew how to do it, but that strange-looking pistol – all organic and somehow insect-like – made me nervous, so I kept fumbling with the spindly legs and clasps. I wiped my sweaty palms on my shorts and tried to calm down.

"You can't do this," Stephen murmured out the side of his mouth. "If they take me back to Research Station Alpha, they'll kill me."

"I don't have much of a choice, Stephen."

"I can feel the shape of something in my pants pocket. Is it the shocker?" Stephen's voice was barely audible.

"Reckon so." I nodded.

"Use it. Get us out of here."

It was a bad idea but the best we had. I leaned down, as if there was a cord to check, and slowly pushed my hand towards Stephen's trouser pocket. My fingertips were touching the metal surface of it when Eva (E.V.A) cleared her throat behind us.

"Part of my enhancements include improved hearing, strength and vision. I even have an X-ray filter I can toggle on or off. I promise you, Franga, if you attempt to retrieve that device and use it on me, I will execute you with extreme prejudice. This is your final warning."

I took my hand off the shocker and backed away.

"I thought you said it'd be a shame to kill me."

"It would be. It's still my job."

"Well, it's a shit job, eh." I hated the petulance in my voice.

"DON'T DO IT!" Stephen roared, and started jerking back and forth out of nowhere. His movements were so violent, so crazed, that the metal carrot had to spring to life just to keep the shunt inserted. "I WON'T GO BACK! I WON'T!"

Suddenly Eva's pistol was raised and her tone lacked any humanity: "Stephen Blentiff, if you don't stop moving, I will be forced to execute your host body."

He didn't stop moving and was jerking around so hard the chair started to move and the thingo was forced to grow additional appendages just to stay upright. I could hear whirring and whining noises from inside. Evidently a host moving this much was bad news.

"I'm sorry, Franga," Eva said, aiming the pistol at Ken's head.

"NO!" I cried and jumped in front of Ken as Stephen made his body dance crazily. "You can't do this! Ken's innocent and even though Stephen's a bit shit, he feels bad for what he did, accidental-like!"

This actually stopped Eva, and she lowered the gun just a tad. "What has he been telling you?"

"That he was gutted at creating muties and wanted to make amends and that, which was why he buggered off into the stick."

"Oh, Stephen," Eva sneered. "That's quite the tale you've told, isn't it?"

Behind me, Stephen had stopped moving. He glared at Eva.

"Piss off, Eva. You're hardly in a position to be sanctimonious."

"What's going on?" I was confused.

"The truth, Franga," Eva looked me right in the eyes, "is that Stephen didn't care one whit about creating mutants. Hell, he regularly vivisected entire mutant families and didn't lose a moment's sleep."

I felt sick and bewildered. "So, why'd he pull his brain out?"

"Because," Stephen smirked, dropping all pretence of friendliness, "I was sick of being held back by primates. Minerva, Garold and Gabriel looked very pretty hanging onto my coattails but their minds were mediocre. I wanted to take my work to the next level. To an organisation that understood what I was trying to do, what I could achieve. I put major aspects of my personality and knowledge of my work into bio-storage, safe from anyone at NanoCorp, and was going to reintegrate with my host body a matter of weeks later. Weeks. Now I wake up, being interrogated by some shit-eyed goblin, and find it's been decades? This is an intolerable nightmare!"

I took a step away from Stephen, shaking my head. "You… didn't do this on purpose? To, like, make amends?"

"Of course not, you imbecilic gargoyle! I was attempting to sell my tech, that's all. I can't even imagine how it all went so horribly wrong."

"I think," Eva was shaking her head in something like wonder, "with you removed from it, your host body grew a conscience."

"You're a fine one to talk about consciences, Eva. Who helped collect all those sweet, innocent mutants in the first place?"

"Regardless." She raised the pistol again. "Your mind belongs to NanoCorp."

Stephen started thrashing about again. "IF YOU THINK I WOULD EVER LET YOU–"

Eva hissed with annoyance and fired. Thrice. There was a *Thruft! Thruft! Thruft!* sound as projectiles shot past me. Then an almighty clang and sparks filled the air. I turned back to see the metal carrot thingo sparking and twitching, legs flailing as it wrenched itself out of Ken's head – roughly and without the earlier precision.

The back of Ken's scalp ripped open, flapping like a torn pocket – and blood geysered out of him. I screamed and ran to Ken. Stephen screamed and then jerked unconscious and Eva lowered her weapon and walked quickly over to the thingo, pulling stuff out of her satchel.

The back of Ken's head was a mess. I quickly grabbed a bunch of rags and applied pressure to the wound. Within seconds the rags were soaked through. I was babbling and crying and begging Ken not to die. I had no idea if he'd even wake up.

I heard a satisfied grunt from behind me. I turned to see Eva staring at the tube of meat. She'd removed it from the thingo to check it for damage and apparently liked what she saw. She then plugged it into a more modern-looking thingo, even smaller and sleeker than the carrot, and shoved it into her satchel.

Eva turned to me, as if I was an afterthought. There was no regret or guilt in her expression when she asked, "How's he doing?"

"I think he's gunna cark it," I sobbed.

I could see the indecision in her face. Just for a second. But then she walked over and gestured I get out of her way.

"Scalp wounds always bleed a lot," she muttered, casually having a squiz at the abattoir on Ken's neck. "However, they're rarely fatal."

Eva swiftly produced a staple gun of some kind, and – with bracing speed – closed the various red flaps with solid-looking staples. She then produced a small aerosol canister – about the size of my thumb – and spritzed the area.

She took a moment to survey her work, then nodded, satisfied.

"He'll live, most likely, although I can't speak for his mental state." She handed me the aerosol. "Use this three time a day. It'll stop any infections and help the blood clot."

"Why did you shoot the thingo?" I asked, numbly taking the spray.

"Safety protocol causes the device to retract the sample if it's heavily damaged. Standard operating procedure."

"Well, thanks for not shooting Ken. Or me."

"I told you: I'm fond of you. The mission's parameters dictated that I only kill you and Ken if absolutely necessary."

I nodded and looked at the bloody, smoking mess in the area of the hab in which I sat.

"What will you do with Stephen?"

"I'm afraid that's classified."

"Oh." I didn't know what else to say. "What about the monster, but? Couldn't you, like, help us with that 'un?"

"That's not within my mission parameters." Eva moved towards the door. "The only way I could help would be... if the creature in question began to damage or destroy NanoCorp property."

"Oh. Righto."

I stood up and slowly began untying Ken's sleeping body.

"Good luck, Franga."

"Thank you."

"Don't come looking for any of us."

No bloody fear of that.

"Or I'll kill you."

And then she was gawn, leaving me alone, waiting to see if Ken would ever wake up.

• • • •

After a restless, tense fifdeen minutes standing over Ken's –

Corpse. Garn, say it.

–sleeping form, I decided my time would be better spent packing the gear away, ready for when –

If

–Ken woke up. The gear was more involved than it looked and it was doubly difficult trying to fit all the stuff into the fiddly little compartments in the back of his chair. I figured he could show me how to do it properly when –

If if if if if!

–he came to.

I wondered how the ruggies were going, what Gia was doing and where the monster was. I pondered over Stephen's story, and how to tell Ken he was, like, one of the shittest cunce I'd ever met.

"Fuggen hell, I dunno," I said out loud.

Speaking to yourself, are ya? Going berko, son?

"You can fuggoff and all, eh."

I took a slash and returned to see the welcome sight of Ken sitting up, wobbly and confused but undeniably back with us.

"Ken, you little rippa."

"Frang, what's going on? Did you find anything out?"

Fark.

"Yeah, mate, I did. Quite a lot of stuff. Do you need some water, bitta food?"

"No, mate, I'm right. Back of my bonce is a tad sore, though."

Ken no doubt had clocked the bloodied bandages, so I appreciated this reaction was a fairly massive understatement.

"There were a few complications," I admitted.

Ken patted the ground next to him. "Carn have a seat. Give us the good word."

"You sure you wouldn't prefer to wait until you've had time to recover–"

"Franga." Ken spoke in a way that suggested he knew or at the very least strongly intuited something was wrong. "Please."

"Righto, then."

So, I sat down and told Kenneth Ages the sins of his body's former owner. It took twenny minutes, give or take, and in that time, I got to see a man's heart break and him lose all hope. After the story finished, with Eva buggering off with Stephen's meat after so generously not killing me, Ken was silent and still for a long time. Then, right when I thought I'd better check for a pulse, he spoke very calmly but loudly.

"I see," he said like he needed to be heard by a large crowd. "Fine. Thank you."

Then, after another pause, softly, "I need a moment."

TWENTY-NINE

It was barely a moment he needed, all told. I'd nipped into the brasco to sponge some of the blood and sweat off my yellow skin when I heard Ken call to me, asking me to come back into the main room. When I walked back out, he seemed sparky, bright eyed, ready to chat. He'd lost a lot of blood, and was still pale as, but the fog of depression appeared to have evaporated.

It was heaps suss.

Ken reckoned he had a real grouse plan but, as he began to lay it out for me, my heart sank. It wasn't the fact his plan was bad, although deadset it was a shocker. It was something else.

In broad strokes, what Ken proposed was that he and I – mainly I – would construct a mounted harpoon gun of sorts, and we could wheel it out into the middle of the streef. When the creature got close to the hab, Ken would launch the pointy thing into it, and "hack the personality matrix" using some biotech he'd flogged from Garold and Minerva.

I didn't understand his lengthy mono-log regarding the science behind the bloody thing but I felt as if I didn't have to. Because when I met Ken's gaze, when I looked at him real hard, it seemed to me that… he wasn't really invested in the words that came out of his gob.

No, more than that, it was like he was hiding some vital bitta info, some key ingredient.

Holding it back for reasons I couldn't fathom.

Regardless, I constructed the sturdy apparatus onto which Ken would slot the harpoon gun. It didn't take long despite the bloody thing being almost as big as me, as the basic mechanics of it were actually much less complicated than the tripod. A bitta push and shove, some latching and she was apples.

"Reckon that'll do us, Ken," I said, strangely flatly, and there was a rumble in me guts, a tension. Something felt skew-whiff.

"That's great, Frang." Ken stirred from a light nap. "Just needs the finishing touch."

Ken lifted the surprisingly light harpoon gun and, with me assisting, attached it to the mount. It looked sturdy enough and I tapped on the side.

"Looks good."

"Thanks, mate." Ken was pouring two generous measures of scotch. "Join me for a drink?"

"Sure."

We sat facing across from one another at the kitchen table and sipped our drinks in silence for a minute or two.

"So…" I began, fortifying myself with an extra big sip, "what aren't you telling me?"

"Eh?"

"Carn, Ken. Don't tell porkies. I know there's something."

He looked at me for an endless moment and then, like a strange dream, started cackling.

"That's a weird reaction."

"I'm sorry," he gasped, trying to get himself under control, "but honestly you never fail to impress me."

I figured he was trying to butter me up, but still, it was nice to hear.

"Do you know what your parents told me when they handed you over?"

I became still; Ken had never said much about my parents. My mouth was suddenly dry.

"No."

"They reckoned you were simple, 'a drongo', they said." Ken shook his head. "They should have taken a look in the mirror to see a true pair of idiots."

Ken stood up, gesturing with his glass yet somehow managing to keep all the liquid safe.

"You pulled yourself up from the muck and became a vital part of the lives of these children, a vital part of my life and all. Despite everything you've had stacked against you – all the misery you face on a daily basis – you manage to be helpful, hard-working and with such empathy, despite being shown barely any yourself."

I could feel my face grow hot but I didn't interrupt; I wanted to see where Ken was going.

"Not only that," Ken said after a sip, "you're far smarter than anyone could credit. Taking imperfect lessons from my buggered-up noggin, you've managed to become a voracious reader – even when the texts are from my messy, muddled mind – you understand and analyse at a level that would be impressive in any cit. It's a credit to you. I sincerely believe you could be a grand murder-poet one day, Franga, if that's what you want to do. You're perceptive, too. Even now you knew I was hiding something. Hold onto that sharpness, it will serve you well in the future."

The heat in my face seemed to have moved to the rest of my body and I was starting to feel very strange and floaty.

"I feel a bit odd, Ken…" I burbled.

"Don't worry about that, just concentrate on what I'm saying: don't get bogged down with guilt or anger, let that bullshit go. Accept that sometimes things go pig's arsehole and you just have to move through it, get out the other side somehow. And, Franga, I just wanna say, mate:

you're the closest thing to a kid I've ever had, and I'd be honoured if you were my biological son."

I was crying now, in a weird, numb fashion, and I whispered the words: "Thank you… Dad. Thank you so much."

"No, mate, thank *you*."

Then a cloud of cottonwool seemed to surround me and it was blissful and calm and I let it envelop my perception and slipped quietly into a warm, dark place.

• • • •

Deadset, I was getting pretty tired of being knocked out, eh. In the past few weeks, I'd been conked on the bonce, slid off a tall building, overdosed on Lord tumours, had a conniption due to monster terror and drugged with chems by a bloke who was like the dad I never had.

Mate, it's a bit bloody rough, is what I'm saying. A bloke shouldn't experience that much bonce-ular trauma. That gear is liable to make a fella dodgy in the skull meats.

Anyway, I woke up on a pile of clean bedding on which Ken had thoughtfully plonked me. It was very early but light out, bit after five. My head felt fuzzy, like I wasn't fully there, but otherwise I was fine. Apparently, Ken had only wanted me out of the picture for a little while. Fordy-five minutes to be precise.

But why? What advantage would he get from me napping?

That's when I saw what was on the floor next to me, or rather – what wasn't. The harpoon gun and stand were gawn, faint tyre impressions wheeling to the front door and beyond. In place of my latest labour was an envelope – a real paper one; musta costa fortune – and inside, a letter, written on the same ancient, brittle paper. It began:

Dear Franga, By the time you read this I'll be somewhere else. Or something else. You see, I was never intending to survive this plan. And I knew you wouldn't have a bar of that, so I had to drug you (sorry about that). The thing is, son...

It said heaps more but I dropped the bloody thing and was scuttling to the front door, yelling: "Ken! KEEEEEEEEN!"

I sprinted down the road, heart thudding like mad, looking around desperately for some sign of Ken. There was movement a few blocks down the streef, cits gathered around and staring at something I couldn't make out. The ground thudded and at first I thought it was my heart kicking up a notch, but no – judging from the scattering of the cits ahead of me, it was something heavy landing nearby.

I didn't need to guess what that something was. I poured on the speed and ran with everything I had.

And that's when explosions of sparkling colour filled the air and the sky.

● ● ● ●

Ken had motored the harpoon stand down the streef, riding it like a wheelchair, and set up a pozzie in the middle of the road, waiting for the roaring menace to get closer. Took a while, just over fordy minutes, but eventually the horror arrived, looking for flesh to absorb. It'd been getting hungrier on account of most cits fleeing for safety and it needed more fuel.

Meat for the beast.

That was when Ken flipped open the harpoon section revealing an enormous collection of fireworks, kept safe and dry from times long gawn. He lit them fireworks and filled the sky with colour, fascinating the few cits unwise enough to still be wandering the streefs and the monster itself.

I was running towards the zone of sparkling colours. The fireworks were building towards a crescendo of incandescence and I couldn't help but appreciate it, despite my panic and confusion.

Neither Ken nor the monster paid any attention to me. The former had his back to me and the latter was enchanted by the sights and sounds.

Its huge bronze eyes shone with something approaching childlike awe and its six hands pawed the air, thick, slimy fingers opening and closing, grasping at the dancing light.

As I suspected, the plan Ken had told me was fiction, beaut bullshit or what he might call "yartistic lie-sense". But then, what was the real plan?

What the bloody hell are you playing at, Ken?

The fireworks spiralled in complicated patterns, bright green and loud violet, pulsing and throbbing like the arteries of an underwater fish with translucent skin. It was strange, it was beautiful and the world seemed to hold its breath to appreciate the rare splash of light and colour daubed across the grimy canvas of the Inasiddy.

Like all beautiful things, it was over too soon. The climax came and went, the glittering lights peaked and faded and then we were just two people and a monster standing in a wafting circle of smoke and ear-ringing silence. The monster's eyes cleared and it became aware of its surroundings once more. Its expression turned from slack-jawed amazement to rage again, the drooping flaps of its body quivering as it growled at Ken, who was now standing directly in front of the thing. Its mouth drooled and there was an unmistakable note of hunger in the sound.

"KEN!" I called out.

He turned slightly and smiled at me, shaking his head in a loving sorta way.

"Goodbye, son."

And then the monster opened up in the middle, unzipped itself from bonce to ballbag in a long vertical slit. Except its guts and innards didn't come splashing out; they hung inside its meaty bulk, shaking with anticipation – a red, shiny nightmarish pit that was obscene beyond anything I'd ever experienced. A kind of ghastly lewdness to the display. Then tentacles – probing, eager appendages – slithered forth. Slowly at first, but then all in a savage rush, dozens of them shot around Ken, into him, piercing him in a hundred places and encircling his old body completely.

Then they pulled him inside the gaping maw and the slit closed with a hideous blurting noise, flesh knitting in seconds.

I screamed in horror, in pain and loss. Ken was gawn, swallowed and absorbed by the creature, who was now vibrating with pleasure. I tried not to think about how it must feel to be dissolved, to have every part of yourself broken down and distributed into an alien lifeform. I tried, I really did, tried so hard.

I failed.

I fell to my knees, sobbing incoherently. I didn't even care that the monster was moving in my direction. Not at first. But I sensed its next forward step and looked up at the fleshy thing looming above me, a mountain of hunger… and yet, it had paused. Something was happening, something inside its mass. Its whole form quivered, shook, a tiny tremor that was getting bigger.

Is that you, Ken? Are you doing something from the inside?

The expression of the thing changed, went from satisfied to pensive to… in pain. It didn't like whatever was going on.

And then it screamed.

Its whole body became a slaughter-choir of mouths, screaming orifices opening everywhere, and shrieking their noisy discontent into the night air. From my perspective at its feet, the sound was deafening. I shoved my fingers deep into my earholes and curled into a ball, willing the dreadful sound to stop.

It didn't.

The wail went on and on and the monster was jerking and twitching as its lament poured out. Then, as suddenly as it had begun, it ceased. The monster stood there, a confused look on its face. Its eyes, the big bronze ones and various others that rippled into being, all turned towards me.

It opened its mouth and burped: "RANGGG."

I shook my head; I didn't understand. But it seemed to be trying to impart something to me, something important.

It tried again: "RANNNGGGGGGGG."

I scooted back half a meater. I wasn't getting the feeling it wanted to hurt me, but who knew with this thing? And yet, it kept trying to get its odd message across.

"RAAANGGGaaa."

Franga?

I looked up into the enormous face, and spoke in a tone that dared to hope: "Ken?"

At first it seemed to almost smile. Or at very least its dripping wound of a mouth curled up at the side, but then it shook and snarled and once again SCREAMED, an ear-assaulting peal of pain-thunder. It started bashing itself on the head and body, slapping its own meat like a panicky cit trying to displace an overeager cockroach. Then, without warning, it leapt away, still screaming, taking three huge loping jumps that took it halfway down the streef.

But it said my name. That's Ken. That's got to be Ken in there.

And, like a prize drongo, I ran after it.

If the monster had been purely focused on escape, there was no way I woulda caught up with it. Those huge muscular legs would have carried the thing to wherever it wanted to go long before I'd been able to make it even a third of the way, but it kept stopping. It would pause and scream and attack itself and then commence moving again.

Still, even with its many stops, it almost got away from me a cuppla times. I jumped as hard as I could, ran up on roofs, leapt off balconies and the like – skinned my knee and smacked my elbow pretty fuggen hard on the way – but after a while chasing the thing, I realised where its destination was.

It was heading towards the New Sydney Harbour Bridge. Why, I didn't know, but that was the unmistakable goal. That or the Big End beyond.

But what would it want over there? And is that Ken or the monster in control?

There were no answers, and the only bloke who could help was currently being digested.

"It's a shithouse situation!" I panted to myself, and leapt between two rooftops, moving at a lung-bursting speed.

When I finally got to the bottom of the bridge – the bullet hole-riddled hellscape and site of the monster riots – it was clear the Pigs had scarpered. Their barrier remained but they'd removed themselves to some location on the other side. But the monster hadn't gawn through the barriers, it had gawn up. I could see it leaping and lurching its way to the top of the bridge – swinging up through the ancient girders crisscrossing its rusting metal bulk – heading to my contemplating spot.

"Don't you even think about it…" I gasped at myself, hoping I'd see sense. I didn't. I took a breath and started following, leaping after the thing.

If there was even a poofteenth of a chance that Ken could still be reached, I had to risk it.

By the time I reached the top of the bridge, I'd chundered twice and almost fainted when I finally stopped moving. I lay flat on my belly, sweat-slicked and gasping. If the monster wanted to kill me, I had no objection. Durries, as rough as I felt I would have taken it as a personal favour.

Once I'd caught my breath, I looked up to see the monster staring at the rising sun, the light diffused through the flock of U-drones that had moved to block the worst of the morning rays. Its eyes, all of its many eyes, shone with a strange sadness as the glowing orb began its daily scorching.

I cautiously approached, ready to leap away if it seemed likely to attack, but there was a stillness to the thing.

I stood next to it and it glanced down at me.

"RAAAAANNNNG–" it started to growl, but then something in its mouth changed, shifted and became more human. "FRAngga."

"Hey, Ken."

"NOt juST KEn. MAny. IN. HeRe."

"Legion."

The creature nodded and winced, something hurtsome happening inside. "YoU SHouLD go," it growled, its tone at once alien and familiar.

"Why?"

"NoT SAfe. FOr. YOU." The words were becoming an effort.

"Ken, the only times I've ever been safe are with you. The only times." I was crying now. The monster seemed to shy away from these words.

"NOt saFE. No huRT FRangAAA. No WANT to…"

"I'm not leaving you, Ken."

"mUST."

"No."

"MUsT."

"NO!"

And then it snarled a grunting snort of annoyance, and in one swift movement backhanded me in the face, the blow knocking me clear off the side of the bridge. Arms pinwheeling, eyes wide, clacker clenched.

● ● ● ●

Everyone in New Sydney has thought about what they'd do if they fell off the bridge. It's just one of those things, human nature. You look up at a bloody high structure and try to reckon how you'd survive falling off the fuggen thing.

Back in the olden days, before Ken's time even, a few blokes fell off the bridge during its construction. Some died, but a cuppla blokes lived and the way they survived was by falling feet first, letting their heavy work boots take the brunt of the water's impact, which at the height they were falling from would be like smacking into concrete, or so legend has it.

Of course, those blokes fell into the drink when it wasn't bubbling poison, so even if you survived the fall these days, your skin would likely melt off the bone by the time you'd swam to shore and slough off like a slow-cooked kitten. And if it happened during a corrosion tide, like there was that very night? There wouldn't be enough left of ya to fill a piss pot.

A shitty way to cark it to be certain.

Still, when you're flailing arse over teakettle through the air, facing a deadset terrifying maggoting from a great height, there are worse things to focus on than your eventual survival. But, in my case, the point ended up being moot as I'd barely fallen a couple of meaters before a tentacle shot out from the monster and grabbed me around the waist. It was strong and firm like an iron bar and it woofed the breath out of me, but it stopped my fall and gave me a few precious seconds to orient myself and grab onto an out-jutting rivet a little way down the bridge.

The tentacle slicked away from me, shooting back up to its owner, and a second after that the monster jumped from its perch, through the bridge and onto the ground that yawned scarifyingly far below. It landed on the bitchy-men with an almighty thud and then began the process of violently dismantling the Pig-constructed barriers, by smacking the piss out of them, sending chunks of rusted metal and reinforced concrete spinning off the edge of the bridge proper.

It was awesome, in a way, just an astonishing display of strength and rage. The power of the thing, it just beggared belief.

Over a period of ten minutes or so, the monster tore apart the barriers that for years had prevented cits from the Inasiddy from entering the Big End. It might have been a powerful moment of emancy-pation had it not come at the six knotted fists of the beast from the Downlow. Once cleared, the monster looked around with what I imagined was a sense of satisfaction at a job well done, although I have no way of confirming that, and it let out a belching roar. Then it turned to the Big End and started off towards it, loping along with a purpose.

Was it Ken, was it Legion, was it something else entirely? I didn't bloody know. Nor did I understand its purpose over in the Big End.

Frankly, I had problems of me own, as I found that I was clutching onto the side of the bridge with a vice-like intensity, my legs shaking with the terrors again.

"No, no, not this shit. Not now. Stop shaking, ya maggot." My legs and body ignored my commands, which was vexing but not real surprising.

"Come on, ya moll, you've climbed this bridge a thousand times. Piece of piss. Sort yourself out! This is nothing!"

Verbal self-abuse seemed to have the desired effect and my hands slowly unclenched and gripped the bridge in the loose, comfy way I was used to. I was still knackered, and I knew the climb down would be hard, but at least I was moving again.

It didn't take long. When I'd touched the ground, I sighed with relief and took a closer look at the trail of destruction left by the monster. A pathway of ruined barriers and scattered debris that led all the way to the Big End of Town.

I guess if I were a different sorta bloke I woulda followed Ken, or whatever was left of him, and strode like a big man after it. But, as Gia had so helpfully and slightly hurtfully pointed out, I wasn't exactly the heroic, action bloke type. Oh, I could give it a red hot go, and I wasn't a coward, but let's be honest: my skills included jumping, looking after the ruggies, reading, telling stories and, recently, rooting. Although I didn't know if I was objectively any good at that lasty.

You're good at reading, though.

The voice inside almost sounded like Ken. But, so what? What's the point of that?

Maybe you'd be good at scribing too?

"And who the bloody hell is that gunna help?" I shouted, realising I'd seem insane if anyone was having a squiz and not particularly caring.

Maybe you could scribe something that helps?

"How can... how can scribing help... anything—"

But I sorta stopped the sentence halfway through. Because an idea was beginning to form, like a garbage-berg moving out of the mist, revealing itself to curious sailors. Maybe there was something I could do. Some way in which my very specific – and extremely limited – talents could give us a chance.

"Probs not gunna work though eh," I murmured.

Might be worth a crack, regardless.

"It might, you know… it just might."

So, I turned away from the Big End, and started walking back to the hab, with one quick stop to make on the way. The sound of gunshots and monster roars filled the air behind me, but I kept walking forward.

I didn't even turn around.

THIRTY

I returned to an empty hab, made all the more lonely by the fact Ken would never again occupy the joint. I could feel the sadness start to curdle in my guts and shook my head, denying the emotion. There'd be time to sook later, if there was a later.

I put the wrapped package from my detour near the door and turned, briefly, to look at the letter from Ken – the one I still hadn't read. The one that began:

Dear Franga, by the time you read this I'll be somewhere else. Or something else...

No, I wasn't ready for that. Not yet.

Put it away.

I did so, then ran upstairs to Ken's room. There, I grabbed handfuls of books, plays and manuscripts and began dividing them into two piles. There was one pile for trading and one pile for ripping. I moved with purpose, not knowing how much time I'd have. It didn't take long.

I took a breath, standing over two piles of precious memories worth more dosh than I could imagine. Then I picked up the first book on the ripping pile – *David Boon's Big Book of Great Sporting Jokes* – and started tearing out pages. Not out of rage, y'understand. I had a plan. A plan that, frankly, probably wouldn't withstand a great deal of scrutiny, but it was the only one I could come up with.

A lot of olden-style books had extra blank pages or pages with just dedications and that on 'em. These were the first to be ripped out and set aside. Then I went with the books where there were two or more copies. I'd pick the least crowded pages in those, rip 'em out.

Next it was stuff I knew well enough that I could re-scribe from memory. Some of the Shakeyspeare – soz, *Hamlit* – then some of the plays we'd already performed that I could recite by heart – *Angels of New Sydney*, onto the pile, love – and so on.

Then it was time for hard decisions. The paperybacks. Those gorgeous prizes. I sacrificed the blankest pages I could find and made myself a promise to replace them one day. I tore pages from the *Word of the Day 2027 Calendar*, from history texts and even some of that Charles Dickens.

Not Guy N. Smith, but. Never Guy N. Smith.

At the end of the process, I had some eighdy-five pages of varying sizes and shapes, mostly blank. It was just as well. I had a lot of scribing to do.

• • • •

I didn't even notice Gia arriving with the ruggies. Not at first anyway. She came up behind me and cleared her throat a number of times to no avail before finally saying: "Oi!"

I turned around, sweaty and distracted, hand cramping from the fast scribing I'd been doing.

"G'day," I said, itching to get back to work.

"One of Lil's sons reckoned you wanted us back here. Brought another wagonload, too. He said you were gunna pay him a whole paperyback."

I nodded, picking up my copy of *Northanger Abbey* and handing it to her.

"That's right. Can you give this to him?" I honestly wasn't sure if I'd be able to physically do it. Soz, Jane Austen, I'll bloody miss ya.

"No wuckers." She took the book, then looked around the room. "Where's Ken?"

"Ken's dead," I stated. "Well, not totes dead but… absorbed. By the monster."

"Oh, Franga…" Gia turned pale.

"He's trynna fight it. From the inside. But… I dunno."

"Some blokes outside reckon it's been tearing up the Big End for ages."

Confused, I looked out the window, then the clock. It was late arvo. I'd been scribing all day.

"Crikey, I lost track of time…" I murmured.

"What are you scribing, Frang?" Gia spoke gently, sitting down beside me.

"Something that I… hope will help. Reach him, like. Wherever he is."

Gia looked at some of the pages I'd written, frowning and moving her lips while she read. She nodded and turned pages, then read some more. Then she looked up at me again.

"Can I take these pages?"

"Yeah, but why?"

"I'm gunna cast and start rehearsals."

Rehearsals. Durries. I hadn't even thought of that!

"Oh," I said, nodding gratefully. "Yeah, grouse, that'd be grouse."

"But scribe quickly, Frang. From what I hear shit's getting hectic in the Big End."

As it turned out, that was an enormous understatement.

THIRTY-ONE

I finished at dusk. My hands were cramping, I was seeing triple, but I was done. I gathered the handful of papers, only about twenny or so – Gia and the ruggies had the rest – and headed downstairs.

I could hear the kids running lines and I entered quietly so as not to interrupt. I was shocked at how awake everyone was and wondered briefly if they'd been necking coffee. Or goey. Or maybe they were just running on fear and adrenaline, like me.

"Franga." Gia was the first to spot me. "You finished?"

"I reckon. First draft, anyway."

"Probs don't have time for a second, though, eh?" She smiled tiredly.

"Probs not," I agreed, handing over the last of the pages and sitting down with a groan.

"Want us to run it from the top?" Gia looked every inch the harried director and I loved her for it.

"Please."

And they began.

Fordy minutes later, I was a strange mixture of proud of the ruggies and Gia, but also wanting to maggot myself for being the worst tryhard murder-poet that ever lived. I'd scribbled angry, self-loathing notes during the run through and handed them out, correcting bits of business here and there, but ultimately it was time to take the show on the road, warts and all.

"Do you think it's ready?" Gia asked quietly as the kids busied themselves, packing props and costumes into the vacant covered wagon.

"Not really but… it sorta *has* to be, you know?"

"If our audience doesn't like it… we could be getting them killed," Gia whispered, nodding at their smiling faces, their innocent features. "That's a seriously fuggen bad review."

"If we do nothing, the same thing's gunna happen." I sighed.

We both knew the stakes; we both knew what this meant; we were just flapping our jaws at that stage, trying to make the insanity sound less so. Unsuccessfully. The whole plan was messy, all over the place like a mad woman's breakfast. But it was better than nothing, albeit only marginally.

"Alright, kids, youse ready to head over to the Big End of Town?"

None of us had been to the Big End before and the first half of the trip over was filled with excited speculation on what it might be like. From the ruggies, at least. Me and Gia were quieter, knowing this wasn't gunna be a fun excursion.

I sat in back with the kids while Gia drove the lead wagon. We'd pulled the covers down so we could talk to one another and, as we moved towards the bridge, passers-by would nod and wave. There was a strangely festive atmosphere now that the monster had gawn over the bridge, and I wasn't sure I liked it. A certain smugness had seeped into the comments I heard.

"Those rich cunce know what it's like to be stuffed now, eh?"

"Serves 'em right for treating us like shit all these years."

"I hope it eats the lot of 'em!"

I could understand the anger, really, I could, but what did these people think was gunna happen after the monster finished whatever it was doing? It wasn't gunna go away, wasn't gunna head bush or nothing. Especially if Ken couldn't control it.

Is he even still in there?

"Franga?" Bella's voice snapped me out of my brain jail.

"What's up, love?"

"Is it gunna be heaps scary, what we're doing?"

I took a deep breath and really thought about my answer.

"Bel, I reckon it is, hey. But only at first. If I'm right, something will… change when we put on the play."

"But… what if it doesn't work?"

Then I'll throw myself between you and the danger because I'll be buggered if I'm gunna let anything hurt you.

"It'll work." I said it like I meant it.

"Then will we get Ken back?"

I opened my mouth but no sound came out. How the bloody hell was I supposed to answer that question? Happily, Gia saved me.

"Oi, Frang?" she called.

"Yeah, mate?"

"Carn here for a sec, would ja?"

"No wuckers."

I patted Bella on the head and climbed around the side of the wagon, moving up to Gia. I sat next to her, grateful for the interruption. Gia didn't even turn to look at me. She was staring off into the distance at something. I followed her gaze and saw what had so mesmerised her.

"Durries…"

We were about halfway across the New Sydney Harbour Bridge, weaving between lumps of detritus and broken barrier fragments, and we were just getting our first look at the Big End. But it wasn't so much the city views that had shocked us into gape-mouthed, stunned mullet expressions, it was the sky.

"It's red, Franga. The sky is red…"

She wasn't wrong. The sky was a bright, angry red, a glowing dome the colour of fresh-spilled blood. Like the skies themselves were wounded, the clouds dripping with people juice. It lent the land below an eerie crimson hue, and I couldn't help but take it as a very shithouse omen indeed.

"Red sky in morning, shepherd's warning… red sky at night, shepherd's delight," Gia murmured.

"What's that?"

"Something my parents used to say. Dunno what it meant."

I looked up at the strange sky. "Doesn't seem very delightful to me."

The ruggies had clocked the sky now, too, and their chatter stopped. They were staring, like us, at the bleeding heavens. I was filled with a sense of almost religious terror, exy-stencil-like. I didn't believe in a particular god, or gods, no matter what the kiddy-fiddlers, God-botherers or Hendoists reckoned, but something strange and otherworldly was happening here.

"It's like the end of the world…" Gia spoke soft enough so only I could hear her.

The wagon rumbled over something soft and lumpy and then we'd reached the end of the bridge and were wheeling into the Big End, the lanky mutie horse pulling us along, completely oblivious to the apocalyptic vibe. I turned and signalled to the second wagon to stop, and do what I'd asked of them, and we kept moving onwards.

• • • •

Cits had come out to stare at the sky and the monster's progress in the Big End. Mostly Big End cits but also some of the braver, curious ones from the Inasiddy. Point of fact, as we moved slowly through the crowd, gently parting them with pleases and thank-yous, I heard a familiar voice.

"Hey, how youse garn?"

I jerked my eyes from the sky and after a beat realised I was looking at Pisshead Michael. He had a bottle in one hand and was grinning stupidly, waving with his free hand.

"G'day Pis – er, Michael," I said, friendly-like.

"Youse wanna hear the good word on what's going on with the monster? I've been watching from the start."

"Eh?" I cocked my head to the side.

"Giz lift and I'll tell youse everything." He nodded to the spare seat next to me and Gia.

I looked at her. She shrugged. Why the bloody hell not?

"Yeah, carn then."

Pisshead plonked himself on the seat and necked from his grog bottle, then offered both me and Gia a snort. We declined.

Pisshead seemed to take a perverse glee in retelling what had occured and he gesticulated wildly. "So, squiz those bones over there? That was the last line of Pigs who were protecting the bridge, y'see. They thought they were gunna have a go, but the monster tore froo 'em like dunny paper, then ate their corpses, shitting out the skellingtons! Anyway, after that, it jumped along the streef over there…"

Michael continued narrating the monster's path in a colourful, albeit apparently accurate fashion. After slaughtering the last of the Pigs, and absorbing their flesh for strength, it had made a beeline for NanoCorp's New Sydney HQ: a fordy-storey-tall slab of nanite-treated concrete and metal. The building thrust into the sky like a morning stiffy, towering over its neighbours. A ring of building-specific security U-drones encircled the top of the place like a halo and ground troops patrolled below. It's no exaggeration to say it was the most important building in New Sydney, the real seat of power. Certainly a more vital part of the city than the guvmint buildings a little way down the streef.

The ground troops were well armed, well trained and all told lasted about four minutes. It wasn't that the raging beast was immune to weapon's fire; it just never stayed still long enough for anyone to get off a decent shot, landing flesh wounds before being smushed into a sticky paste and then absorbed. The final troop managed to shout for help into his walkie talkie before he was crushed into pie filling and reinforcements arrived, in the form of EVAs. Or as Pisshead put it, "Six of the spunkiest sheilas I've ever bloody seen dressed in what looked like fuggen oil slicks!"

Eva has a bunch of clone-sisters? Strewth.

NanoCorp's New Sydney HQ had six EVAs on staff, ready to be deployed only in the direst of emergencies. This more than qualified. So, six sleek, corporate-branded "assistants" emerged from the front of the building. They hit the ground running and moved in perfect sync, biological augmentations making them fast and deadly.

Three of the EVAs held back and aimed rifles at the monster, while the other three approached, unleashing tether-whips and corrosion-charges, deadly ordinance hardly ever seen outside of a battlefield.

The whips lashed out and for a second it looked like they'd tangled the thing up, caught it in the sparking, nanite-infused razor wire. It roared in pain and the first of the corrosion-charges exploded on its middle section. Blood, flesh and fluid sprayed in a wide arc. Half its torso was gawn and it was standing there, its insides on its outside. But then… they shifted. Moved back into place, the torso thickening up and extending over the holes.

"And durries, it had the shits," Pisshead intoned solemnly.

The monster grabbed one tether-whip with a group of three hands and the other with the same, reefing them inwards and causing two of the EVAs to fly over and smack into one another with a horrible crack. Then it grabbed both EVAs and just… smushed them together. Like a stroppy baby breaking its own toys in a bathtub. They were simply obliterated. The third one who'd gawn close tried to chuck another corrosion-charge but the monster just flowed onto her, and pierced her with tentacles, absorbing her in seconds.

Then it turned its attention to the other three. Credit where it's due; they didn't back down. They were still firing right into its face as the monster snapped the first of them in half, still shooting when it absorbed the next and the last EVA. She was still screaming and punching it —

barehanded of all things – as it knocked her corporate-branded head off her shoulders, and then absorbed the corpse.

"And then it climbed up the building, right up to the top…"

Once there, the beast from the Downlow was attacked by the U-drone security halo, that swooped and attacked like "angry magpies".

The monster fought them off in short order, limbs bursting from its body and fighting back in a three-hunnerd-and-sixdy-degree radius. But one U-drone? One it saved, and held, almost gently in its hands.

"At first, I thought it was pashing the U-drone," Pisshead mused, "but that's stupid. When I squinted, it was clear the thing was spitting on the U-drone, like spewing on it. Like, how birds chunder in baby birds' mouths to feed 'em?

"Anyway, the drone seemed to settle down a bit, like the flashing emergency lights dimmed down to a steady red, and it, like – floated, but real calm, off into the sky, heading towards the rest of the U-drones in the sky."

Once the monster had cleared this final hurdle, it only had to enter the building itself. Security shutters had closed over all the windows and doors, the kind of gear designed to withstand a nuke-lar explosion, but as the monster started banging on the NanoCorp HQ's rooftop – fists pounding with a strength nothing natural-born could possess – those inside had to know that it was a question of when not if.

"But what's the go with the sky, Michael?" Gia asked.

"Oh, that? Yeah, it's them U-drones. They're, like… whatcha call it? Infected, eh."

We both stared at him like he was the town drongo – which, let's face it, wasn't far from the truth – but he shook his head, insistent.

"Nah, yeah – fair dinks. The monster, like, spagged on one of the drones like I said, and changed it somehow and then it flew up, heading over to all the others. And then, like, one by one they started glowing allred. Took ages, like most of the day, but eventually they all turned. S'why the sky looks like that. Lights from the drones."

As if he'd timed it, a hazy shelf of cloud moved aside, clearing our view of the heavens, and we could see that the red lights weren't a solid thing, but rather the product of thousands upon thousands of U-drones, all beaming the eerie light. But frankly that just raised further questions, like:

"How can U-drones get infected?" and,

"What does that mean for their future use?" and,

"What happens next?"

Pisshead knew the answers to precisely none of these questions, and he just shrugged and gestured with the bottle. He didn't know what was going on, and didn't even have any theories; he was just glad that the madness had proven real and that others cits knew he wasn't, in fact, a crazy person or prize bullshit artist.

"You'll see the monster when we go around the next corner. Top of NanoCorp, you can't miss it, fair dinks."

We moved the wagon through the thickening crowd, past the streeflights, and craned our heads up, to see what we'd come over the bridge for.

To see the end of our journey.

• • • •

Despite our mental preparation and planning, despite having faced the monster before and barely escaping with our lives, it was still a shock to see the thing. The whole approach felt like a bad dream.

The road led directly to the courtyard below the fuggen heaps tall NanoCorp HQ building. More lights lined the road and then seemed to flow up the sides of the building, e-loomy-nating the lush grounds around the place. At the top of the building, fordy storeys up in the bloody sky, the monster stood in silhouette against the scarlet light, bashing the fuggen crap out of the steel shutter, seeking entrance with methodically brutal consistency.

WHAM! WHAM! WHAM! WHAM!

The crowd was thickest at the bottom of the building and we parked the wagon just in front of them. I was worried they might get the shits with us but they barely paid any attention. It soon became clear why.

"Thing's gunna get in... any minute now."

"Those shutters won't hold. The employees are gawners."

"Poor bastards. Why is it going after them, do y'reckon?"

Theories, half-baked and reasonable alike, shot back and forth amongst the audience. I felt like I could give them a bitta helpful mouth-gear but I had other priorities. With an effort, I dragged my gaze from the monster –

Ken, say his name, it's Ken

–and its attempts at a hostile takeover and turned to Gia.

"We should get the stage unpacked and ready."

"Yeah, righto," she agreed, turning her head away from the fearful view. "Come on, guys, let's bump in!"

Back at the hab, Gia and I had worked out a plan to turn the wagon into a stage. It was just a matter of removing the metal struts from the covered area and spreading some of the pallets we'd brought from home, making a crude but effective stage that we could move as needed. The whole process should have taken ten minutes tops but the ruggies kept getting distracted by the monster and the sky, staring upwards, fear on their little faces.

"Is that really Ken?" Bella whispered.

I looked at the thing, those powerful limbs beating a way inside, and had to wonder myself. What if we were too late? What if he was already gawn?

"Ken's not one to give up. He's still in there."

I hope.

We finally got the stage assembled and my cast of ruggies got dressed, with help from me and Gia, and I was about to start the next part of the plan when Pisshead, who'd just been drinking off to one side and not helping us at all, yelled out: "It's got the shutter open!"

We followed his shaking finger and saw the monster peel a thick metal shutter off the roof, flinging it to one side like it was made of light plastic and not reinforced steel. It leaned inside the hole it had wrenched open and yelled once, short and bark-like.

Then it did something strange, or rather stranger. It turned to the sky and roared in a way I'd not heard or seen before. The sound moved upwards into the sky, like he was signalling someone or something.

"That's new." Pisshead spoke agreeably, slurping his booze.

"Why's it waiting?" Gia whispered to me.

"Dunno," I whispered back.

The red sky changed a moment later. Got brighter in one section and seemed to shift. It took a bit before we could get our heads around what we were seeing, but it was like a glowing red tendril from the blood-coloured sky was separating itself from the main group, some U-drones breaking off from the flock. Probs hundreds of 'em, but compared with the larger mass, it seemed a small number.

They moved gracefully, spiralling through the sky and twirling, a beautiful display that felt out of place on this weird, dark night.

"Something's going on with its bonce... I can't see it properly..." Gia murmured and I squinted to get a better look, but it was too dark atop the building, too far away.

I scanned the crowd around us and saw one nearby bloke had a pair of binoculars.

"Oi, mate, can I borrow your binocs?"

The bloke took one look at me and almost fell over. Seemed to be a Big End cit and had probs not spent a lot of time with uppity muties. I took his shocked silence as a "yes" and grabbed the binocs, putting them up to my scab-coloured eyes.

The monster was holding onto the edge of the building and staring up at the sub-flock of U-drones. Its featureless, triangular growth of a bonce was moving back and forth, circling around and around. I looked further into the sky and saw the sub-flock was moving in the same fashion. His bonce was controlling the bloody things! Directing them like a demonic composer.

"Fuggen durries…" I took the binocs away from my eyes and felt faint.

Gia snatched them off me and had a look too. Once she'd worked it out, she wore the same expression.

"It's controlling them." She shook her head in disbelief.

That much was clear but the bigger question was: what did it want to do with them?

We didn't have to wait long to find out.

The sub-flock of U-drones flew down at a feverish clip, their twirls and pirouettes ended. Now they were all purpose and they were heading straight for the monster. As they got closer, I could see the improved design of the Big End U-drones. Sleeker, spikier and more durable. They looked sorta eerie with their red lights glowing, but like they were angry, like they had murder on their minds.

I remembered Ken's or rather Stephen's tales of the U-drones containing organic material… was that how the monster was controlling them? A bit of itself living inside them all?

"I don't like this, Frang." Gia nodded at the cloud of whirring red as it moved atop the roof, with the monster.

The slab of a beast looked at the U-drones around it, features lit up, red and sinister. Then it nodded its bonce and barked once. The floating drones started whirring something fierce and began to move inside the open doorway.

They started as a trickle, then a stream, then a thundering torrent of drones, madly heading inside like a swarm of bees. But man-made bees, with spiky exteriors, deadly propellers and no capacity for pain.

"What are they doing?" Gia asked.

But she knew. We both did.

When the screaming started, our suspicions were confirmed.

The crowd around us began to murmur. As the last of the U-drones slipped inside, the screams got louder, accompanied by the sound of small arms firing and even a couple of explosions. After a minute or two, the security shutters shunted open on several of the upper floors. NanoCorp workers began jumping out of windows, screaming. Some tried to climb to lower floors but the black monolith of a building didn't come equipped with handholds or anything to latch onto.

A number of poor bastards were dragged, kicking and screaming, by rogue U-drones that bashed through the windows, sending employees shrieking into the air. People gurgling, screaming, flailing as they fell. Cits impaled on drone spikes, cut to ribbons by propellers, falling, falling. Landing with slaughterhouse smacks, people-puddles rendered black in the red light.

It was a piteous, horrible slaughter, one that I can only imagine was much worse inside. What of those poor office workers who were just doing their jobs, beavering away at their tasks, only to be confronted by a buzzing swarm, watching their friends die, knowing they'd be next? It was hideous.

Blood coated the inside of many windows, and limp arms and legs dangled from windowsills and the like, ripped torsos, severed heads, unidentified parts. The screams began to take on a more plaintive, pleading quality. I looked away. I couldn't take anymore.

I noticed Gia had moved the ruggies from the horrendous scene and was holding them in a group hug. She looked up at me; she'd been crying.

Many of the ruggies had too. In fact, there was scarcely a dry eye in the crowd. This audience had got more of a show than they'd bargained for.

"You should take them back. This plan was a bad idea." I spoke sadly.

"What about you?" Gia was stroking the weeping heads of ruggies.

"I'm…" What? Just what did I think I was gunna do? "… doing the play."

"You've got no actors."

"It'll be a one-man show."

"Everyone hates one-man shows."

"I know, but…"

"That's not Ken up there, Franga."

"I have to try anyway."

Gia could see that I wouldn't be swayed. She nodded and sighed, then gathered the kids and started walking them away, pushing gently through the crowd.

"Can I come?" Pisshead, lower lip trembling, stepped up, looking scared. "I'll help. Fair dinkum."

Gia nodded and he joined their little band, moving away from me and into the night.

I wondered if I'd ever see any of them again.

I turned back to NanoCorp HQ which had now gawn as silent as the grave. The U-drones were beginning to return from their dark work, covered in blood and chunks of flesh. Through the binocs, I could see the monster strutting back and forth, a triumphant goose step, revelling in the slaughter, the grisly victory.

Then it opened its mouth wider than insanity – flesh tearing and reforming, tearing and reforming – and issued a blood-curdling roar that was so loud it burned. Everyone jerked back a step, shocked by the power of the noise. And then everything seemed to go redder, as if the drones were glowing brighter.

"What's goin' on?"

"Look, up there!"

"Faaaaark."

No, the drones weren't brighter, they were moving closer. All of them, all of the "infected" U-drones that protected the Big End of Town, were moving as one, moving to the monster's command, and coming to visit the very city they orbited.

The sky was falling and everyone was absolutely stuffed.

THIRTY-TWO

It was an awesome sight to behold, the crimson sky moving downwards like a vengeful God. If I'd been an articulate type of murder-poet, I probs could have come up with some grouse way of defining it, a lovely turn of phrase or similar. Instead, I'll just say it looked like doom was descending, red as a well-smacked bum.

Cits were freaking out, of course. Running for the bridge, heading back to their own habs and the like. I wished 'em all the best, even though I pretty much knew their efforts would amount to nothing. But crikey, who was I to talk? I was about to tread the boards!

Even the mutie horse, previously so oblivious to everything around it, began to whinny and pull at its reins. I untethered it and let it run into the red night. If I survived, I could track it down later.

First thing I had to do was get the monster's attention. After searching Ken's room, back in the hab, I'd found a bunch more fireworks, like the kind he'd used on the mounted gun, so I wasted no time firing them up and stepping back, watching the fuses quickly burn.

I reckoned we didn't have long, so I had to make every moment count.

The first of the crackers exploded bright green sparks into the night, whistling loudly. I held a handful of sparklers in one hand and lit them up, waving them over my head like a bo-kay of fire-flowers. The final few crackers were going next, banshee-wailing into the night, all colour and prettiness.

I turned back to the NanoCorp building, ready to take a squiz through the binocs to see if I'd caught the monster's attention, when a bone-jarring, ground-shaking thud alerted me to the fact that I already had it.

Screams erupted all around me – loud enough to hear over the fireworks – and I turned to see the monster walking along terror firma. In the juddering, rainbow-coloured lights of the fireworks, the monster looked to me a little like a hand opening up. Its multiple arms were fingers, its nuggety body a coarse, uneven palm and its legs just the start of a sinewy wrist attached to some much larger beast, hidden below ground by the night. It was an unsettling optical illusion, but one that I couldn't seem to shake. A hand coming to crush me. To squeeze me into pulp.

The creature was staring at the colourful explosions, an enchanted expression on its face. The blank bonce no longer swivelling and moving, and a quick glance at the sky confirmed that the descending canopy of U-drones had, for the moment, stopped moving, or at the very least slowed to a point where they appeared stationary, poised as if awaiting further instructions.

Cits fled left and right, leaving only a very few of the hardier souls. I didn't take it personal-like. This show was for an audience of one.

I stepped to the front of the stage as the fireworks dwindled down to low sparking tremors, holding a lantern to light me from below. I was never much of an actor, better suited to brief walk-on roles and that, so I prayed the words I was saying would cut through, make an impact.

"Uh, yeah, so this was originally meant to have a bigger cast," I stammered, deliberately looking over the top of my audience's bulbous noggin. "But now it's gunna be a one-man show."

The monster growled, low in its throat.

Gia was right; everyone does *hate one-man shows.*

I figured I'd just launch into the opening mono-log. I was no Bella, but I could probs do alright.

"The life of a mutie is a hard one," I said, all actorly, "a life of… uh, rejection and disgrace."

At this point in the show, some of the ruggies were meant to act out what I was saying, dressed as normies pushing around mutie kids and such. It really lost a lot of its impact without the rest of the cast. I skipped ahead to the next bitta hefty mouth-gear, desperately trying to ignore the mounting growl from the monster.

"B-but there was one man who wouldn't let these poor wretches be treated like that… one man… who… who…"

I've lost me fuggen place!

The growl increased and I started backing away from the monster, when I heard:

"One man who didn't care what the rest of society said, one man who saw injustice and said, 'Yeah, nah – mate, that seems a good deal like bullshit, eh.'" It was Bella, sweet Bella, coming on stage as an angel, totally ignoring me and fully committing to the part.

Chookas, love.

"Bugger off, mutie, we don't want ya here!" That was Debs, striding onto the stage as "The Parent" – a character that sorta represented all of our parents, every one of them who didn't deserve the title.

"Oh no, where will I go? I have been cast out onto the streef and now my life is cactus." That was Claire, playing the part of "The Child".

"That's not true, young mutant. You can come stay with me. I'll look after ya." And Tommy, stepping onto the stage and into the role of Ken himself.

I smiled at them and stepped back, relieved to be off the stage and delighted to have been rescued. The play continued as I stepped down, and there was Gia, arms crossed and waiting for me.

"You came back." I was real happy.

"Yeah, you know. Nothing else to do."

"Thank you."

"Is it working?"

"We're still alive, for now. Ask me again in twenny minutes."

And so, the play went on. It was about a whole buncha things, really. I scribed it as a journey through the Inasiddy, talking about how shithouse life was for a mutant kid, and delivered a fair whack of mouth-gear about the quality of the kind of bloke who would take the time to rescue ruggies from that dark fate, for no reason other than a desire to do good. The kids performed marvellously, especially for a work that was so unrehearsed. Even when they stuffed up a line, they made it look natural, part of the show, and the whole caper felt slicker than a greasy grunter.

Gia and I barely had to do anything other than shoot the ruggies encouraging looks and thumbs up, plus assist with the odd costume change.

The monster had a look on its face, a kinda far off expression that was also, somehow, attentive. Mesmerised-like. It didn't take its many eyes off the stage and barely moved at all. The U-drones stayed right where they were, still casting a baleful red glow across everything but not moving, not killing. We'd been granted a reprieve, but I couldn't help but wonder for how long.

"And thanks to Ken, the mutie children of the Inasiddy had a place to be, somewhere safe. A home."

Bella was about to launch into her mono-log that led into the final section of the play, and I nodded to Gia, ready for the next bit. Bella walked to the front of the stage, the warm light of the lantern softening the red hue that dripped over everything. She smiled right at the monster, like it was Ken sitting there and not some fleshy grotesquery, and began.

"This story has been told by angels, but the truth is: I'm not an angel." Bella started unclasping her wings. "'Cos angels aren't real. They're something made up to make us feel better when life is hard or unfair.

When you're born with mutations or parents that hate you or sold into slavery: that's when angels comfort you. It's a lie, but a nice one."

Bella's wings fell to the stage.

"But in the Inassidy, we don't need no angels because we have Kenneth Ages. He saved our lives and made us safe, made us feel like we belonged. We didn't just survive; we lived. So, thank you, Ken, thank you for my life."

Tommy was next to step up.

"My parents tried to kill me because they reckoned I was the devil. But the devil isn't real, he's something God-botherers invented to scare cits into obedience or explain the bad things humans do. In the Inasiddy, when you're a mutie, you don't need no devil – because the devil lives in the hearts of other people. But not Kenneth Ages; he looked the everyday devils in their eyes and told 'em to pull their heads in. He saved my life and gave me a better one. So, thank you, Ken, thank you for my life."

One by one they came up, each dropping character and breaking the fourth wall. It's not a technique I normally approve of in the yarts, but I reckoned this counted as a special circumstance.

"My parents tried to sell me to the circus…"

"… and after they beat me up, they abandoned me in the Garbage Plains…"

"… but then I found a home, with people I love. So, thank you, Ken, thank you…"

"Thank you, Ken…"

"Thank you."

"Thank"

"You."

As each of the ruggies delivered their thanks directly to the monster, a strange thing began to happen. It vibrated, softly but noticeably, and its eyes were widening and growing wet. Fair dinkum, it looked like me when reading a sad book and trying real hard not to cry in a room fulla other people.

"Is it crying?" Gia whispered.

"Hard to say. But something's happening."

And then it was my turn to get on stage. I took a deep breath and stepped up.

"It's easy to be a sinny-cool, to crack the shits and look at everyone and say, 'What a packa cunce,'" I began, looking right at Ken. Like I've said before, I'm not much of an actor, but I reckoned I could tell the truth and hope like hell it got through. I was gunna give it my all. "And, to be fair, there's a lot of that out there. People deadset fuggen suck sometimes, being cruel and vicious and greedy to one another, letting others suffer because it's easy. I reckon I've been guilty of it myself, giving in to despair, throwing me hands up at the whole caper and not caring. I've fair dinkum come close a lot of times. But you know what stops me?"

The multiple wet eyes of the monster widened as it looked at me. I kept staring right back.

"I imagine what it would be like to wake up in a body that didn't feel like mine. An older body, the body of a cit who had lived through the biggest parts of Strayan history. I imagine being in that body and knowing I was guilty of the former occupant's sins, terrible sins, sins committed by a deadset arsehole named Stephen bloody Blentiff."

The monster growled softly, eyes still not leaving mine. Mine not leaving his.

"I wonder what I'd do, but I reckon I'd head down the pub. Start myself a beaut little grog habit and drink myself into a sad and sorry state like half the poor cunce in the Inasiddy. Sometimes I reckon better of myself, sometimes I think I'd just leave. Maybe go work on one of the protein farms, even join the army, hide somewhere, anything but face the truth. Hard to say, really. Tell you what, but, I don't reckon my instinct, my first thought would be, 'I'll go and look after mutie children, make sure they're safe and well cared for. Make sure they're loved.'"

My voice cracked on 'loved' but I kept going.

"And that's because I'm not as strong, as loving or as caring as Kenneth Ages. The man who saved me and my family. The kind of bloke who has the fordy-tood and honour to accept the heavy burden of responsibility and make Straya a better place."

Okay, we were getting to it now. The big moment.

"And *wherever* Ken Ages is right now, I know he'd be fighting hard to take control of… whatever situation he finds himself in. And, like, if Ken could hear me right now, I would say to him: Ken, wake up. Wherever you are, fight your way back and wake up."

Looking right into those bronze eyes, I said it again.

"Wake up, Ken. Take control and wake. Up."

The monster's tremors increased. It was rippling, shaking, changing. And it was hurting because of it, the growl turning into a groan from multiple mouths. A keening, hurtsome sound.

"Carn, Ken, you can do this. WAKE UP!"

"CARN, KEN-AAAAAAA!" Bella bellowed next to me.

"Carn, Ken, you've got this, mate!" Gia joined in.

"CARN, KEN!"

"CAAARN!"

Soon we were all shouting at the monster from atop the stage, looking right at its twisting bulk and heckling Ken to carn the bloody hell out. Calling him, summoning him.

"CAAAAAAAAAAAAAAAAAARN!"

And the monster stopped, looked up into the sky and SCREAMED. Everyone shoved their hands over their ears and the monster stumbled a few meaters, plonking down directly in front of the stage, close enough to touch.

Then it looked up at me, a familiar expression writ across its massive face.

"FRAnga?"

I almost started sooking on the spot.

"Ken?"

"IT's me. For nOW."

"You've got to take control, mate. That fuggen thing is trynna bring the drones down, kill the whole city."

Ken followed my gaze up to the red, temporarily stationary sky. It growled a noise like a sigh, but from a steam train-sized set of lungs.

'That'S not gOOD."

"No, it's really not." I laughed, somewhere between sorrow and his-terrier.

The monster turned its eyes back to me.

"iT'S Too HaRd. To. ContROl. Mate. ToO maNy VoICEs. All. SCREAMing," it gasped out, with considerable effort, a sheen of slimy sweat sliding down its mass.

"You can beat it. You're beating it now." I was begging him for it to be true.

"NoT FOr LoNG. TOo hARD."

"But… the whole city, Ken. Wiped away like a chunk of snot."

The monster/Ken shook his head and I could swear its/his mouth curled up in a slight smile.

"Not guNnA Let THat happEN."

I was confused. "So, what are you saying?"

"SayinG THAnK YoU AlL. FoR tHe PLaY."

Ken reached out with one huge hand, extending a finger the size of a bloody table and held it there, right in front of my face. Reacting like a deadset drongo, I reached out and shook the enormous appendage. Like me and it were just two old mates, shaking hands and saying thank you. Touching one another's skin and saying hooroo.

Saying goodbye.

"What are you doing?"

But the monster turned from me and strode a short distance away. Then it looked up at the sky and roared, bark-like as before. And the drones responded instantly, moving downwards again, even faster than before.

Descending like a flood.

"Oh, durries, it didn't work," Gia murmured.

But it was different; we could see that pretty quick. The drones were moving into a funnel formation, sort like a huge red tentacle, the pointy end of which was heading towards a specific target.

The monster.

Ken.

Heading right for him.

"KEN!"

The tentacle's tip dropped through the air, the drones moving at a speed that practically defied the eye's ability to keep up.

No, Ken. Not like this, mate. Not like this.

My feet hit the ground and the blood pulsed in my ears. I gave it everything I could but I was still too slow. The tentacle slammed into the monster's enormous body, dwarfing it completely, and destroyed U-drones exploded everywhere as the non-Ken parts of the monster started to fight back. Some arms were open and welcoming the flood of 'em, others battered them away, shrieking from newly opened mouths and glaring from freshly formed eyes.

The monster was at war with itself, new arms bursting from within, dozens of the bloody things, tearing at its own flesh as the drone torrent thickened. It fought like a madly mutating gladiator, roaring and screeching and evolving strategies to combat the flood of destructive tech. But despite the valiant battle, the numbers simply weren't on its side. The monster of the Downlow was a dark miracle of science but, despite its many personalities, it was singular, alone.

The U-drones were in numbers too high to count, and they just kept coming.

So, the monster turned and ran, loping across the ground as the U-drones followed. This was exactly what I hadn't wanted to happen. I couldn't let it go deeper into the Big End.

One way or another this had to end tonight.

I turned to my wrapped package on the stage cart and pulled back the dirty old sheet covering it. My faithful old U-drone sat there, ready for use. It had seen me through many scavenging missions into the Downlow, but tonight, I'd be asking more of it than ever before.

I powered it up, used my fingers to manipulate the direction controls and I was airborne in seconds, rising high over the monster's stop-start escape.

Once I'd drawn close, I cleared my throat.

"OI!" I yelled out as loud as I could. "TRAYVOR'S A PISSWEAK GRONK WHO ROOTS DIRTY OLD DOG CLACKS AND IS THE SHITTEST MONGREL EVER!"

It wasn't my, like, most articulate mouth-gear, but fuggen hell, it got the monster's attention. The dominant personality quickly switched over to the former Mongrel clan leader and the creature stopped and turned, giving chase and leaping into the air at me. I managed to dodge just in time, but I could feel the heat of the bloody thing as it passed me. I spun quickly, speeding up. Heading back towards the Harbour Bridge.

• • • •

My plan had always been to bring Ken fully out of the monster, to have his personality take total control. It was a bold idea, some might even say deluded, but I wanted to give the old fella every possible chance I could. Of course, I'd have to be a total drongo not to at least consider the extreme likelihood it would fail.

And a prize dickhead not to have a Plan B.

So, as I pelted through the air towards the bridge, with the monster roaring right behind me and the massive cloud of U-drones further back behind it, I stuck my fingers in me mouth and let out a high-pitched whistle. Ahead of me, on the end section of the bridge, I saw heads pop up from behind the overturned wagon. The faces of twitchy, broken men. Cits who'd fought in debilitating wars and survived. Cits who, most importantly, had held onto their weapons and were keen to earn a whole paperyback book apiece.

See, I'd told Old Lil's son to make the offer to anyone at the Arr Ess Ell who was keen for some dosh and fancied a blue. I flew over the top of these former soldiers, and watched as they took aim, readying their projectile guns, plasma launchers and beam weapons from across dozens of nameless conflicts; the deadliest weapons ever held by human hands. There were twenny soldiers all told, Unsteady Eddy and the limbless fella, Stumpy – strapped into a clever mouth-operated cannon apparatus – amongst them, and despite their various physical and mental disabilities, they were quick on the trigger when the monster thumped down in front of them.

A variety of gunfire started up. Cracker-popping sounds, deeper thunking noises and the *zuun! zuun!* of beam fire, stitching holes and scars in the monster's meaty bulk, boiling whole sections of flesh away in an instant. It snarled, surprised, looking down at the new subtractions from its flesh, and then turned its eyes up to me, realising I'd led it into this ambush. It snarled up at me, squatting down, ready to launch, rasping one word that it loved so well: "CUUUUUUUNCE!"

I desperately jammed my fingers into the U-drone, trying to get it to turn away, knowing I had seconds to live, when suddenly there was a whistling noise followed by a *CRACK* that seemed to split the night in two.

I managed to hold onto the U-drone, just, and hung there for a bit, ears ringing, shaking my head in confusion. I looked down at where the monster was standing, smoke wreathing its massive body. I couldn't hear a bloody thing, but somehow something had taken a huge chunk of flesh out of the bastard! I could see some of the soldiers from the Arr Ess Ell craning their necks up the bridge and I turned to see a woman on a strut above us, holding a flash, insecty-looking rocket launcher, aiming it for another go. It was bloody Eva! She'd decided to help us after all!

Or she's just protecting NanoCorp property, ya goose.

Eva saw that I was looking and gave me a slight nod with just the barest hint of a smile, aiming the weapon she was about to fire again and – oh, fug!

I held on tight as the second rocket launched. It shot through the hole the first had created and the explosion was much chunkier, spraying unnamable fluids and gobbets of flesh all over the shop, spattering Eddy and Stumpy behind the cart; some fluid even landed on me. Encouraged, my ambush team started firing again and the monster looked less like a solid thing. It now resembled two big slabs of meat leaning against one another, linked by quivering tendrils.

"CuUUuuNNNcccEee?" Multiple mouths mewled, confused and in pain.

I had no doubt it could fix itself, given time. However, before that process could begin in earnest, the swarm of red-eyed U-drones arrived and started in on the beast, like a flock of seagulls after a bag of chips. Soon drones were stuck in the monster's flesh, buzzing and clicking, unable to extract themselves and stuck too deep to be squeezed out. As more drones slammed into it –

THUNK! THUNK! THUNK!

–I saw the tendrils begin to form between them, the mesh linking the drones together, to form some kind of… what?

I got my answer soon. The drones started lifting, the hundreds of linked bodies pulling the thing up into the air, off the ground and away to destinations unknown. The first attempts were failures; they managed to lift it off the ground, only to drop it down along the bridge a piece.

But they kept at it, forming a stronger, wider mesh, linking to yet more drones, digging deeper into the transforming flesh.

It was like a swarm of flies, weak on their own, but together they could move mountains.

Move monsters.

Eventually there were enough so that even with the creature's hectic movements and outraged screeching they could lift and stay airborne. The monster was being pulled into the sky, wailing and gnashing.

The drones pulled the monster out from the bridge and into the air above the waters of New Sydney Harbour, which bubbled and churned with a corrosion tide. I followed, staring at the twisted thing held in the grip of the U-drones, the thing that was even then tearing into two halves as it fought within its very own mass.

It might have been my imagination, but a section of the thing, face-sized, seemed to look at me for just a moment and I think it was grateful. I knew this was Ken's final gift, his attempt at redemption, but it fair broke my heart.

The Ken-thing, the monster, split into two dripping pieces and I watched with a kind of numb horror as both of those slabs fell down into the toxic waters of New Sydney Harbour. They landed with a splash of flesh, drones and furiously bubbling water, a body of sludge that devoured and dissolved on contact.

The water churned, then calmed and it was over.

And cheers started to fill the night.

THIRTY-THREE

The celebratory beano kicked off about two hours after the last remnants of Ken and the monster dissolved into the deadly waters of New Sydney Harbour. It happened impromptu-like, with some of the grateful and relieved cits of the Big End bringing out huge kegs of goon on trolleys and declaring it open slather to all who wanted a bevvy.

Turned out pretty much everyone did, eh.

To be honest, two hours is longer than I would have expected from the Strayan populace, but I reckon the lag was due to the U-drones losing their red light and slowly, very slowly, heading back up into the sky to their predetermined pozzies. Once the influence of the monster ended, they just sorta returned to business as usual, slinking back to work in a fashion that seemed almost shamefaced. It was something the drones were programmed to do if they ever went skew-whiff, but I reckon cits didn't quite trust 'em right away. Once they were back in the sky, albeit with some pretty large gaps due to the dead and destroyed ones, everyone sorta relaxed a bit. Unclenched their sphincters and so forth. And then out came the grog.

You might reckon there'd be some awkwardness due to the, like, fiscal disparity between the Big Enders and Inassidy-ites. And admittedly at first the mood was a bit cautious. However, once everybody had necked a few, and possibly snorted or hoofed a bitta this or that, the cits of New Sydney kicked off in fine style. Inhibitions were shed along with clothes, and all manner of cunce were singing, dancing and – of course – rooting to show their extreme happiness in the face of a narrowly avoided mass maggoting.

Not me, but. I couldn't face it. I was on top of me perch on the New Sydney Harbour Bridge, staring down at the little people enjoying themselves far below. I was watching what appeared to be a conga line of cits pissing off the edge of the bridge. I dunno if they thought they were sending the monster a cheeky farewell, or they just needed to have a slash, but it did nothing to improve my mood, which was blacker than Satan's clacker. I'd headed up the bridge pretty much straight after I landed my drone and made sure the ruggies were safe. I knew Gia would be able to get them home for the night and I just couldn't face them or the rest of the people. They were happy, you see, gleefully running down grinning streef and all because I'd help kill the best bloke I knew. I couldn't get my head around that and, rather than be the mopey bastard everyone hates, I took myself away and up.

I needed to have a think. About the whole strange bizzo I'd been through, about the things I'd found out along the way and about the bloke who was now gawn forever. And I needed, finally, to have a read of Ken's final scribed work.

Dear Franga, By the time you read this I'll be somewhere else. Or something else. You see, I was never intending to survive this plan. It's why I had to drug you (sorry about that). The thing is, son, this was always going to be my battle. The sins of my past returning for one final fight. I sincerely hope I did okay; I hope you and the ruggies and Gia are all safe. I hope I made my ending a braver, more righteous thing than I did my life.

"You did, Ken," I assured the letter. "You did that and more, mate."

I suppose we should talk about practicalities and the notion of a will. Basically, I bequeath unto you every-bloody-thing. The hab is yours to do with as you see fit, all my possessions – yes, that includes the books –

are now the property of Franga. Also, you'll find a safe with a generous amount of dosh and barterable items. It won't have you set for life, but it should help.

"Oh, Ken, I'd give it all up to have you back."

And finally, son, know that I loved you best in all this world. I believe you're destined for grand and beautiful things and my one regret is that I won't be there to see them. Stay strong but kind. I know you'll kick it in the dick, mate. Love, Kenneth Ages.

I cried bitter tears as the sounds of badly played but loud music came wafting up.

"Waltzing Matilda, who bloody killed her, lying on the grass with a dagger up her arse..."

I sat there, bare legs dangling over the side of the bridge, my lab coat fluttering madly in the breeze, and thought about all the times I'd had with Ken, all I'd learned from him, all gawn now. Forever.

"Oh, for fug's fuggen sake." A voice, a sheila's. Coming from down the bridge a bit.

"Why the bloody hell does he haveta always be up here?" Getting closer.

I couldn't help but smile. I recognised the voice and temperament.

A few minutes later Gia, sweaty and grumpy, crested over the ridge of the bridge, holding a half-full jug of beer. She staggered over to me and sat down with a flop, breathing hard.

"Gia."

"Christ on a bike that's a climb anna half," she wheezed. "Wanna beer?"

I didn't much feel like it, but it seemed rude to say no after all the effort she'd put in. I had a generous pull of the warm sudsy liquid and, I had to admit, it didn't hurt.

"So, what are you doing up here, Frang?"

"Having a think. About stuff."

"Wanna share with me?" She raised an eyebrow.

"I… I'm just thinking it's like… we're all heading down a body chute, in a way. Sliding down a path that's well lubed with other people's blood and what we don't know is… there's probably not even a fat grunter waiting at the end. There's just… cold and darkness." The words came out in a rush and were slightly ruined by the fact my voice was shaking, my eyes teary.

Gia looked at me for a long, dark moment and then started laughing.

Fair dinkum, *laughing*.

"What's so bloody funny, ya moll?"

"You, ya goose!" she cackled, swigging the beer and passing it over. "You're like the loosest bloody unit."

"What do you mean?" I drank more, glaring.

"Like, mate, you just saved pretty much everyone down there. You're the fuggen hero of the hour, all the blokes wanna be you, all the sheilas wanna root you and here you are, stuck up the top of a bloody bridge, coming up with ways to make yourself feel even more miserable."

"Ken's dead, Gia!"

"Yeah. He is. And that's a deadset tragedy but, like, he's gunna be dead tomorrow, too. And the next day and the next. But right now? People are celebrating being alive. Because of you."

"They're never gunna know, G."

"What?"

"That Ken was the one who saved us, really. All he was, all he used to be, all he sacrificed for everyone. They're never gunna know."

"So, tell 'em. Get your arse down the bridge, have a drink, sing a song and tell 'em what happened here today. That's the only way people are gunna know. Durries, start talking to the survivors and get the full story! Scribe it into a play or a paperyback and let 'em read about it. That's the only way the story's gunna be told, isn't it?"

She was right. I suddenly felt like I had a purpose. I was gunna tell this story and tell it proper. I'd interview those I could and put it all together. Make something of this whole mess.

"Besides," Gia continued, "we're outta beer."

We were and I felt a sudden and all-encompassing thirst for anothery. I stood up and held out my hand, which Gia took, and together we clambered down the bridge, just as the sun began to rise and e-loomy-nate the shonky shenanigans going on in the streefs. I descended with the full intention of knuckling down and taking some notes on the project that would tell the whole tale of what had transpired.

That's not what happened, but.

As soon as my feet hit the ground, I heard: "Oi! It's that yellow bloke!"

I turned around, my fight-or-flight response ready to do either, but what faced me was strange and unexpected. Normie bloke, huge, but smiling all sincerely, grabbed me in his beefy hands, lifted me up and hugged me.

Deadset hugged me!

Cheers greeted this and I found myself being held aloft over the bloke's head and passed around like a sack of cats. And strange noises started up from the crowd and I realised with a shock they were chanting. But, like, they were chanting my name.

"Franga! Franga! Franga!"

I caught glimpses of Gia following my progress down the streef, laughing and pointing, and after a few moments of getting used to it, I have to admit, the whole thing felt pretty grouse. Eventually I was placed gently down and had my hands filled with grog, which I was encouraged, extremely vocally, to drink quicksticks.

It seemed rude to refuse, so I did as I was told. Again and again.

The rest of the night is a bit of a blur. I know we went inside somewhere fancy-looking to escape from the sun and then there was more grog, some party chems and a whole bunch of talking to cits, explaining what had happened and all the rest. I'd never had so many people, normies no less, hanging on my every word, and it was a surreal experience.

Eventually, things began to move in a curious fashion and I blacked out a number of times, coming to in a series of unexpected circumstances. One time I was singing, badly, yet being applauded by a large crowd. Another time, I was running through what appeared to be an abandoned bowling alley, starkers, with a buncha blokes and sheilas who were also starkers, including Gia and some other good sorts. A third time, I was getting an extremely skillful gobbie from a blonde-haired, freckle-faced sheila while sitting on the edge of a pool, chatting with some cits. Gia was there too and no one seemed terribly bothered by the fact I was having my tocko gargled, so I sorta just went with it. Gia caught my eye and gave me a 'cheers' with her drink and I returned the gesture, just as the sheila was working me up to the vinegar stroke.

I laughed as I came, and everyone cheered – including the hardworking blonde sheila – and we drank beer and talked shit well into the day, afternoon and evening.

Dunno exactly when or how I ended up back at the hab, but it was late enough that the ruggies were asleep. Me and Gia headed straight upstairs and crashed on Ken's old mattress. Gia was snoring before her head hit the pillow and I managed a sip of water before I lay my aching, satisfied body down.

I smiled as I closed my eyes and – though I knew an epic hangover, a season of mourning and the slow, painful rebuilding process awaited me and the rest of New Sydney – for those brief, blessed, crazy moments I felt bloody wonderful and I took that feeling with me into my dreams, wearing it like a long-sleeve shirt tied around my waist.

THIRTY-FOUR

It's a sad truth of life that all parties must come to an end and New Sydney faced that uncomfortable reality about twenny-two days into the epic piss-up that occurred post monster. I'm not saying every bastard kicked on for that long, mind you – sleep and medical emergencies took most cunce out of the running, at least temporarily – but once the goon vats had run dry and most cits had a sorta gaunt, haunted look on their chops, it was clear it was time to call it a day. Food stores needed to be replenished, buildings repaired and cleaned, plus the guvmint had to conduct some kind of sense of law and order. See, I reckon most cits were expecting NanoCorp to come back, drop in a battalion of augmented office drones, and rebuild the HQ building.

Didn't happen, but.

Every day the HQ stood there, alone and devoid of life, a grisly tombstone. A fitting tribute to a corporation that once ran everything and now seemed to just not matter anymore. In an emotional way, it felt like we'd been abandoned by God or a stern parental figure. It was a bit hurtsome, but also liberating. Of course, it left a power vacuum that the blokes and sheilas over in the guvmint district eventually decided to fill. Although their first attempts weren't exactly smooth.

The now legendary first public guvmint meeting had the acting mayor of New Sydney, Nathan Boonta, begin and end with the infamous words: "Ladies, gents, esteemed colleagues, I'd like to put forward the motion that everyone has spent the last few weeks getting thoroughly rinsed – and we're all feeling a bit tired and emotional. I'd like to further put forward that we postpone any additional guvmint action for one week, or until such time as the room stops spinning." Mr. Boonta then chundered loudly into a nearby bin.

The motion was carried unanimously.

Not exactly a stellar start to the new rule of New Sydney, but one week later, Boonta and crew came back and this time they seemed to have things under control, at least partially.

For a start, the bridge was now to remain open. The divide between the Inasiddy and the Big End was declared unlawful and unStrayan. Of course, there'd still be some snobbery on both sides, but I have found it's difficult to be too judgemental of someone after you've necked their grog or snorted lines off their noras.

The biggest project, of course, was rebuilding the Inasiddy and hundreds of jobs were created by the guvmint for that exact initiative. Cits who'd never worked a day in their lives suddenly had jobs that paid well – in food, dosh and credit – and the change in a large portion of the populace was swift and stunning. Over the next four months, the Inasiddy was rebuilt better than it had ever been in my lifetime, with the Big End providing sturdier building materials and even an electric generator and limited access to running water. It still wasn't as flash as the Big End, mind you, but a marked improvement over the shit state of affairs from before.

It was approximately month five when I was called up during the guvmint meeting, which surprised the shit out of me. I'd been helping building crews and tending to the ruggies with Gia, so I'd not been keeping a close eye on local politics. I'd been advised to attend that meeting, but, and I figured I'd lob over and have a squiz.

Nathan Boonta was a Firstie, an Aboriginal bloke with twinkling eyes and an audacious halo of grey hair around his bonce. It looked like he was trying hard not to smile when he started talking.

"The guvmint would like to call a mister Franga Ages," Nathan called, voice reaching me all the way in the back of the room.

"How come?" I called out.

"Please, Mr. Ages, this won't take long."

I walked to the front of the room like a man facing his own execution. There were only about thirdy people in the crowd and a half dozen on stage, but I still felt horribly self-conscious, my cheeks blushing a pinky-yellow colour.

"Mr. Ages, it's come to our attention that the government of New Sydney has been rather remiss in its dealings with you," Nathan began sternly, then paused like I should probs interject.

"Oh yeah?"

"Indeed. We have yet to thank you for your heroic, if somewhat bizarre, actions during the Monster Crisis. Your quick thinking and selfless behaviour saved countless lives and brought to an end the most destructive event in New Sydney since the dark days of the Water Wars. So, Mr. Ages, thanks, mate. Let the record reflect that the guvmint reckons Franga Ages is pretty grouse and a top bloke."

And then Nathan began to applaud. And then the other guvmint cunce started to applaud. And then the bloody crowd started to applaud! It was all a bit much, to be honest.

"Oh yeah, no worries and that," I muttered and turned to go sit back down.

"Before you return to your seat," Boonta stopped me with his kindness, "we'd like to offer you some… concessions for your actions. Firstly, I believe you have a number of young charges in your care?"

"You mean the ruggies?"

"That's right."

"What about them?" I narrowed my eyes.

"Well, we understand that their education may be somewhat… lacking. I would like to offer all of them full scholarships at our illustrious New Sydney School."

I couldn't breathe for a moment. My head was spinning.

"All of them?" I murmured.

"We rather think it's the least we can do, to be dinkum."

"You know, they're uh… muties. Like me." I didn't want to get the ruggies' hopes up over something that could be snatched away.

"Indeed we do," Nathan agreed, "which leads me to my next point. Our previous laws regarding muties have always been draconian. So, we've decided, not quite as unanimously as I'd like, to grant full citizenship to every mutant of New Sydney."

The crowd went wild, both angry and happy. The guvmint cits also seemed divided, with one bloke in particular huffing and puffing, mouth puckered shut like a cat's date. Still and all, it was a done deal and with the saying of it, I was now Franga Ages: solid cit. Receiver of guvmint nutrition bricks, legally employable. Of course, what kind of job would a bloke like me get? Well, seemed Boonta had that sorted too.

"Further to that," he continued as if the uproar didn't even exist, "we will be employing Mr. Ages as the first New Sydney Mutie/Normie Liaison Officer."

The crowd got even louder, a mixture of "Fug yeah, Franga!", "Nice one, mate!" and "Don't want no muties!", "Normie pride!" and so on.

I leaned in real close to Nathan's ear, whispering: "Mate, I've got no idea what a Mutie/Normie Liaison Officer is."

"No one does," Nathan smiled. "We'll make it up as we go along."

Back to the whole room, Nathan continued: "Not to mention the fact we will be granting Mr. Ages the Key to the City."

Applause. Shouts. Confusion. The latter from me, mainly. School for the ruggies, guvmint recognition, a job and a key to the city? What the bloody hell was going on?

After the meeting eventually concluded, Nathan beckoned me over and explained a few things. I was sad to learn that the key to the city wasn't actually a physical key that unlocked everything.

"What it means," Nathan explained, "is that you're welcome to visit and take part in the many official buildings of New Sydney."

Oh, okay. That's, you know, nice... I suppose.

"You can visit the museums, the art galleries…"

Yeah, righto.

"The libraries."

Wait, hold up.

"Libraries, you say?" I spoke with a grin, eyes widening.

Nathan nodded and smiled too. It seemed genuine.

"Right this way, Mr. Ages."

• • • •

The New Sydney Library was one of the fanciest buildings I'd ever set eyes on. Huge stone pillars, tall-like, seemed to hold up the roof like thrusting arms. There was a sense of concrete importance, of a place unwearied by the passage of time.

"Looks grouse," I murmured, thinking covetous-like about all them books inside, getting my fingers on them, smelling that old book smell.

I couldn't wait.

Nate took me up the stairs and inside the building, down a flash-looking hallway and into the huge interior… whereupon I was struck by a crushing sense of confusion and disappointment.

"Where are all the books?"

The only books in sight were in a small bookcase near the front desk. Certainly, the shelves were full, but it was mainly historical texts, a few versions of the Bible – Satanic, God-botherer and Hendoist – and a bunch of official maps and such of New Sydney and the outlying suburbs. The rest of the joint was bereft of tomes and, somewhat inexplicably, full of old blokes and sheilas, who were standing up straight, not reading, and staring blankly into the middle distance.

Deadset, there must've been like two hundred of these old ones, just stood there, mellow and perhaps a little vacant. I noticed there were tubes all connected to them, leading up and down from their bodies into areas of the library I couldn't see.

"Books are all around you, Mr. Ages," Nathan insisted.

"I reckon Ken had more than that." I gestured to the shelf. But Mr. Boonta just smiled and walked over to one of the senior cits.

"This bloke here," he said, tapping the old dear on the shoulder, "is the complete works of William Shakespeare."

I didn't correct his mispronunciation of the bard's name. Seemed rude and I didn't want to embarrass the bloke.

Nathan strode over to a short, ancient sheila with big hair. "This here? The complete Agatha Christie."

He moved himself further into the library and pointed at a whole row of 'em: "This entire row is true crime, and that one," he gestured to another row, "is crime fiction. The best detective stories ever written."

"Are you taking the piss, Nathan?"

He laughed gently and walked over to the Shakeyspeare bloke. "*Hamlet*, Act three, scene one."

Straight away the old fella raised a hand and in a beautiful, flowery voice started in: "'To be or not to be, that is the question: whether 'tis nobler in the mind to suffer the slings and arrows of outrageous fortune, or to take arms against a sea of troubles, and by opposing end them.'"

"Stop." Nathan spoke gently, and the old bloke stopped, face turning slack once more.

"So, all of these cits are…?"

"Most of them are from back in the day, a time when they had life-extending nanotech. Thousands of them were left essentially brain dead after their nanotech stopped working and pretty much had no function in society… until we worked out they can remember and record information with photographic precision. Most physical copies of books have been lost or destroyed, but these cits are now the largest library in Straya. Possibly the world."

Nathan walked me up the next four floors, where row upon row of senior cits stood, gathering dust and waiting to be asked for the information they contained. It was surreal and a little sad. Eventually we ran into the librarian, a short sheila with thick glasses, who was wandering from elder to elder, wiping them down, making sure their food and sewage tubes were properly connected.

"Ah, this is our new member." She spoke no-nonsensey, nodding at me with neither approval nor dislike. "I'm Beryl. Well, what do you think?"

"It's not what I expected," I said diplomatically.

"Bit of a shock, I reckon," Beryl agreed. "But then this represents three times the amount of content the old State Library contained. You just need to know what you're looking for. Also, you have to keep the shit tubes clean otherwise they get clogged. Such is the life of a librarian, I suppose!"

She barked out an alarming sound that, after a moment, I realised was a laugh.

"I'll leave you to it, Mr. Ages." Nathan started moving for the exit.

"Franga. Call me, Franga, please. Mr. Ages was my father."

"Righto, Franga. I'll see you tomorrow for your first day on the job."

First day. Durries.

"So," Beryl spoke crisply, "what do you want to read, or hear, first?"

And there it was. The ultimate choice. All of humanity's knowledge – or at the very least an absolute shitload of it – spread out before me, ready for the sampling. What did I most want to know, to learn? Whose wisdom would be my first choice to hear? What dose of the yarts did I want inside me? And then it came to me and I realised it was never really a choice at all. It was actually pretty easy once I put my mind to it. I looked Beryl right in the eye.

"Youse got any of them Guy N. Smith killer crab books?"

AFTERWORD

I started out this whole writing caper working on screenplays which, generally speaking, is a collaborative process. Lots of meetings, table discussions and bouncing ideas back and forth; it's surprisingly social. I'd always fancied that writing novels would be the opposite, an extremely solitary pursuit. Romantic images of a lone (and very handsome/ windswept) writer stuck in a lofty garret have always appealed to me, and for most of the novel writing process it's quite true. Well, not the garret bit. To be honest, I had to google what the fuck a garret even was because I'm nowhere near as bright as my eyebrows and facial hair would suggest.

But while the writing itself took place alone in a series of dank, dark rooms and eerie sub basements, what came afterwards took a village.

So, a little backstory: the seed of *Straya* has been stuck in my head for decades. It used to be this nebulous thing I tentatively titled *Body Chute* and the main premise was the same. Devastated city, personality-absorbing monster on the loose, hijinks ensue. However, I didn't have a main character, a point of view. Early concepts featured a cop from the rich part of town and a cop from the poor part of town forced to join forces to defeat the thing.

The problem? I know nothing about cops and, frankly, care even less. With respect to those members of our vaunted constabulary who aren't thick-necked, power-tripping bullies, it's just not an occupation about which I have anything new or interesting to say. So, the tale languished. A few years back, I had this weird idea about a bunch of mutants who put on amateur theatre productions to keep their home and like a mysterious beast from the Downlow, *Body Chute* rose back up and transformed into *Straya* and here we are.

Of course, when you pitch an idea like "a mutant who is bad at violence battles a monster with theatre - oh, and everyone talks in bastardized and frequently obscure Aussie slang" to a publisher, not only will you *not* make their slush pile, you're likely to be forcibly ejected from the building.

Like a prize drongo, I started writing the damn thing anyway, it simply wouldn't leave my head otherwise, and as I neared the end, I pitched it to long-time friend and frequent creative partner Jonathon Green (who has acted as producer and co-writer on a bunch of film and book projects with me). Somewhat inexplicably, he loved the idea and wanted to be involved. So, the reason you're reading this in a nice book with a pretty cover and fancy pages with numbers, as opposed to a pile of tear-soaked napkins stored in a milk crate, is due to the shepherding of JG. Thank you so much, my brother. You continue to believe in me despite all evidence to the contrary.

The text of the book itself benefited from the intervention of others as well. An early edit from Kate O'Donnell kept the characters consistent and emotional arcs singing, whereas a structural and copy edit from the superhuman editing Valkyrie, Samantha Sainsbury, improved things no end. If you flat out hated this book, you should have seen it *before*, holy shit! That latter relationship was forged by my agent and fellow cheerful misanthrope, Elizabeth Troyeur, who managed to read the whole thing despite the gross violence and swears.

Further kudos belongs to people who have helped the book along in various ways, like James Bradley, Steve Worland, Joel Naoum, Tom Savini, Jodii Christiansen, Kiah Roache-Turner, Nicholas Hope,

Alex Proyas, Malla Nunn, Helen Bethune Moore and Gina Flaxman. Not to forget the ladies of Impressum: Sheree Chambers, Zoë Hale and Emma Biddle.

Plus, my early readers who gave valuable (and occasionally hurtful) feedback: April Cleaver, Kara Emerton, Christopher Lee Frazer, Annabelle Gigliotti, Suzanne O'Connor and Michala Kowalski (who eventually realised it wasn't a children's book!).

And of course, the staggeringly talented Aussie artiste, Chris Wahl, whose stunning cover art is almost certainly 90% of the reason you even stopped to have a closer look. Working with him, and his super-agent Clara Marcus, was an absolute dream and the result is a legit work of art that, in a right-thinking society, would be hanging in the fanciest art galleries and tattooed on the softest skin.

Further, I want to thank all those who created the books, comics, video games and movies I adored growing up that influence me as a writer to this day. *2000AD* comics first and foremost, with specific love to Judge Dredd, the works of John Carpenter (particularly *The Thing*), the *Mad Max* movies, Frank Henenlotter's *Brain Damage* and *Basket Case*, Joe R. Lansdale, Stephen King, the *Fallout* series and every single genre writer who took an unlikely premise and ran with it.

And, finally, you: the reader. Thank you for picking up a weird book with a strange title and taking a chance on it. Let me leave with one little piece of (unrequested) wisdom:

If anyone tells you, you can't accomplish something, or that your dreams are foolish or unrealistic: just remember Guy N. Smith published ELEVEN FUCKEN BOOKS and one short story collection about killer crabs and tell 'em to get stuffed.

Cheers ta,

Anthony O'Connor
Old Sydney, February 2021

ABOUT THE AUTHOR

Anthony O'Connor is a writer, reviewer, teacher and journalist. He has written original screenplays for the indie Aussie romcom, *Angst*, and the blood-soaked, allegorical office horror, *Redd Inc.* (aka *Inhuman Resources* in the US/UK). He bangs on about film, TV and video games for numerous outlets and, occasionally, disinterested cats.

O'Connor regularly contributes dialogue, story beats and additional writing for film and TV projects.

For more information head to www.anthonyoconnorauthor.com

9 781922 588036